D1564080

THE UNSPEAKABLE

THE
UNSPEAKABLE

Peter Anderson

C&R PRESS

PRESS

The Unspeakable © 2014 by Peter Anderson

FIRST EDITION HARDCOVER

ISBN-13: 978-1-936196-37-1
ISBN-10: 1-936196-37-9
LCCN: 2014931876

The skull of Paranthropus boisei
Copyright © 2012 Bjørn Christian Tørrissen

Cover & book design by Terrence Chouinard
The typeface is Janson.

Scorched Earth

I KNOW HOW THE WORLD BEGAN. It began with a pepper tree. A giant old pepper tree, it must have been there before the farmhouse, and the farmhouse was now part of the dorp.[1] Magnet Heights. There was ironstone in the koppies,[2] and something that made compass needles spin every which way, but no ants except white ants which built tall socks of red sand round the fence posts until Pa replaced the old wooden posts with iron.

Pa was a big man. He had tattoos on his arm, a snake twining round a dagger, and when he tensed his muscles the snake's hood would spread. He was proud of that. He laughed a lot, so the veins in his neck stood out. He also liked to stare at you fixedly, in silence. Then, he said, he was 'thinking'.

Pa slung a swing for me in the pepper tree: an old tyre turned inside out. I used to bellyflop into it and spin around, twisting the rope over on itself all the way up to the branch to which it was knotted, and then let go and spin back again, round in the other direction until it had unwound all the way and I just hung there, hardly moving.

Beyond the house lay the veld that caught fire one winter – flames leaping and coming close, bright and huge like a beast, smoke roiling away or coming towards you, thick and choking, and after the fire there was black stubble everywhere and fine soot that settled even between your teeth. It was then, too, that Pa brought home the baboon.

'A big black bastard of a baboon,' he said.

A lean old dog baboon, gaunt as angle iron, and terribly strong. And grey, I saw, not black. Grey, like any other baboon. He had scars on his flanks, where he had once been shot and left for dead.

Pa chained him up under the tree on the side opposite to my swing.

'We'll call him Ou Willem,' said Pa, and I laughed and tried to hide my face against his trouser leg, because everyone knew there was one Ou Willem already——Ou Willem who worked for Pa. How could a baboon be Ou Willem, too?

The baboon sat down and began picking at the lock on his iron stake with clever, puzzled fingers.

1. *dorp*, small town
2. *koppies*, hillocks, boulder clumps

'There's the devil in a baboon,' said Pa. 'So watch out. If he catches you, he'll squeeze your ribs until your eyes pop out. Then he'll pull your head off and suck the blood. Baboons like little boys. They think you taste better than mieliepap.'[3]

I could never look at the cracked white mieliepap curling in his bowl without fascination after that.

The rest of the backyard was loaded with broken-down tractors and ploughs and other farm equipment, not our own, which Pa was always fixing. Ou Willem, [4]the old black man, sometimes lent a hand. He would pass Pa the spanners, or hold the funnel while Pa poured petrol into a tractor's tank, or spend hours cleaning something – a windscreen, say – with a rag. Ou Willem was very old. He moved slowly and rumbled in his chest a lot and coughed. At lunchtime, he would sit in the sun and eat his bread and drink his mug of tea. Then, if he didn't fall asleep, he would tell me how things used to be, long ago. He could remember a time before our house was built, he said. When the only white man in the area was Mr, Zuckerman, a trader, a round fat man who puffed when he walked, and stared. Ou Willem showed me how. He stuck out his elbows and blew up his cheeks. One day, when Mr Zuckerman was on his way home from Ou Willem's father's kraal, a flash of lightning knocked him over dead. (Ou Willem shut his eyes, lolled his head to one side.) The people of the kraal smelt out the witch, however, and killed her for sending the lightning, and piled big stones on her body. The stones could still be seen on the koppie, not far from here. Ou Willem would take me there one day. He promised.

But when I asked Pa if I could go and see the witch's stones, he said I mustn't be a fool, Ou Willem was mad, or more likely, lying.

'You can't sit and listen to the kak[5] he talks, day in, day out, or you'll go mad, too,' Pa warned. 'He stinks of kaffir [6]beer like vomit. One of these days, I'm going to tell him to take his children and his wives and his dogs and his two sticks of furniture, and go. He's good for nothing. He must get out.'

It wasn't a time for laughing. My face was burning with shame. I felt I distrusted them both, my father as well as Ou Willem. How could I have made such a mistake?

'Leave him alone,' said Pa. 'Haven't you got better things to do? Go and play.'

I went outside and began flopping around in the swing. It was Sunday

---

3. *mieliepap*, mealie meal porridge

4. *Ou Willem*, old Willem

5. *kak*, crap

6. *kaffir*, (offensive) South African equivalent of American 'nigger'

morning. The baboon was searching his fur for fleas. Ou Willem was painting the wall of the shed where Pa kept his tools.

I dragged my toes in the dust. Spun round.

I really wanted to go right up to Ou Willem and have a look. What if Pa was right?

In the seedbed beside the wall, spring onions were sending up their thin leaves. A broad patch of the wall was already a glistening creamy white.

I expected Pa, who always had an eye on me, to shout from the kitchen and call me back, but nothing happened.

'My baas!' Ou Willem greeted me.

His teeth looked like a mule's, I thought, and his lips hung loosely. The paintbrush kept making sticky sounds on the wall.

He stopped to stuff his pipe with tobacco. His arm dropped to his side. He looked down at me, considering.

It was hot in the sun.

I plucked up a spring onion and bit at it.

Ou Willem grinned, the flap of his lips pulled back.

'Ja, my basie!' he said. And chuckled so that he coughed.

I said nothing. He straightened up and turned back to his work again. Dabbling the paintbrush in the paint, he tested it on the wall.

'Look, my baas.'[7]

He showed me how the brush dragged.

'We must make this paint thin-thin, so it goes nice again,' he advised. 'Mix it!' Making a lively gesture.

Then he asked me to fetch the methylated spirits – to mix, as I understood it into the paint. I ran, only too glad to get away. I must be seen to be actually helping, I thought. Under the sink in the kitchen stood the bottle of methylated spirits. I brought it back as quickly as I could, anxious because it was less than half full.

'Is this enough?' I asked.

Crouching down, Ou Willem reached out both hands to the bottle.

'Ja! Is enough,' he replied with the utmost satisfaction, rubbing his hands. 'Enough, my basie!'[8]

He uncorked the bottle, wiped its top with his palm. First, he peered around cautiously, then he threw back his head and drank, his Adam's apple working painfully.

7. *baas,* boss

8. *basie,* little boss

'Hai!' he gasped, sitting back on his heels.

Then he began again, and continued until the bottle was empty.

'Yagh! Agh!' he coughed, choking, almost retching. He shook his head vigorously.

Then he got shakily to his feet and stamped or shuffled around, reeling off a stream of words I could not understand. The metallic smell of the meths caught me. Pa was right, Ou Willem stank.

Now, he was clapping his hand and pointing to the horizon, telling me something.

The big day was coming, he said. Look! It was coming. It was small, now, like a hand, but one day it would be big like a cloud of rain. On that day, Morena[9] would come. He, Ou Willem, had seen Morena once. Morena was tall and stretched right up to heaven. The angels and all the people who had died and gone to heaven wept when they saw Him walk, because they knew why. His eyes were like a tiger's. Morena would walk from stone to stone, and the world would shake under his feet.

'And next time He comes,' Ou Willem warned, 'next time He comes, He will kill.'

He went silent. Leaning the knuckles of his fist against the wall, he picked up the brush, but it slipped and fell. I had to fetch it for him. Unsteadily, he tried to wipe off the coating of sand with his fingers, and dip the brush in the paint again.

'My baas!' he chuckled hoarsely, fondly. 'My little big baas!'

'Ja, Ou Willem?' replied Pa.

Pa was standing under the pepper tree with his arms folded. He was staring hard at the two of us, 'thinking'.

'My baas!' Ou Willem exclaimed.

He turned to the wall and began slapping the paintbrush across it.

But Pa couldn't be put off so easily.

'Ou Willem,' he sang out. He moved forward in a leisurely way, almost as if he was lazy. 'Ou Willem, I want to talk to you.'

Ou Willem put down the can of paint and laid the brush across it very neatly. He stood at attention, upright, his hands at the seams of his trousers.

'It seems to me, Ou Willem,' said Pa, 'it seems to me, you don't know what's what. Do you, Ou Willem?'

'Baas?'

'You heard me. You don't know ... Or maybe you don't want to know. Am I right, Ou Willem?'

---

9. *Morena,* God

'Ai kôna!¹⁰ Ai!¹¹ My groot baas.'¹²

'You were born black, kaffir, and you are going to stay that way, if I have to wring your neck. And that's the truth.'

'Is true, my baas. Is true, my groot baas!'

'That's right!' said Pa, walking slowly round Ou Willem and smiling at him.

'That's the story. But it doesn't mean you can steal, Ou Willem.'

'Baas?' There was fright in Ou Willem's voice.

Pa caught him by the collar of his shirt and twisted it round. As Ou Willem stared at Pa, his knees seemed to cave in.

'You can't steal from me, you can't lie to me, you can't drink on the job, you can't talk nonsense to my child, you can't make him do your dirty work for you. That's what I mean. Understand?'

Ou Willem seemed more helpless than ever.

Pa let him go.

The old man could see what was coming. His hands flew up around his ears in an effort to protect himself, but Pa punched him in the face. Once, twice, three times. I remember the smack of it, the sense of flesh grinding against bone. Then Pa caught him by the shirt again, which tore, an unnatural sound.

Pa was cursing heavily, breathlessly. He pushed or tripped Ou Willem, and the old man fell flat.

Pa gripped him by the back of his collar and began dragging him backwards. Ou Willem had to pedal on his heels as he squatted, his backside scraping the ground, and stretch his arms out wildly on either side to balance.

'Sit there,' said Pa, dropping him in the dust on the baboon's side of the pepper tree.

Ou Willem sat. He wiped a glistening drop from his nose with his wrist, and stared at it.

Pa sent me to the shed to fetch a length of chain and two padlocks. Wrapping one end of the chain around the trunk of the pepper tree, he clinched it with a lock. Then he locked the other end of the chain around Ou Willem's neck.

'Now, kaffir, you're going to sit,' he said, 'where you belong.'

Ou Willem looked old and shrunken. There was blood on his knuckles, where he must have hurt himself when he was being dragged backwards. He began to cough. A bubble of blood swelled up suddenly from his nostrils and burst.

10. *Ai kôna*, No

11. *Ai!* phatic exclamation, here of fear

12. *groot baas*, big boss

I clutched at Pa's trouser leg.

'What's the matter with you?' said Pa, looking down at me.

There was the rattle and snapping-taut of a chain. The baboon had retreated as far as it could. It was grimacing at us, and lifting one black paw in gestures that seemed to say, 'Go away!'

Pa laughed aloud.

'Ou Willem and Ou Willem! You know where kaffirs come from, don't you, Rian? I'll tell you. It happened not so long ago. A white man chopped off a baboon's tail and set him to work. Then he caught another baboon and made it that one's wife, and soon there were hundreds all over the place. Too many, in fact. Don't move, Ou Willem. I'm going to make you eat shit.'

I wanted to run inside and hide, but Pa wouldn't let me. He got me to scoop some dusty baboon turds into the aluminium dish, and to set the dish down in front of the old man.

'Now, eat!' said Pa.

I know how the world began, therefore. I also know how it will end. But I don't know how to tell anyone, how to speak.

It is so long ago now that our speed steadied out that we seem as though stationary on this flat and unchanging road, heading north.

Bucs, beside me and driving, looks sullen in profile, remote. I watch the blunt red needle of the kombi's speedometer for want of something more real to do. In the end, I wonder if I will speak.

In the back, the two lovers, Vicky and the professor, Digby Bamford, have fallen so quiet that they might be asleep. Though I don't turn around to check.

Instead, I try shutting my eyes, too. But I can't.

Anyway, it was Bamford who had the last word. Back at the tree where we stopped for lunch.

'We're all in the same boat now, you know!'

I know. At the bottom of this vast dry ocean of veld.

The white metal shell of the kombi[1] trembles slightly, leaning head-on into the wind, the engine at full throttle kicking up a flat roar under the strain.

Bucs is wearing those sunglasses with lenses like mirrors and a baseball cap with the peak flipped up. Every now and again, he reaches out a hand and adjusts the rearview mirror by tilting or tapping it exactly once – as though that might do the trick at last, and allow him access to what lies behind us at a glance. A polished bullet swings from a locket chain around his neck, and the muscles beneath his T-shirt are deft and supple in movement. He is meticulous, Bucs, ambitious to get things done, impatient of me and all my constraints. His heavy mouth protrudes in what might be disgust.

This morning, during the video shoot at the zoo, he wanted to get right up on top of the leopard's cage and sling his microphone down over its nose to pick up its purring as it licked at the piece of raw meat between its paws.

'Ah, shit! Why not?' he objected when I stopped him. 'I can't hear a thing from here. It's no good.'

Headphones over the baseball cap. My own reflection distorted in the chromed lenses. His querulous frown and my fixed and stilted grin.

'And if it takes a swipe at you?' I wanted to know. 'Or bites a hole in the mike?'

Bucs looked down at the ground as if on the verge of coming up with the whole odd and ugly truth right to my white man's face.

1. *kombi*, minibus

Then, grudgingly, he gave way, scuffing his tackies² in the dust and turning his back.

Yet whether he stood in front of me and to one side after that, or squatted on his heels with the microphone out at arm's length, he still seemed only to be hanging around, waiting to grab the chance to do as he liked. While I completed the camera work.

I already had most of the shots – including the leopard, sprawled lazily at full length, switching, and the leopard, becoming totally intent and alert when it heard the clatter of the keeper arriving to shove a hunk of meat between the bars, and the leopard, the haunch of unflayed goat's meat in its jaws, springing up to pad back along the log in its cement cage. A quick, silent, deadly, brute cat. It crouched and paused for a moment or two to gaze at us: I got in close on the head. Eyes like glass, menacing. Split pupils in the light.

Then the quick, deadly crunching of the hairy blooded goat's meat.

'Got it,' I told Bucs as I turned off the equipment. 'That's a wrap.'

Vicky and Bamford were whiling away the time beside a cockatoo, a bedraggled white and pink bird on an open perch. Bamford was trying to coax it to climb onto his finger.

'Mind he doesn't bite!' cried Vicky, almost with a shriek, but terribly fond and excited.

'Why?' scoffed Bamford, twiddling a thick red forefinger in the bird's breast feathers. 'How do you know? Perhaps 'he' is really a 'she'? Looks a bit like a hysterical, fussy old whore—now, don't you? Come, come, now, big daddy wouldn't hurt you.'

But his clumsy finger-poking had ruffled the cockatoo. Its crest flicked up sharply and it uttered a screech of protest. Then it wound its head round and almost upside down as though surveying a very great oddity.

'Saucy thing!' said the professor.

In a high good temper, very pleased and self-satisfied, he stepped back and folded his arms, his beer-drinker's belly big—within a stitch, it seemed, of splitting his fly. A flat, squashed cap, like a quirk or a devilry, topped his handsome head. With a tight smile for Vicky, he began tapping his foot and glancing around, waiting.

His brawny arms were bare, and unexpectedly milky above the elbow.

'Aha!' He lifted a hand in salute as he caught sight of us. 'Finished at last, have you? Good lads, good lads. Well, then. What's next?'

'You,' I said. 'In the veld. Talking straight to camera.'

2. *tackies*, sneakers

If gold-rimmed glasses made Bamford look benign, it was only because the eyes behind the lenses had not yet been taken into account. A hot dark brown, these could as easily sharpen and nail you as melt and turn inward with self-pity.

'Oh, really?' he said. 'Me? Right away? In the buff?'

'No. In the veld.'

'I know, I know. Just joking. But seriously, I couldn't be more pleased. The African Creation Myth. My opening harangue. It's about time. Well, we'll have to get moving, then, and no delay. It was delay, wasn't it, that broke the camel's back? Made it impossible to hump. Come, sweetie.'

Draping a heavy, affectionate arm round Vicky's shoulders, he drew her to him, and together, like some ungainly, two-headed animal, they moved down the row of cages toward the exit. Bamford's broad hand fondled her shoulder, then slipped down her arm and casually cupped a buttock. Quickly, she glanced back, catching my eye. Her small face went tight, hostile. Her eyes were a deep blue. I don't know you, was the message, so direct and determined she might as well have spoken aloud.

The fetor of the zoo caught me by the throat. Oh, you don't, don't you?

'Ready?' I asked Bucs. 'Okay. Let's go.'

In the back of the kombi, the only corner free of Bamford's overflow was the space set aside for the TV equipment. The rest was a jumbled mound of luggage, on top of which a nest of sleeping bags had been slapped together. There the two of them lay now, Vicky with her head on his lap.

Though the petrol gauge was perilously close to the red E, Bucs took the first on-ramp to the highway. Like water, bright little mirages rippled across the road ahead.

One by one we fell silent, as though spellbound by the heat. Then a spanking new Shell sign rose above the low monotonous scrub, together with another sign:

TAKE-AWAY EATS

'Well, well,' observed Bamford. 'An oasis, I see. In the middle of nowhere. Lucky for you. A fine old restaurant, a la carte and cordon bleu.'

Once, in all likelihood, Bamford's fine old restaurant had been the only brick house on that remote and empty stretch of veld. Now it looked badly humbled, or worse, half-derelict, beside the shining, all-too-modern sweep of the filling station.

'I can't imagine why they've allowed it to stand,' I said.

'For our sake, of course,' Bamford replied.

At that moment, the kombi coughed, jerked and cut out.

'Luck of the devil!' remarked Bamford, adding: 'You do like to take chances, don't you?'

Bucs was able to coast the last hundred meters or so, then he swung the wheel, and the kombi went bumping across a stretch of rutted red earth to the smooth concrete apron around the pumps.

'Made it,' I said.

'Ooh, quick!' Vicky piped up. 'I have to wee or I'll pop!'

She clapped a hand over her mouth, and rolled her eyes up at Bamford, who let his hand rest on her belly just below her belt.

'Shall I squeeze?'

'Don't you dare!'

I opened the sliding door for her, and she pushed her way down through the luggage.

'Thank you,' she said as I pointed. 'I can see.'

Her plastic sandals clacking on the concrete, she hurried away to the door marked:

WHITES ONLY LADIES

SLEGS BLANKES DAMES

'Here,' said Bamford, clambering out to stand beside me. 'Whee-ew! Can you believe it? Christ almighty, this heat . . .' Reaching over his shoulder with one hand, he started to scratch his back. 'Here,' he said again, turning and stuffing, or trying to stuff, the ends of his T-shirt into his pants. In a gap, the bulge of his white belly flab and the coarse curling hair. 'What do you say to lending me a hand with the eats?' Without waiting for my reply, he whispered: 'Watch!' Crossing his legs tightly, he began to totter forward. 'Wee wee!' he squealed as though desperate. 'Wee wee!'

On tiptoe, tying himself into knots, he toiled on for a few steps. Then, pirouetting like a dainty if obese ballerina, he posed and said: 'The dying swan.'

'Go on,' I urged, giving him a few ironical hand claps.

He smiled. Throwing off his role with a show of easy strength and manly pride, he sauntered up to the toilet door and began to pound on it with the flat of his hand.

'Hey, lady,' he called in the earnest labored tones of Afrikaner petty officialdom. 'Tell me, lady. Did you got a comfortable seat?'

Bucs was round the other side of the kombi, I found, exchanging comments in an undertone with a thin old man in crumpled overalls who stood watching over the filling of the tank. They paused as I came up, and Bucs said:

'This trip, bra'. Without music, it's bad, man. Really! There is no life.'

'For sure,' I said. 'What's wrong with your tape-deck?'

All along, he had taken care to keep a little tape player on the seat beside him, but had made no attempt to use it.

'Nothing! Nothing is wrong!'

'Then, why . . . ?'

'It is the batteries, is fucked.'

'Fucked?' I said, and Bucs burst into laughter. So did I. Even the old petrol attendant opened wide his pink mouth, and wheezed.

'Ja, is fucked,' said Bucs. 'But maybe . . .'

He gave a nod over his shoulder.

'At a take-away eats joint?' I said. 'Batteries?'

In the twin bulbs of the mirror lenses, images of the filling station stood transfixed. Bucs's lips, still plucked up at the corners in a smile, sought, slightly contemptuously, to frame the correct friendly words.

'Ag, please, bra' Rian. Just try. I'll pay you back, man. Please. Four little batteries. Hey, okay, bra'? Please. Try. Why not?'

'Okay, okay,' I said, relenting.

'For example!' he said, holding out a number of small dead batteries in his palm.

I selected one.

Without waiting for Bamford, without even looking round to see where he had gone, I crossed the newly laid tar to the café.

It looked like a stranded farmhouse. What with its red corrugated iron roof and wide rambling verandah, the place seemed to reach all the way back to my childhood and beyond.

The sieve-door clapped to behind me.

I could almost feel the stale smell of hot fried potato chips hanging in the air. Directly in front of me, and close – so close, in fact, that we could almost have leaned forward and bumped our pale and sweaty foreheads together – sat a fat, hostile white woman, wedged in behind the old fashioned till, and knitting something dainty. Her small mouth was sucked in, petulant.

'Middag, tannie,'[3] I said in my most agreeable Afrikaans. 'Tannie does not perhaps sell batteries? Torch batteries?'

3. *Middag, tannie,* (Good) afternoon, auntie. A traditional greeting, both familiar and respectful.

I upended the black and shiny object on the counter, and watched it topple and roll round.

When I raised my eyes again, however, I found her as determined not to budge as before. There was a silence. Politeness made it impossible for me to utter another word. A hitch had developed in the knitting, it seemed, and I would have to wait.

At last, with an abrupt little click of needles, the tannie set aside her knitting. 'Ja-a,' she sighed.

'You have?' I said – conscious of taking her too literally, but oppressed by a sense of endless hot afternoons with nothing to do. 'Then could I have four, please? No, wait. Eight. Let it rather be eight.'

For Bucs, a set of spares. As long as he understood. Not charity, solidarity.

Just then, the screen door flapped again, and in bustled Digby, muttering under his breath about the murderous bloody heat, and the delay, and women. He didn't think to check his own impetuosity, nor did he seem completely satisfied, until he was standing right beside me again.

He turned up a menu lying face downward on the counter, and began rubbing his hands together with relish.

'Right!' he said. 'Let's see. That'll be, what, Spanish burgers, three Spanish burgers, with plenty of hot sauce. Make 'em doubles. And... Well?' Turning to me. 'What'll you and your sidekick have?'

'The shrimp cocktail for starters,' I said, rubbing my hands together, too, in unconcealed parody. 'The shrimp cocktail first, and then the roast duck with almonds.'

'Oh, really?' said Bamford, and his eyes went curiously intent while his lip curled in a smile. 'Well, you can go and suck for that in this hole, my friend. So. What'll it be?'

I drew the menu towards me. Pretended to be studying it.

'How about a double Spanish burger each?' I demanded, as if acting on a hunch.

'Right! Good! So that makes, what – five, am I right? Five double Spanishes with hot chili sauce. And now: salads. What salads have you got?'

'Egg,' responded the fat lady. 'French with lettuce. Greek salad with that nice fatty cheese. Ag,[4] anything. Whatever the gentlemen would prefer.'

'Mm? Yes,' muttered Bamford, leaning forward with both elbows on the counter so that his swag belly hung down. 'And chips? Tell me, do you make sloppy chips?'

4. *Ag*, phatic, 'Ah'; cf. German, 'Ach.'

'Excuse . . . ?' It was as though she couldn't breathe, or take her eyes off him.

'Limp chips, sloppy chips! Don't you like limp chips, Rian? We can't go a week without 'em, the girl and I. Scour the town for all the greasiest fish 'n chip shops. Limp chips! You swallow them whole, with salt, soaked so long in vinegar that they almost taste sweet.'

'All our food is fresh-prepared on the premises,' said the fat lady, her mouth as prim as a turtle's. She reached for her knitting again.

'Oh, quite!' returned Bamford. 'Well, that'll be one French salad only, then.' And to me: 'For Vicky. She needs it to keep her insides oiled. And chips? What shall we say? Two packets? Three? Two ought to be quite enough, don't you think?'

I nodded.

Painstakingly, on a stubby pad beside the till, the proprietress noted down the order in ballpoint. Then, sitting back and letting her arms flop to her sides, she raised her tremulous little voice piercingly: 'Anna-tjie!'

Immediately, from the kitchen came the reply:

'Miesies?'[5]

A buxom young black woman appeared, shyly trailing the beads of the curtain over the doorway through her fingers. She smiled back when I smiled. Her breasts pushed up against her housecoat, straining its creases as she breathed.

'Posh place, ain't it?' the professor remarked chattily, turning and leaning back against the counter. 'What do you think it once was? The voorkamer?'[6]

Altogether too close to my face.

I looked down at my fingers, tried to make some remark. But Bamford was simply too shrewd.

'Oo-er,' he crooned, dropping his voice so low that only I could hear it. 'How I'd love to nibble her noombies! Make women my size in the platteland,[7] don't they? Boobs like dumbbells. Imagine the miesies and the maid on the same bed. Side by side, on hands and knees, bums up and plump. 'Oh, no, sir, please don't!' All-in wrestling all night, man.'

'For sure,' I murmured, twisting up my face in an embarrassed grin.

I took a pace aside as though I was drawn by the nearby paperback stand. Put out a hand. Nothing much sold here. *Apocalypse Now.* Napalm in technicolor explosions on the cover, helicopter gunships, Marlon Brando's face. John D. MacDonald. James Hadley Chase. A chic blonde in a sprawl as though

5.   *miesies*, madam

6.   *voorkamer*, parlor

7.   *platteland*, rural areas

strangled, her hair spilling out wide around her. Another blonde, the tall sophisticated type, her evening dress slit up the thigh to expose a snub-nosed revolver tucked into the top of her stocking. Unreality. Murder. Sex. I suddenly wanted to sit down on the floor and press my head into my hands, and sink, black out.

But Bamford, whistling monotonously, pushed in beside me and ran a finger down the rack. Then, squatting comfortably on his haunches, he began flipping through a bunch of comics on the bottom shelf.

'Donald Duck,' he said. 'Dagwood. Dagwood and Blondie. Popular culture, Rian. You really ought to try and get into it, some time. All of it about Vicky's mental age, it would seem. We'll have to get her something, won't we? Keep her happy. Baby Huey, Baby Huey. Li'l Archie. Aha! What's this? Captain Marvel? Superheroes? Now, that's more like it. More my style. It's a pity they've never made a Wonderboy hero, though. Could have included it in the shoot, couldn't we? As a – cutaway, is it?'

'It's an idea,' I admitted, swallowing.

From him, bulky, preaching, to the flash heroics of the comic – cut.

WHIZZ! BLAM! POW!

I pressed my fingers into my eyes, let the pain turn over into floating lights. From the kitchen, I caught the sound of hamburger patties kissing the skillet and starting to fry. Meanwhile, the fat lady was shifting, rolling almost, from side to side – trying to smile, perhaps. Or to fart.

'Yes?' I said.

'Your batteries!' she fussed.

Rinds of pink gum, no teeth. You could almost taste the spittle.

'Thank you.'

Exactly the right batteries, too, wrapped in plastic.

I paid. Hung around.

The sounds of frying stopped. The fat lady paused, cocking her head – critical only of what Annatjie might be up to in the kitchen. Time had stood still here. You needed gills to breathe the stagnant air. Bamford, holding his comic at arm's length so as not to overbalance, stayed squatting on his heels, a little smile of rapt curiosity on his face. I headed for the door.

The smell of the tar closed over my head, sluggish, rich. The sun seemed also not to have moved.

I crossed to the pumps. Bucs had landed up slouched in the cab of the kombi, asleep or pretending. The old black man was nowhere in sight.

'Hier's hy, my bra',' I called, opening the driver's door. Here you are, brother.

He sat up with a jolt, a soft yelp.

'Yoh!'

Cupping his palms, he reached out across the steering wheel for the precious goods.

'There's the luck!' he grumbled throatily.

Perhaps he really had been asleep? I watched him ripping at the plastic with his teeth. I wanted to stay, if only to be satisfied that the tape would work. But those hamburgers weighed on me.

As I set foot on the verandah again, the screen door sprang open and out stepped Bamford. In one hand, he held a few comics, furled up. In the other, a paper bag packed with soft podgy things. Lunch.

'Aha!' he greeted me. 'Where did you disappear to?'

I gave a nod back over my shoulder. (The toilet, perhaps?) In an attempt to make up for it, I started forward.

'Let me....' I offered.

'Oh, no, no, no,' he insisted politely. 'No, thanks. Not at all.'

Lifting the packet high out of my reach, and cradling it there. His trophy.

Then I made a mistake: I tried to take the bag, anyway. He put out the hand containing the comics and caught me square in the chest, like a punch.

I would probably have gone over backwards if he hadn't grabbed my shirt with the same hand, full of comics.

I caught hold of his wrist. It was broad and rock-solid.

'Fuck you,' I said.

'Oh, come, come,' he proposed quietly, as if there was no room for pretence between us any more. 'Don't take it so hard!'

I found I couldn't speak.

With a high whine of gears, the kombi came banging and swaying in reverse across the tarmac. Vicky, I noticed, was lying on the sleeping bags in the back, staring straight up.

Bamford blew a raspberry at her, and bundled himself in, while I slammed the door on the two of them with a wrench.

I felt tired out or reluctant or something.

The air in the cab was charged. Reggae. Like the blood in my head, the beat. Trite words. Ethiopia, Utopia. The little speaker gleamed like a coin through the perforations of its leather jacket.

> *I – a warrior*
> *You – a warrior*
> *We – a warrior*

Bucs seemed to be musing, his hands resting slack on the wheel. He was waiting for orders. I felt glad. I felt quite capable of murder.

Bamford's voice cut across from the back:

'The very first tree, remember. The very first imposing tree!'

'Ja, baas, the tree,' Bucs replied, struggling deftly to engage the gears. 'It's baas Bamford's trip.'

The kombi rolled forward, tanked up, ready to go.

3

BAMFORD'S TRIP IT IS, ALL RIGHT. It's his ego at stake, his script, his woman. I am X, the faceless cameraman. Bucs is along for the ride. It is Bamford who is lying sprawled across the mound of booty in the back – the Wonderboy skull, the boxes of booze, the English shotgun with dozens of fat red cartridges strewn around loosely, the birthday cake and candles, the Yank Army pup tent that zips up snug as a dinghy at night. It's his belated attempt to recoup a failing reputation.

In the early sixties, Digby Bamford, then a bright young field researcher, made a discovery in a dried-up watercourse in the far north of the country that drew worldwide attention – the intact skull of an upright-walking ape, the 'missing link' of popular imagination. On the strength of it, he proclaimed:

'True man first arose in southern Africa!'

The skull is in the back, now. I've seen it, handled it. Mineralized almost purely into stone, it is a kind of marvel, more than two million years old, if you believe him. The inexplicable point about it seems to be its cranial capacity – over twice the size of any other of its kind.

'This is no ape up an evolutionary cul-de-sac. This is man. *Homo. Ipse.* Adam, if you like.'

In a memorable photograph, the twenty-five-year-old Bamford, already fat from too much beer, is sitting with the skull on his knee. The press dubbed it (and him) 'Wonderboy'.

Today, mainstream scientists openly debunk Bamford's theory. Wonderboy with its swollen brainpan is regarded as an anomaly, a freak. If not a fraud. In the years between, moreover, nothing has turned up to back the skull's discoverer.

Later in the sixties, world attention swung to the Olduvai Gorge, and the Leakeys' discovery of Zinj, the massive skull of a root-chewing man-beast. It was Zinj, too, who gave Kubrick the idea for the opening of *2001: Space Odyssey*, I guess. There's this dry sunken desert landscape. A water pan in a hollow. A group of shaggy ape-men crouching around, picking at a pile of bleached bones. Next thing, a rival gang arrives, and there is plenty of grunting and shrieking and snarling around the water pan until a squat shambling thug from our group plucks up the courage to rush forward and sock one of the gatecrashers over the skull with a bone. The intruder drops flat on his face in the water, and our ape, capering about in victory, sends the bone spinning high overhead into an unforgettable match-cut, a spaceship rotating on its axis. . . Don't get excited, though. Nothing like that is likely here. ACE-TV is a Mickey Mouse outfit. The Wonderboy tapes will be a teaching series for undergraduates.

In recent years, the Leakeys' son, Richard, has staked out a rich territory for himself among the fossil deposits in the volcanic ash around Lake Turkana. It was the young Leakey, too, who scripted and presented the highly successful BBC-TV series, *The Making of Mankind* – which probably gave Bamford his big idea.

More recently yet, world attention has swung to the deserts of Eritrea, where sun and wind have laid bare millions of years of prehistory as if on a plate for the Americans to pick at.

Bamford has been forgotten. The reason, he thinks, is political.

'We have everything the rest of Africa has, and more. Every fossil hominid found elsewhere has also been found here. Except for Wonderboy. Which strengthens my case, don't you see? Wonderboy is unique.'

I don't know very much more about Bamford. Except, of course, that he is with Vicky, now. Vicky, who is being so icy, pretending not to know me.

The first tree was a solitary blue gum . We sat at a round white concrete table beneath it.

No one spoke.

Digby divided up the junk food as though it were some kind of square meal. It was two o' clock. There was a good strong sense of silence. Full force of the afternoon.

Flipping open a comic and spreading it before him, he took a first mouthful. Vicky drew a comic towards her, too, and placed a dinky little Japanese stills camera on top of it as a paperweight.

'Yours?' I said.

She nodded but wouldn't look up. She was wearing a checked shirt like a boy's, and faded blue jeans, as usual.

Bucs, who had taken a large bite out of his hamburger, began rolling it round and round, as though he wanted to spit it out.

'What's all this hot shit?' he demanded.

'Spanish sauce,' I announced.

'Why?' said Bamford. 'What's wrong?'

In the end, he had to get Bucs a beer to cool his mouth down. Helped himself to one, too, while he was about it. And seemed to find it highly unsatisfactory that I could refuse.

'You're sure you don't want one?'

'Quite sure, thanks. I wouldn't like to be all thumbs when I am trying to shoot you.'

'I see. What you are saying is that you can't hold your booze.'

I crinkled the corners of my eyes, grinned merrily.

'For sure!'

He slipped the ring of the tag from the can around his little finger, and sucked at the beer in one long, almost endless pull. Patted his paunch with pleasure at the finish. Clipped the tag off a second can and sat down again. Belched.

As for my hamburger, it must have been at the bottom of the packet: it was squashed. Thick reddish sauce had smutched the wrapper. I couldn't eat it. But for the first time, I could look steadily across the table at Vicky.

Her face was pale, strained, but as triangular and interesting as ever. Her shoulders had thickened slightly. Her fair hair had lighter streaks in it from the sun. To my consternation, I noticed the first signs of crow's feet at the corners of her eyes. I had the impulse to lean across and try and smooth them away with my fingers. It must be possible. Gently. Gently. To touch her mouth that I remembered so well, her small mouth. Her sudden hot ardor, the way she bit and twisted, the whimper forced from her:

'Do it, do it . . . Oh, please, please, do it. Oh, Jesus, Jesus, Jesus, Rian – please!'

I got up from the table and chucked my hamburger across to Bucs. I felt shaky. I felt I couldn't understand. I feared I might even puke.

'Got to go and set things up,' I said.

I made my way back to the kombi, hauled out the camera case and dumped it at the side of the road. Sat down. Tried to let my mind go empty. Drained.

A long droning, growing bigger and heavier, made me look up. Trucks. An army convoy. I didn't move. Canvas flapping, and the smell of diesel and hot rubber as they ground by. The pale faces of very young soldiers in the back. Where were they going? I could have jumped up and clambered on as they passed. Gripping their rifles between their knees, in their hands, the young men looked down at me.

I waited until the whole convoy had gone by before I lugged the camera to the point I had already decided on, facing a clump of boulders. There he could deliver his opening speech, for all I cared. Boulders big enough to make a koppie, almost. Beyond, the blue gum, and flat and forever, the veld.

I scanned the area in a long pan, feeling the flow as I turned, zooming in and out easily on the boulder where Bamford could stand.

There were footfalls in the grass behind me.

'He wants to know,' came Vicky's voice, 'must he get ready?'

'Please,' I replied mechanically, my eyes fixed on the viewfinder. It was my turn not to look up.

The professor took his time, chatting with Bucs and pointing out something to him in his comic. Finally, he emptied a can of beer and walked over to the koppie with another two full cans in his hands, stowing them out of sight but not out of reach behind a rock.

Then he pulled off his T-shirt and struck a pose. Flexing his biceps, sucking in his belly and swelling out his chest, he stood there like some flabby failure in a Mr Universe contest.

'How's this?' he grunted, glancing with open admiration at his own muscles. His face was very red.

'Try again next year,' I advised.

Bucs, busy untwisting the microphone cable, looked at me quizzically, uncertain whether or not to laugh.

'Aaaurgh!' roared Bamford, dropping down on all fours, and hopping up and down, hoo-hooing like an ape. Vicky took a snapshot.

'When you're quite ready,' I said.

'Coo-ee!' cried Vicky, and took another picture.

Then she helped him change into a clean shirt and used a little mirror to show him how she combed his hair. At last, he sat down on a boulder and folded his arms. Leaned back. Looked at the camera and me aloofly.

'That's better,' I agreed. 'But you could afford to be more casual.'

He made some effort to relax, crossing one leg over the other and linking his hands together over his knee.

'We all wonder how the world began. Who are we? Where do we come from? Where are we going to? Rhubarb, rhubarb, rhubarb, rhubarb.'

Bucs gave a thumbs-up for sound.

'Right,' I said. 'Hold it. Stand by.'

I got Bamford in midshot, midriff and upward. Triggered the camera: the red recording light in my viewfinder blinked on, red like a bead.

'We all wonder how the world began,' Bamford ventured – for real, this time. 'Who are we? Where do we come from? Where are we going to? One idea that I personally like is derived from a Central African genesis myth. In the beginning, there was only a tree. A big tree, lots of leaves. And on the tree were ants, thousands and thousands of ants. The ants ate and defecated, ate and defecated, and as the mound grew, it turned into our world, as we know it. With a tree.' He gestured at the blue gum . 'A world tree.'

'Good,' I said. 'Cut. I think that's a take.'

Bucs and I shifted the video equipment over to the clump of boulders so I could record the tree from his point of view. Slender branches, white as bone against the drab hanging foliage, the bark round the trunk withering and curling back in strips. Like burnt and shredded skin, I thought.

Bamford clipped open another beer. Took a long swig. Wiped his mouth on the back of his hand. His eyes glinted resentfully.

'That was very quick,' he muttered.

'Sure. But I got what I wanted.'

'Spend all morning over bloody baboons' bums and only a minute on me?'

I laughed a little.

'You I don't have to try and catch on the off-chance. I can always set you up. Tell you what to do.'

'Telling me you can!'

He tilted his head back again, swallowing from the can.

He would have said more, but Vicky put her hands round his arm and began caressing his biceps, pressing her fingers into his arm, distracting him. Restraining him.

I turned away as soon as I could, trailed the camera over to the tree and hunted around until I found a line of ants trickling up and down the bark. Anything is interesting, if you watch it closely enough. Black ants twittering along, like the prickle of blood returning to a numbed limb. I leant back, rubbed my eyes. Tried to feel what was needed from the shot.

At that moment, a lizard flicked round and sat on the trunk. A nimble little thing, throat pulsing. Delicate. Agile. Silver as a leaf. I wondered if it ate ants. And if so, could I catch it on camera? I sank down on one knee.

'What the hell are you up to now?' said Bamford, bellicose.

The lizard was gone.

I checked the viewfinder. It was blank: a small flat space excised from reality. Over the camera, perhaps, I had some control.

'I'm not going on,' I stated calmly, and stood up.

I hoped Bamford would make for me again. I wanted to smash him in the face with the camera. My fingers trembled slightly as I snapped the lens cover back on.

He made some demand. I didn't hear it.

'I'm not going on,' I repeated. My heart began to beat. 'I'm through. This is it.'

I looked around. I couldn't believe what I had done. Flat horizon, level all around. Bamford's big face looming, his lips twisted like a child's, his hair beginning to recover from Vicky's attention with the comb. The odd thing was, I hadn't expected to say a word. It had simply happened. If he had been taken unawares, so had I. I swung the camera on to my shoulder and walked back to the kombi. Bucs came too, and climbed into the driver's seat, while I stayed outside. He lit a cigarette, exhaling the smoke in angry puffs. I ignored him.

Vicky appeared round the back of the kombi, in a hurry. The little black Jap camera was swinging round her neck, between her breasts.

I looked down. The sand underfoot was very clean. It gets that way, sometimes, beside a main road.

'Adrian?' she said timidly.

She'd always had to wear a bra one size too large because, she said, her back was too broad. The first time I uncovered her breasts, she had squirmed and tried to stifle her giggling.

'They're such minis!' she had declared.

Nipples tightening under my hands.

Anyhow. I began trying to shove the camera plus its cables into the carrying case in the kombi. She put her hand on my shoulder.

'Adrian,' she said. 'Please.'

I tried shaking her off, but she only held on more tightly, and her voice stung me like a cord.

'Can't you grow up?'

'You want *me*,' I panted thinly. 'You want *me* to grow up?'

'Oh, please,' she said, exasperated. 'You know what I mean. Please ... It means so much to him. You don't understand. He's like a big baby. Oh, he's shocking, outrageous, I know, but he doesn't mean any harm. *You* know. ...'

'Yes, I know. I know, all right. But does he?'

'Does he what?'

'Know.'

'Know what?'

'About us.'

'No. Oh, come on, Rian. Really. That was years and years ago.'

She sat down beside me and took my hand. To my chagrin, the gesture eased me. Her fingers were sweaty, worried. I wanted to kiss them. Instead, I got up and went over to Bamford, who was sitting at the table again, rolling a single eucalyptus seed round and round between his palms.

'Professor,' I said, and it was harsh, like sand in my mouth. 'I'm sorry.'

He said nothing, but looked at me distantly, broodingly. Opening his hands, he glanced at the eucalyptus seed. Smelt his palms.

'Want a smell?'

I shook my head awkwardly.

'We'll make it to the Wonderboy site tonight,' I promised. 'I really did get a good shot of you back there, you know. In fact, I've had nothing but good shots all day.'

'Of course,' he agreed politely, reassuringly. He tipped up the last beer can. It was almost empty.

'Guess I wouldn't mind a beer now myself,' I put in.

'Too late,' he replied with evident satisfaction. 'The cold ones are all gone. As for the others, well – do you like boiled beer?'

There was a pause.

'Don't mistake me,' I added in an undertone, a warning. 'I'd like to ditch this show. I'd like to walk out and leave it flat. I would, too, if I could.'

Bamford gave me a disgruntled glance.

'We're all in the same boat, you know!' he retorted, and got to his feet, stretching so that his bones cracked.

He went over to Vicky, put an arm around her and sought her mouth out with his. Showing me something. She resisted for a moment, then melted. Perhaps I ought to have had the camera on them. At length, he broke away, wiping his lips. Turned her round by grappling with her and twisting her arm up behind her back, and smacked her bottom.

'Ooh, don't!' she squealed. Or not in front of the others, anyway.

'And so?' Bamford invited. 'On with the show!'

'Right,' I said from where I sat.

When we drove off, I leaned my forehead against the dashboard. Bucs didn't try to play the tape again. I'd have been glad if I could have felt anything. I wanted to get it over with – this unreal situation.

Bucs says nothing. There is silence in the back. I shut my eyes, listen to the engine.

I want to tip the horizon upright. Slowly, toiling for years, perhaps, but let it hold. Like iron. The road keeps coming at me – the same road, I have known it all my life. I am five or six years old and standing on the seat of my father's pick-up truck, his bakkie. The sky beyond the trees is red, but whether with dawn or sunset, I cannot tell. My father is beside me. He is dead, I know, but his big white face is wagging at me, trying to tell me something. I wish I could hear him over the roar of the engine, but I can only catch one word, whether it is 'liar' or 'fire,' I cannot tell. I try to repeat it, only to find myself in the kitchen of the take-away café, beside the stove. The oven is open. The tannie is looking inside it, for change, it seems, but out she comes with a fluffy day-old chicken, half of a bloodied eggshell still sticking to its back. The chicken cheeps and struggles. I don't want it to die. I sink my thumbs into her fat neck, trying to throttle her. Her flesh is soft, powdered, sleepy-smelling: I am engulfed. She sighs, splutters: Ag, no. I'm only smiling!

And I awake with an erection.

It is late afternoon. The kombi sails on. Grass in waves and the slow jigging of a barbed wire fence.

I try to keep pace with its measured leaps from pole to pole.

Bamford calls from the back:

'Stop a minute, will you? I have to pee.'

On the spur of the moment, I get out and stand beside him. His own trick. He splits open his zip and fumbles. The pink little head of his penis, smaller than I had expected. I try to concentrate on something else. Unzip my fly, too. Careful not to show him. Stand waiting.

'You say this whole area was once under water?' I remark for want of anything better to say.

'All of it,' he replies promptly, pissing from side to side. 'Two billion years ago. A vast inland lake or sea, bigger than the Sea of Galilee, and more miraculous. Bubbling with life. Tiny shellfish raining down on the mud at the bottom incessantly for millions of years. . . . That mud is now the outcrop stone around here.'

Stunted scrubby trees. A koppie. What made the water dry up, I wonder. The same thing as happened to me?

'Every little drop helps,' Bamford remarks comfortably, stowing his penis away after a cursory shake. 'See you back in the bus.'

I nod, glance down. My own prick, still lazily thick between my fingers. It has a will of its own. I try and hurry up.

4

BAMFORD IS THRIVING. His face is redder than ever, he goes around in a spotless pith helmet and dark glasses and acts as if he owns the place. He likes lecturing me on camera work, Bucs on being black. If black men didn't have such long penises, they would never have been oppressed, he says. The whole of imperialist history in Africa can be boiled down to the black man's dangler. Apartheid, for instance, is penis envy, pure and simple. The boer[1] can't live in the shadow of the black man's cock.

'Oh, stop it!' cries Vicky.

This is at breakfast.

'What?' says Bamford, his mouth full of baked beans.

'All that. It's old hat.'

'Whose cock is old hat? Not mine, I hope.'

'No,' agrees Vicky lightly, laughing but going scarlet. 'Not yours. Definitely not.'

She doesn't even glance at me. She doesn't have to. It is nearly two days since we arrived, and she hasn't spoken a word to me.

I consider what remains on my plate. Ignore her. Bucs and I have shot a whole clutter of tapes, more than I expected. Bamford on the Cradle of Man. Bamford on Other Famous Skulls of South Africa – the Taung baby; Mrs Ples. Bamford on Bamford. Bamford in silhouette against the dawn. We arrived here on Friday afternoon and today is Sunday. Today we are going to shoot Bamford brushing his teeth. Tomorrow is his birthday: he is in his mid-fifties, I guess. He wants a party, he says. Balloons and booze and a birthday cake. Vicky will prepare it.

'I will,' she promises. 'A pretty cake with icing and candles, and bowls on the table with sweeties.'

'You're the sweetie,' he murmurs, pouting his lips.

Yesterday we set out on our first expedition to where he claims to have found the skull: Bamford with a shotgun over his shoulder.

'You never know,' he pointed out. 'We might get something for the pot.'

I followed, my camera on my shoulder, and behind me came Bucs with the rest of the equipment.

---

1. *boer*, Afrikaner (literally, farmer)

The land around here is very flat. Spectral, ashen-grey thorn trees which seem only to crack and wither further in the silence and the heat. Ahead of us, two ground hornbills flapped heavily into the air. I was glad to see that Bamford didn't consider them candidates for the pot.

'What do you hope to shoot?' I called out.

He motioned impatiently for me to shut up, and stood still, crouching and staring ahead.

I stopped, and Bucs walked into me with a grunt.

'Oh, God!' groaned Bamford, as though about to blow his top.

'Sorry,' I said. 'It's difficult to lug this stuff around quietly, you know. What did you miss?'

'I don't know, damn it! I saw horns, though. Distinctly. I'm almost positive...'

'Some sort of buck?'

He didn't reply.

I looked ahead. There was no sign of life, only the bush. You could almost have stepped into it and disappeared.

The riverbed, when we came to it, was as dry as a stick and littered with boulders. At our approach, a small herd of goats broke away and began scrambling up the banks. One old goat refused to scare, though. He blinked. Evil eyes. Flies twiddled round his ears. A piece of rope was knotted to his neck like a lead. I pitched a pebble at him but he wouldn't budge.

'Your buck?' I asked Bamford.

'Possibly,' he admitted.

He couldn't squirm out of it. It was too obvious. The horns.

The only other thing that happened was that a little herd boy ran by – ragged shorts and a big Army bunny jacket, eyes rolling, teeth bared in a whimper of fright. I expected Bucs to call out to him, a joke or some kind of reassurance, but Bucs wasn't in the mood. His cap was twisted round so that the peak projected backwards. From his armpits, patches of sweat had spread.

'Yebo, Bucs,' I said. It's okay, Bucs. But he only grimaced.

We pushed on through ankle-deep sand and over boulders. God knows when last there was any water here. High banks to make you feel cramped. The perfect place for an ambush. Wicked slicing sound of arrows – the thud of one finding its mark. The solar topee'd leader turns on his own axis and staggers with an arrow through his throat. Ga, ga, ga, he tries to speak, to point. He topples. Cut back to the camp. The leaves of a bush are stealthily parted. A face, daubed with war paint, but black, peers out. (Movies distort history.) Vicky, in a shirt that might be Bamford's, and tight jeans, is lying back in a deck chair. Innocently, she bites into a big juicy red apple as she turns the pages of a magazine.

'You'll tell us when we're getting near the place, won't you?' I said.

Bamford stopped and stood with his arms akimbo. Turned around. Looked right and left.

'You know,' he remarked, pinching his nose as if it was itchy: 'any place will do, really. Any bend in the stream. The landscape reconfigures itself. I'll probably never find the exact spot again. After all these years. You can't step into the same river twice. Why don't *you* choose? Go on.'

'You're not serious,' I said.

'I am,' he said. 'I am, indeed.'

Bucs sat down on a rock and began singing to himself, some monotonous refrain, over and over again.

Bamford folded his arms, putting me on the spot.

'What the hell, then!' I retaliated. 'This is it. It was exactly here that you found the Wonderboy skull, professor.'

I directed him to walk up and down. I got him to peer up at the sky, to stand as if musing. I got him to kneel down to examine the front of a rock minutely. I got him to stand with his back to us, twiddling his thumbs. Then I told him it had all been only a rehearsal, and got him to start again – this time I'd do it for real, in heroic angle. And I did.

In the end, he stood on a rock, his hair slightly awry, his face stern, perspiration beading his upper lip.

'It was along here,' he announced, 'over thirty years ago, that I made the discovery. I was walking along, I remember. Not a cloud in the sky. A day very like today, glaring hot. I tried to rest my stick on a round stone, but the stick slipped. 'Hello,' I thought. 'What have we here?' I picked up the stone, turned it face upwards. Of course, it is common knowledge today what I held in my hands. Proof. Solid proof. Here, in this far corner of the world where no one would have dreamt it. . . Granted, I can't tell how the skull arrived at my feet. Perhaps, as some of my critics have suggested, it fell from the sky. It seems more likely, however, that it was washed from a cave by an underground flood, and simply got deposited here, where I found it.

'But look at it, I ask you. A perfect skull. Not a heap of fragments stuck together with glue, like the monstrosities from Olduvai and Lake Turkana and that dustbowl, whatsitsname, in Ethiopia. Look at the teeth, the eye-sockets, the cranium. Can there be any doubt? We existed first. Before the degenerates, the man-apes, came man. Perish the sceptics. This is man, true man. Man with a brain, a mind of his own, man capable of standing on his own feet, of conquering the world. My skull predates all the little subhuman creatures put forward by Dart, the Leakeys, Johansen, and all the rest of the gang. Look.

'In Wonderboy, you are encountering your own most ancient self. Yourself before history. Millions of years ago, when the whole continent was a hotbed of evolving life, volcanoes still active, sunsets streaked with fire right around the horizon, strange animal forms groaning and crying out... South Africa, like it or not, was the birthplace of man. This is it. Here, right where I am standing. All right, cut! Enough, I've had it.'

Waving his arms above his head as though helpless, Bamford stepped down from the rock.

I sat back on my heels.

'Shit,' I said. 'How could you do that?'

'Do what?'

'What you just did. I mean, make up what you like, and ad lib. What about the script?'

'What about it? Is there no space to improvise?'

'Christ, all that rant about critics.'

'Well, since we can't find the actual spot, I thought...'

'Oh, no. Not 'we' can't, professor. You can't.'

'What do you mean?'

'You can't find the spot.'

'Oh, all right! I can't. I can't, then.'

'Another thing. How can you ask people to look at the skull if you don't have the bloody thing in your hands?'

'Oh, come on, man! Can't you just splice it in, make it look good?'

'You mean... A slow dissolve from your face to the skull?'

Through his hot sweaty flesh, the petrified bone emerging.

I liked it. I almost laughed.

'Yes,' I admitted. 'Okay, I'll try.'

Bucs was already wrapping the mike in its cord. I packed up the camera. I had no intention of ever coming back.

The kombi is parked in the shade of a massive spreading wild fig, the only green thing around. Bits of white cloth are tied to its lower branches, making me wonder if the tree might not be sacred. I've asked Bucs about it but he doesn't seem to know. Vicky, for her part, admires the tree. The smooth limbs fascinate her, especially where they fork upward. They look like the human groin, she says. Bamford claims to have camped here on his first trip, right under the branches. Only, the monkeys were a nuisance, he says. They tore up his books.

'Monkeys?' says Vicky, frightened. 'Tore up your books?'

'A pocket Darwin, I remember. And a copy of *Adventures with the Missing Link*, by someone less famous. It seems that the little blighters objected to being seen as the progenitors of the human race. Can't really blame them, can you?'

'Oh, you!' cries Vicky, and pummels his arm with her fists.

I delight in her flushed face and bright eyes. I'd love to slip my hand into her jeans. I want that lingering, delicate softness, that heat.

Bamford, whose glasses have been knocked askew, looks round like a halfwit, enjoying only the moment, as I get up from the breakfast table and mention going to see what Bucs is up to.

Vicky swipes at his hair, ruffling it.

'I think,' he remarks. 'I think I'm going to have to... Ha!'

He grabs her, mauls her, draws her backward into his lap. She looks small in comparison to his bulk, almost a child. She struggles. As, I imagine, at night. Turn away.

Bucs has been setting up the props for the shoot. A shaving mirror for the professor, a plastic tooth mug, a new tube of toothpaste and a ruby red toothbrush. This is to be the part about teeth, about the way a chimp's bottom jaw forms a V, and a human's a U. I know every line of the script. It's tedious. My idea is for Bamford to jazz it up a little by brushing his teeth. Let him lecture while he foams at the mouth, and spits. I'll catch the reflection in the mirror to make it doubly riveting.

'All ready?' I ask Bucs, unnecessarily. I can see that it is.

To one side, a chimp's skull. Like a dog's, its teeth. Not far from it, in a box whose sides fold away, the Wonderboy skull on black velvet. It is smaller than I thought. And remote, terribly remote. Unimaginable span of time.

I hold it in both hands, look into the empty eye-sockets but can't see into it.

'Speak to me!' I beg.

I wish I could make the teeth snap.

'He's hungry,' I warn Bucs. 'He wants you.'

Bucs grins in a pained way and ducks. (My father's kind of joke. Scare the kaffir, see if he plays along.)

Ashamed, angry with myself, I stop, but don't know what to do next.

Bucs touches the dome of the skull with his forefinger.

'This is a man?'

'Not just *a* man. The first man. Ask the professor.'

'How does he know it is not a woman?'

'A woman?'

I pick up the microphone and blow into it.

'We interrupt this program for an important announcement. For the past million years or so, we have thought Wonderboy was a man. We were wrong, folks! A case of mistaken gender. He is a girl. I repeat, Wonderboy is a girl.'

I push the microphone under Bucs's nose.

'Your reaction, sir?'

We both laugh. Bucs with a wary eye on me.

'Bra' Rian,' he ventures in a tone I already know well. 'Please, bra'. Ek sê[2]. . . . Let me have a chance with the camera today. Please! I won't fuck with it, I promise.'

'Why not? How big a prick do you need for a camera?'

'Bra'?'

Suddenly, I feel it is all a waste of time. I sometimes feel terribly old. And tired.

'Go ahead,' I say. 'It's yours.'

'Bra'?'

'The camera. It's yours.'

The camera, the bush. History and prehistory with all its mistakes and dead ends. Take it, brother. It's yours.

In the last couple of nights round the fire, when Bucs smoked his weed, I tried stealing a drag or two, although the taste was harsh and I disliked the limp spitty paper in my mouth. Bamford, boozing solidly, whisky and soda, hung around, too, staring into the flames, and brooding. Last night, for instance, he was full of the philosopher, Hobbes.

'Hobbes,' he said. 'D'you know him? Know Hobbes? Brain like a combustion engine. Said reason – reason is a motion in the head. I admire him. Admire Hobbes.'

I thought about this for a while.

'I don't get it,' I said. 'Emotion in the head?'

'No, no. Motion, a motion!'

'Oh, I see,' I said, turning a finger round at my temple. 'Like. . .?'

'Yes,' retorted Bamford. 'Like. . .'And he turned a finger round at his own temple.

With a strangled snort, Bucs rolled over, unable to hold back the giggles.

---

2. *Ek sê*, I say

The firelight kept twinkling on his glasses.

'Awu,'[3] he crooned helplessly. 'Abelungu.'

Abelungu. Whiteys. That's us.

I feel wrung out, dry mouthed. Reckless.

Bamford and Vicky come wandering over at last, their little fingers linked.

'Would you like to join me for a drink?' I inquire.

'No!' says Vicky, tugging at his hand as though to drag him away. 'It's too early.'

'It's never too early,' declares Bamford, wresting himself away. 'Or, for that matter, too late.'

I fetch a new bottle of whisky from the kombi, breaking the seal on the way. Bamford, who has folded his arms, continues to watch me with great interest.

'One virgin less,' I laugh, displaying the cap.

He doesn't react. Nor does Vicky. Maybe it isn't that funny. I splash the tooth mug half full, and knock it back in one go.

'Lachaim,' I say.

Tears prick my eyes. I fear I might cough but force myself not to, though it somehow becomes difficult to breathe. I smile at Bamford. Pouring himself rather less than I did, he swallows it in the same way.

'Down the hatch!' he agrees, wiping his mouth on the back of his hand.

I cough. Take a swig straight from the bottle.

'Oh,' says Vicky in a cold and tiny voice. 'You big brave men!'

Turning her back on us, she begins to make a show of interest in Bucs and the camera. Bamford shrugs. We spend a few minutes discussing the next sequence.

'I wish we had a pair of false teeth,' he fusses.

'I think your own will be better,' I reply. 'I could always do a zoom into your open mouth. Just tell me what to go for beforehand.'

Ignoring my encouragement, he pokes a finger into his mouth, and rubs it up and down while he looks into the shaving mirror.

'B'this looks stupid,' he mumbles.

'It doesn't!' I insist with a laugh. 'Come on, let's begin.'

I fit the headphones on.

Vicky smiles at Bucs.

'Look how funny he looks!' she says of me. 'He thinks he's you.'

Somewhere in the bush, a bird is crying monotonously, sweetly, 'Blood, blood, blood, blood. . .' There is a scratch and a squeak as I touch the mike, followed by a roar as I blow into it.

---

3.   *Awu*, phatic exclamation; cf. 'Wow!'

'Testing, testing. . .'

I decide to go and check Bucs's camerawork. He has Bamford framed in mid shot, too small and at a slight slant. I couldn't care. My belly is hot and full of whisky.

'Good,' I call. 'Go for it! Roll when you are ready.'

First, as planned, we do Bamford brushing his teeth. He ends up baring them at himself in the mirror.

'Our teeth are what incline us to being human. . .'

Then the lecture on the ape's jaw.

'A v-shape. And look at those canines – made for tearing.'

Then, with the Wonderboy skull in his lap:

'Alas, poor Yorick. What lips hung here, I wonder? What tales could they have told? Did he use fire? Did he make and keep his own tools? Did he hunt? Worship a god? Did he have only one mate?'

Vicky hangs round with her little Nikon again. She has shot quite a few rolls of film already.

In a pause in the taping, I help myself to another tot of whisky. So does Bamford. His face looks swollen. His eyes are red. Too many late nights, I guess.

'Why don't we have a break?' I ask. I'm beginning to feel bold, loose tongued. Maybe I will speak? 'Come on, professor. Let's do something we would like to do.'

Bamford takes the whisky bottle and tilts it up for a swig, as I did before. He regards me speculatively.

'All right,' he agrees. 'I'll get the shotgun, shall I? You throw a bean can up in the air as a target, and we'll see what we can do to it.'

I go and collect a couple of bean cans from the garbage hole Bucs and I dug when we first arrived, while Bamford fetches his shotgun from the kombi and stands polishing the barrels with the end of his shirt.

'You should see little Vicky use one of these,' he remarks. 'You've never known anything like it. Clay pigeons. Bing! Crack! Dust.'

'I'd like to see that,' I say.

He leans the shotgun barrel down on his toe.

'Isn't it a beauty?' He strokes the butt.

I eye it apprehensively.

He grins.

'Whatsamatter?'

I don't reply.

Slinging the gun up again, he breaks open the barrels and feeds in two fat red cartridges.

'Okay,' he commands. 'Chuck the tin as high as you can.'

I fling the thing, though it's too light really to do more than spin. Bamford follows it in an arc, and pulls the trigger just as it begins to drop.

The gun bucks with a heavy explosion.

The tin sails back to earth undamaged.

'Damn it! Again.'

I walk across, pick it up. Vicky and Bucs are sitting in the kombi, at the sliding door. They seem to be getting on very well together. They watch me, but don't stop talking.

I pitch the tin up again, and this time Bamford gets it glancingly. It is knocked to one side and wavers as it falls.

He smiles, looks more satisfied.

'That took the oomph out of it.'

'Could I have a go?'

I've never laid hands on a shotgun before but the more whisky I drink, the easier it begins to look.

'All right. Just hang on. One more shot.'

His 'one more' turns into two. He misses both. He tries to argue for more, but I won't listen. I get hold of the gun and manage to load it.

He walks away to fetch me a tin.

Out of the corner of my eye, I catch sight of Vicky passing her fingers through her hair. A preening gesture. For Bucs?

'Vicky!' I'd like to call, but the word sticks in my throat.

I take another swig of whisky, shake my head. If I swing round now and pull the trigger. . . . I can see it all taking place in slow motion: the roar of both barrels simultaneously, Vicky flinging out her arms as she tries to rise to her feet, the sudden burst of red across her shirt, it's wet, she is stumbling, going up sideways and backwards, knocked into the side panel of the kombi, her hands fluttering and clawing at her shirt, her face set in a scream. I can't hear it, I can hear only the music, Rasta stuff, a heavy beat, cut back to me as I reload, squeeze the trigger again, both triggers, one set slightly in front of the other, the silver filigree work along the stock of the handsome English shotgun. You don't see my face, only the barrels, and then again the kick and the flash of the flame and the smoke curling, completely satisfying, nothing like it. And Bucs collapsing, sprawling beside her, his outstretched hand groping to touch hers in a last trembling effort, a spasm, as a trickle of blood begins its way down the corner of his mouth, and – but, no, wait, that's too heroic – as he tries to crawl under the seat for protection, screaming, gibbering, eyes rolling, his blood spattering the white enamel of the kombi. Cut back to me.

'Vicky!' I call out loud, and raise the gun.

She gives me a dirty look, and her hand comes up as though to wave me away.

'Don't play the fool!' she says.

I squint along the barrels. Black. Shiny. Long. I laugh, turn back. Take another mouthful of whisky. It burns, but I'm used to it, now.

'Are you ready?' calls Bamford, who has been waiting.

He throws the tin can high, I follow it, but it seems to slip by too quickly – I can't quite aim.

'Try again?' he calls.

'For sure. Throw it higher, this time.'

In the movies of my childhood, flocks of white birds always erupted to hover above the African treetops when the great gun boomed. Their cries were weird, desolate. Here, nothing has stirred. The explosions seem only to have added to the silence. Bamford retrieves the bean can, waves, and throws it up in the air again.

The gun kicks harder than I expected. A hard mechanical thing, unwieldy.

'Did I hit it?'

'Dear God, no! Here, give it back to me.'

I relinquish the shotgun. Drink more whisky. He leans the gun on the toe of his shoe, shoves more cartridges in, closes it. As he reaches for the whisky, it happens.

The gun kicks right out of his grasp, falling with a clatter and a roar, or roars first with its mouth close to the earth, and then falls, I don't know.

But Bamford sits down, his face very white.

A thin noise comes from him.

Part of the toe of his shoe is missing. I can't believe what I am seeing. There is no blood, only a chunk of shoe missing. I am on my knees, struggling to undo the laces. His hand comes out at me, trying to push me away.

'I've got to see!' I tell him.

I pull the shoe off. I can smell the odor of the inner shoe. It's dark, sweaty. Now I can see the blood, the ripped flesh on the outside of his big toe.

'It doesn't look too bad,' I say. But I don't know.

Helpless, big bellied, rolling around on his back, Bamford tries to grab his foot and see for himself. I manage forcefully to pull off the sock. Beside me, Vicky is on her knees, too, now.

'Digbee-ee!' she wails.

'Goddamn it,' he bellows.

I hold his foot still and try to examine it. There is the pattern left by the sock. The big toe is bleeding copiously. A bit seems to have been nipped out of the flesh. Nothing too terrible. I drop his foot roughly.

'You're lucky,' I say.

'Digby, baby,' cries Vicky. 'Oh, my baby, are you all right?'

Bucs has brought the first-aid kit from the kombi. I fold a bandage into a pad, hold it to the wound. The pad quickly soaks through, but I wind more bandage round the toe, tightly.

'We'd better pack up and go back to town,' I remark. 'Get you to a doctor.'

'To hell with that,' Bamford grunts. 'I'm not going.'

'Oh, please, please, you must, baby,' cries Vicky.

He shoves her away and sits up.

'No, leave me alone. I've got to see if I can walk.'

I warn him: 'You'll force it to bleed.'

'That's all right. As long as I can walk.'

He gets up. Holds on to Bucs. Limps along for a few steps.

'Jesus, Jesus,' he mutters furiously. 'Fuck it! Fuck, fuck, fuck it.'

'What a stupid thing to do,' Vicky says flatly under her breath.

'What?' I demand. 'Walk? Or blow your toe off?'

She ignores me.

I pick up the shotgun and trail behind.

We make the professor as comfortable as possible in the back of the kombi, his bandaged foot resting higher than his head. He is soon attempting to smile again, although his face is white and shiny with shock. In the crook of his arm, he cradles the whisky bottle. Vicky sits beside him, her head on her knees.

Bucs climbs into the front of the kombi and switches his tape on softly.

I – a warrior.

I feel as if I have been through all this before.

Flies are beginning to find the place irresistible. I suggest we shut the doors and windows.

'It'll be like an oven,' Bamford objects.

'But maybe you'll be able to sleep.'

His toe has almost stopped bleeding. I change the dressing, decide against disinfecting it: it has probably bled enough to be clean. A broad but shallow wound. It could have been worse.

Bamford grasps my hand as I tie the last knot.

'Thank you,' he says.

I deflect the sentiment with an ironic jab.

'We're all in the same boat, you know.'

'I know,' he replies. Smiles.

'You old fool.'

'No fool like an old fool,' he chirps.

'You can say that again,' says Vicky.

A fly tries to settle on his foot but I wave it away.

He shuts his eyes and a ripple goes through his jaw muscles.

'Is it very painful?' asks Vicky.

He nods irritably.

She helps him to some aspirin from the first-aid chest, and he swallows the tablets with whisky.

I find some shotgun cartridges on the floor and stuff them into my pocket. We talk desultorily for a while, then, after a silence, a light snore escapes Bamford's lips.

I shove back the door and quietly step outside.

'Where are you going?' Vicky whispers sharply.

I lift the shotgun, point at the bush.

'Why? What are you going to try and shoot?'

I roll my eyes, mouth the words silently:

'Myself, maybe!'

'Don't be stupid, Rian. Come back.'

My head is aching dryly. Too much whisky. Too much excitement. The bush is hot. Empty. Desecrated. I can't turn back now. Five greasy cartridges in my pocket, one in the gun. Vicky, I keep thinking. This is for you.

5

THE FIRST BIRD IS A BUSH DOVE, its drowsy seductive cooing making the sunlight throb. I circle the tree, staring into the thorns. Nothing.

The shotgun is heavy, unwieldy, like a third leg. My headache is worse.

I lean back against the tree. I've already puked, an acid gush of whisky and things from breakfast. It doesn't matter. A feast for the ants.

In among the thorns, I make out a thicker shadow than the rest. The dove, no doubt.

The sights of the shotgun dip and sway.

'Squeeze your trigger, don't jerk it,' I can almost hear Bamford advising. 'Squeeze it. Like a woman's tit.'

I laugh soundlessly, try not to breathe. Nestle my cheek against the stock. Brace myself.

I am astounded and deafened. It feels as though I've been kicked in the face. Thorns and feathers have burst through a hole in the twigs. I start forward. Very little seems to be left of the dove. Feathers and blood. I stick a few of the feathers in my hair, daub the blood across my cheeks. Check my nose to see if it is bleeding, but it isn't. I am distressed. On impulse, I would like to pick up the pieces and put the bird back together again. One wing is perfect. I spread it on my fingers. But I can't find the head.

With my back to the tree again, I slip to the ground and sweat. I'd like to turn back the clock. Let the dove call again; I'd leave it alone this time. I'd avoid all but the most innocent thoughts – a dove is love, love is a dove. Jesus could never have walked here, his feet were too white.

I used to help pour hot water into the zinc tub when Pa took a bath, hot water from a pot.

'Ah,' said Pa, and flung back his head.

I don't want to hate, I want to think.

In the vlei at the foot of the hill lived an old grey heron called Dawie. When he spied us coming, old Dawie would jack himself into the air and sail away downwind with a croak.

Pa refused to shoot him

'Heron tastes of fish oil,' he said with disgust.

Mushrooms grew in the vlei. We would pick them. They tasted black like iron, fried in a pan on the stove.

Sometimes, though, Pa would shoot anything that moved. Once even a big black eagle that was spiraling over the house and that fell in a heap of sooty feathers in the yard. Pa didn't know what to do with it. He threw it over the fence. He killed a little family of warthog in the vlei, too, laughing afterwards at the way they had run, their tails in the air 'like aerials'. His great dream was to shoot a leopard – a 'tiger,' as they said in our district – but he never did. Tarentaal on the other hand were an everyday affair. He would dump them on the kitchen table. Sky-blue with red wattles, the birds' heads dangled from long skinny necks. Their eyelids looked shriveled like ash. It was my job to hang them in the shed by the tail feathers. As soon as they dropped, said Pa, they were good enough to eat.

Once, too, he returned from a hunt with the whole severed head of a hippo roped to the back of the bakkie.

'We're going to boil it,' he told me. 'Boil it and take out the skull.'

He had shot the hippo, a cow, while she was sleeping in the reeds on the banks of the Limpopo, two white birds on her back.

'I crept up close,' he said. 'You can't take chances with a hippo, you know. And this was one hell of a hippo, Rian. Big like a kaffir hut, and fat. A hippo's got jaws, too, let me tell you. They can chop a man in half. First a hippo runs you down, then she chops you up. I went down on one knee in the mud and took aim, like this. I was so close I could have hit her with a stone. It takes cunning to creep up so close to a hippo, let me tell you. I kept thinking she can't be alone – she must be part of a herd. I looked over this shoulder, I looked over that. The last thing I wanted was to be stuck in the middle of a hippo family when I shot their Mamma. I heard her grunt when the bullet smacked, and I knew she was finished. I yelled. I danced. 'Got you!' I shouted. 'Got you!' But all of a sudden, the reeds blew up like a bomb. 'Jesus, God!' I thought.

'She's charging.' Mud and reeds went flying away on all sides like the birds. 'I'm dead,' I thought. I wanted to throw my rifle away and run, but it was too late – she was already on top of me. A hippo's got small little eyes like a frog, only red. I couldn't shout, my voice was gone. I just waved my arms, and she stumbled and fell, rolling over at my feet, dead, and fat, like a ton of bricks. I went up to her and took out my hunting knife. 'Ja, Madam Hippo,' I said. 'Excuse me, but I want your head.'

Domed and bloated, black and rubbery, the head was covered in dust.

Pa slapped it between the eyes.

'Now, you try,' he said.

It felt hard as iron, unbudgeable.

It took many days to boil to the bone, I remember. In a zinc tub tended by one of Ou Willem's daughters, Seraphima, beyond the jumble of tractors and broken-down threshing machines, in the hope that the smell of the cooking would not penetrate the house. It did, though, in a waft that brought the saliva to my mouth. Twice a day, Pa went down to see how things were going. I followed him one afternoon, I don't know why, but couldn't find him.

'Pa!' I called at the top of my voice. 'Pa, where are you?'

A bucket lay kicked over beside the tub, but neither Pa nor Seraphima was in sight. The hippo's head, shrunken in some places and swollen in others, jutted out above the rim of the tub. One stiff ear stuck up. Most of the water had boiled away. A scum of fat was bubbling on top. The mouth seemed ready to smile, to split open and talk.

'Pa!' I cried.

He didn't hear. Or if he did, wouldn't reply.

I dodged back through a row of tractors, trying to take a shortcut, and found them.

Seraphima was bending over and holding the mudguard of a big yellow cultivator. I could see her thumbs. Her heavy pleated skirt was rucked up, as was the tattered man's vest she was wearing – one of Pa's own, cast off from last year – her large breasts hung down, and her buttocks stood out. Pa's hand was under her buttocks somewhere, moving round and round, so that the flesh of them kept shaking.

'Eeeeee!' cried Seraphima. Her head was rolling backwards and forwards. She seemed to want to curl up.

'You like it?' panted Pa. 'You like it? You like it?'

'My baas!' she groaned, toppling forward on her hands and knees. 'Awu, my baas!'

Pa proceeded to unbutton his pants. Seraphima stayed as she was, on all fours, her head hanging, and then, as Pa mounted her from behind, her head jerked back and her face twisted up heavily, angrily, I thought, and she cried out again:

'Eeee-eeeeee!'

I didn't stop running until I was in the farthest room of the house, the one we never used, the living room with its china ornaments and large immobile furniture. I hid behind the door. I burrowed into the cushions of the couch, swallowed dust, choked. I got up, sat down. Lifted the leg of my shorts, took out my penis. I squeezed it, pulling back the skin. Time went by. Nothing happened. I looked around.

Over the mantelpiece hung a photograph of my mother, the only one we had. I climbed on a chair to get closer. Dressed as a bride in lace and kid gloves, my mother looked like a girl, and smiled. Long-stemmed flowers – irises, I think – lay in her arms. Color had been added to the photograph in crayon, giving her pink cheeks, cherry lips and bright blue eyes. Behind glass and in a thick black frame, she seemed cold and flat. Pa seldom spoke of her, and all I knew was, she was dead.

I pressed my face to the glass.

It was not until years later, therefore, when I saw Vicky for the first time, that I had any inkling of what the picture would have looked like, alive.

It was at a suburban party, snacks and drinks and a little illegal roulette. Vicky, in a slinky silver dress for which she moved too coltishly, was coming toward me through the crowd. I couldn't take my eyes off her. All she lacked was an armful of flowers. I touched her sleeve.

'I've seen your photograph,' I said.

'Oh?' she replied, full of curiosity. 'Where?'

People jostled me. There was too much to tell all at once. My throat swelled, my ears felt hot. She was breathing softly, leaning towards me. Her lipstick gleamed like wet paint; her lips were slightly parted. I couldn't dream of kissing her.

'It was a long time ago,' I confessed. 'You were in your wedding dress.'

'My wedding dress!' She giggled, wrinkling up her nose, intrigued and disbelieving.

'How do you know it was me?' she pursued.

'I looked.'

She was holding, toying with, a thin-stemmed wineglass.

There was an awkward silence.

Her hands were too large, I saw, and she bit her nails. But now, suddenly, I wanted to touch her. I wanted to slip my hands down the back of her dress and feel her zip splitting open. I wanted to press my face between her breasts, and drop my hands down further, and cup her buttocks.

Instead, of course, I asked her name.

'Vicky. Vicky Daintree. And yours?'

'Adrian. But call me Rian. Rian Erasmus.'

She smiled.

'Vicky is short for Victoria. But I don't like Victoria.'

I caught myself staring at her collarbone.

'What *do* you like, then?' I said. 'Do you like roulette?'

'Only the Russian kind,' she laughed, squinting and pointing a finger at her head. Pa had other photographs, too, of course, that I never told anyone about. Of a stranger this time – a fancy lady in ostrich feathers. On Sundays, or the days he called 'Christmas', when he was drinking, he would take out the pictures, a dozen of them in chocolate and cream, and give them a loose shuffle. From across the table, I could make out the pale humps of the lady's body, the frozen smile on her face. In the final picture, she had nothing on at all, and Pa liked to pause and fumble longingly with one finger at the space between her legs.

'Hey, lovely thing!' he mumbled, breathing heavily. 'Got a lovely thing?'

I reload the shotgun and lean on it deliberately, the way Bamford did. Scuff sand over the remains of the dove. Cupping my hands around my mouth, I yell: 'Vic-toreee!'

No reply, though I do listen for a while. I must be too far from camp.

I begin to scan the sky with long sweeps of the shotgun as though I am aiming at something. I feel hard. Intent. This is how I'll do it. . . I pull both triggers at once. I'm not resting my cheek against the stock, so it's okay, I'm not stunned. The gun rocks me back on my heels, jars my shoulder. The sky looks as empty as ever.

Three rounds left in my pocket. I'll have to save. Worst of all would be to return empty-handed.

Dead dry landscape, withered and grey. I have walked far from my childhood, but it walks with me still, I know. At the same time, it is (I am) an old, old man. I split away, and I am I, but he, too. My lips are cracked, covered in dried spit. My eyes are sunken in my head. I walk. I am the last man. I have seen everything. Snow falls sparsely around me. Soon it will be night.

I recognize an outcrop of rock. Good. That's where I'll go, then. Where Bamford says he found the skull.

I step from stone to stone. Past reeds which could catch fire, a wall of flame, swaying and roaring if you dropped a match. I pat my pockets. Nothing. I am tracking the beast up the riverbed. You have to be cautious, tread lightly, keep your eyes peeled. The beast, the man-eater, might be anywhere. The beast has sickly sweet breath, it is huge and fat, you smell it before you see it. Then it comes with a stifling roar, you are embraced, engulfed, its talons dig into your back, its mouth is open and mumbling at you, you are paralyzed, your only hope is to stick your shotgun down its throat and pull the trigger. If you are lucky, its head will come off, and the heavy body will fall like a rug, like cushions.

Suddenly weak in the joints, I sit down. It seems futile to carry on. I stare at the shotgun, trail my fingertips across the silver inlay work, realize that the tears are running down my face. I must still be drunk. I lift the shotgun, try to balance it on its butt in the sand. I have to heap up sand about it until it is balancing, however. I fear I may retch: the touch of the barrels on the roof of my mouth is cold, oily. Why can't I do it? I force myself to pull the triggers. Which click on empty chambers, sending a faint thrill through my head. I gag. Enough.

When I return to camp, it will be as one returning from the dead, then. Vicky will spin round, her eyes will pop out, she won't believe it.

'Rian!' she will cry. 'Oh, Rian, is it you?'

I'll gather her in my arms. The camera will crane away lyrically into long shot, we will seem smaller and smaller as figures, the music will soar overwhelmingly into the theme melody, so true love does triumph after all, la la la la la la dum, the credits will begin to roll, that's all, folks. The End.

The first time we did it, Vicky and I, she unbuttoned her shirt and dropped it on the floor. A pink shirt, pale pink, with big white buttons that seemed to ogle things.

'Hurry,' I urged softly.

'I am!' she said. Her arms went up awkwardly behind her back and the bra came loose. She slipped it off, slung it over a chair.

Naked already, I sat on the edge of the bed. I felt breathless, trapped by desire, waiting.

Her hair was in pigtails. For a while she was busy, worrying the elastic bands off them.

'Don't stare,' she said, crossing her elbows over her breasts.

'You look like a girl of thirteen or so. . .'

'I'm old enough, don't worry.'

She shucked off her jeans.

I made a cage out of my fingers, but did not shut my eyes.

Her naked body was very white at the end of the room, and her legs looked long.

Quickly, she moved to the bed.

'Switch out the light,' she begged.

'Not yet.'

I touched her. I could smell the slight acridity of her skin. She seemed very tense.

'Kiss me!' she commanded.

I did, but her eyes stayed wide open, fixed on the ceiling.

Gently, I trailed my fingers down from her throat to her breasts and her belly, then to the small tangle of coarser hair, to a liquid softness I could penetrate.

'Why don't you switch out the light?'

I sat up.

She began looking down at herself, following my eyes.

'What are you thinking?' she asked narrowly.

I tried to kiss her again but she wouldn't let me. We struggled and she laughed. I pinned her down, pressed my knee into her groin, and she parted her legs, arching her back.

'You want it?' I panted. 'You want it?'

Vicky nodded.

I wanted to bite her, to force her – beat my way blindly into it, into her, be on top of it, of her – but I was afraid. A pulse was throbbing in her throat.

'I don't want to hurt you,' I faltered.

'Oh, please,' she replied cynically.

She shut her eyes. Which was enough. I didn't switch out the light. I wanted to see.

I have no idea that I have been asleep until I wake up. The shadow of the reeds has advanced. I am cold. It is as though I'm at the bottom of a well. It must be getting late. My mouth is full of grit, sticky. I'm thirsty. I sit up, aware of a rustling, a disturbance, all around me. Then a goat goes tripping across the rocks in the sunlight. I get to my feet, reload the shotgun.

I know what I am looking for now.

Halfway up the bank is yesterday's goat. He chews, taking no notice of me, as I clamber up and stand beside him. I point the shotgun at his flank, then gradually move it up to his ear, which twitches.

'You old fucker,' I say. 'Your time has come. I'm going to blow a hole in your ribs. I'm going to chop off your head and stick it on a pole. I can't stand you any more. I can't stand your smell, I can't stand your voice, I can't stand the way you stare, I can't stand your chewing and the thought of your teeth, I can't stand your horns, your long skinny neck, your guts. I can't stand the balls of shit you leave lying around all over the place. You must die, you devil. You goat.'

There is a cry from the bank above me. I look up. It is the little herd boy, waving a stick. He seems to be saying no.

With unexpected agility, the goat leaps up the bank. I throw the gun to my shoulder, but he keeps picking his way higher in a zigzag. The gun goes off. Pellets thrum like bees in ricochet. I have lost my chance, I know. I laugh. Bamford's goat! He leads a charmed life.

I scramble up the side of the bank and look around. Not ten steps away, the goat has stopped and is tearing at the leaves of a bush. I can't believe my luck.

I approach warily, one hand stretched out as if to soothe him. I don't dare breathe a word.

He braces his front feet. Just as he seems on the verge of bolting again, I fire. I have to.

He somersaults. I don't know what I expected, but I drop the shotgun and snatch at the loop of rope around his neck. I miss and have to grab hold of his horns. Vigorously, he shakes his head. I don't know what to do now – I can't hang on forever. If he pushes, he will knock me off my feet. I hammer at his head with the flat of my hand.

'You old fool!' I shout.

He sneezes blood, bleating in a way that I don't want to hear. Blood spurts from the hole in his throat, it splatters across the stones, I can smell it. I am sickened, appalled. Panting, I throw my body across his. I want to drag him down, make his legs buckle. He simply staggers sideways under my weight, bleating again. I can't stand the sound. I kick him, punch him. I still have hold of one horn.

I grunt, 'For God's sake!'

The muscles in my neck and shoulder are becoming strained and knotted. I stumble, I am lifted off my feet, the struggle goes senselessly on and on, man and goat. Goat bucking, man trying to hold him down. Then the goat goes head over heels and I follow, sprawling at his side and losing my grip. The goat's head lies twisted in the dust, his mouth is open and his tongue protrudes, spotted with blood. He gives one long shudder after another, his legs raking backwards and forwards. One eye stares fixedly, then the lid comes down in a slow blink.

'Die,' I whisper. 'Please, die.'

Flies have fastened themselves on to the blood already. There are flies on my legs, my hands. I get to my feet, wave them away. I am shaking. I'm smeared, spattered in blood. I try to swallow but my mouth is too dry.

There is no sign of the little goatherd. Perhaps it is just as well. I would ask him for a knife. I'd like to cut off the goat's head, or maybe only one ear, the way they did in the bush war in the north, and present it to Bamford.

'Yours, I believe?'

But now I have a problem. When I try and shift the goat, I find him unwieldy, inert. I sit down on the ground again. Taking hold of the horns, I roll the head from side to side. I wish it could come off with a wrench. The carcass is too heavy to drag back to camp. I'll have to leave it here. In the fork of a tree, perhaps, as though a leopard got it. Which is what happened to the Wonderboy creature, isn't it? On one of the tapes, Bamford can be seen, tapping significantly at two neat holes in the base of the skull.

'Bite marks!' he claims.

I manage to shove the goat up into the nearest thorn tree, not very high: the legs dangle. They'll go stiff like that.

Then I return to where I left the shotgun. I am still shaking and sweating, sticky with blood. I fear I may puke again but I kneel and hold myself tight, and gradually the feeling passes.

I take off my shirt and pants, my underpants, shoes and socks, and roll them into a bundle which I hang from the barrels of the gun. It will be better to walk naked through the late afternoon, I hope. Cleaner. More peaceful, too. The river spreads like a giant crack in the landscape. Yawning, bone dry. The Great Rift Valley, they tell me, can be seen from the moon.

Pa and I ploughed a whole hillside one winter's afternoon. The moon hung high in the sky, remote. The tractor juddered and sprang forward as Pa spun the steering wheel. Behind him, I stood on the iron footplates, hanging on. Whenever we reached the end of a row, he would sit for a moment or two, 'thinking' – listening, perhaps, for a faulty tick in the motor he had just repaired. Then we would be off again, bumping over the hard ground, the plough making the earth behind us smile, while a flock of white birds came down to settle on the lips of the furrow, looking for grubs to eat.

'We're making it!' shouted Pa, but the wind snatched his voice away. 'Look!'

He braced his arms squarely against the wheel while the tractor champed on. 'Hot shot, hey?' he called out over his shoulder. 'Doesn't she go like a dream?' I nodded and cried: 'Yes!'

My hands were numb with the cold but I would never have let go. The moon was a faint polished skull in the sky. I stared at the ground racing by beneath my feet. I could almost feel the earth tilt.

I overhear a distinct metallic clinking in the reeds. Tarentaal. I force another cartridge into the shotgun, drop my bundle and cross the riverbed, intending to cut them off. Instantly, they are silent. I wait for a while, then try to wade among the reeds. I can see nothing, only the waving stems which touch me all over like so many cool impersonal fingers. I shake my head, stretch up vainly on tiptoe.

'Come on, come on,' I fret aloud. 'Catch fright. Fly!'

Nothing happens.

I pick up a big flat stone and heave it at the spot where last I heard the clinking. As it falls there is a racket of wings and a single tarentaal starts up.

'Oh, yes?' I shout, taking aim and squeezing the trigger.

To my own surprise, the bird is knocked down. Feathers float.

I rush forward, pushing my way through the reeds to find it flopping around in a circle. Other tarentaal start up into the air around me, a whole flock of them, but I have eyes only for the one at my feet. I club it with the gun butt. After another flop or two, it stops struggling. I pick it up.

'Got you,' I murmur. 'Got you.'

My second bird.

I press my fingers through to the skin, avoiding the wound in the back. Its feathers are crisp, cool, speckled. A drop of blood has appeared on the open beak.

I wonder what Bamford will say?

I break open the shotgun, fit the final shell into the barrel. I can hardly move, I feel so battered. But grateful, too. Slowly, I get into my clothes again.

It won't be difficult to find my way back to camp. The wild fig protrudes above the surrounding bush, its foliage rich and green. It must be fed by some secret spring. Or each leaf turns into a tongue to lick up the dew, perhaps. The little bits of white cloth tied to the lower branches show white, signs of prayer. To whom? Morena?

I am Morena. I step from stone to stone, the bird's wings shaking like a bush. I am as white as the dead. My hands smell of blood. My eyes are like a tiger's and I can kill.

'ISN'T IT A LOVELY THING?' says Bamford. 'A lovely, lovely thing.' He picks up the tarentaal by the tail. 'A pity you bagged only one, though. How come?'

I make an effort at wit.

'Oh, you know. A bird in the hand. . . .'

He chuckles.

'Telling me,' he agrees. 'I'll pluck her for you, shall I?'

He is sitting in one of the deck chairs with his foot, wrapped in more bandages than ever, on the seat of another.

The goat. I can't tell him about the goat.

He drops the dead bird into his lap and begins to rip out the odd pinch of feathers, scattering them under his seat. On the table lies a packet of sweets. It would seem that he has broken further into the goodies that Vicky has been saving for tomorrow.

'Have a peppermint.'

'Thanks,' I say, taking one. 'Where's Vicky?'

'Oh, she and your black sidekick went off into the bush together some time ago. Searching for you, it seems. I told her not to worry. I said you could take care of yourself. After all, you're a big boy now!'

'Right.' I smile faintly. Roll the peppermint around in my mouth.

'Don't just stand there,' he adds, wallowing around to show me he can't get up. 'Go grab yourself something to drink. The beers are in the back of the kombi – you know where. Go on. Help yourself. I expect they'll be hot as hell, though.'

True enough, my beer spouts as I open the can. I scoop up the foam to wash off the blood which has dried into a kind of rust on my hands and face, then tip up the can to drink. As I do so, I catch sight of myself in the rearview mirror. My hair is sticking up like Pa's (his 'devil's peak,' he used to call it), my Adam's apple bobs, the beer goes trickling down my chin. I must be about as old now as he was then. He liked to laugh and wink at himself in the shaving glass: 'Hullo, good looking.' I used to watch.

Collecting another couple of cans from the case, I go back to the table. Walk round him.

'How's the foot?'

'On fire, thanks.'

'You ought to get it to a doctor, you know.'

'Yes, yes, I know. Tomorrow. Tomorrow.'

I offer him one of the cans, which he takes but doesn't open. He seems to be brooding.

Like a molten coin, the sun is poised on the horizon. The light is pure gold. You could fill your head with it, relax. If that were possible.

I take a chair opposite him, finish my beer and stare into the bush.

'You agree with me, then, Rian?' Bamford observes, leaning forward. 'You do agree?'

I recognize the gambit but don't want to play. I belch.

'Gesundheit,' he says, and raises one finger.

When I still say nothing, he continues as if I had acquiesced, anyway.

'I have an idea. A simple one, really. All the same, it has occupied my mind, off and on, for a good many years, now.'

I can't believe I am going to have to sit through another one of his lectures. To begin with, I am dead tired. But also, I am watching the bush.

'I know your theory, professor.'

'Do you? Then don't you agree it's worth it?'

'Worth what?'

'Look, my friend. Something happened. Something big. Wait, listen to me. Don't interrupt. I like to think it was triggered by the sun. Let's picture it in the simplest terms. The biggest stories do unfold like a picture book, don't they? One day, the sun rolled over and looked down here, right here near this tree, wound himself up like a clock, and WHAM! Our brain sprang into being. Like it or not, that's how it happened. In one blinding flash. Call it the evolutionary Big Bang theory, if you like. Because that's what it was – a blast of solar-nuclear energy that split the genes and sent the DNA spinning in unprecedented spirals. The result was an anti-Darwinian somersault – your bulging human brain and mine, an organ that resembles nothing so much as a mushroom cloud. Mind you, everything else around here went through the same thing. Trees' leaves turned into mouths and spoke. Grass lifted up its roots and crawled, walked. Sand became liquid, and flowed clear as glass to the sea. I kid you not, my friend. I am telling you my dream as I dreamed it.

'In fact, the land around here has never recovered. I'd like to take a walk in the bush some day and prove it. Trace the roots of our human brain in the dust. Man was made of a pinch of this dust – of that I am convinced. For me, the old slow-but-steady theory cuts no ice. No. Something happened. Something that made us what we are. Oh, I don't doubt there were other prodigies, too.

Flamingos with tits like women. Two-headed ostriches. Cliff-climbing fishes. Whatnot. Monsters, tons of them, but none like us. And we survived. We alone survived. That's how we come to be sitting here now.'

I settle back in my chair.

'Don't you agree,' repeats Bamford, 'it's worth it?'

'Worth what?'

'Worth more, I mean.'

'More?'

'More than this hokey little video. Why not aim for the giant screen, a block-buster? I want to fly a little – especially with this damned foot. Let's give them Africa, as they never thought of it, man. Africa, where it all began. D'you know what I mean?'

'A blockbuster?' I am watching the bush.

'You're not listening. Think of sex, damn it. Hot sex. Think of the hottest, sweetest, drippingest, wide-openest, little cunt you can. That's what I want my movie to be like.' He throws back his head and laughs. A tooth glints gold in his mouth.

My breathing becomes difficult. I swallow. I may try to speak.

'Professor Bamford.'

'Yes?' he says. 'What?'

'I'd like to know. . . .' My voice trails away. I find myself watching his fingers as he tears at the tarentaal's plumage with a steady thump, exposing the wretched skin.

The silence grows.

He pauses. Looks over his glasses.

'Well?'

'What do you know. . . .'

'Yes?'

It would be easier, somehow, to snap the legs off the chairs, break the table in half, pick up the pieces and shove them in his face. See, professor?

But I manage at last, quite casually: 'About me.'

Baffled, Bamford passes a hand backwards through his hair, leaving it standing up.

'What do you mean, about you?'

I swallow. Rub sweaty palms on the slats of my chair.

'I mean . . . about me and Vicky.'

'Vicky?' he repeats inadvertently. 'And you?'

I can't add a single word. I nod.

'I see,' he says.

He reaches for his beer and pops it open, slips the ring down over his little finger. Considers it pensively.

'My guess,' he continues, 'is this: I'd say you're an old flame. From what I can tell, not a very serious old flame. Also, it all ended a long time ago. You haven't, I hope, become involved again, have you? Not on this trip?'

'No,' I admit. 'Not now. Not for a long time now. Years.'

I remember, long ago, Vicky's hot breath in my mouth.

'I love you,' she mumbled. 'I love you, I love you.'

Biting my tongue in the dark.

Bamford shifts his bulk uncomfortably. The seat creaks under him as though it would split.

'Thank you,' he says gravely.

For a moment, he stays exactly as he is, as though helpless. Then he fidgets, so that a tiny feather is left sticking to the corner of his glasses.

'Thank you,' he repeats, rubbing his chin.

He is suffering, I see. I almost want to reach out, pat his hand, lift him out of it. We sit around without speaking while he drains his beer.

'Well,' he remarks, with the faintest quirk of a smile, crumpling his beer can: 'that's that.'

The last slice of the sun is gone.

Where is Vicky?

'Shouldn't we light the gas lamp?' I suggest.

'Good idea! Why not fire a shot or two, too? You never know, the bang may bring them running.'

'Okay,' I say. 'Why not?'

The flare of the lamp is bone-white, intense. I place it on the ground and pick up the shotgun. Study his back. Slumbering muscle under all that fat: a strong man, once. He'd never know what hit him. Pointblank.

'Hello, hello,' Bamford mutters, lifting his head to peer at the bush, as I break open the barrels. 'Our rescue team has returned, I think.'

A single brass-butted shell gleams at me.

'Hello, is that you?' Bamford calls into the bush.

Is it? I can see nothing beyond the lamplight.

The trigger you have to squeeze. Like a tit. From here, the blast would take the top of his head right off. His fat hands would fly up, the chair go toppling over with a crash, and the breath come bubbling out of him. Good God, I'd say. It was an accident. Can't you see? An accident.

Bamford leans back, cupping his hands round his mouth.

'Come on, hurry up, you two! We can't wait forever.'

Pa shot himself in the kitchen, I remember. He fell over backwards across the stove. The blood tapped and sizzled.

My finger stays stiff and white-knuckled on the trigger.

You can still see the mark of the bullet in the wall of the house at Magnet Heights.

'That's the place,' I told Vicky. 'Above the stove. The bullet hole.'

'Oh, no,' she cried.

Like a spotlight, the lamp casts my shadow, a jagged giant, up the white sides of the kombi. What shall I do with this thing, this heavy, loaded shotgun – drop it, break it over my knee? I take a step backwards, stand the gun leaning up straight against the kombi.

'Here's light,' I say, and dump the lamp on the table.

'Banzai!' yells Bamford, and suddenly begins to swing the half-plucked tarentaal round his head.

Its body must be elastic, it stretches so. I wish I could grab it, hide it under my shirt, run away and bury it. But it's too late.

'Hello-o?' comes Vicky's voice, quite close.

I can't take my eyes off the tarentaal.

'Behold!' calls Bamford. 'A bird! A plump bird! How do you like it? Ain't she a beauty? A plump little sweetheart? A bird in the hand! What's it worth to you, Vicky? Two in the bush? The pubic bush? Come on, come, hurry up. Where the hell have you been?'

When I look up again, Vicky is at the table. Her face looks taut and tired in the lurid upcast light of the lamp. Behind her comes Bucs, stumbling, another big shadow.

Bamford pinches out a few feathers and flicks them at her.

'Oh, disgusting!' she cries with a glance at me. 'Did *you* kill that poor skinny little thing?'

Before I can reply, Bucs begins slapping me on the back.

'Bra' Rian! Hey, bra'! It's good to see you! Hai! We were so worried, bra'! We thought you were. . . .' He rolls his eyes, pokes a finger into his mouth, and makes a cork-popping sound.

Everybody laughs.

'We did, indeed,' says Vicky, and seems on the verge of adding more, but Bamford stops her.

'Let's get a fire going,' he argues, testily shifting his trussed-up foot. 'I'm starving.'

Bucs and I build the fire together. Bamford orders us about. Glad of the activity, I go around collecting loose twigs, thorns, a large dead branch. We spit the guinea fowl carcass – which looks smaller, punier than ever – on a stick, and start to roast it.

'This fire is too high,' I remark. 'We'll have to wait.'

'No! Don't wait,' says Bucs.

'Why, what else can we do?'

He shows me. Twisting the carcass away from the fiercest heat, he secures the stick in position with a stone.

Vicky is watching every movement through the flames.

'Adrian Erasmus,' she says. 'I want to talk to you!'

I get up, wipe my hands on my jeans.

She leads me round the back of the kombi. Deep shadow. I can't see her, but I can feel her breathing. I shut my eyes as tight as I can, open them wide. It makes no difference.

'What the hell are you up to?' she whispers fiercely.

'Up to?'

She is so close. I take her by the shoulders and draw her to me. Her breasts are flattened against my chest. They seem much softer, laxer than I remember. I bend, searching for her mouth.

She whips away.

'Are you mad?' she whispers, panting.

'No, listen, Vicky. I just want to. . . .'

'No, *you* listen. I don't want you to touch me, understand? I know what you are thinking. Don't. Don't stare at me all the time. And Jesus, Rian, stop pointing that gun at people. Okay?'

Before I can put in another word, she turns and marches back to the fire, head up. I clench my hands, trying to get rid of the feeling of her. Her crumpled shirt, warm body.

We eat the guinea fowl, which seems to bleed in my mouth, and only tastes good charred. I can't stomach it. I open a can of peaches, dish out a few to those who want (Vicky doesn't), and finish the remainder myself, sipping the clear slow sweet syrup from the can. Bamford is expounding the secrets of creation again. What was the universe like before the beginning, he says, but black? Black and shiny. Death is like that. In fact, death is the identical state. We all fear death, prefiguring it as a total blackness, the ultimate loss of self, but surely the lack of self before birth is or was equally black? In this sense, the end and the beginning are one. The deep upon which only the spirit of God may move. (I find it tedious to listen, but at the same time impossible not to.) In the beginning, says Bamford, what happened? At a point already computed down to the nearest micro-millisecond, came the Big Bang, the ongoing orgasm, the expanding universe in which we live. I lie back, clasp my hands under my head, and stare at the stars. Plenty of black up there. Do I fear I shall lose myself? Bucs, unperturbed, rolls himself a joint and lights it from the fire. Vicky, opposite me, is sitting with her chin on her knees.

I want to ride you, Vicky. Ride you. Bite you. I want to feel our skin sticking together because I know you get wet with sweat when you fuck. I want to see your hair go all tousled and stiff, I want to hear you pleading for more, more. I want you to go down on your knees while I stand over you. I want to see your mouth all distorted, I want to feel your tongue working, rolling round my cock. I want to lick you, too, bite you. But more than anything else, I want to take you from the back, the way I never did. I want to hear you panting, whimpering, crying out, oh, God, yes, yes, fuck me, Rian, fuck me. I want to see your head lolling from side to side, your breasts hanging down, swinging, slippery with sweat. I want to see your face twisting up. I want to see you as I know you, Vicky.

A branch cracks in the fire. Far away, a jackal howls. I think of the goat.

Vicky stretches, stifling a yawn.

'Haven't you had enough for one day?' she asks Bamford.

'Yes, indeed – for one day!' he admits. 'Let's hit the sack.'

Wiping greasy fingers on his pants, he struggles to get up, but the deck chair totters. He seems to be stuck.

'Wait a minute,' Vicky says. 'Let me help.'

He heaves himself up, and, using her as a crutch, begins to hop.

'Help!' he calls out. 'This is an abduction.'

I laugh. Wave.

'Good night.'

I watch them heading for the kombi, which offers ampler space than the pup tent, no doubt.

I wonder whether I shall sleep tonight.

Bucs is sitting staring at the fire and pinching his lower lip.

'Tomorrow – it is our last day?' he asks. 'For sure?'

'For sure.'

He says nothing more, but rubs his face with his fingers and yawns.

We seem to have curiously little to say to one another.

Bucs pats at his pouch to check what's left of the dope. He pours a little into his palm, seems to think better of it, and starts coaxing every last precious twig and morsel back again.

'Bucs.'

He looks up.

'That goat yesterday. . . .'

He frowns. Without his glasses, his eyes look sore and red and somehow smaller.

'Goat?' he queries. 'What goat?'

'The big white one, remember? The one that the prof nearly took a pot shot at on the stones in the riverbed, man. Well, say it's dead. Lightning killed it. Or maybe it jumped into a tree and hanged itself. Stranger things have been known to happen. But the big white goat is dead. I know it is. How do you think the people who owned it will feel?'

'Not happy,' he says. Unable to help it, he snorts with laughter, wiping his nose on the back of his hand.

'Why? What's a goat good for?' Hairy white carcass up a tree. Old Satan.

Bucs looks wary.

'For milk,' he proposes after a pause. 'And goats are like money.'

'Wealth?'

'It's right. And sometimes the people, they kill them, for sacrifice. Then the people, they eat the meat.' He picks at imaginary meat.

'I'll take your word for it,' I say. Should I tell him? Hey, Bucs, I killed the goat. My palms are sweaty. I feel sick.

But I say nothing.

'Cool!' says Bucs.

We stare one another hard in the eye, and burst out laughing, I don't know why.

Bucs is keen on the pup tent, so I leave him to it. It is too small for the two of us, anyway. I spread my sleeping bag on the ground under the wild fig and lie gazing up through the branches at the night sky. Bright crust of stars. You could reach up and catch a whole handful, if you liked. I shut my eyes and feel I am falling, long and rapidly away from myself. I am just about to disappear completely when I snap awake.

The air smells cold. The stars have wheeled round but it is nowhere near dawn.

A twig cracks and a flame curls up. Someone is sitting at the fire.

Should I move? But already I am up.

Except for a few embers and the crackling twig, the fire, I see, is a heap of white ash. Vicky has a blanket draped around her shoulders. Her head is resting on her knees.

'What is it?' I ask, crouching beside her.

She rolls her head from side to side but will not reply.

'What's wrong? Tell me!'

'Nothing,' she says. 'Go away. Please.'

I put an arm around her, ignoring the clumsy blanket. She feels small and stays very still. I shiver, being nearly naked – no shirt or pants.

I coax another twig to catch alight.

Vicky presses her face fiercely into my shoulder, and moans: 'Oh, Adrian!'

'What is it?' I urge softly. 'What's wrong?' I take her hand and try to force my fingers in between hers. 'Tell me!'

She rubs her face against my chest. Her whole body quakes, but whether she is laughing or crying, I can't tell. I try to see her face.

'No,' she whispers finally, relaxing, going calm again. 'Forget it. Go back to sleep.'

'Is it Bamford?'

'Oh, no!' She smiles. Shakes her head. 'No, no.'

'What, then?'

She won't reply. I sit drawing circles in the ash, wondering. Flame goes creeping along a thorn.

'I should never have left you,' I say at last.

For the first time she nods.

'Yes.'

There is a silence.

'I've told him, you know,' I add. 'Bamford. About us.'

She stares at the fire a little. Shrugs, looks at me.

'Why?'

'Don't you think he deserves to know?'

'Know what?'

'About us.'

'There is nothing to know. I was just a girl.'

'You were eighteen.'

'Eighteen!' She smiles sadly, touching a twig to the flame.

'And now you are – what – thirty-two?'

'Thank you. I always like a little reminder.'

'I'm thirty-eight.'

Leaning her head on her knees, she stares at the candle-like flames of the twigs. 'Tomorrow,' she remarks, 'is Digby's birthday.'

'Oh, yes. Digby. I'm almost beginning to like him, you know. The Great White Hope. Nobody believes in him and his freak monkey skull any more, so he's prepared to sell out completely, pull out all the stops, look like a fraud, but enjoy it. Make everything ridiculous without even trying.'

'What did you tell him about us?'

'Not much, come to think of it. I can't think why you didn't tell him yourself.'

'Me? Oh, no.'

'Why not? He's not Humpty Dumpty, you know. He won't fall to pieces. More likely, he'll bounce like a ball. He's got an ego like a Flying Fortress.'

'You're wrong,' she replies flatly. 'To me, you know, when it really matters, he has always been unbelievably sensitive and kind. Jesus, Rian, try and understand, why don't you? To begin with, the rejection of his work isn't scientific. It's political. The Wonderboy skull is real. It's human. And it's far, far older than anyone expected, or anyone – except Digby – can explain. The real problem is, Wonderboy happens to have been discovered too far south.'

'You believe him, huh?'

'Yes, of course. Don't you? He's a victim of politics, like all of us. What I love about him is his bounce. 'If all my life I was meant to fail,' he says, 'then no one can say I haven't succeeded!' That's the kind of man he is. He has a wonderful, witty, fighting spirit. He won't go down, even with the whole world against him. And everyone, everyone cheats him and laughs at him and lets him down. Why? Why do they do that?'

She leans, rolls her brow against her knees. I press my lips to the crown of her head.

'No,' she warns. 'Don't.'

I kiss her hair.

'I should never. . . .' I breathe.

'Yes,' she retorts with an abrupt little laugh, turning her face aside. 'How could you? I'll never forget it. Pushing me out of the car in the middle of nowhere like that, you bastard! I didn't know which way to go. I was such a child, I sat down and cried. I had no idea where the nearest town was. I had to hitch hike back. I got a lift from a fat old boer in a bakkie, who showed me his penis.'

'Oh, yes?' I mock. 'And what did you do?'

She bites her lip and says nothing.

I stir the embers of the fire, trying to get a glow from them.

'Cold?' says Vicky. 'Oh, shame, Rian! Poor thing.'

She opens a wing of her blanket and suddenly I am very close to her again. The warmth is so good I am grateful.

'And you?' she asks curiously. 'What did you do?'

'Nothing much. Kept going.' I wrap closer. 'I didn't want to live.'

'You, too?'

I kiss her cheek, and, when she offers no resistance, run my hands up over her breasts, and down to her belly, but she shakes her head.

'No, no, I can't. It would be too much. Not with you. Stop it!'

I swallow. Relax. Breathe evenly.

'Then with who?' I ask.

She ignores the question.

'Feed the fire,' she says.

I snap a few more twigs. Behind us, not fifty paces away, stands the kombi, a glint of starlight on its windscreen. I stop to listen, but all is quiet.

'Did you,' I ask, 'think of me at all in the time between?'

She tilts her chin. Considers the question.

'Not too much, I suppose. Life goes on. Sometimes, when I brushed my hair, I would think of how you used to like it. You used to say it tumbled like a stream in the mountains. You don't write poetry any more, I suppose?'

'No. Not for years.'

I wrap her hair around my hand. It is brittle, longish – just hair, after all. But I do manage to pull her down and kiss her. Her mouth is as sweet as I remember. Her belly seems thicker, while her breasts hang lower. Her ribs stand out. I could count them, one for each year, but I don't. Instead, I fondle a breast. She allows it. I press my face to her skin and take a nipple between my lips. It starts to tighten. When I lift my head again, she is breathing faster, even whimpering a little.

'Come on,' I urge. 'Vicky! Come.'

She pushes me away.

'No. Not now.'

'Why not?' I insist. 'What's wrong?'

For awhile, she says nothing. Then she sighs and begins to explain mechanically.

'I'm not who you think I am, you know. I never was. That's what really split us apart. In your eyes, I was this funny fantasy about a photograph. But I'm nobody's fantasy – not yours, not Digby's, nobody's. I'm … well, just me. Ordinary. Older now. And I've been with a lot of men. Do you understand, Rian? I'm not your mother's face come to life off the wall. I never was. I'm just … me.'

'I see.'

'Do you?'

She buttons her shirt decisively and holds both my hands in her own, knotting our fingers together.

'Stay like that,' she insists. Then: 'Talk to me. Tell me about Nando.'

'Nando? What's Nando?'

'Not, 'What'! 'Who?' 'Who is Nando?' Nando is Nando, the man you call 'Bucs'. Nando Killing Boy Ndhlovu–don't you know? Nando is nice. He thinks the world of you, bra' Rian! He ran all over the bush this afternoon, just because I was scared you had blown your stupid head off.' She grips my hands more tightly. 'Don't do that again,' she says in a low distinct voice. 'Don't ever do that again.'

We sit in silence for a while. Then she gives me a willful little shove with her shoulder.

'Tell me!'

'Okay, but what do you want to know? He joined ACE-TV about three months ago. Trainee technician, grade one. He's okay, is Nando. Overbold, sometimes, and maybe he thinks too much of himself, but then he hasn't had the edges knocked off him yet, the way all the rest of us have. He's bright, he catches on quickly, he doesn't have to be told anything twice. Watch when he wears the headphones, though. He rocks on his heels, clicks his fingers. I think he fancies himself as a Rasta, although he hasn't got the dreadlocks or anything.'

'Oh, he is more than that,' she remarks with quiet self-assurance. 'Much more.'

'Oh? How do you know?'

'Well, to begin with, he's very earnest about things, is Nando. Especially TV, so you'd better watch out! He grew up on the township streets, played soccer all day among those swarms of kids. He was the star. They had a bald tennis ball, he used to look after it–it was his most treasured possession. Do you know, he once scored a hundred and four goals in one afternoon? You must get him to show you how he kicked. He can keep a pebble up in the air by sort of juggle-kicking it with his toes. He's lovely, so supple and serious. He laughs about it now. He is very special when he laughs, Rian, you must admit. Pele was king in those days, he says.'

'I see. And who is king now?'

'Nando himself, I suppose. But that isn't all. He must have been through the fires of the townships, too. He won't tell me about it, but he has, I know he has.

Just imagine, Rian. He has seen the army and the police shooting people. He has seen petrol bombings, necklaces – terrible things. And he has come out of it so proud, and like a dancer, afraid of nothing. Do you know, he is only twenty-two years old? He won't stand any shit, he says, and I don't blame him. He wants to learn, he says. He wants to master the technology which white men like you have kept away from black men like him.'

'I'm not stopping him.'

'Ah, but are you helping him, Rian?'

'Am I not? He's an audio technician, remember, but only this morning I let him work the camera.'

'Good.'

'I could do more, I suppose. What about you, though? How do you hope to help him?'

'I don't know yet.'

'You're sure you haven't helped him already? To a little hot pussy in the bush?'

She whips around, struggling to slap or scratch me, but I slip out of the blanket, wrap her heavily in it and pin her down. She swears at me and tries to kick.

'So you *have* got the hots for Bucs!' I say.

'Oh, yes!' she taunts. 'Yes! Isn't it obvious? You should see him move. He's like – liquid, oh, lovely, all muscle and grace. I can't get him out of my mind. I thought you were him. I was waiting. He's wonderful, so uncomplicated after you men. Oh, you men!'

'Don't count on that,' I say and let her go.

She rolls on her side, her hair trailing in the ash.

'Oh, Jesus,' she cries, gritting her teeth. 'Jesus. Why can't you just leave me alone, Rian?'

'Is that what you want?' I say, getting up.

She grips my hand. Wipes her hot face.

'No, wait,' she says. 'Don't go.'

'Go away, don't go?'

'Oh, you don't understand. Listen. I don't have to answer to you, or to anyone, do I?'

'All right. You don't.'

'Because. . . . Because. . . . Oh, God! God!'

Pressing her face into her hands, she begins to cry in dry, jerky sobs. I kneel down, gather her up, and hold her, rock her in an attempt to comfort her. Slowly, she grows quiet again, her head heavy on my shoulder.

'I want to go back to the kombi, now,' she whispers at last.

'You do?' Twining my fingers into her hair, I pull her head back. Her mouth is salty, sticky, warm. I press my lips to her neck, the hollow of her throat. Then I kiss her eyelids, too, very gently. 'I could fuck you now, you know.'

Her eyes glisten in the dark.

'I know.'

'Good,' I say.

She does not speak.

I let her go.

7

Oom[1] Frikkie cried a lot, I remember. He sat in his chair by the door and cried. His no-color old man's hair stood straight up, and he kept munching at his cheeks so that his lips pouted and rolled, but he couldn't take his eyes off us.

'Who is he?' whispered Vicky.

'Pa's uncle,' I said. 'Don't worry. He's harmless.'

Oom Frikkie shook his head.

'Hnnh,' he said. 'Hnnnnh.'

Vicky clutched my hand and shifted closer on the sofa.

'My uncle, too,' I added. 'Remember me, Oom?'

Oom Frikkie sobbed, spluttering spittle. He was wearing a pajama top with braces, and his fly seemed permanently undone.

'Let's go home,' said Vicky. 'Please. Right now.'

'Why?' I said with a laugh. 'It'll be all right.'

The old man stopped to scratch at the stubble on his chin where the tears had collected. He rolled his eyes. A fly buzzed.

It was hot and cramped and dull in the room. I could smell the dust from the sofa cushions, and Seraphima's piercing cry seemed only just to have vanished in the air. It was here, too, on the table in the middle of the room, that Pa's coffin had once lain, although only a strip of sunlight lay there now. My mother's photograph hung over the mantelpiece. Nothing had changed at Magnet Heights.

In the kitchen, I could hear the clatter of crockery. Tant[2] Koba was making tea.

Vicky nudged me.

'Look!'

Oom Frikkie was busy cramming his fingers into his mouth and sucking or blowing at them as if to stifle his own noises.

'Pan pipes?' I said.

'No!' she said and giggled.

She shifted closer to me, squeezing her thigh, bare beneath her apple green skirt, against mine. I caressed the hair at the nape of her neck.

---

1. *Oom* – uncle
2. *Tant* – aunt

'Oom,' I said – not for the first time since we had arrived. 'This is Vicky, Oom. My fiancé. Don't you want to say hullo?'

Oom Frikkie shook his head heavily.

'Unh-unh. Hnnnnh.'

Spit dangled. The fingers came out of his mouth, he made a slurping sound and sucked in both cheeks.

'No?' I said.

He shoved a wet finger in front of his lips.

'Shh-shh.'

'What is it, Oom?'

His eyes looked weary, red. He opened his mouth, showing his tongue and vacant gums.

'It is the devil.'

Vicky's grip on my hand tightened.

'Oom – ' I began.

'Sometimes, she looks like that.'

'Oom,' I said. 'Don't start. This is Vicky. My bride-to-be.'

He stared at me, set his lips grimly and shook his head.

'Look how she smiles,' he mumbled. 'Look! You don't believe me, but she does. She knows me. She has come to me before. She comes through my door when I am sleeping. I open my eyes and she is there. She smiles at me – like that, look! She shows me her fig.'

Vicky was pinching her nose in an effort to shut off the giggles.

'Enough now, Oubaas,'[3] I warned.

I would have gotten up, too, and shaken him or cuffed his head to try and bring him to his sense, but she wouldn't let me.

'No, please,' she said and hung on to my arm.

'Go, Satan!' cried Oom Frik, pointing at the door. 'Get behind me. I don't want to smell you again. Don't tempt me. Annie, Annie, I don't want to. No! I see you. Scarlet. Scarlet woman.'

'Green,' Vicky said, and flipped up her skirt at him.

The old man's eyes bulged. He looked as if he was choking. Lifting one trembling finger, he pointed.

'The sin! The sin! No, please, Jesus!'

His lips curled, his chin puckered up and he began to cry.

I laughed.

'You see?' I said.

3. *Oubaas*, old boss

Before I could say any more, Vicky bit me. She pressed her face into my shoulder and bit me.

'Hey – stop it,' I said, rubbing hard. 'What did you do that for?'

Her face was red and angry and her eyes were full of tears.

At that moment, Tant Koba pushed open the door.

'Pee-beep!' she called. 'Here comes the bus. Pee-beep! Mind out the way. Here we are. Everything is ready.'

On the tray stood the best teapot and cups, as well as a plate piled high with beskuit[4] in honor of our visit.

There was a silence.

'What's wrong, now?' said Tant Koba. 'What's wrong with *you*, old boy?'

She was a huge, obese and dissatisfied old woman. She put the tray on the table and began to wipe her fingers on a dishcloth.

'Hnnh-hnnnh,' said Oom Frikkie.

'Pop Eye!' she snapped. 'Don't sit there and bawl, man. You're making the youngsters feel funny. Get out. Go on. Give us some peace. If you want to be morbid, go and sit alone in your room.'

'My little brother, Frederikus,' Tant Koba explained, more fondly once he had gone. 'Don't let him worry you. He is full of all the sorrows of the world. I've looked after him all these years. I was father and mother to him and Rian. Did Rian tell you? He was always up to mischief, was Frikkie, you won't believe me! It was like having two small children to care for at once. I always said, 'I've got two small children to care for, and not one of them is my own.' I never married, you know. He's not quite right in the head, is Frikkie.'

'I'm sorry,' Vicky said, wiping the tears from her cheeks and trying to smile.

'It's not your fault,' observed Tant Koba. 'So I don't see what you've got to feel sorry about.'

She placed both hands on the teapot, as if considering.

'And Adrian?' ventured Vicky. 'What was he like as a boy?'

'Him? You would think the butter wouldn't melt in his mouth, but I knew better. Don't give him an inch. He was always watching, Mr Mouse Eyes. With his pale little face and his sharp little eyes. It was as if he wanted to get right inside of you. He wanted to know, he used to say. 'Well, I don't know what you want to know,' I used to say. I used to chase him right out of the house. Sometimes, to fix him, I gave him a big dose of castor oil – remember, Rian?'

'Uhmm,' I grimaced through a mouthful of beskuit.

'That will fix you, my man,' I said. 'A tablespoon of castor oil.'

4. *beskuit*, rusk

'All it ever did was give me the runs.'

'Hai!' She flapped the dishcloth at me, chuckling. 'How can you talk like that in front of your old aunt? Show some respect.'

Vicky looked solemn. Tant Koba poured the tea.

'Sugar, sweetie?' she asked Vicky.

'Yes, please.'

'Milk?'

'Milk, too, please.'

'Rian's late father used to idolize his son. It was wrong, I think. His father was always telling him things, talking to him as if he was a grownup. No good for the child. It's better for a child not to know, if you ask me.'

'I'm sure you're right,' said Vicky.

Tant Koba sipped her tea pensively.

I got up and went to the mantelpiece and took down my mother's picture.

'Here,' I said, and passed it to Vicky. 'Don't you think it looks like you?'

'This?' She held it at arm's length, and put her head to one side.

'That's Rian's mother,' Tant Koba sighed. 'I helped her sew her wedding dress. It was the best one in Doornlaagte, where we lived. White silk and ostrich feathers. We bought it from old Bham Jee, the coolie[5] trader. He was a crook and I told him so to his face. 'I hope you roast in hell,' I said, 'the way you cheat poor Christian folk.' Lovely white silk. Yard and yards of it because she had a train. 'It's best to be in fashion,' I said to Rian's Ma, 'and anyway,' I said, 'it's only once in a lifetime.' Which is true, for some people. Though nowadays, even to get married seems to be going out of fashion. Rian's Pa's own mother was my older sister, Elisabet. She is long dead now, God rest her soul. We've all got to die some day, I suppose. When Rian's Pa and Ma got married, they stayed with us for a while. I was mother to the whole family. I was the youngest girl, and the last child in our family was poor little Frederik. He was the eleventh child, the late lamb, as we say. Now, my dear, Rian's mother was a lady, as you can see from the picture. A wild one, I sometimes thought. She liked to dance. She had a gramophone and a bad case of the nerves. It was the nerves that killed her, if you ask me. She used to sit here, pregnant, in this room, and cry. 'Jakoba,' she said, 'I'm so afraid I'm going to die.' And I would say, 'Come now, of course you won't.' Then, after Rian was born, she got the fever, the purple fever, and it was all over in a day or two.'

She sipped her tea.

5. *coolie*, offensive; Indian

'Never cremate *me*,' she added. 'They say your body goes stiff like this'—she held out a finger—'and then it moves, sits up. I don't want to dance around after I am dead. Rian's Pa used to keep her ashes in a vase on his dressing table. I couldn't stand it. I threw the vase and all away in the veld after we arrived. God can sort it out on the Day of Judgment, I won't!'

Vicky turned the photograph round in her hands.

'What was her name?' she said.

'Anne,' said Tant Koba. 'An English Anne. To Rian's Pa, she was the Queen of Sheba. He loved her so much you would think he was out of his head. Then, when she was dead, he loved Rian the same way. Mad, if you ask me.'

Vicky put down the photograph and took a sip of tea.

'Rian says I look like her,' she said. 'Do you think so?'

'I don't know,' Tant Koba remarked, pouring tea into her saucer and blowing across it to cool it down. 'I haven't looked at that old picture in years, and now my eyes are growing dim. But won't you help yourself to some beskuit, my dear? It's home made.'

Vicky took a piece and began to dunk it in her tea.

'I eat like a horse,' she told Tant Koba.

'Eat,' Tant Koba said, comfortably helping herself to another piece of beskuit, too. 'It makes the heart grow sweet.'

The talk shifted to recipes. I retrieved the photograph and put it back in its place.

'Tante, excuse me.' I gave a nod. 'I need to go. . . .'

'Go. We're not stopping you.'

I went out the back.

It was very hot and still in the yard. All that was left of the swing I'd had as a child was a frayed rope-end hanging from the tree. In the dust the baboon's stake stood upright. The veld beyond was bare except for the rusting hulk of a tractor without wheels, a relic from Pa's day. The wire netting of the fowl run sagged: Tant Koba made a little money from the sale of poultry and eggs. I walked to the privy and shut the door.

I stood breathing the fetid odors of the two old people in the half-dark. A crack of sunlight lay across the cement floor. I thought of Pa's coffin. It had looked too small, I remembered.

'Pa,' I whispered. 'For Christ's sake, Pa!'

I slammed my fist against the corrugated iron wall of the privy. Dirt and dust rained down on me from the roof. A spider skittered away across the smooth wooden seat of the toilet. I could feel the sweat on my face. I nearly prayed.

PA'S COFFIN looked too small.

The room was choked with people who tried to hold me. The dominee[6] put his hand on my head. This was a young dominee I had never seen before, a Pentecostal. His hand was soft and smelt of soap.

'Child, do you know of the kingdom of God?'

'No, dominee.'

He shut his eyes and his lips moved soundlessly. Behind him on the table was Pa's coffin, and on the coffin stood a glass vase of lilies: I could see the cut stems looking too large, distorted by the glass. The dominee pinched at the bridge of his nose. He seemed to be thinking.

He waved his hands.

'Brothers and sisters!' He stretched out his arms and frowned as if to concentrate harder, and the veins stood out on his forehead. He leaned over backwards.

'Do you know the face of God?'

'No!' wailed someone and a woman sobbed.

'Who is there in this room who can say, 'I – yea, I – even I – have looked on the face of God?' Who could look on the naked sun and not be blinded? Only the dead, who are all around us, can see. The dead see, I say, and rejoice! All but one. Sinner, self-murderer, turn away. Go, gnash thy teeth in outer darkness. The face of God is not for thee. O Lord, what is man that Thou art mindful of him? Man is dust, and less than dust. Thou art the voice in the whirlwind. Thou art thine own son in the place of the skull. The mountains that have been from everlasting unto everlasting know Thee. Thou wert before them. Thou art God.'

'Amen!' cried several voices. 'Praise God!'

And someone groaned, 'Halleluia!'

'Dust,' cried the dominee, 'to dust. I see myself in the dust at my feet. My name is dust. And yours. And yours. I see myself in the shadows of this room. I hear my name in the silence when the chatter dies down and guilty people who deny the Word eye one another in fear. My own name is Gerhardus Lodewikus du Plessis, but my other name is death. What is yours, brother?'

'Kotze,' confessed a fat man in a brown suit, our neighbor from across the vlei[7].

'Hendrik Kotze.'

'Called?' said the dominee.

'Kot for short,' muttered the fat man after a moment.

'Death!' said the dominee. 'And your name, sister?'

6. *dominee*, pastor

7. *vlei*, marsh

A woman in the crowd, slim and tall and well-dressed, wearing a black veil, whispered her name so softly that he saw fit to repeat it after her.

'Crystal . . . Crystal le Roux.'

'Called? Called?'

'Death.'

'Praise God!' said the dominee. He turned to me again. 'And your name, child?'

I told him.

'Adrian Erasmus,' he said. 'Little Adrian, the child of death. And before us lying cold in his blood, the dead man, Theodosius Ocherse Karel Erasmus, called Tok.

The damned. Of him we will not speak. But there is another name, brothers, another name, sisters – the name of the conqueror of death, written in the sky at night, and in the light of dawn, forever. Let us now say His name together, silently in our heart.'

He paused for a moment, then continued:

'Brothers and sisters. Come. Let us sing.'

They all stood up and there was more of a crush in the room than ever, and they sang a hymn while the dominee stretched out his arms like Christ on the cross, and moved his hands, conducting the singing. Then he took the lilies off the coffin and gave a sign to the men in the front row who stepped forward and lifted Pa's coffin and maneuvered it, stumbling a little and groaning between their teeth at its weight.

They buried Pa in the new cemetery on the outskirts of the dorp. The dominee preached again, raising his arms and pointing to all the quarters of the horizon.

'Who shall be here to witness the glory at the end of time? Who shall be here to see the terror? Who but you and I, brothers and sisters, you and I! On that day the sun shall stand like a sword in Christ's right hand, and the fire of His judgment shall be loosed upon the world, and the hosts of the angels shall shiver the heavens with the blasts of their trumpets. Well, are you ready? I ask you, brothers and sisters. Are you ready?'

At the brink of the grave he stopped and looked down. For a moment, I thought he was about to jump in, but he didn't. All he did was say, 'Amen!' You could see the way the spade had cut the sides of the grave, and bits of roots. You could smell the earth. At the bottom lay the coffin. Then everybody began throwing handfuls of earth into the grave. Clods knocked against the lid, and spattered and sprawled. I couldn't stand the sound. I pressed my way to the back of the crowd, past all the legs.

A black man was squatting behind the nearest headstone, smoking.

'What are you doing here, outa?'[8] I asked.

With one eye shut against the smoke, he gave a nod at a shovel leaning against the headstone behind him.

'It is my Pa they are burying. Did you know?'

'Awu! The small basie's Pa?' He shook his head, clicking his tongue. 'How old is the small baas?'

'Six.'

He murmured sympathetically in his own tongue.

I stayed beside him. His cigarette was no more than a twist of brown paper and spit and tobacco, but I liked the strong smell of the smoke.

At last the people began to turn and move away, and I had to join them. It was over.

'Not a word about the shooting,' remarked a man with a broad back in a brown suit, the same Kot Kotze who had spoken.

'No, not a word!' agreed the man beside him, who had a moustache. 'Or the drink and the debts and the black kaffirmeide.[9] But he sent old Tok to the right place!'

He laughed, a high yelping, like a dog.

Not Pa, I said to myself, not Pa, not my Pa. I was burning with shame but I could not cry.

Back at the house, the dominee took me by the hand and led me to a fat old woman in a black dress, who was eating cake and wiping the crumbs off her bodice with her fingers. I knew her. She had moved in the day before. Pa's wardrobe was full of her dresses. They swayed and smelt of her when I pushed my head in amongst them. His own clothes lay on the floor, tied together in a bundle.

'Jakoba Alida Hendrina Erasmus!' exclaimed the dominee. 'Sister Jakoba. Look up. The face of the Lord is made to shine upon those who shelter orphans.'

Flustered, the old woman wanted to smile but couldn't, because her mouth was too full of cake. She nodded.

'Do you accept the Lord's charge, sister Jakoba?'

She touched her fingers to her lips, and one cheek bulged. Beside her sat a man with his hair oiled and combed straight back. He nodded at me and waggled his fingers.

8. *outa*, elder

9. *kaffirmeide*, offensive; African women servants

'Genesis, Exodus, Leviticus,' he said, 'Numbers, Deuteronomy, Kings.'

'Ag, dominee,' said Tant Koba, 'dominee doesn't after all have to ask. Dominee knows.'

The old woman pulled me on to her lap and told me to sit still, holding me close to her soft heavy bosom. A brooch pricked my ear. The man next to her smiled at me.

There was cake on his trousers and a smear of lipstick on his cheek – no doubt, someone had greeted him with a kiss.

'Hullo,' he said. 'Hullo, 'lo, 'lo, 'lo, 'lo.'

'Enough!' said Tant Koba. 'But I haven't introduced the dominee. This is my brother, dominee. Frederikus Johannes. Another charge of God.'

Meekly, the young dominee inclined his head.

I tried to slide off her lap but she held me tight.

Next morning – and every morning from then on, I found – when I ran through the house to the kitchen, the old woman was waiting. I would try and get past her to the back door but she would pick me up.

'Come,' she said.

Tying a dishcloth round my throat, she held me on her lap and began to feed me. Lumpy mieliepap in a large spoon.

'Don't vomit,' she warned. 'Chew.'

Then she tied Oom Frikkie up, too, and fed him in exactly the same way, except that he had to sit in a chair, and the pap ran down his chin, and his eyes bulged, and he made smacking noises with his lips.

After breakfast, she put the two of us outside.

We played together under the pepper tree.

Oom Frikkie was very strong. He could wrap my whole face in his hands. ('Who?' he said. 'Who are you?') It was dark in his hands and difficult to breathe. Then my nose began to bleed, all over his fingers and pants. Big soft drops of blood. It was startling. He wanted me to stop but I couldn't. He beat me over the head with the flat of his hand, and when that didn't help, he started hammering his fists up and down on his own head and pulling at his hair, and crying, 'No!' Then he climbed up my tree by way of the swing. The baboon howled, barked, hopped up on to the roof of its kennel. I watched Oom Frikkie's bare toes clench at the rope, which spun slowly round. The branches shook as he got higher, and he turned.

'Come! Hey, little boy! Come up here, quick!' he panted.

I saw his big scared face among the leaves, and I ran away down the hill, to the vlei far from the farmhouse, where the black women were washing clothes on the stones. They smiled a greeting and called my name. They were soaking the clothes in the water and scrubbing and slapping them on the stones. They gave me dry bread to eat. My nose had stopped bleeding. A dragonfly hung over a lump of cow dung at the edge of the vlei. It had jeweled wings – they shimmered, and you could see right through them.

When the women had finished the clothes, they went around collecting as much dung as they could find, and carried it back to their kraal in a bucket. I helped. The best dung was wet and green and soft, and slipped through your fingers. The women laughed and showed me how to pick it up. You had to cup your hands and pat it into the bucket. At the kraal, the dung was made runnier yet with water, and then the women smeared it all over the yard where it dried into a smooth crust, cleaner than dust. On their knees, while it was still wet, they scrawled patterns into it with their fingers. I drew patterns, too. I played with the kraal children. One little girl in particular. She had big warm friendly eyes, and snot running down over her lip, which she licked. I told her my name but she didn't understand. She ran round the side of the hut and I ran after her. Dead dry sunflowers stood behind the hut, tall against the sky. In the yard lay a thin dog with floppy teats. I wanted to suck the teats to see if there was any milk in them. The girl and I tried to suck the teats together. The dog turned on its back with a puzzled frown, and then squirmed to its feet, snarling and snapping. We both laughed.

But Tant Koba was angry.

'You come home plastered with cow shit,' she said. 'What is the matter with you? You can get sick like this.'

She was washing me in the zinc tub in front of the coal stove. She had poured disinfectant into the water. It was dark brown in the bottle but turned a milky white in the water. I liked the smell.

'Now you stink like a drain,' she said, rubbing me dry with a towel. 'Go and call Frikkie. Tell him he can't take all night to milk old Boland.'

The light of the lantern cut through the sides of the shed. Inside, giant shadows leapt up the walls. I could hear Oom Frikkie wheezing and moaning even before I saw him. The cow's back legs were tied with a riempie, and her hoofs rubbed together awkwardly as she shifted. Oom Frikkie was sitting on the upturned bucket with the tin can of grease for the cow's udder between his knees. He was rubbing the grease all over his face and into his hair, and he smiled, loose-lipped, when he saw me.

'More?' he said.

Dipping a finger into the pot, he held it out to me, capped with grease.

His fly was open, and his big thing lolled out.

'Watch me,' he said. 'I'm going to put it up – put it up Boland.'

'What!' cried Tant Koba when I told her.

She got to her feet and hurried out into the night. When she returned, she was leading him by the ear.

He tried to resist, but the more he twisted and whined, the grimmer her silence became. She took a piece of newspaper, crumpled it, and rubbed and scraped at his face. Then she washed his neck and ears with soap and hot water. As soon as his face was clean, she got him to take off his pants and scrub his belly and between his legs while she burnt the newspaper in the fire. Then she forced him to sit at the table while she took out a pair of scissors.

'Sies!' [10]she said. 'With a cow. With grease. And you told the child to stay and watch. Sit still! Sit still, or I'll cut off your ear.'

Frikkie's hair fell in sticky bunches, and she wiped her fingers on the collar of his shirt.

'Sies!' she said.

He looked even stranger with his scalp all bald and patchy.

'No,' he moaned, 'no, no, no, no. . . .'

'Shut up. Sit still. And when you see your head in the mirror, I want you to remember.'

'Oh, Jesus,' cried Oom Frikkie. 'Jesus! I have sinned.'

'Telling me. Now stand up, take your trousers, and go to bed.'

Whimpering and gnawing at his knuckles, Frikkie picked up his crumpled trousers from the floor, slung them over the crook of his arm, and went.

Slowly, the old woman set about clearing the kitchen.

Her slippers made a dry papery sound as she shuffled about, and she sighed, while the hair she threw into the fire filled the room with the smell of its singeing. Then she went out into the night again and milked the cow, and brought back the bucket full of foaming milk.

'Here,' she said, and gave me a cup.

The heat of the stove made me sleepy. My mouth was sticky with milk. I shivered.

On a bench by the fire, the old woman began rocking back and forth, gesticulating.

'Is this my life? Grease and shit and hair!'

10. *Sies!* phatic exclamation of disgust; cf. American 'Yuck!' 'Eww!'

Plucking off the doek[11] she wore during the milking, she ran her fingers through her own thin hair. Then she leaned back, covering her face with her hands, and began to laugh and cry at the same time. She looked swollen and fat when she did that. Helpless. I felt very frightened but all I could do was watch. Eventually, she got to her feet, and began to fill every available pot with water and crowd them all together on the stove.

'I am going to bath,' she said. 'Don't look!'

In a short while the tub was ready. She pulled her dress over her head, struggled out of her underthings, and sat down in the water. She rubbed soap into her face and under her armpits, and splashed it off again and snorted and sighed. But when she tried to get up at last, it appeared that she couldn't. Her legs were tucked up. She was stuck.

'And now?' she said. 'Am I going to have to sit here, like a tortoise on its back, forever? Rian, come here!'

I could hear the water slopping as she struggled. I could smell the soap.

'Come, child, come!' she said. 'I won't bite.'

At last, reluctantly, I went. I kept my eyes fixed on the floor.

'Now,' she said. 'Let me see.'

Her fingers pressed into my shoulder. They felt unusually soft and warm. She paused for a moment, then heaved herself up with a heavy splash of the rocking water and stood dripping. I saw her bulging white belly and huge breasts with their nipples, and a wet hairy splay-mouthed cleft, which opened as she moved, stepping out of the tub.

'Hai, don't look!'

I shut my eyes and pressed my face against her leg. I hated crying, but I couldn't help it – the tears began to squeeze out between my lids, burning.

'And now, little man?' said the old woman, laughing and placing a warm hand on my head. 'What do you know now?'

IN THE SLUGGISH HEAT OF THE PRIVY, I opened my fly, took out my cock and squeezed it. I liked to feel the soft weight of it. I liked to see the whole thing stir and grow bigger.

'Dumb buddy,' I said. 'You'll just have to wait.'

I ran my fingers down to the base and the hair. Then I shoved it away again and shut the zip. Allowing a minute or so for the bulge to subside, I hooked back the door to let in a little sunlight and air, and crossed the yard again to the house.

11. *doek*, scarf

Vicky and Tant Koba were talking together in the kitchen.

'You know, my own big trouble has always been the heart,' Tant Koba confided. 'It swells up in my throat like a football, and I get hot all over and full of longing, and it's as though I'm going to die. The worst is at night. I can't breathe, then, even if I open all the windows and undo the top of my nightie.'

'Have you seen a doctor?'

Vicky was being polite, rinsing the tea things and stacking them beside the sink to dry.

'Now and again,' the old woman replied. 'But I take Steel Drops every morning for the heart. Essence of Life gets rid of morbidity and gives you that spring feeling, and Steel Drops strengthen the heart. Ask Rian,' she added. 'He used to give them to me.'

'It's true,' I put in.

'Rian!' said Vicky. 'What took you so long?'

'Cramp,' I said. I pressed a forefinger to my temple with a grin. 'In the head.'

'In the . . . ?'

'Don't listen to him,' said the old woman. 'It's just his nerves. He takes after his mother, that's all. She always used to look like that.'

'Like what?' I wanted to know.

'Go and look at yourself in the mirror.'

Vicky touched my face with nimble wet fingers.

'You're white as a sheet,' she said. 'And hot. What's wrong?'

'Want to see a bullet hole?'

'Ag, no!' objected the old woman. 'Don't show her that, man.'

'Why not?' I said.

Tant Koba folded her arms and considered me in a leisurely way from head to foot.

'If anyone in the world knows why, that person is you, Adrian Erasmus. And you know it.'

'Come on, tante.'

'Don't 'come on' me!'

I dried a cup and stacked it away. Vicky let the water drain from the sink. The old woman moved around the room, collecting a sieve and a broad enamel bowl, both of which she put on the table.

'How long are you planning to stay?' she asked.

'All weekend,' I replied, 'if it's all right with tante.'

'I thought as much. Well, you are welcome, child. But then I must bake some bread. Do you,' she asked Vicky, 'like home-made bread, fresh from the oven?'

'Delicious!' smiled Vicky, flicking her fingers to dry them.

I caught her hand. Her fingertips were cold.

'That's the place,' I told her. 'Above the stove. The bullet hole.'

'Oh, my God,' she said.

The old woman put her fist on her hip. Tilting her head, she raised her chin and glanced askance at the wall.

'If I was a young lady,' she remarked. 'If I was young again, I would like to see the Seven Wonders of the World, not just a hole in the wall. Or even something nearer to home. Like the Rand Show. They bring things from all over the world to the Rand Show. All sorts of things. The latest model cars, fancy new gadgets, chickens with two heads, sweet stuff like clouds that you take pinches out of, and eat, called candy floss. Rian's Pa told us. He used to go to the Show. Once, he brought us back a bar of soap that smelt like all sorts of different fruit when you washed your hands. Now it was apricot, now it was pear, now it was peach. Just like the fruit. If you closed your eyes and used only your nose you would think it was real. Then Oom Frikkie went and ate half of it and got sick, so I had to lock it away in a drawer. The Rand Show.' She sighed. 'Sometimes I think everyone in this house is funny in the head. So many wonderful things in the world to see, but you go and show her that. Why don't you take your young lady and show her the spruit,[12] show her the tree where your swing used to hang, show her the fowl hok.[13] Go on, go! Get out from under my feet, now, I'm busy.'

Pouring a pile of flour into the sieve, she began to tap and shake the sieve over the bowl. Soon, her fists would be kneading the dough, folding it back on itself, thumping it, pressing it into oblong black pans smeared with lard.

'Can't we stay and watch?' I asked. 'Vicky has never seen how bread is made.'

'Oh?' said the old woman. 'And why not?'

She stopped and rested the sieve on the rim of the bowl. Her fingers were white to the knuckle.

'I'd rather go outside,' said Vicky.

'The voice of wisdom,' said Tant Koba with a nod. 'Go, then. Don't be too long.'

We went out the front door. Vicky was still smiling, but her face was tight and two small spots of red stood out on her cheeks.

'What's wrong?' I said.

'The Rand Show!' she whispered, rolling her eyes.

At any moment, I knew, she would burst into giggles.

12. *spruit*, creek

13. *fowl hok*, chicken coop

Vicky came from a wealthy home. Across wide lawns beneath jacaranda and bougainvillea, peacocks went trailing their gorgeous tails, and cried out, shrieked. In the walls of the great white house were niches where statues could have stood. The house itself breathed peace, a mixture of opulence and ease, but somehow I always felt out of place. The wooden staircase creaked, and there were more rooms than anyone ever used. Round the back lay a swimming pool, but Vicky wouldn't swim. 'I don't like cold water,' she said.

Before meeting me, she had been involved with an oil tycoon, Russell MacKay, Rusty, from Aberdeen, Scotland. I'd seen him once, a short and stocky man with bushy ginger eyebrows, dancing what he claimed was the Highland fling on the patio. He was very drunk and put an arm around my neck, and tried to kiss me, too – a wet-lipped kiss on the nose – but I ducked, and stepped back. 'Rusty has a sea-going yacht,' Vicky told me. 'And a castle near Forres. You know, like in Shakespeare: 'How far is't called to Forres?' When I said I didn't believe it, she said: 'It's true. He's not only rich, he's waiting to inherit a fortune.' Then, what did she want with me? I asked. We were sitting cross-legged on the kelim carpet in her room, having abandoned the patio to the Scotsman. Vicky, opposite me, was tracing the intricate pattern of the rug with one finger. 'I don't want him any more,' she said. Her eyes were bright with sincerity. Harsh. 'You've got to understand. I've always gone with older men, my father's friends. Doggy old men. Smelly. I've had to be their little girl. You don't know how disgusting it all was. I don't want to do that any more, Rian. None of it. I want you. I'm glad it's you.'

It had been her idea to get married, and she had wanted to do so quickly. But first, I had felt she must see my mother's photograph, among other things.

We stopped on the front stoep,[14] now. The hippo's skull stood in place just as Pa had left it, its jaws tied together with bloudraad. [15]

'How'd you like to meet an old friend?' I said. 'A hippo. She almost told me something once.'

'Oh, grisly! Why do you keep it?'

'I'm waiting. You never know. One day she may whisper in my ear.' I tapped at the teeth which stood out like stumpy tusks. 'Solid ivory,' I said.

'Watch out! What if it bites?'

'Oh, yes?' I said, holding my shoulder. 'Once bitten. . . .'

She laughed and squeezed my hand.

'Let's go,' she said.

14. *stoep*, porch, stoop

15. *bloudraad*, heavy gauge fencing wire

It was a long walk down to the vlei. The grass was chest-high in places, and tiny grasshoppers kept chipping up ahead of us. Grass seeds stuck to my face. We
stopped at the derelict tractor, but didn't go up close. Spears of khakibos[16] had
shot up around it, spreading a bronze odor, like urine. The sun was heavy. Mid-
afternoon. I pointed out the big round stones scattered all over the veld, and
the high spine of the ironstone ridge in the distance, and told her Ou Willem's
story of the witch.

'Is it true?' she asked. Points of suspicion had appeared in her eyes.

'Oh, yes. I believe it.'

'I mean, I only want to know what is true.'

'Well, it is true. It happened. But even if the old man had made it all up, I'd
still believe it. It's a story, not a lie.'

'What do you mean?'

I pinched at the bridge of my nose, concentrated.

'I mean, I think, a way of speaking the unspeakable.'

She said nothing. Her lipstick was flaking: she was biting it off.

'Where are the witch's stones?' she asked.

'On that ridge up there. One day, we'll find them, you'll see.'

The vlei was a winding green stain at the foot of the slope. We followed a
footpath round the edge of it and then, avoiding the softer, more treacherous
places, cut across to a pool I knew of, walled in on all sides by reeds. The odor of
the marsh was heavy, dank. Vicky took my hand. The pool was dead still.

'What are you most afraid of?' she asked.

'Me?' I said with a laugh. 'The Creature from the Black Lagoon.'

Vicky looked at me.

'Are you making this up?'

I shook my head. 'I've seen the movie. At a drive-in with my father, when
I was very small. It scared me stiff. Imagine. This black shiny water, and the
monster poking his head out of it. Spiny. A face like a fish-frog, and webs and
flippers. Totally silent. The monster, I mean, not the movie. I'd laugh if I saw
it today, I guess. But there are moments when I suspect it is still there, only just
out of sight. If you shut your eyes, it's there. The monster kidnaps this beautiful
girl and carries her into the lagoon. She is wearing a white dress like a bride, and
hangs limp. They go into the water and sink, and the water closes over them,
black, and you see bubbles bursting, big ones. And then silence. You can almost
feel its scaly grip, its hands. All slimy, cold . . . what's wrong?'

'Oh,' she said, 'that horrible old man! That horrible, horrible old man.'

16. *khakibos*, khaki bush

I laughed. Sucking in both cheeks, I crossed my eyes.

'Don't,' she cried. 'You look just like him.'

'Not me. I look just like my father.'

She sat down on the dry sand of the bank and smoothed her skirt toward her knees, while I sat beside her. She looked out over the dull water.

'Why didn't you tell me?' she said.

'Tell you what?'

'About him. Who he really is.'

'What do you mean? He's my uncle. Oh, come on. I told you, all right. Long ago. Don't mind Oom Frik, I said, he's off his head. He doesn't know if he's a Happy Clappy or a four-year-old. And my aunt is this hefty old tannie, one hell of a gossip. You'll like her, I said. And you do, don't you?'

'I knew they were funny people, but. . . .'

'But what?' I said, my throat tightening. I didn't like to hear her say things like that.

'Nothing. I want to go home. I don't want to stay the weekend any more.'

'Too late. We're staying.'

She crossed her legs, picked up a stick and began digging at the sand. I recollected Oom Frikkie's face when she had flipped up her skirt, and I smiled. The sun was hot.

'Why can't we go home?' she asked.

A kingfisher – electric blue, flame orange and white – alighted on a bent reed.

'Hey, look,' I said.

Like a rock, the kingfisher sat – alert, watchful, his dagger bill poised. We hardly dared to breathe. Suddenly, he dipped down at the water, hitting it with hardly a splash. For a moment, he seemed to hover over the ripples as he rose, then he mounted high into the air and was gone.

'Did you see that?' I said.

'Did I not?' said Vicky. She smiled. Her eyes were dark and her face seemed drained of all color by the sun.

'Are you the witch of the pool?' I asked.

'No. Not of this pool.'

'Why not?'

'It's obvious.'

'I want you,' I said.

'Watch out. I may bite.'

'Oh, yes?'

I leaned forward and she bared her teeth at me. I opened my mouth wide but when I tried to kiss her she kept her teeth clenched, and all I could do was run my tongue over them. I expected her at any moment to bite, but she didn't. I began to lick her cheek, her eyelids, with the tip of my tongue. I took her earlobe between my teeth and bit it.

'No!' she cried. 'How could you?'

But this time when I kissed her she opened her mouth and it was all sweet and warm and deep, and I trailed my fingers down across her throat, aware of the pulse there. Slipping my hand between her shirt collar and her neck, I undid a button or two. She leant forward and I found her breast, small, a swelling beneath my hand, and then she bit my tongue.

Difficult as it was, I began to laugh. I twined a finger into the hair of her armpit, which was warm and wet, and tweaked it. She sank her teeth harder and then released me and I sat back.

'Jesus,' I said. 'How do you talk with a hurt tongue?'

'You don't,' she pointed out. 'You behave.'

Her sweaty hair framed her face, and she pushed it back with both hands. Then she kissed me.

I pushed up the apple green skirt, running my fingers across the skimpy bikini panties to feel the springiness of her pubic hair. Still kissing her, I pressed my fingers into the slick liquid warmth.

'We can't,' she breathed, moving, almost bucking, to my hand.

'No one is around. We can. Right here.'

With my free hand, I unzipped my pants. She trailed her fingers down my standing penis, then put her mouth over it.

'Don't bite!'

She shook her head and laughed, a throbbing feeling to me.

'Lie back,' I urged. 'Quick.'

It was hot and sweet, unbelievably hot and sweet, but over all too soon.

Afterwards, she lay with her knees up and her arm across her eyes. I wiped the sweat off my forehead with the back of my wrist. Then I put my hand on her pubic hair and cupped the soft, pendulous lips beneath.

'Again?' I said.

I squeezed the lips together and spread them wide. She began to tremble. Coral pink, the splayed cleft. I was about to put my mouth to it when I realized she was crying.

'I want to go home,' she whispered, trembling. 'I want to go home.'

Tears were sliding down her cheeks and her fists were clenched. I took one fist and gently pressed the knuckles.

'All right. If it's that bad. We'll go.'

Tant Koba's kitchen was full of the smell of freshly baked bread. Four loaves wrapped in white cloth stood on the table. The old woman herself, broad and squat in her black dress, was bending over the oven.

'Tante,' I remarked, 'we've changed our minds.'

She looked round, her hands on her knees, and wiped a few wisps of hair from her face.

'What now?' she said.

Inside the oven stood another loaf of bread.

'We're going,' I said. 'We can't stay the weekend, after all.'

'Why not? Where is your young lady?'

'In the car. She finds Oom Frikkie too funny, I think.'

'Ag, I would look after him. She wouldn't have to worry. Go tell her that.'

'It wouldn't do any good. She said I must say goodbye.'

Tant Koba reached for the last pan of bread. Putting a hand to the small of her back as an aid in straightening up, she muttered with a grimace: 'Old age.'

She turned the bread pan over on the table, and tapped at its sides with a spoon. When she lifted the pan, the loaf lay upside down but free.

'I'm sorry, tante.'

'Ja,' she said. 'I heard.'

She took off her doek. Her hair was thin and white, and her shoulders humped. Untying her apron, she folded it into a small neat square.

'Some people don't know what's what,' she observed. 'They just don't know. What is going on with you, Rian? You go away, we never see you or hear from you. Not even so much as a postcard. Not even: 'Hullo, old people, remember me? I'm still in the land of the living. Are you?' And then one fine day, there you are on my doorstep. 'Meet my bride-to-be,' you say. I look. A fine young lady, I see. A bit wild, perhaps. And very young. Quite pretty, too. But I don't say a word. I make tea for you. I give you beskuit. I bake bread all afternoon. Next thing, 'Tante,' you say, 'we're leaving.' 'Why?' is all I ask. Your teacups are not even cold.'

'It's too much for Vicky, that's all. She is just not used to it.'

'Oh? And what is she used to, the madam?'

'Pearls and champagne. All the wonders of the world. Everything money can buy.'

The old woman opened her mouth as if to speak, then shut it again as if equally determined not to.

'You must at least take some bread,' she remarked. 'Your uncle and I can't eat five loaves by ourselves. And I'm fat enough as it is.' She tugged briefly at the waist of her dress by way of demonstration. 'Frederik!' she called. 'Go and open the gate for the visitors. They are going, now.'

I picked up two of the loaves and stood with one under each arm.

'Tante,' I began, 'I just want to say thank you. I'm sorry. I wish we weren't leaving, but....'

'Don't be sorry, child. And don't thank me, eitht me er. I don't want your thanks. Just be happy, if you can. Here, you can kiss your old aunt on the cheek before you go.'

She turned her cheek up to me. I don't know why, but I expected the withered skin to be tough and dry as bark. Instead, it was soft, almost incredibly soft. I couldn't stand it. I stepped back again as soon as I could, forcing a smile.

'I'll write you a whole lot, tante,' I promised. 'Not just a postcard. It won't be like last time, you'll see.'

'Over my dead body,' she said. 'I don't even read the Bible these days. I sing. The psalms of David and all my old favorite hymns. I sit here in the kitchen on my own and sing. Sometimes, your uncle joins me, and then it's a real cats' and dogs' choir, I'm telling you. But if the heart is in the right place, then where is the harm? Your uncle likes 'Onward, Christian Soldiers'. You should see him march. Up and down and round and round. It's better than letting him lie in his room all the time. He is also a human being. He gets lonely, too, sometimes. Ag, ja. Even if we don't remember the words any more, the tunes are enough. Now, why only two loaves, Rian? Come, take three.'

Oom Frikkie stood at the gate, squinting against the sun. As I eased through the gate in my car, he began banging flat-handed on the hood.

'Dominee must call again soon,' he begged. 'Okay, dominee?'

'No,' I said. 'Never. Amen. Goodbye. Go fuck yourself, Oom Frik.'

Shifting into gear, I tore up the dust around him. When I looked back, he was still waving.

'God, am I glad we are leaving,' said Vicky. She was biting a nail. She spat it on the floor. 'I hope you don't mind.'

'Mind? Why should I? They're such funny people. The problem is, I may be one of them. Or don't you think so?'

'Oh, please,' she muttered, looking away and ignoring me.

I wound down the window and let the warm draught blow in, drying my sweat. On the back seat lay the three loaves. I reached over, tore a corner off one, and chewed it. It was crusty, flaky.

'Want some?' I asked.

'Mm, yes, thanks. I'm starved.'

Vicky sat curled up, bare feet on the seat, picking at the ragged end of bread and staring at the road. In a corner of the dashboard, a trapped fly buzzed.

'What are you thinking?' I said.

She shook her head and swallowed, the muscles in her cheeks shifting, but made no reply.

We left the dorp with its church steeple and cluster of shops, took the fork to the highway, and drove on through the late afternoon. I couldn't believe I was leaving, somehow. The wind pressed in, hot and dry and exhausted. If I had had nothing more to lose, I would have gone to sleep.

'Do you know what he said?' Vicky asked abruptly.

'Who?'

'You know who. Your so-called uncle.'

'Oh, him.'

'He said, 'Annie, I don't want to.'

'Is that so? I don't remember.'

'Don't want to what, Rian?'

'Who knows? He's got sex on the brain. Wank, suck or fuck, no doubt. Forget him. He's not worth worrying about.'

'I know he's not worth it, but I can't. . . .'

'Can't what?'

'Stop worrying. Annie was your mother?'

'Yes, Anne or Annie was my mother. My pretty mother. You saw the photograph.'

'Yes. And he called me Annie, and said he didn't want to. Didn't want to what, Rian?'

'Oh, come on, Vicky. What is this?'

'It's the truth, Rian. He may be your father, for all you know. Your real father. That funny old man. He may be. I can't take the chance.'

'Listen, Vicky. . . .'

She shut her eyes tight and pressed her fingers into her ears. I laughed.

'Hear no, see no, speak no evil, huh?'

'Shut up!'

She stayed curled up, and I was obliged to speak to her just as she was.

'Listen. Oom Frikkie didn't want Annie, and you know it. He wanted you. Hell, his brain is full of crossed wires, Vicky. He called you Annie, me dominee. He would call himself Jesus Christ, if only Tant Koba would let him grow a beard. You didn't know my father. He would have broken old Frikkie's neck if that idiot had done so much as lift his eyes to my mother. Anyway, what makes you think my mother would have seen anything in him? Why should she? I mean, would you?'

'No, no, disgusting!'

'Well, then.'

'You don't understand, Rian. I kept seeing him in you all afternoon. I saw his face instead of yours when we made love.'

'You did? I can't think why.'

'I've told you why.'

'And what was it like, making love to him?'

'Shut up! Shut up!'

'Okay, okay. Let's both stop saying stupid things for a while, okay?'

My broad old Dodge seemed to be the only car on the road. It rolled along steadily but at no great speed. Vicky and I sat for some time without speaking. A row of electric pylons came up, stalking toward the horizon. Six, seven, eight of them in sight.

How many hours of driving ahead?

'Listen,' I said. 'Let's find ourselves a place to spend the night. A small hotel. Get ourselves a decent meal and a bed. Take it easy, huh? Have a beer. Sleep over.'

Vicky looked tired. She lifted her hair in a bunch and leaned on her hand.

'No,' she replied. 'I don't want to.'

'It's a long drive if we don't. Maybe you could take the wheel for a while later on?'

'No, it's too heavy for me, this big old tank that you drive. You know that.'

'Well, I don't feel like pushing on and on forever after dark.'

'Couldn't you just take a nap sometime? I'll wait.'

'Vicky, please. What's going on?'

She looked at me, and then out of the window.

'Even if your father was your father,' she said. 'It's still in the family.'

'What?'

'You know what. It's in your genes.'

'And so? What are you saying?'

'I don't want funny babies, Rian.'

I let the car coast to the side of the road and stop. All around lay bare veld, flat to the horizon.

'If that's how you feel,' I said. I felt very tired. 'Get out.'

'What?'

'Get out.'

'No, Rian, listen.'

'No. Out. Go on.'

'I won't.'

'Won't you?'

I opened the car door by leaning over her and she was out. I didn't even have to push. I locked the door after her. Breathing was painful. I didn't look. I didn't have to. She was clutching at the handle and beating at the window, crying, 'Rian! Rian! Don't be stupid.'

For the space of an instant I saw her face, surprised, twisted, appealing in the mirror as I put my foot flat and the Dodge drew ponderously away.

I kept trying not to think.

I pressed on for about twenty minutes before I doubled back, recognizing the place by the pylons. The Dodge's tracks stood out on the verge. Twenty or thirty meters farther lay another set of tracks. Also, her footprints in the soft red sand. A lift, then. Where to? And what now? I switched off the car.

The sun was beginning to set. Through the hot and glassy air, I could hear the sound made by the current in the cables, a rippling, droning, humming sound, like a distorted babbling of human voices.

Late that night, I checked into a cheap hotel.

Too tired to sleep, I lay for a long time, staring. At fixed intervals, the room was flooded by the bone-pale glare of the neon hotel sign outside the window. On the far wall, like a pool, gleamed a mirror. The pillow beneath my head gave off faint whiffs of a woman's perfume. Thirsty, I sat up and took a mouthful of water from the bedside carafe. Tepid. Metallic. Then, wrapping my head in the sheet, I lay down flat.

The road was still coming at me, it seemed, moving silently through the wall. I thought of pressing my mouth to her armpit, and the taste of the hot moist hair, as the sheet collapsed to my breathing and clung to my face. Now you are dead, I told myself. In your shroud, you hang suspended. Dead.

Don't breathe. Don't move.

8

I AWAKE TO THE CHATTER OF MONKEYS – a whole handful of them, scrambling and crashing through the wild fig. They cling overhead and peer down at me with lively little faces, gibbering.

I get to my feet with a laugh.

'Bandits! Come down here and say that!'

Astonished, outraged, they tumble over one another and scatter. A bit of white cloth, torn off, comes twirling down from the leaves as the monkeys vanish.

I stretch. No one else is up.

It is a perfect morning, wide and calm and quiet.

I pick up the cloth but it falls apart between my fingers. Brittle, sun-dried. A smell of dust.

The pup tent sags, as though sucked in by Bucs's breathing all night.

What I should do next is fix breakfast, I know. Eggs and bacon. Toast. But first, I wander over to the kombi, press my hands and face flat against the window, and bare my teeth.

Bamford's head pops from the sleeping bag. His hair is sticking up straight and he blinks.

'Sweet fucking Jesus!' he says.

On the pillow beside him, I can make out her sleeping head. Her hair is spread out, the rest of her no more than a small huddle in the military surplus sleeping bag.

Bamford seems to think it can only be himself that I want.

'Hang on! Half a minute.' Behind the glass, his voice sounds distant, small.

After a struggle, he manages to shove open the sliding door. Then he slings his legs out and just sits there, humped.

'Sweet Jesus,' he groans. 'Dear God. Dear fucking ballbag of God. What time is it?'

'Just after seven.'

'You must be joking. Bloody crack of dawn.'

'No, it's getting late. Want a cup of coffee?'

He nods, leaning his head on his hand. Without glasses, his eyes look malignant, swollen.

'Oh, Jesus, I've had it. I'm broken in pieces. I ache. I must be growing old. Coffee, did you say? All right, then. Coffee.'

I fill the kettle. The water-level in the 50-litre tank is low, I notice, but I couldn't care. We're leaving today. I unscrew the lamp from the gas canister and fit the stove-top into place. The flame makes a low flapping sound under the kettle. First we shall celebrate Bamford's birthday – shoot the table and the cake for luck, maybe – then strike camp. I can't wait to lay hands on the camera again. I am in high spirits. It is a clear and perfect morning.

'I – a warrior!' I repeat under my breath.

I go and slap the sides of Bucs's tent.

'Hah?' he groans.

'You'll suffocate if you lie there any longer. Up, brother. Up and greet the sun.'

By the time I reach Bamford with the coffee, he has almost completely un-wrapped the dressing on his foot. The end of the bandage is stuck to it. His toe must have bled again in the night.

'What do I do now?' he grunts.

'Soak it, I suppose. Be patient. I'll go and fetch you a basin of water.'

'Not on your life. Forget it. I'm not going to sit here all day like an old hag with a cold. Why don't you just give the damned thing a jerk, like a tooth?'

'Why me? Do it yourself, if you imagine it'll work.'

'Go on, man. Give it a try.'

'You want to lose a pound of flesh?'

'I can afford it. Go on. Try.'

I catch up the trailing bandage and wrap it round my open hand. As I do so, I look him in the eye.

'You asked for it.'

He gives me a queer, lopsided grin.

'Cheese.'

Only when I am within an inch or two of his toe do I stop winding up the ban-dage. I can feel the heat of his body, count the pores on his nose. The fuzz on his chin has a coppery glint. His breath smells.

I tug once, sharply.

Bamford suffers in silence, squirming and puffing.

'Sorry,' I tell him. 'It's still sticking a bit. Wait.' I try again, twisting it this time. 'That's better. Did it hurt.'

He hisses through his bottom teeth.

'Not much. Oh, no! Jesus Christ. You'd make a bloody good axe-murderer, you know.'

His whole foot is swollen, I see. The skin is shiny and tight, inflamed around the wound. Blood has pricked up at the point where the bandage was stuck.

'You're mad if you don't take this to a doctor.'

He shuts his eyes.

'I am fifty-two years old today,' he says. He looks drained and grey, and his voice sounds hoarse, a kind of whisper. 'Fifty-two. Count it.'

'What do you mean?'

'Go ahead, count it. I want to hear you. Count it out loud.'

His lips move without a sound, keeping time with mine.

'Fifty-two,' he says impatiently, a little ahead of me. 'How long did that take?'

'About a minute. Maybe less.'

'A minute. Dear God. It's less than the life of a fruit fly. Old,' he muses. 'How old is old?'

'Wonderboy is old,' I quote from the script. 'The mind of man is young.'

It's good to get an opportunity to rub it in.

'Oh, balls,' he says. 'I mean it man. Can't you see? Here I sit in the sun and sweat. It makes no particular sense, you know. I am fifty-two years old. What does it mean? A certain sum of circles, ellipses, or whatever, around the sun. I know, I know: the question can't even be asked. It's like the silver stick they keep in Paris, isn't it, to fix the length of the meter? Arbitrary. How long is long?'

'A lecture is always long, I think. Too long.'

He sits for a while without a word. Then he wipes the sweat from around his mouth with the back of his wrist.

'Old. I'm getting old. And I drink too much. My toe is the cherry on top.'

'If they amputate that toe, you won't be able to walk again. You'll waddle. Use a cane. Hup, hup.' I show him how.

'Thanks, I can manage.' He starts to pick at a stain on his chest. 'Look at my hands. Wrinkled, aren't they? And spotty. I've got the shakes this morning. Booze is what does it. Blows the synapses like fuses. But I don't give a fuck. What was I saying?'

'Something about your toe.'

'No, wait, I know. Birthdays. Birthdays are nothing but simple arithmetic – x plus one, plus one, and so on, until you get the sum. Linear rule. Pass the meter stick. July the twelfth, nineteen eighty-four, and I'm exactly . . . let's see. Eight short of sixty. But what does T.S. Eliot say? 'Time present is time eternal.' Is that it? And Nicholas of Cusa, fifteenth century: 'God is a circle whose centre is everywhere, and whose circumference, nowhere.' Renounce calculation, my friend. Admit eternity. Bliss is our element. Don't you forget it.'

'Enough already, professor. You're not dead yet. Who knows, you may have a year or two left. We'll see. Happy birthday. Drink up.'

'You think so?' He slurps at his coffee. Frowns down at the cup. 'How about a drop of the real thing?'

'Only if you crave it.'

'Oh, I do. You know I do. Just a drop.'

I go and fetch the whisky from the folding table.

Bucs is rolling up his sleeping bag outside the pup tent.

'Want some?' I call, holding up the bottle.

He grimaces and shakes his head. His baseball cap is back to front, and the long muscles in his arms move quickly, casually. I almost see what Vicky sees in him, and I turn away.

'Take the tent down, too,' I tell him. 'Roll it up, pack it. We're leaving before lunch.'

Vicky is sitting up when I get back, brushing her hair, a scuffing sound. Bamford, in lecture mode, is holding up one finger in what I take to be a strict request for silence.

'If little girls are made of sugar and spice, then why do they all smell of fish?'

He smells his finger. Vicky raps him over the head with her brush. Not too hard. I foresee another day of these little games, and I begin to feel tired.

'Coffee?' I ask Vicky.

'No, thanks.' She won't even look at me. Last night didn't happen, I see. Okay, then. I'm also growing old.

I add a drop of whisky to Bamford's coffee.

'Fill 'er up!' He gestures, and I do. 'Ah,' he says, taking the mug in both hands and savoring the odor. 'That's more like it!'

Vicky goes back to brushing her hair. I cap the bottle and put it away. With his glasses on his nose now, Bamford holds up his foot as though trying to dry the wound in the sun.

'Tell me,' he remarks. 'You know about these things, Mr Director. After all, you are the knowledgeable sort. Why are there suddenly two black men in the camp?'

For a wild moment, I suspect him of riddling.

'Two?'

Afraid of making a fool of myself, I don't turn round.

'Yes,' he says, 'two. One, two. Look behind you.'

A young black man, younger than Bucs, is kneeling on the ground beside him. Bucs, sitting back on his heels, is winding up a guy rope from the topple pup tent. He looks round at me, his forehead wrinkled questioningly.

I swallow the rest of my coffee and cross to them.

'Yes?' I ask the newcomer. 'What can I do for you?'

He does not look up and meet my eyes. Instead, he speaks very softly to Bucs. It is a mark of respect, I know. He is wearing a vest so tattered it is no more than a loop or two across his bare skin.

Bucs indicates him with his thumb.

'This boy,' he remarks. 'This boy comes from. . . .' He extends his arm in a sweeping motion, revealing the patch of sweat in his armpit. 'Over the river.'

'The little dried-up spruit?'

Bucs and the boy talk together again.

'Yes,' says Bucs.

The boy is still kneeling with downcast eyes.

Bucs listens. The boy talks with some animation, using his hands to explain. Not once does he glance up at me. His eyes are heavy, thick-lidded. He nods often, and his lips move quickly. He seems somehow willing, but also, it seems to me, quite apprehensive.

Scratching his head, Bucs gets to his feet.

'This boy says,' he explains. 'This boy says, we kill his father's goat. Yesterday.'

'Oh? A goat. And what did you say?'

'Ai kôna, I say. No. Baas Rian, I say, he shot the tarentaal.'

'This goat. It belonged to his father, you say?'

'Yes,' says Bucs. He pinches his lip and looks at the boy. He begins to talk to the boy again, waving his hands, but I interrupt.

'A white goat?' I ask. 'With a piece of rope around its neck?'

I put my hands around my neck and mime the rope.

Bucs's face changes as he looks at me. He seems to wise up. He smiles. It is not a smile that I like to see.

The boy is making motions in the air to indicate the size of the goat, I think, and talking quite urgently, but Bucs doesn't seem to listen to him. Instead, he puts his head to one side and says to me:

'Did you kill this goat?'

'Me?' I grin hard. 'A goat?'

Without taking his eyes off me, Bucs murmurs to the boy again. The boy speaks, pointing down at the ground and raising his voice for the first time.

'This boy says,' Bucs tells me. 'This boy says you must come with him now. To the madala, the old man.'

'Why?'

'Speak to him. Speak to the madala, the old man.'

'And what will this madala want, do you think?' I rub together my forefinger and thumb. 'Money?'

Bucs shrugs. The boy nods as if he has both overheard and understood, and then simply sits, waiting. There is a pause.

Bamford calls from the kombi: 'Hey! What about us? Come on, man. What the hell is going on?'

'Nothing much. I've got to go and see a man about a goat.'

'You're joking. A goat? What goat?'

'Your goat,' I say. I can't resist spelling it out. I even walk back to the kombi again. 'The one you missed, remember? Big and white and hairy. On top of a boulder. Stinking. Shaking its ears.'

Bamford pushes his fingers backwards through his hair.

'My goat, you say? Well, what about it?'

'I shot it. Yesterday. In the riverbed.'

'You?' He opens and shuts his mouth. 'You . . . ?' He almost chokes on his own gurgling, whistling laughter. Phlegm. 'Shot? My goat?'

'Right. And now I have to go to the kraal and pay for it.'

'Really? How much?'

'I don't know.'

'What about breakfast?'

'Yes, why don't you fix yourself some? I'll skip it.'

I go and collect my wallet from the cab of the kombi and check it for cash. Not much, but it will have to do. My ears are burning and feel too large. If I had a razor, I'd take each ear by the lobe, tug, and with a single upward stroke, sever it. See, Vicky? I'd shake my head and grin, scattering blood. Allow me to present to you, in your lap. A perfect pair. Twins.

'Be back as soon as I can,' I call. 'Okay?'

'If you insist,' grunts Bamford.

Vicky's hair is shining in the sun. How good it would be to wrap my face up in her hair, tight, dark.

'Okay,' I tell Bucs, slipping the wallet into my pocket and patting it. 'I'm ready. Let's go.'

The young man in the vest takes the lead. Well-built, walking springily. Only too pleased to be leaving, I'd say. He knows his way around. Bone-white grass and withered grey bush. Silence. His land.

Not far from the camp, the little goatherd in the Army bunny jacket jumps up from the grass and runs ahead of us.

'Who is that?' I ask.

Bucs relays my question to the young man.

'This one's small-small brother.'

'What's his name?'

'Mfana,' says Bucs, without asking.

'Just that?' I remark, annoyed. I know that 'mfana' is no name. All it means is 'boy.'

'Hai, mfaan!' Bucs calls, to show me. The little boy stops and looks around, scared.

'It's okay,' I call. 'It's all right, mfaan. Go on.'

He runs ahead again, but just as I drop back, another possibility crosses my mind.

'This goat, bra'. Did it have a name of its own?'

'What?' says Bucs as if he can't understand.

'Ask if this goat had a special name,' I insist, and he and the young man discuss it.

'No,' replies Bucs. 'No name.'

'Good. Then at least it wasn't a pet.'

Bucs queries the word with a frown.

'A pet,' I explain. 'Like a dog or a cat. You know.'

'A cat?'

Bucs laughs a short dry laugh and I feel a fool. Like any other guilty person, I have been talking too much. I decide to shut up.

We follow a footpath. Cicadas are drilling the air. It is beginning to grow hot. I wonder how far it is to the madala's kraal.

Bucs looks round again, wiping his face on his T-shirt.

'Yesterday, we come this way,' he says with a smile. 'This way. Me and . . . and. . . .'

'Vicky?'

His teeth shine. Between his teeth, a stalk of grass he has plucked presses softly into his lower lip.

'We were so afraid!' he exclaims. 'Awu!'

'Afraid? Of what?'

'Of you, bra'!'

'Me? Why?'

'You take the gun. We hear it shoot. 'Ra-bow!' 'He has killed himself,' cries the madam.' Bucs laughs, shaking his head. 'He has killed himself!' The madam, she holds on to me.' He takes hold of the chest of his T-shirt and pulls at it. 'We go that way,' – he gestures – 'looking for you. 'Rian!' I shout loud. 'Rian, bra' Rian!' I look. I run. I look.' He shades his eyes and crouches, a parody of hunting around. 'Where, where? 'Rian, bra' Rian, bra'!' Is he dead? You, are you dead?'

He laughs again, slapping his knee.

'And Vicky?' I pull at the chest of my T-shirt, giving myself pointy tits. 'What did she do, hey, Bucs? Hang on to you all the time?'

He avoids my eyes. Laughs.

'Sometimes,' he explains. 'She is frightened.'

We cross the dried riverbed near the tree where I hung the goat. The fork is bare, accusing me. This tree could go up in a sheet of flame, a shriek – charred to the roots. Scorched earth.

On the far side of the watercourse, large boulders stand leaning together beside the odd flat-topped thorn tree. We climb the crumpled spine of the ridge, closer to the sun, in silence. The landscape stares. Where are the witch's stones?

The boy in the vest points.

'Madala's place,' says Bucs.

At the foot of the ridge stands a small cluster of thatched huts, only four in all. No stirring of life that I can see.

The little herd boy sprints the rest of the way, shouting.

'He's happy,' I suggest.

'Happy?' says Bucs.

'Sure. Bliss is our element. Ask Bamford.'

Bucs does not bother to reply. We descend along a sliding, stony footpath.

As we draw closer, a woman comes out of the farthest hut and peers toward us with her hand over her eyes. A small child clings to her knee. A few more children gather and watch us over a low mud wall.

'I've come about the goat,' I try to explain.

'Baas?' she replies as though scared, and Bucs puts in a brief word.

The young man, too, launches upon an explanation. I watch his slow-moving jaw. The woman smiles. Bucs squeezes his hands self-consciously into his armpits.

'Just wait,' he tells me.

I stand to one side, the ignominious white man. I smile at the children, who back away, shy. I should have packed my pockets full of sweets – could have, too. Bamford would never have noticed. Here, kids, catch! It's a party.

A fowl hops up on the wall with a flap. Darting its head from side to side, it crouches. I watch its scaly toes gripping the dirt. A creaking sound comes from its craw. A comment on me, I reckon. If I had a good strong stick, a kierie, I'd knock the scrawny creature high over the nearest roof. A cluck, a screech. A bomb. Watch out, I've lobbed. BLAM! Feathers.

The huts look decrepit. The thatch is sunken, falling apart. On the wooden door nearest to me stands a number daubed in blue paint: 5 2. (Remember to tell Bamford.)

'Postal address?' I point ironically.

Bucs does not smile.

'Removals,' he tells me. 'Any day, now, these people.'

'Removals? How come? Surely, these things are not supposed to take place any more.'

Bucs shrugs.

'For three years, now, these people, they wait. GG[1] can come tomorrow, can come next year, any time. Everybody, they must be ready.'

'Why the numbers?'

'The government paints the numbers, writes it in a book. You are not allowed to fix the houses, otherwise you pay. Spot cash, big fine. One hundred, two hundred Rands. No money? You go to jail, long time. It is better you wait for GG. Let it all fall down. Too bad.'

I shake my head, feel helpless, say nothing.

The boy in the vest has disappeared round the side of a hut. With one hand on her hip, the woman stands talking to Bucs.

'What's happening?' I want to know.

Bucs shakes his head, frowns at me and steps over the wall.

'Come,' he says, crooking a finger. 'Now. You talk.'

The fowl bundles away with a squawk underfoot.

'Fuck off,' I mutter.

Bucs swings round. He can lift his ears by contracting his scalp, I see – a talent I envy. He opens his mouth but before he can speak, I say:

'Go on, bra'. Lead the way.'

We land up side by side in the broad round shadow of a hut, Bucs and I, while the woman goes and fetches a couple of chairs – straight-backed dining room

1. *GG*, government trucks used in apartheid's forced removals of people

chairs of the ball-and-claw variety. Too old-fashioned for some white madam, no doubt. Sold, carried here on this woman's head. Proud possessions. She places them face to face in the middle of the yard. Our interview promises to be a formal affair. How do you do, madala? My name is Erasmus. Adrian Erasmus. Fine, thank you, madala, fine. The goat? He was a menace, madala. Knocked me head over heels, could have broken my bones. Mind you, I'm not claiming self-defense. I did you a favor, that's all. He was a devil, madala.

But forget the goat. I have something more important to tell you. Pa says: Take your two sticks of furniture and go. Right away, yes. Now, if not sooner. Are you ready? The trouble with you is you don't know your place, so we are going to find one for you. Far away, ja. Bye bye. Don't give me lip, kaffir. Bring all your fleas and your chickens and your children and your wives, they can sit on top of one another for all I care. We've given you more than enough time already, do you hear? I'm sick and tired of you people. The GG truck is waiting. I am waiting. Don't make me wait all day, madala. You can build your hut again, don't tell me you can't. One kaffir nest is the same as another – mud and sticks, dirt and disease. You will know your place as soon as you see it. A brand new tin shithouse is already standing waiting for you like a sentry box in the middle of the veld. Compliments of the state, ja. Cleanliness is next to godliness. Understand, madala? We will ensure that you kaffirs shit clean, for once. Shit your heart out. Die, if you want to. Old kaffirs like you and the little ones always die first. Why? Because there are too many of you, that's why. Ask Pa.

Big talk, Pa's talk. I test the hinges of my jaw with my fingertips and open my mouth as wide as I can. Will this do?

Pa? I said. Pa called? And the screen door clapped shut behind me.

He was standing at the far end of the kitchen, I remember, the rifle in his hands.

As I watched, he turned the rifle round and grappled it close.

He began to bend over backwards.

Outside in the back yard the baboon lay flat on his side in the dust, flipping his narrow black paws at the flies. In a fork of the pepper tree the transistor radio hung gleaming. I had switched it off and run up the back stairs and into the kitchen, where at first I had not been able to see.

Pa's face was very white and his eyes shut tight.

His fingers kept reaching, scratching for the trigger. He seemed to hang there. The barrel of the rifle went straight up into his mouth, while the shabby black shadow of the coal stove hung over him.

Purely as a practical measure, I take out my wallet and slap it against my palm. My mouth is dry.

'How much is a goat?'

'A lot of money,' Bucs replies, eyeing me.

'How much at a guess?'

'Maybe one hundred, one hundred and fifty.'

I have exactly twenty-eight Rands, I know, but I leaf through the notes, which do not multiply in my hands.

Bucs warns: 'The madala!'

I can't tell which of the huts he has appeared from. A tall and gaunt, and terribly old, old man. His eyes are turned up, as white as eggs. Despite the heat, he is wearing a greatcoat, which flaps aside to show the bones of his chest. The little goatherd has hold of him by the fingers of one hand, leading him. The old man clutches a stick in the other hand, a knob kierie. In the middle of the yard, he stops and begins to wave the stick over his head. Turning his face up to the sky, he begins to clamor in a hoarse high voice.

'What is he saying?' I ask Bucs.

The old man swings round, pointing his stick.

'You!' he cries. 'You!'

'He says you must go to the hut,' says Bucs.

'Which one?'

Bucs juts his chin. Behind me, the young man in the vest is dragging open the door: number 52.

I haven't been inside a hut since I was a child. At first, I can make out nothing but throbbing after-images of the sun like a headache in the dark. The smell of goat is strong – a rank smell of goat amid the first taint of putrescence. A large, dim, white blotch seems to come floating up at my feet. I crouch down and stretch out a hand, but recoil from the wet sticky hairiness. The goat has been half flayed, I see, and left in the dust. I sit back on my heels, allow my eyes time to adjust. The pelt is curled over in flaps. The chest is narrow and shiny, all lean taut interwoven muscle sheathed in what seems to be a membrane. Pushed aside in a pile, the guts are still attached to the hollow of the abdomen by what looks like a string. I bend my head. What should I do? It's hot in the hut, and I have an itchy feeling as though fine grit is sifting down on me from the grass roof. I get to my feet and wipe my hands on my pants.

'That's where I got him. In the neck, see?'

Bucs gives a low whistle.

'Why you do this?'

I'd like to say, 'For Vicky.' I'd like deliberately to take Bucs by the throat and rock him back and forth. Instead, I ask:

'What are they going to do with him, now?'

He puts the question to the boy, who grins and looks at me for the first time.

'Eat it,' says Bucs.

'Like Christmas?' I say. Pa speaking.

To my surprise, they both burst into laughter. Bucs's teeth shine. He slaps the pockets of his jeans, and stamps, half doubled up. I can see all round the hut, now. Spokes of sunlight penetrate the thatch overhead. The floor is of earth, bare except for the goat.

The boy takes out a knife.

Squatting on his heels, he cuts a wavering line down the back of one foreleg. I watch, fascinated, as he starts to tug and peel back the hide like a sock.

'Let's see that knife?'

An ex-kitchen knife sharpened to a point. I run my thumb along its edge.

Pa would have said, '*My* knife!' and pocketed it. Another joke.

I test it by the tip.

'Balanced like a throwing knife,' I remark.

Unable to comprehend, the boy grins. When I hand him back his knife, he sets willingly to work on the other leg. I watch him sweat.

A thick sweetness begins to collect at the back of my throat.

Without waiting for Bucs, I step outside again. The weight of the sun seems concentrated on my head. On all sides, the huts surround me, dry walls of red earth, crumbling, as if down on their knees. I look at the old man and the child. Is it all my fault? The phlegm drags as I swallow. I'd like to spit.

'Madala!' I call. 'I am ready. Come, let us talk.'

I take the chair nearest me while the child leads him to the other. The old man moves his hand all around to be sure of the seat. His eyes are still rolled up, I see. Blue-blind.

'I am here, madala,' I say, leaning forward, half expecting him to take my face in his hands.

But the old man sits back, very stiff and upright. He clutches the stick to his chest.

He lifts one skinny finger.

'What do you do here?'

'Madala sent for me. I have come. I killed the goat.'

'I know, I know! But what do you do here?'

'Madala?'

He screams. His spit flies into my face, and he raises his stick – I feel its shadow cross my head. Again, he wrangles, as if with the sun. I look up at the stick, unable to understand a word until at last, coughing, almost retching, he switches back to a perfunctory English.

'You people, you come. You come. You do not ask, 'Whose land?' You bring your bus, you bring your guns. You do not ask. You shoot. You kill. What for?'

I have no ready reply.

'What for?' he repeats.

I look at the ground between my feet. What can I say? Yes, I killed your goat, madala, for no reason? I killed your goat, madala, because I wanted to see it kick its feet and roll over? I killed your goat, madala, because I was feeling horny? I killed your goat, madala, because I really wanted to kill myself?

I decide to try and push my luck.

'Madala, yes. I killed your goat, it is true. I killed your goat. For my father.'

'Your father? Who is your father? Where is he?'

'Madala?'

'Why does he send you? Why does he not come himself?'

'I'm sorry, madala. My father, he is dead.'

The old man tilts his head. He turns his face from side to side in what I take to be a refusal.

'What is this you say?'

'It is very long ago, now, madala.' I find myself smiling fondly down at the little goatherd while he, squatting almost under the old man's chair, scowls back at me. 'I was small, like this mfaan. My father . . . I am sorry, madala. Has the madala ever killed a goat?'

The old man stays very still. Even after my words have ceased, he seems to be listening, carefully.

'You kill this goat,' he repeats. 'You kill this goat for your father? For your father, who is late?'

'Late?' (Like the 'late Theodosius Ocherse Karel, called Tok,' I realize. A euphemism. Respect.) 'Right madala. It is for my father, who is late.'

For a moment longer, the old man sits without moving, holding his stick upright between his knees. Then, with one hand, he gropes around in his greatcoat pocket, producing from its folds a snuff tin. He taps a pinch of snuff on to the back of one knuckle and sniffs it up, squeezing each nostril askew in turn. Finally, he sits back and blinks, ruminating.

'Your father?'

'My father, madala.'

'You come far?' He nods in the direction of the ridge. 'Far? You walk far?'

'Not so far as the madala, I think. Not nearly so far. Tell me, madala. How old is the madala?'

The old man chuckles, swaying from side to side, and almost crows.

'Awu! The madala! How old is the madala? How old? He is the father, he is the grandfather, many times, many times.'

'Seventy years?'

'Seventy years, eighty years, maybe more.'

Still chuckling, he helps himself to more snuff.

Across the courtyard comes the young woman, carrying a tray. On the tray stands a tall silver coffeepot of the same vintage as the chairs, and a couple of enamel mugs.

'You drink some tea?' the old man asks.

'Thank you, madala. I would like to. But I certainly didn't expect. . . .'

'You come far?' he says, and chuckles. 'Far? A long walk.' He reaches out his hand. 'Jonas,' he says.

I take his hand, which is large and light, like cork.

'Rian,' I tell him. 'Rian Erasmus.'

'Rian!' he repeats, pleased. 'Ja, Rian.'

The tea has been sweetened with condensed milk. I swallow, loudly to my own ears. Old Jonas sits with his mug on his knees but drinks nothing. Beside me, the woman stands waiting for my mug. Chickens come timidly gawking and pecking around our chairs. Except for the little goatherd, the children are nowhere to be seen. Bucs, wearing his sunglasses again, is sitting sprawled with his back to the hut.

I sip my tea and smile at the woman, who keeps her eyes lowered. A fine-boned face, pouting mouth.

Old Jonas is talking.

'Crown Jewellers,' he informs me. 'Kruis Street, Johannesburg.'

'What, madala?'

'Crown Jewellers. You can read? 'Importers of Highest Quality Time-Pieces. Established nineteen twenty-two.' First, you go past the law courts. You know the law courts? Right. Turn right. One street, two streets. Kruis Street. It is easy, nobody can go wrong. Kruis Street. In brass, the numbers on top of the door. I polish them, they shine. One forty-four. In front of that door, I stand all night. The nightwatch.'

'The nightwatch, madala?'

'Many years, many years. I work for Mr Fine, the oubaas. I work for Mr Fine, his son. I work for Mr Fine, the kleinbaas,[2] the son of Mr Fine the son.'

'That's plenty Mr Fines, madala. Three generations?'

The old man smiles, and his face twitches, splitting open at the eyeballs, so to speak, as he remembers.

'Mr Fine, the kleinbaas, he has the sour stomach. Marie biscuits, boiled milk, is all that can make his stomach happy. Every morning, seven-thirty, he opens the shop. Then Jonas must boil the milk, sweep the pavement, buy the biscuits. 'Crown Jewellers,' I always say. 'This is a very fine shop!'

I laugh. He laughs. I think of Ou Willem.

'Everybody knows! Everybody knows Jonas! No trouble in those days. Everybody is happy. In the windows, the light is strong, you can see all night. Blue pillows, red pillows. Velvet. You know velvet? What the madams wear – gold and diamonds, rings for the fingers – all these things sleep safe on the pillows. Jonas is there. Jonas! Yes.'

'What would you do if they broke your windows, madala? What if they broke your windows and stole your things?'

'Who?'

'Tsotsis,' I say. Hoodlums. Like me.

He lifts his stick again, waves it. A skull-cracker, the polished knob. This peril I have escaped. I can almost feel the blood in my hair, the hollow smashed place at the back of my head, and the pavement pressing cold and flat against my face, the breath slurring between my lips as I lie staring, knowing I am not screaming, but dying.

'Awu!' I say. 'The madala is right.'

I touch the hem of his coat. Hairy green khaki stuff.

'And this coat, madala? Is it not too warm for a day like today?'

He shakes his head.

'It is my good friend, this coat. In the winter, when I was the nightwatch, I have my coat, I have my stick. I stand in the doorway. I wait. Many years, many years. I am old already, I have grey hair, when the king comes.'

'The king, madala?'

The old man smiles. He makes a remark to the woman who goes into a hut. Then he pinches up more snuff.

'Mr Fine is happy. He tells everybody: 'This is the king's shop. The king will like this shop.' Jonas must clean the windows. Jonas must sweep. But the king

2. *kleinbaas*, small boss, young boss

rides down another street. He is a boy, the king. I see him. No beard.' Old Jonas laughs. 'Smooth cheeks. He rides by in a car without a roof. All the people wave. I hold up my stick. He is the king of England.'

'The royal visit? That was a long time ago, now, madala.'

The old man nods.

'Long time. Long time.'

He takes a mouthful of tea. The woman returns with a small box, which she hands to me.

'Open it,' urges Jonas.

On a bed of watered silk, grimy at the edges, lies a large and glittering gold wristwatch.

'And this watch, madala?'

'This is a tip-top watch,' old Jonas replies, very pleased and dogmatic. 'Tiptop! Yes. But it does not go.'

'Oh, really?' I lift the watch out of its box, shake it and put it to my ear. Too lightweight for gold, I feel. A junk watch.

'You can read?' the old man continues. 'Read the back, Rian.'

Like an epitaph, etched in graceful cursive:

JONAS
1936–1962
Quality, Fidelity, Eternity
Crown Jewellers
144 Kruis Street
Johannesburg

'Go on,' says Jonas. 'Read, Rian. Read. The jewels.'

'Waterproof. Stainless steel back. Thirty-two jewels.'

'Thirty-two jewels!' He swallows more tea, smacks his lips and nods. 'Is right.'

'This,' I remark significantly. 'This is a very fine watch, madala.'

Which is as close as I can come to telling him.

If I could spit in his eyes and make him see. Smash this watch. Grind it under my heel. Walk. Sweep clean. Tower like Morena. Wreak havoc. I would crush, burn, ransack. Restore to this old man his years, his land, his dead. I? Who am I? The white marauder who killed his goat.

'I must leave, now, madala.' Quickly, I replace the watch in its box and take out my wallet. 'Madala. Thank you. I want to pay you for the goat.'

'Ai kôna! It is for your father,' he objects, shaking his head and waving me away. 'For your father, you kill the goat.'

'No, madala....'

But he won't hear of it. He calls the boy in the vest. I get to my feet. The old man does, too. As I shake hands with him again, I try to press the litter of bills into his palm.

'No!' he says, removing his hand. It is final.

The woman begins carting away the chairs even before we leave.

'We have a birthday party to go to, remember?' I tell Bucs, who shrugs.

We leave the kraal the way we came, taking the footpath to the ridge and making the long climb among the stones, but the boy in the vest calls out and comes running after us, and we must wait.

His chest heaving, he holds out to me a ragged wedge of blood-stained newspaper.

'What's this?' I want to know.

'For you,' says Bucs. 'The old man says.'

'Oh?'

A slice of the pie for the guest of honor, no doubt. A hair of the goat that bit you. Well, what will you do? In its torn wrapping, the slab of raw meat sags. The boy keeps his eyes on the ground.

'Bucs, ask him if I can buy his knife.'

'What is this? Why you want his knife?'

'Just ask, man. Ask.'

For once, the boy seems to grasp my words on his own. With alacrity, he produces the knife from his pocket, while I turn my wallet inside out.

'Here. For you. For everyone. Understand?'

He stands staring at the small pile of notes he has cupped in his hands. To him, perhaps, it looks like a lot of money.

I examine the knife, pick the blade clean of dried blood, and rub it on the leg of my jeans until it shines. Then I take the goat's meat, a weight, in my hands.

'Let's go,' I say, and Bucs agrees.

Soon we are climbing the ridge again. We hardly speak. Aloes grow among the stones, dripping fiery blossoms. The heat is huge. It is as though we are under a dome of glass, a bell jar. Cicadas scream. Stones scatter beneath my feet. I wipe my itching forehead.

'I want to make one – just one – real movie,' I announce at the top of the ridge. Bucs quirks an eyebrow.

'You?'

'Yes, me. Why not? Don't you think I can do it? Listen.'

But before I can begin, Bucs pushes ahead of me down the path. He, too, has had enough, it seems. His T-shirt hangs limply, soaked down the back with sweat. I let him go.

I shall talk to myself, then. Aloud, sometimes. With my face turned up to the sun.

'Ss-sssst!' Bucs hisses, and stops dead in his tracks.

Half-crouching, he stares straight ahead at the bush. With one hand he makes a violent gesture to me to shut up.

I look over his shoulder. Nothing ahead as far as I can see but the stillness of the bush. A fly tickles my hand. As I wave it away, the newspaper makes a slight shuffling sound. Then, not a stone's throw from us, I catch sight of a kudu bull, as silent as smoke, gazing at us over the thorn scrub. Large, liquid eyes. Spiraling, upswept horns. Majestic, calm.

Next moment, with a startled plunge, the kudu breaks away, clearing the scrub in a single high crash, and is gone. I yell and run a few steps as if I would follow. Bucs is grinning beside me.

'Where did he go?'

Bucs shakes his head.

A minute or two later, we see the kudu cross the dried riverbed, leap up the bank and disappear through a screen of white thorn.

'Did you see that?' I say.

Bucs laughs.

'Now, you want . . . !' He raises an imaginary gun to his cheek, swings round and clicks the trigger. 'Ra-bow!'

'No, fuck the gun. I'd never kill a creature like that.'

We try to track the kudu for a few hundred meters, then double back in a loop, talking together and laughing.

We approach the camp with the kombi parked between us and the wild fig. For that reason, we see nothing of what is going on until we step round the back of the kombi.

'Hey, listen,' I cry. 'You'll never guess what we just saw – '

I catch my breath, cut off.

Vicky jumps to her feet with a strangled little scream.

'Go away!'

I feel as though the top of my head has been cut clean off. With a bright keen blade, a sword. I am left without words. She is naked except for a large straw hat.

Bucs laughs abruptly.

While Vicky seems all legs, all desperation.

In an effort to cover herself, she claps one hand, fingers spread wide, to the top of her thighs, and I catch a glimpse of the frail hair hiding what I know to be the plump pussy. Then she turns her back, and I see the imprint of the deck chair's slats across her buttocks – pink and angry.

'Don't look!'

I don't. I look all around me. At the sky, the tops of the trees. Nothing has changed. I hear the grating of her zipper, loud in the silence, as she does up her jeans, followed by the hasty flapping of her shirt.

'Sorry,' I say through a thickening ache in my throat, a slow tight squeeze that makes me pant. 'We didn't mean to gatecrash.'

Bamford, fully clothed in a safari suit, I see, is bending over the little camp table. His broad back is turned to us. He is helping himself, it would seem, to another drink.

I pat at a bunch of party balloons, drooping in the heat, tied to the back of Vicky's chair. The balloons barely bump or bounce. I smell my fingers. The dull smell of rubber cloys. I cross to the table.

'Quite a party,' I observe mildly. 'What happened?'

The table is crowded. In the middle lie the ruins of the birthday cake, hacked and carved and half eaten. In silver letters across the icing, HA BIRTH, stands out like a piece of wit. Beside the cake, on the lid of its open black velvet box, squats the Wonderboy skull. A handful or so of shotgun shells are scattered around, and upside down between the cake and the skull lies an ornate silver trowel.

I drop the goat's meat almost on top of the cake. The paper uncurls a little.

'Do you mind?' I ask, looking up.

Across the table from me, Bamford is leaning heavily on the knuckles of one hand. Askew on his head is a green-and-orange paper crown, the sort you find in a Christmas cracker. In the other hand, he is holding my camera.

'Oho!' he jeers, slurring drunkenly. 'The whiz kid returns. We're having a spot – a spot of fun, you see. A peep show.' He gestures with the camera, waving it around, trailing the cables across the remains of the food on the table. 'Problem is,' he adds, pondering. 'Problem is, I can't get – can't get – a picture.'

I am finding it difficult to breathe.

'Give me the camera. Give me the camera, Bamford. If you don't, I'm going to stab you in the throat.'

'Oh, really?' he replies. His eyes behind his glasses are hot and derisive. 'You, and which army?'

I hold up the knife. It catches a glint of the sun.

'Wait. Wait a minute,' says Bamford, putting up one clumsy hand and smiling. 'Lemme – lemme ask you something. First.' He turns the camera upside down, and fumbles as if to peer into the lens. 'Tell me, you, Mr Pro-bloody-fessional. Tell me. How much real knowhow does it take to work one of these things? Wait. Lemme see. This gadget is yours, isn't it?'

He heaves the camera at me across the table. I manage to grab hold of the carrying handle – awkwardly, because of the knife – only to find that he has not yet released his grip.

'Listen,' he says in a hiss, close to my ear. 'Don't make me strain myself, cute boy. If I wanted to, I could take away that knife of yours and stick it up that little button of hair on your arse – get it? Give up. You can't beat me. You don't have the muscle.'

'You're drunk, man,' I tell him.

I could sink the knife to the hilt in the hollow beneath his ear. I could watch him go staggering, gurgling, his tongue wagging like a stump, blood mixed with drool hanging from his mouth like a bib.

'I'm going to count three,' I continue. 'One. Two.'

'Drunk? Who's drunk?' He throws himself forward, muttering: 'I'll break your back,' and trying to exert his huge, overwhelming weight. But his bandaged foot undercuts him and he totters.

We go into deadlock. I manage to loop the cable round my wrist, securing my grip.

'Drop the camera, Digby. Give it up.'

He stands on one leg, sweating.

'All right,' he says. 'All right. I just need to know one thing. How does it work?' His glasses glitter in the light. 'Show me. Show me, and – you have my word for it – you'll get what you want.'

'Oh? And what do I want?'

'You think I don't know?' A small smile plays about his lips, but his gaze on me is merciless. 'It's written all over your face, my friend. What you want is slippery like a mango, a fat fruit. It's so wet you could almost drink it. What wouldn't you give to dip your dick into it, all the way? As for me, all I want is to shoot the pictures. Hear me. In less than five minutes – get it? In – less – than – five – minutes, you and your black buddy could both be screwing little Vicky. Sweet, sweet little Vicky. How about it, man? Him with his whanger like a mule's, and you. One down her throat, and one from behind. Or one underneath, and one on top. One in the little place, one in the big. Ah, Christ, how she'd love it!'

'She would, would she? How do you know?'

'Don't tell me *you* don't know, lover boy. Listen. It's staring you straight in the face. Opportunity knocks but once, remember. You still don't believe me? Go on, then. Ask her yourself. She's ready to try anything once, as you well know. Isn't that her motto? You saw her with your own eyes, didn't you? I mean, there she sat, legs wide apart, fingers in all the right places. . . .'

'I saw nothing.'

'What a pity. You should have heard her, then. She was talking aloud, my friend. She was telling me all she wanted to do, as soon as you and Bucs came back. And she said . . . she said . . . well? Wouldn't you like to know?'

'No.'

But my heart is beating heavily, in surges. I shift my hold on the camera. I am lying, I know.

Vicky is standing where she was, knotting her shirt tails over her belly. Her face is flushed, her eyes lowered. Bucs is leaning back against the kombi. He seems indifferent.

Bamford hiccoughs. One eyelid droops by way of a wink.

'I'll get her to – you know – show you. Let her do it for camera, as planned.'

'Let her do what?'

'You'll see.'

'Tell me.'

'You know. You know what she's like.'

'What is she like?'

'Well, once I watched her use a champagne bottle, ice cold, freshly popped, as a stand-in for a . . . you know what.'

I let the camera drop, or seem to, and he comes lurching towards me across the table.

'And you?' I say to his face. 'How's it for you? Sex, I mean. You like it hot?'

The paper crown seems stuck to his forehead with sweat. His face looks huge and red, swollen. He laughs. His lips stay curled.

'Some do.'

'I know. I've seen the movie, too. But come on, Digby. Tell me. What about you?'

'Me? Oh, yes, my friend. Hot. I like it hot.'

'Like fire?'

'Oh, yes. Like fire. Like real fucking fire.'

'I get it. Okay, let's do it, then.'

'Do it?'

'Yes, let's do it. Let's shoot the picture, hot.'

'I knew it! I knew you'd come around.'

He relaxes a little and leans away from the table, and I very nearly get to lift the camera out of his hands. He tries to retaliate, slamming the camera from side to side. The skull gets knocked over. A couple of bottles go rolling.

'Go on,' I urge. 'Break a few things. Why not?'

'Why not?' he jeers, stumbling to a halt. 'Why – for fuck's sake – not?' With a jerk that breaks my hold and sends the knife to clatter in among the bottles, he raises the camera high, out of my reach. His big rounded shoulders begin to shake, and he goes staggering back – helpless, it would seem, to control his own laughter. 'The champ!' he roars, drunkenly swinging the camera round above his head. 'The king!'

And then he drops it. The camera strikes the corner of the table, rebounds. I throw myself forward and just manage to catch it, hold it.

'If this thing is broken. . . .'

I cradle the camera, running my fingers over it in a vain attempt to check for damage.

'Why?' jeers Bamford. 'What'll you do? Cut my throat?'

We pant, eyeing one another across the shaky camp table.

9

THE KNIFE IS LYING WHERE IT FELL among the bottles, but I don't touch it. I don't need to. I lean across the table, pinch together a few cake crumbs, and sprinkle them into my mouth. Warm sticky fruitcake.

I know what I am going to do.

Bamford pours himself a paper cup of soda water and tosses it back. 'Teetotal?' I mock.

'The thirsties. First the thirsties. Then the munchies.'

He crams a handful of potato crisps into his mouth, and munches with a smile, rolling his eyes. Then he opens his mouth wide to display the sticky mess, pronouncing silently:

'Let's — get — going!'

'Going? Where to?'

It takes him a moment or two to swallow.

'The shoot,' he says. 'What about the shoot?'

'Aren't you overlooking something?' A quick once-over of the switches can tell me next to nothing. Besides, he forgot to link up the power pack. 'You don't know what a camera is, do you?'

'McLuhan?' he offers, adding another crisp to his mouth. 'Extension of the eye'?'

'Old hat, Digby. Out of date, way out. No, it's not just a question of optics. A camera like this is a mechanism for thinking. I think with this camera.' I lift the camera to my shoulder, and turn as though scanning both him and the table. 'It's an extension of the brain. Film is like a language, every image a neologism.'

He hiccoughs, sways and holds up one finger.

'Then we're not — not, after all, in total contradiction. Western thought is always already visual, isn't it? In some fundamental way, I mean. Fun. Da. Mental. See? But wait. Wait. He who drinkee whiskee, go too plenty pee-pee. Confucius.' He gives a drunken, lumbering hop or two, and halts just short of the tree. 'But, pray sir. Tell me. You do, don't you, agree?'

In order to pan with a hand-held camera (even a dead one), the first rule is: Don't move your feet. What you would most like to do is describe a full circle. If I were a searchlight, raking. Nothing from here to the horizon but the odd squat thorn tree clenched against the sun, and a wall of dry white grass like a great sheet. The ridge. More bush. Fuel for the flames. I am sweating under the shoulder pad, but the weight of the camera feels right, secure in its place.

I catch the sound of his spouting trickle. In a moment, the odor will hang in the heat. I don't want to smell it.

'You don't have a snowball's chance in hell,' I remark.

He looks back over his shoulder.

'What's that?'

'Not a hope. You've got to understand, Digby. A camera like this is jam-packed with sensitive electronic circuitry. It's a state-of-the-art E.N.G., built for free-range news gathering, bright as ten thousand eyes, but fragile. Knock it out of kilter, and the whole thing goes haywire. If you bump it around the way you have, you get nothing, see? Nothing. Not even a zigzag, never mind a picture.'

'Oh, I did nothing to your precious bloody camera, man. I dropped it and it fell, I know. But you caught it. Bully for you.'

I pause.

'You'll get zilch,' I warn him again. 'Zero.'

But now, as he comes limping, hopping back, I go down on one knee and pretend to film him.

'R-r-r-r-r-r-r. Do something!'

'Me?' he sticks his thumbs under his armpits as if only too proud to present his lapels. 'Here I am, as you see. The last man in Africa. . . .' He frowns, puckering up his mouth as if brooding. 'The last stand. Of the last white man. In Africa.' Still hamming, he rolls over into the nearest deck chair, exclaiming: 'For this relief, much thanks!'

'Fuck Hamlet. This is Hot Mango, remember. Thrills, Dills and Dig the Dick. Digby's Dick. The real thing.'

'In that case —' He lifts the leg of his safari shorts. In the pit of dark hairiness, I catch sight of the bud of his penis, squeezed to one side as if crimped.

'How about that last stand?' I prompt.

'Alas!' he pats his paunch regretfully and reaches down to fiddle with the tip of his prick. 'You know what they say. Nothing can grow in the shade.'

With a laugh, the camera still on my shoulder, I lean across and retrieve the knife. I stow it in my belt. In addition, I scrape together a last few cake crumbs and sprinkle them into my mouth. A rich taste, dark, like a secret. Then I turn and make for the kombi.

'Hey, what the hell? Where are you off to?' Bamford cries. 'What about the movie?'

'Sit tight. I won't be long. First, let me collect the proper equipment.'

This time the fifty paces or so seem a long way. Compact on my shoulder, the camera makes me feel tall. A trained head.

Vicky and Bucs are standing side by side with their backs to the kombi, not talking. She is studying her toes, it seems. Chipped red paint on the nails. As I approach, Bucs turns his mirror glasses on me.

'Bra' Rian, let's go, bra'! What you say, let's hit the road? Make dust.'

It seems odd to be standing so close to Vicky after the way Bamford and I have been talking of her.

'We've still got one or two things to do,' I point out. 'Okay?'

She looks up.

'Oh? What do you still have to do?'

'Shoot the cake. Shoot the camp. Shoot you and Bucs together. Have a party, go home.'

'Very funny. What was the fight about?'

'You.'

'Me?'

'Yes, you. Bamford wants to shoot this movie, see. It's all very new, hot and blue. Starring you. I tried to object, but he said I know you, and you'd love it. Anyway, all he wants to do, as I understand it, is what you were doing, or were about to do, before. With a few variations. For camera.'

Giving half a wry giggle, she wrinkles her nose.

'What did he say I was doing? I was sunbathing.'

'Well, sunbathe again. We'll all sunbathe. You, me and Bucs. A gang bang, that's the plan. Aren't we ready to try anything, once? Later, we'll all watch the movie.'

She stares at me icily for a long moment.

'Fuck *you*.' Pushing past me, her shoulders squared, she cries out: 'Digby!'

Only too pleased, I turn to Bucs with a smile. I would like to predict: 'It looks like nothing is going to happen, after all, bra'. It looks like we'll just go home, and forget it.'

But all I do is smile. He shifts the glasses up on the bridge of his nose, sweating — and in a flash I seem to see her again, all elbows and knees, her slack little breasts slapping every which way, her face, her eyes, bright. Here I am. Don't look. For shame. Smooth and white, like milk, her body. Sunbathing? I shut my eyes. I don't want to think.

Urgently, Bucs puts in:

'This is no good, bra'. No good. Let's go. We don't have to wait. Why do you want to wait?'

'I want to see.'

'What you want to see?'

I don't respond. I can wait.

'No good,' murmurs Bucs. 'This is no good, bra'. I'm telling you. We must go home. Now.'

'Oh, nothing is going to happen, man. Don't worry. Listen, why don't you go grab yourself a beer and a slice of cake? It's the only breakfast we're likely to get, you know. Or lunch.'

He is reluctant to leave, and takes more persuading. Only when I start methodically unpacking the equipment from the back of the kombi does he push off, muttering.

Inside the kombi, it is airless, like an oven. I squat on my heels and lay the camera down beside me on the floor. If only I could sink down flat into the metal underfoot and sleep. I rub my eyes and press, put pressure on my eyelids. Slow lights turn over in my head. Let the flames wrap around me. Let me go turning, twisting, a fiery tower.

I open my eyes a crack, and see at my feet Vicky's hairbrush lying tangled in a pair of Bamford's discarded underpants. I want to see this kombi explode. I want to see its white metal shell buckling and charring, the windshield shattering, the flames flapping outward and rolling.

I overturn a pile of kitchen things. A packet of sugar splits open, a bottle of coffee breaks, but at last I find what I want: a box of matches.

'Plan everything,' I remind myself aloud as I pitch the matchbox up into the air and catch it again, for luck. 'Everything, down to the last pin. And why? Because you can't predict what will happen. When the balloon goes up, you will want to know where you are. So, plan.'

Doubled up under the front seat of the kombi is a duffel bag stuffed with our soiled clothing. I find the knot at its throat too tight to undo, and I don't want to waste time fumbling, so I rip open the bag in slash after slash with the goat knife.

I—a warrior.

Is this what you want?

My hands are shaking. I dig out and spread the clothes in a heap across the floor. Then I begin to tear the shirts into strips and knot them together. A close, musty, sweaty odor.

I know what I am doing. I am making a fuse.

I STUFF THE KNOTTED FUSE DOWN the long steel gullet of the kombi's petrol tank. The fumes are heady, and I breathe them in.

'Balloon, balloon, fly to the moon,' I say aloud.

I place my hand on the white, sun-hot side of the kombi as if to acknowledge a living creature which has to be coaxed through this. I leave the tag end of the fuse sticking out like a tuft of bandage, and half-fit the petrol cap back into place.

Bucs is sitting on the grass. His legs are stretched out in front of him and he is tilting up a beer bottle, letting the last trickle go straight down his throat. Vicky has planted her deck chair closer to the table and settled in, her knees drawn up under her chin.

Everything seems very peaceful.

I begin to set up the equipment. Although I take my time to unfold each leg of the tripod in turn, measuring and then pegging out places for the bronze-tipped feet as well as watching the slow sidelong drift of the bubble in the spirit-level, I feel very tense. I can't help but wonder what has happened in the meantime. Who has said what to whom? And what now?

In a slump in his chair, Bamford surveys me with hooded eyes. Red-faced, drunk and drowsy, he looks exactly as he did before, except that across his belly now he is cradling the shotgun.

'Going to blow away tin cans again?' I ask.

'Who, me? Not on your life, my friend. Black boy brought me the gun. Seems it was leaning up against the kombi all along. What's this he tells me about a kudu?'

'A greater kudu, yes. A bull. Magnificent head. But he's well over the horizon by now – like an arrow from a bow. A pity you didn't get to see him.'

'Ah, but I did, I did. You forget. Yesterday. Yesterday in the riverbed. I told you so at the time. Glad you saw him, too, at last.'

'Oh, yes?'

Smiling vaguely, I wipe my palms, which are still grubby, it seems, from the soiled clothing, on the pockets of my jeans. Then I lift the camera and lock it into place.

Vicky is sitting back with her eyes closed, a gleam of sweat visible on her upper lip. Bucs has begun some kind of juggling game with the beer bottle, trying to get it to balance upside down on one forefinger.

Casually, I go up to Bamford's chair.

'Where would you like the Wonderboy skull, professor?' I ask. A bogus question, but it will do. In a much lowered voice, I add: 'Look. Are you dead set on going on with this?'

He rakes a hand through his sweaty hair, splitting the paper crown, and stares around as though baffled.

'Why? For what other earthly reason do you think I am sitting here, man?'

Neither Vicky nor Bucs seem to be paying attention, probably because they are used to our pre-recording wrangles.

I don't reply, except to raise my chin.

Bamford smiles. Behind his glasses, his eyes look malignant.

'If you mean, have I popped the question yet,' he says, 'then, no. Not yet. But all is well, my friend. Never fear. I have a touch with these things. As for you, I don't know what the hell you said back there, but you came very close to blowing it.'

'I could still blow it now.'

'What do you mean?' He stares at me sharply. 'Go and put your camera in order. As soon as you're ready, we'll opt for action. Get it?'

Back at the camera, I link up the power pack, which is slung in a specially-built bulky belt around my waist.

'Everything all right?' Bamford calls.

'Too soon to tell.'

I kneel to check the test-pattern on the portable video monitor. Glowing rainbow bars, like the colored ices you once had as a child, but now almost invisible in the light.

'Look,' I say, lifting the small monitor.

'Is that the go-ahead?'

'No. Bars are nothing, I'm afraid. Internally generated. Not a picture, I mean. Very pretty, though, don't you think?'

I straighten up again.

'Go ahead,' says Bamford. 'Entertain yourself while you wait.' Like a genial host, he passes Bucs another bottle of beer. 'Bottoms up, friend.'

Vicky, her eyes wide open again, is sitting back, looking bored.

It is very hot. Nothing moves. I use the panning handle to turn the camera, and feel the gliding motion, the perfect, liquid precision. Far in the bush, the same bird as yesterday begins to strike up, drop by drop, its slow, sweet cry of blood.

I look into the viewfinder. Dark. A pinpoint of white light pulses, stabs. As I watch, it stops, trembles, then expands suddenly to twice its size and erupts, and the first useless image, inchoate and grainy, goes flipping and rolling on the screen. I shut my eyes.

I can feel the sweat running down my ribs. On my head, on my back, is the sun: a fierce incandescent silence. Underfoot is the dried bed of the ocean, a vast cracked plain littered with stones. Again, I am far from here, at a very great distance, it seems, a hooded figure wrapped in a robe. You can't see my face. I am rigid, forbidding. I smite with my staff the desolate earth. All around me, black birds cry out and rise into the air. Their wing beats form a clamor. I am older than this earth. Older than this dust. My lips move, form words. Hear me.

The image in the viewfinder is still rolling over, a soundless chatter. Better to stay at the surface, then. I swear under my breath and slap the sides of the camera. I am sweating, thirsty.

'Fuck.'

'What's wrong?'

'The horizontal hold.'

'The what?'

But before I can explain, a long ripple runs through the screen, which steadies out and slowly settles into place. Without waiting to check for stability, I zoom in on the side of the kombi and set the white-balance, the reading of light that holds in place the spectrum of color.

Softly, I begin to whistle to myself.

'Well?' calls Bamford.

'We'll see. Wait.'

The kombi stands as though nothing could ever rock it.

For the first time, I am aware of a slow, weighty swelling in my groin. Aware, too, of the tinny taste of fear in my mouth.

I pan in an arc across the bush, the ridge, and then skim the company for a close-up. Vicky has not yet spoken a word. Why not? I wonder. Is she too tired? I go in close on her mouth. Blood, cries the bird. Blood. Blood.

I drag my fingers down my face to rid myself of the itch of sweat.

'Image-stability, A-one and holding,' I sing out. 'Star Trek log, year sixty-nine, sixty-nine, in a new galaxy on the frontiers of time. Ready when you are, Captain Kirk.'

Bamford smiles. Shifting the shotgun on his belly, he scratches himself.

'So. The camera is working. Good. I must admit I never thought otherwise. Technological mystification. Don't try it again – I won't fall for it, next time. All right, my friend. All right. Carry on.'

'I thought you wanted some instruction in how to use a camera.'

He does not move, not even to answer me. I think I can see why. He is too drunk, too lazy, and has eaten too much. He seems to be studying the tip of his nose.

'What would you say to a change of plan?' he proposes at length. 'You work the camera. I direct. Well? How about it, my man?'

By way of reply, I begin to loosen the wing nut under the camera.

'Bucs,' I say. 'Pack up. We're leaving.'

'No, no, wait! You're right, you're right.' He sits up, smiling waving. 'The time has come,' the walrus said, 'to speak of many things.' Why don't you go and tell your black friend what we want? Go, and I'll tell the lady. Then we'll get on with the show.'

'What show?' says Vicky, alert now. She sits forward, her head balanced to one side. 'What are you talking about?'

Bamford pushes a hand through his hair again, and smiles.

'Come. Come, sit on my knee, sweet, and we shall all the pleasures prove, that hills and valleys . . . hills and valleys. And then, let's see, prove, prove – should rhyme with 'love'. Maybe it did, once. As it still does in Yorkshire. You know the poem? Come, and I'll tell you. You'll adore it. Just wait till you hear.'

Vicky's eyes are sharp, determined. She studies him coldly.

'This isn't that same old stupid game, is it?'

'Game? What game?'

'That stupid movie, that you said . . . that Rian said. It's not that same old stupid thing again, is it?'

'Is it? I thought I was the only stupid old thing around here.'

'I hate it. You promised. You said it was only a joke.'

He pats his knee and smiles again.

'Come, my sweet. Come and sit here, and we'll prove. . . . Don't be shy.'

'No. Sit on your own lap.'

'Is that possible?' As if hugely tickled, he starts rolling around in his seat with a squeal, gurgling: 'Oh, please!'

Vicky's own mouth begins to twitch — against her will, it seems.

'I couldn't sit on your lap, even if I wanted to,' she remarks. 'Your toe is too sore.'

'My toe? Don't you worry about my toe,' he says, falling back in his seat again. 'My toe is all right. My toe is just fine. It won't feel a thing, you'll see. You can cure me at a touch, if you like. Of course, it all depends on what you touch. Come, my sweet, come and sit in my lap.' His voice changes, becomes gravelly, imitation Louis Armstrong. 'Come my sugar. Come, my honey. Come, my sweetie pie.'

She giggles, but for some reason seems fascinated. She stirs one leg.

'Come, come and I'll tell you,' croons Bamford. 'Don't you want to come?'

This could go on forever. I feel the old swelling ache in my throat. I look at my hands on the camera, and then up again.

Bucs is sucking at the beer bottle, his tongue stuck out of his mouth and showing very pink. To me, what he is doing looks studied, a way of ignoring.

'Hey, wena,' I say with a grin. I feel quite friendly. Hey, you.

I cap the camera, unbuckle the power pack and place it on the ground.

As soon as he sees that my summons is in earnest, Bucs gets to his feet, stamps and shivers.

'Eh-weh?'[1]

'Come and help me fetch something from the kombi.'

Wary, ready to leap away, Bucs trails a step or two behind me. When we get to the kombi, I turn to him with a smile.

'So. You want to fuck the white madam?'

He rubs his face. Warm, beery breath.

'Baas?'

It is the first time he has ever directly called me that, and we both feel it, the abasement. But I won't be put off.

'Just think, Nando. Nando Killing Boy. Your big chance. Bamford thinks she'll do it, and so do I. All you have to do is stay in front of camera. Dip it in — mid-shot. Pull it out — close-up. Black mamba rising! What do you say?'

Bucs purses his mouth, stubbornly silent, but I insist.

'What do you say?'

He twists around as though about to spit.

'Ai kôna! No! Not me.'

'No, is it? Why not? Don't you want to? She wants you, you know. She told me so, last night.'

He breaks into a clamor of words that I do not understand, ending in a reiteration of, 'Ai kôna!' No.

'Why not?'

'Because, why? Because I am not a mad dog, is why.'

I touch his arm. He recoils into a crouch.

'Yes?' I say.

But he does not speak. All he does is stand slowly upright, shift the peak of his baseball cap round to the front and walk away, straight into the bush.

1. *eh-weh*, uh-huh

I open the kombi's door, scoop up the tape recorder from the front seat and go after him.

'You wouldn't want anything to happen to this,' I say, catching up with him in the meager shade of a thorn tree.

Calmly, he takes the tape recorder from me and twines the slim leather strap around his fingers. He still refuses to look at me, but turns on his heel without a word and sets out again as if more determined than ever. Where to? I wonder. The road is over twenty kilometers from here. His back is very straight, almost rigid. The tape recorder, dangling, knocks at his knees. His cap is tilted down over his nose.

'Go, brother, go. Don't look back,' I breathe.

Vicky is sitting on Bamford's lap. She is busy squeezing his cheeks between her hands so that his mouth gapes like a fish's, and planting light kisses on his bulbous lips. His eyes roll over as soon as he sees me. He makes an effort to push her off but she resists. The gun, lying cross-wise over his belly, begins to slip, but he catches it in one hand.

'Where is Bucs?' he demands at once, suspicious.

'Nowhere. Don't worry. What's going on?'

'Nothing,' says Vicky. She bends over and presses her lips to his as though to stop him from speaking, but he pushes her away with one hand flat to her chest.

'Him? I've already told him,' he says, looking directly into her eyes and smiling. 'Him, him! Your old lover.'

'You haven't,' she says softly. 'You haven't.' Placing a finger on his lips, she gives him a warning look.

Under pressure of the finger, Bamford can only mumble stiffly: 'What do you mean, I haven't?'

Before she can reply, he opens his mouth wide. Her finger slips inside, and he traps it, biting down with a grunt of satisfaction.

'Stop it!' she cries. 'Stop it! Stop! Please! Let go!'

She tries to force his jaw open with her free hand and when that fails, starts slapping his chin. He splutters with laughter. She snatches away her hand, slips the finger into her mouth, and still astride him, starts sucking it.

He stares at her smugly.

'Oh, but I have,' he resumes. 'I have told him. Want to see? Here, Erasmus. Listen. You'll know the answer, I'm sure. Tell me. Here it is, a little trick. When is a shotgun like a champagne bottle?'

'I can't think.'

But I seem to see it. In close-up. The sparse curling hair, the open wet lips, the shining wet steel. Her hands gripping the barrels tight, her thighs parted wide. The only sound the slight slip-slap of the moving, prodding barrels, and her own stifled whimpers and panting. Cut. To the slow, steady squeezing of the trigger. Once. By whose hand? Mine?

God forbid.

'Go on,' urges Bamford. 'Give it a try, man. Why not?'

'What do you mean, 'a little trick'?'

'Trick, schmick, a good stiff prick! Don't tell me you need a clue.'

'You see,' says Vicky. 'He doesn't know.'

'Oh, but,' Bamford maintains as if in polite disagreement, raising his eyebrows, 'I have told him. I have. And I will again, in case he has forgotten. But I think we have talked too much, don't you? Action, my sweet. How about it?' He draws her closer and fondles her buttocks, but she pulls his hands away. 'Come on,' he urges. 'Take off your clothes.'

'What makes you think that I want to?'

With a laugh, he begins to tug at her shirt. She places both her hands on his and looks at him with utter straight sincerity, leaning her forehead on his.

'No.'

'Why not?'

'Because I said so.'

'That's no reason. What do you say, Rian? If she doesn't remove her clothes of her own free will, we'll have to strip her, won't we?'

'Sounds democratic enough to me. One vote to her, three to us.'

'No,' says Vicky, looking around. 'Two to you. Only two.'

Where is Bucs?

She puts a hand to the top button of her shirt and looks down at Bamford.

'If you promise to stop,' she says, 'if you promise, I'll take off my shirt. But only my shirt.'

She begins to unbutton.

'Never say die,' says Bamford.

'I didn't.'

'It's a start.'

'It's also where it ends,' she asserts, pulling off her shirt.

If only I were a little closer, I might be able to cup both her breasts in my hands and cover them from sight — a simple act. She drops her shirt over Bamford's head. He snatches it off. He, too, would like to reach out and grab her, no doubt, but she has already stepped away from him and turned to face the camera. Her nipples are flat, like pale pennies in the sun. I am aware of her looking at me, but I can't meet her eyes or look up. In search of a cool place, I press my forehead to the camera. The blood in my head is thudding. Blood, blood. My mouth is dry.

Vicky is smiling, her hands on her hips. In the viewfinder, her image is all charcoal and silver, sparkling round the edges.

I have seen your photograph.

I adjust the focus.

In the dark beyond the stars, I drift. An old, old man, I am locked into my iron sarcophagus. White-haired, gaunt, grieving mutely. My eyes are shut. In the cold, the dark.

I trigger the tape. The bead of the recording light blinks red.

'Wait!' I hear Bamford's loud laugh or yap. 'Wait for me!'

I look up. He comes stumbling out of his chair, pulling off his shirt, and staggering, hopping, kicking off his pants, while his big belly bulges. Except for his forearms and wrinkled neck, which are brick-red and rough, his whole body is a smooth, milky white. Compared with the bulk of him, his buttocks seem small and slender, almost childish. His genitals jiggle, close to lost in the pubic bush.

'Ha!' he says in triumph.

Rotund and self-satisfied, quite naked now, using the shotgun as a short but handy crutch, he begins to hobble toward her, the bandage loose on his toe.

She gives a brief, high-pitched, uncertain laugh.

'Go away!'

'Go away?' he takes her in his arms and swings her round as if to commence ballroom dancing. 'Ta da!'

'No!' she cries. 'Leave me!'

To camera, he says, posing: 'First shot?'

I watch as he folds her to him and kisses her, mauling her slowly, smothering her into silence, putting her head back, kneading her breasts with one hand and tweaking the nipples, while she squirms and gives a sidelong stare at camera, hostile, hating it, and trying to push him away. She tries to hide her face, while he ends up gazing directly into camera. He waves the shotgun.

'How about a little trick?'

He turns her hard toward the camera and pins her to him, holding the shotgun up horizontally under her breasts. Her breasts are lifted. The nipples, I see, are stiff. I had not expected. My throat is shut tight. In order to breathe,

I might have to use the knife to pierce, slit my windpipe. Carefully, carefully. Just enough to suck at air. Otherwise, I would undo her zip right now, and drag, work, ruck the jeans right down to her ankles. Spreading her small hairy cleft with one hand, I would place the head of my penis in position. Remember me? Or I'd turn her round, and find that tighter place, her anus, and enter more sharply there as she cries, pleads, calls out. Oh, no. Oh, no. Oh, please, please. Please stop.

Stop this, yes, I tell myself. Now. At once. But can I?

Bamford is still talking to her, murmuring, coaxing.

'Tell it to camera, my love. Tell us how much you want it. Talk. Say how much you usually like. . . .'

She is twisting against him, fighting. Her face looks pale and small.

'No!' she wails. Her lips are thin. The shotgun barrels are not lifting up so much as pressing into her small soft breasts. She bends and tries to twist away. 'Stop it. Stop it. Can't you see I don't want to?'

'Oh, just say it, for God's sake! Say it. Go on. Tell everyone. Or shall I? All right. Allow me. Do you know what she would really like?' he says, looking straight into camera.

Very deliberately, he measures off two hand spans along the barrel of the gun.

'No,' cries Vicky, struggling to push or pull away the gun.

'No, is it? No? Wait. Let me tell the story. First of all, she would like to be deep-throating this big black cock. Oh, yes. Oh, yes. Isn't that what you said, Vicky? Isn't it? On hands and knees, you said. At the same time, you said, you'd like to be reamed from the back by the shotgun, both barrels. And then to swap, as we will see, soon enough, when you demonstrate. To suck the gun and fuck the cock. Isn't that what you'd like? Isn't it? Well, then. Say so. Tell your tale to camera. Speak. Go on. Don't be afraid. Say, 'I want to feel the shotgun reaming my cunt.'

I warn, very steadily and calmly:

'That gun is loaded, Digby.'

'Loaded? That will be a novelty. But tell me, you. You'll know, I'm sure. Tell me, where the hell is Bucs?'

'He hasn't disappeared, I'm sure. Do you want me to go and fetch him?'

'No!' cries Vicky, but Bamford slips the shotgun higher, so that it rests like a bar across her throat.

'Fetch him,' says Bamford. 'Fetch our hero. We'll get him to pluck his weapon out of his pants, and measure it for size against the shotgun. How's that for an opening shot? Your director has a touch of talent, evident in his sense of humor, you see. Well, go on, man! What are you waiting for? Fetch him.'

I lock off the camera and leave it recording the scene. Unbuckle the power pack, drop it. Taking care not to seem in too much of a hurry, I cross to the kombi. The sky overhead is a faded white-blue. I listen for the bird, but the bush seems silent. Around midday the heat is immense. Stifling. I do not even think of Bucs. I unscrew the petrol cap, lead the fuse out and lay it across the grass. Then I kneel and strike a match, cup it in my hands.

In the sunlight, the flame runs invisibly. The soaked cord blackens, smokes, seems to shrivel. Then there is a single, blunt and concussive thud, as when the air is knocked out of you, and the kombi, I see, is standing in a pool of bright orange flame, the grass all around it is flattened and crackling, flaring, while a fine line of smoke is going twisting up from the opening to the petrol tank, but no other, or hardly any other smoke, and then in the growing blast of scorching heat I hear the crash of the shotgun and a scream from Bamford.

Before he can reload, I turn, double up and run. Ashen dry, spectral trees go by me in a wavering row. In the small of my back I have a shrinking feeling. I expect at any moment to feel the blow of the gun. Then I am out in the open and thrashing, swerving from side to side through the waist-high grass. The breath is burning in my throat, my chest. My eyes are itching, streaming. Tiny grass seeds are sticking to my face like parasites. Nothing can curb the spread of the flames now, I know. A wind will spring up. It will roar, whipping up the blaze to a towering wall, rolling and spreading the smoke. I will climb to the top of the madala's ridge. I will stand, looking out over the plain.

Pa, where are you, Pa? I am trying to find you, can't you see?

Ice in Winter

I

IT WAS STILL BLACK SHINY DARK beyond the windowpanes when Pa woke me. I could smell how cold it was. I could smell the fresh paraffin of the lighted lamp. He placed the lamp on the dresser and let the handle drop.

'Rian,' he said softly. 'Little Rian, you must wake up now.'

Sleep lay like an ache in my throat. In the glass chimney of the lamp, the bud of the flame stood tall and still.

When I opened my eyes again – years later, was it? – the door of the wardrobe had swung open, and my own face stood reflected, small, pale, like a fist, in the glimmering varnish of the wood. Pa reached into the wardrobe, and slung the odd piece of clothing over his arm.

'Here you are, now, little boy. Come. Sit up.'

And my head got pressed – a tight fit – into the prickly wool of my school jersey.

'Wait!'

'Why?' asked Pa, tugging the jersey down to free my face. 'What's your problem?' Squatting on his heels, he pushed back his hat and smiled. 'Hey. Your head's not getting too big for your boots, is it?' He put out a hand and ruffled my hair. 'Come, stand up, little mister. Where are your shoes?'

The linoleum floor was like ice. I tried working my way into a shoe.

'It's cold!' I stammered.

'Is it?' said Pa. 'Here, let me help you. First, the socks. Now, the shoes. No school today, you know.'

'Pa?'

'That's right. No school. I'm not joking. Today is a big day. You'll see. I've got plans. Big plans. But first things first. Let's finish getting you dressed.' Outside in the solid night, Vaaljapie¹ the rooster crowed. 'You hear?' said Pa as he helped me to buckle my belt. 'Even the boss of the backyard says, 'Get a move on. Here comes the sun. Up, up, up you get!'

Jagged shadows leapt and swung before the lamp as we went down the passage to the kitchen. In the corner, like a fortress, stood the black-and-silver coal stove, making slow, quiet, cracking sounds. Smoke came curling up through chinks in the iron plates.

---

1. *vaaljapie,* a cheap, rough wine

Pa put the lamp on the table.

'Sit, little boy. Egg and toast for breakfast?'

I climbed up on to the bench.

Across one wall stood the shadow of a cupboard, like a giant wing. A dishrag, grey and shrunken, with holes for eyes, stared at me from the taps at the sink. I am waiting, the dishrag said.

The curtains, too, seemed to be waiting.

'Today is the day,' said Pa. He smeared a pan with lard, placed the pan on the stove beside the coffeepot. Then he laid out flat two or three pieces of bread between the pan and the coffeepot. 'Today, my lightie, either we win.' He smiled, and stood staring at the pan. 'Or we lose . . . Ja,' he added, cracking an egg into a saucer. 'Today, we go to Oude Hoop and talk to Oupa[2] Gert van Dyk. Him with his finger in every pie.

The fattest, richest boer in the district. Citrus, citrus and citrus. But first – breakfast. After all, a man needs to eat. Sunny side up, okay? We just have to wait a bit for the stove to get properly hot.'

You could hear the dull roar of the flames being drawn up the inside of the stove pipe. With a buckle and a crash, the wood gave way, and the coal packed on top of it came rumbling, spilling down. No school today! Soon the whole kitchen would be warm. I pressed my hands in between my knees and squeezed. How to stop shivering? My eyes felt big and hot and heavy. I yawned.

It seemed that I could see the oranges at Oude Hoop. Big, round oranges. Heavy. Hot. It seemed that I could feel the weight of the sun, too, on my back. Beneath the trees stood Oupa Gert. His fingers were limp and white and very long. They hung down past his knees and went trailing away across the ground and then up into the trees again. He was feeding, I saw – sucking at the oranges with fingers like tapeworms. He smiled at me. His face was fat and round and white. He was sweating. The sun, he said, his face close to mine. The blood of the sun. You want a taste?

I sat up with a jolt.

Pa was still busy at the stove.

'It won't be long now, don't worry. Just wait.'

Shifting away from the back of the bench, I pulled up close the pillow that lay in one corner. Very soft, like a paunch, the pillow, and warm. I pressed my face into it, and it seemed to me that I could smell the dust of the thorn hedges that surrounded Oude Hoop. I could see, too, the jet of sprinkler water we had once seen, Pa and I, high above the orange trees. And, cutting through the sprinkler

2.   *Oupa*, Grandpa

jet, little rainbows–fleeting, quivering, almost invisible. You see? said Pa. Oude Hoop is the pot of gold. Can you imagine, he said, how many hundreds of tons of export oranges they pull from that land in any given year? And then, if the overseas prices aren't right, aren't high enough, do you know what they do? They go and dump all the oranges into the sea. Ship after ship full of export oranges, a whole year's harvest, the finest quality–they go and dump just over the horizon. Who, Pa? Who go and dump all the oranges? Oupa Gert and the government, that's who, said Pa. They're in cahoots. But why, Pa? Why are they in cahoots? (I was drifting. Was I an orange?) Because one hand washes the other, that's why, said Pa. That's why the waves break white, from all the soap. (Deep and soft, the pillow, the bench. Deep water.) And then what happens? No, nothing, said Pa. In the end, those few that still can float, roll up on the beach, spoilt, split and burst, full of salt. Where, Pa? Where, anywhere, if you ask me. Ask Oupa Gert where. Isipingo, Durban, Umhlanga Rocks. Maybe further up, too, like Mozambique.

I was looking into the lamp.

'Don't go to sleep again, little boy. Okay?'

'I wasn't asleep.'

'No?'

You could still smell the cold. It smelt of wood smoke and coal.

Let a boer like me tell you, said Pa. Never trust a boer. Not with a pin, not with a penny. Just look at what old Oupa Gert has done to that lovely old house of his. One day he went and pulled up all the thatch, and stuck in its place two lorry loads of red Spanish tiles. And what does it look like now, that lovely old Cape-Dutch house? Like it's wearing a wig of scabs, dry scabs.

If you shut your eyes you could see it, the big white house, standing out against the sky like a summer cloud. What kept it tethered to the ground, I wondered.

At the end of the driveway was a fishpond. Beside the fishpond stood the statue of a woman, dusty and white, bare to the waist, a vase on her shoulder. From the lip of the vase trickled water. If you looked down into the pond, you could see goldfish, their long wavy fins barely moving, packed together and dreaming, gleaming like long brass knives.

Crystal le Roux, Oupa Gert's niece, painted her mouth and her fingernails bright red. She baked biscuits, and sprinkled sugar on top. She said I could dip my biscuit in my milk if I liked. When I told her I wanted a goldfish, she laughed, holding her throat with one hand, and looking at me with her big wide eyes that were so difficult to look back into. She told me not to forget to bring a bucket next time. Why? I asked. She opened her eyes wider, in astonishment, and said, Well, how else will we go and catch your goldfish?

The kitchen was beginning to grow warmer.

'Pa, where's the bucket, Pa?'

'Why?' he asked, but added without waiting for a reply: 'In its place, of course. Under the sink.'

I pushed away the cushion and slipped off the bench.

Thick with the smell of scrubbing powder, the air beneath the sink closed around me. A den. My own. Damp and gritty, the concrete floor. Ahead of me, doubled up in a cramp, bulged the U-bend pipe. At the back of my den stood the bucket; beside it, a stack of tins of red stoep polish. A stiff crumpled red rag on the lid of the top tin.

It was Seraphima who made the front stoep of our house shine. She tucked up her dress, and went down on her hands and knees, rubbing the rag, smearing the polish round in circles. Under her breath, she sang a song in words I could not understand.

'What are you singing, Seraphima?'

'I am singing, I am sad. For home.'

'Why, Seraphima?'

She was home, wasn't she? I said. She smiled and shook her head, and sang again, a little. I could see the muscles in her back working beneath her shirt as she rubbed.

Oupa Gert van Dyk was a very short, fat man who clung to the handle of a thick bamboo cane. His trousers he kept jacked up high on his belly by means of a pair of braces. (A man's pants, Pa warned me in private, should never reach halfway up to his armpits.) When he climbed the steps to the stoep, Oupa Gert clung with one hand to the handle of his cane, and with the other, kept his knuckles squeezed hard into the small of his back. All the bones of his back were collapsing into one another, he told us. It was murder, he said. There was no other word for it. Murder, in the worst degree. And the doctors were useless. Useless. All they ever did was send you bills. In the meantime, he said, it was like a mountain on his backbone, slowly getting heavier. Each month, he felt he was growing a little shorter. He could hardly move now or breathe. He would not wish such suffering on any other Christian person, he told us. No, he said. Not even on his own worst enemy.

Oupa Gert drove a very long car, a butter-yellow Mercedes-Benz, its windows dark and smoky, like sunglasses. Jesus, said Pa. A Merc like that is wasted on a fat old ballie[3] like Oupa Gert. A Merc like that is a sleeping tiger. Do you know, he said, it can cruise – cruise! – at over a hundred? And Pa made a joke. He called the Merc 'ou tamaties', old tomatoes, because, he said, it was well known that Oupa Gert had refused to take delivery of the brand new vehicle until the English 'automatic' written on the back had been altered to the Afrikaans, 'outomaties'. Pa also sometimes called it 'vrot tamaties', rotten tomatoes, because, he said, of the smell that hung round old Oupa Gert. The smell of money, said Pa. I used to try not to breathe inside the Mercedes-Benz. I kept close to the open window, and tried to take bites of the air from outside.

When Oupa Gert was driving, he wore his hat, a soft grey panama in suede. In the back pocket of his trousers he carried a pair of small brushes with wire bristles.

Whenever he had to sit and wait for Pa, as he sometimes did, in our front room, he would settle the hat very carefully on his knees and begin to brush the suede this way and that. The trouble, he said, was all these spots. You get these spots, he told me, from tipping your hat to the ladies. Shiny spots, especially round the brim. But what could a man do? You tipped your hat. Sometimes, however, there were no spots, or none that I could see, let alone any ladies, but Oupa Gert would take great care to buff the suede with his brushes, anyway.

When he was driving, Oupa Gert used to take out his dentures and place them on the dashboard. It was more comfortable like that, he explained. He himself was a man of peace, a churchgoer and one who feared God, but he could not endure these things stuck in his mouth all the time, the size of a bathroom basin.

Hot fat sputtered. Pa poured the egg into the pan, and I dragged out the bucket and stowed it under my chair.

'What are you up to?' he wanted to know, scraping busily at a piece of toast with a kitchen knife.

'No, nothing, Pa.'

'What do you mean, nothing?' But at that moment, he put out a hand to the coffee pot, and had to wince away, blowing hard at his fingers. 'Jesus Christ!' he whispered in a fury, and pushed back his hat. 'I never bloody well *think*. And then I go and do a thing like that.'

He slid the egg from the flipper to my plate. He himself did not bother to eat, but sat opposite me at the table, sipping black coffee. His eyes looked very dark and heavy, and he stared at the wall, thinking.

Sometimes, Pa did not sleep at night.

3.   *old ballie*, metonym for an old man: old cock, or rather, old balls

'Ja-nee,' he said at last, sitting back. Yes and no. 'A man must pay his debts. Eat your breakfast, little mister. You want to grow up big and strong like your Pa, don't you?'

I crunched at the burnt toast.

Outside in the pepper tree, the first birds were beginning to twitter.

'Listen. Do you hear? They make one hell of a noise, don't they? And do you know why? Because they are all so busy shouting: 'I've got no pockets! I don't need any! I've got no money!' Listen. You hear how happy they are?'

Above the growing swarm of the rest, a single bird began to whistle. Pa concentrated, put his head to one side, and imitated it perfectly. I asked him to do it again, and he did. The coffee was black and strong, and I tried to drink it, but couldn't until Pa added a little milk. I told him about the bucket and the goldfish, and he laughed.

'Oupa Gert won't give you ice in winter. Or me. You'll see.'

But he let me take the bucket.

The sky was beginning to grow blank with dawn by the time we made our way into the backyard. I felt very excited to be following Pa. It was a dry cold day in early winter. You could smell the dust. The boughs of the pepper tree stood out, dark against the light. In his kennel, the baboon was nothing but a shadow, a smell and a rattling chain.

'This way,' said Pa. 'We've got to go and milk a tractor.'

I ran to keep up. The veld grass, stiff with frost, whipped my bare legs. Soon, I was wet and shivering. I let my breath pour out like smoke as I ran. Pa was carrying a petrol can. I had my bucket.

'Look, Pa!'

I began to run faster. I had to hold up my arms, the grass was so high.

'Go, little Rian, go!' called Pa. 'Today is the day. Okay?'

The bucket was heavy to wield, and clanked.

I knew where to go: the circle of parked vehicles, Pa's open-air repair shop. Today, there were only a couple of bakkies, a broken down tractor and a car in the circle.

Pa was the best mechanic this side of the Ysterberg. A genius, said Dominee Roelofse of the Dutch Reformed Church. A genius with his hands. Dominee Roelofse was not our dominee. We never went to his church, the huge white church with the loudspeakers in the steeple. On Sunday mornings, Dominee Roelofse would broadcast the sound of bells from a gramophone record. It was a scratched record, and the needle hissed. If too few people turned up for his sermon, he would go and play the record again. And again, he warned from the pulpit, if he had to.

Pa liked only the Pentecostals, who came to the dorp in a tent. Because they still hear the Word, he said. If you watch, you can see it happen, he said. They tune in. It's not the same old gramophone record over and over again, no. It's like a radio, where you fiddle around a bit until you get the proper station. All of a sudden, he said, they jump to their feet and wave their arms. Happy? You can see it in their faces. It's so good – they can't help it – big tears run down their cheeks. They shout and cry and stamp their feet. And then they begin to talk. Not so that you can understand, no. They talk in tongues – but it doesn't matter, because you know what they are saying, anyway. You can't help it. You can't understand, and you can. It goes both ways. Until you want to jump up and speak in tongues yourself.

'And you, Pa? Can you speak in tongues?'

'Me?' Pa laughed.

In the middle of the circle of broken down vehicles, I turned my bucket upside down and sat on the iron bottom. Wet grass seeds sticking to my legs itched, and I scratched. Breathed out smoke.

Pa had a story to tell about Dominee Roelofse. The Story of the White Mudguard, he called it. On the day the dominee first visited Pa with a motor vehicle problem, he wanted to know how Pa knew what he, Pa, was doing. My philosophy, dominee? said Pa, and smiled. It's like this, he said. We fix it or we fucks it. You see? Still smiling, he tapped the hood of the dominee's bubble-shaped, milk-white Morris Minor with his hard, oil-blackened fingers. The tongue of the devil! swore the dominee. And for two Sundays in a row, according to our neighbor, Don Coetzee, he preached on the evils of a loose, clever tongue.

But when Tant Hattie, the dominee's wife, who played the organ in church and wore pretty lace gloves and made the arrangement of flowers for the niche before the pulpit, went driving one day and knocked over little Sonja van der Merwe, a girl in the class below me at school, the dominee again brought the Morris Minor to Pa. He came after sundown, said Pa. He sat in the kitchen and drank tea. Or rather, he spilled a little tea into his saucer, and sat staring at it. And told Pa that Sonja's mother and father were going to sue, because the hospital in Pietersburg said it was brain damage, and little Sansoentjie, as they called her, would be silly in the head for life. It was Tant Hattie's own fault, the dominee cried. Her handbag had opened, spilling all of her woman's vanities, lipstick and powder and mirrors, and she had taken her eyes off the road for a moment, and the child must have wobbled on her bicycle, or something, and bang! Don't panel beat the mudguard, Tok, he begged. I want you to take it right off. Replace the whole thing.

Why? said Pa. What's the problem? How big is that dent? I mean, can a little girl's head do so much damage? No, no, said the dominee. You don't understand. I've got that dent on my conscience, Tok. Too bad, said Pa, I can't panel beat your head. Please, Tok, man, the dominee begged, and added in a whisper something he would not say in church. Please, he said. Please. We must fix it, not, not. . . . He kept his eyes down, unable to say the word, but trying, said Pa, really trying.

As a result, Pa removed the mudguard, replacing it with one he found in a scrap-yard in Pietersburg, as good as new, not milk-white but sky-blue. You can't beat it, he always said with a wink when he told me the story. The tongue of the devil.

When at last he came into the circle of vehicles, Pa went and slapped the saddle of the tractor.

'This,' he said, 'is my iron cow. You don't believe me? Watch.'

Taking a coil of plastic piping from his back pocket, he fed it into the tractor's tank. Then, squatting on his heels, he took the end of the pipe between his lips and began to suck.

'Aaaa-gha!' he said, and spat. 'There is nothing,' he told me, and gasped. 'Nothing worse, I tell you, Rian. Than a full mouthful of petrol.'

The petrol rattled into the can between his knees. Wiping the dribble from his chin with the back of his wrist, he shook his head. And spat.

I looked down into the can. I liked the way the petrol swirled around – not only in the can, it seemed, but also in my head. And I spat to one side, too, like Pa.

As soon as the can was full, we went and decanted the petrol into the bakkie that stood in the lean-to behind the fowl run. Pa stepped up on to the back bumper, and began to rock the bakkie from side to side.

'I want you, you, you!' he sang, his head thrown back, his Adam's apple working, his lips fluting. 'No one else will do, do, do. . . .'

I turned my bucket upside down and stood on it, hanging on to the wire. I liked to feel the fence sag and sway and hold me like a great net. Inside the fowl run, Vaaljapie, the white Leghorn rooster, strutted and stalked among his crowd of busy hens. His comb, thick as if swollen, and red, kept flopping over his beak. He jerked his head as if to keep an eye on me – a fierce eye.

'Pa.'

'What?'

Vaaljapie flapped his wings, scattering dust and bits of dried chicken shit. He crowed again. His wattles shook.

'Pa!'

'Ag, ja, Vaaljapie,' called Pa with a laugh. 'Enough, man! Don't worry, I'm not going to chop off your head. A boer doesn't eat his alarm clock. And just look at you. All muscles and chest, too big for the pot. You don't have a snowball's hope in hell.' Stepping down from the bumper, Pa wiped his hands on his pants, and glanced up at the sky. 'We must get a move on, now, Rian. The sun is up. It's getting late.'

On any other day, I would not have been allowed near the junkyard – the cemetery, Pa called it – for fear of snakes. It was a paradise, said Pa, for snakes. A bare plot of ground in the shadow of the windmill, it was there that every last broken, twisted and useless thing landed up. Mudguards and bumpers lay jammed, stacked on top of each other. Old bald tires were toppled together in mounds. Dumped, dead engine blocks, some with radiators and fans still attached, some without, together with axle shafts, gearboxes, chassis frames, and whole hulks of cars, stood everywhere. In the middle of the dump, as if in disgrace, leaned the white bulk of a fridge, its door hanging by one hinge. A slow smell of seeping black oil hung over the place. If you stopped there in the heat of the day with the sun on your head, you could feel in your bones how the ground would drag you down, too, in the end.

It was different, today, though, I could tell.

'Look,' said Pa, and pointed.

On the roof of a car hulk beside the round concrete water tank sat a crow. It greeted us with a rattling croak.

'Ja, crow!' replied Pa. 'Good morning to you, too. You're lucky I'm not carrying my shotgun, I can tell you. I take no shit from a bird.' But he smiled and stood watching as the crow sailed away, low and without flapping, across the veld. 'Rian, my son,' he said to me without looking down. 'We need fifteen bottles. Can you go and find them?'

'Now, Pa?'

'Now, ja. Go get us some bottles. We need a whole bunch. Penny a bottle. We'll take them all to old Mr Abie. You like Mr Abie, don't you? 'Hey, Mr Abie,' I'll say. 'Pay us in cash, man.' Fifteen bottles, fifteen pennies. It is enough. Enough is enough. And then,' he said, smiling and half-shutting one eye, as if taking aim. 'Then we will pay our debts.'

I took a shortcut along a broken ploughshare, and jumped down. I knew where to go because I knew where the empty bottles were kept. At my feet, like a huge chromed eyeball, torn out and still trailing its wires, lay a car's headlight. I kicked it, and the headlight rolled round in a circle, and the glass burst. Ahead, a crooked bundle of barbed wire lay rusting away to orange powder under the sun. Beyond stood the chassis of a car. Tall spears of khakibos had shot up everywhere. A paradise for snakes.

I crossed over a stack of warped brown sheets of corrugated iron, stamping my feet. Passing by the fridge, I made my way along a pile of scaffolding planks, soft with old thick cement, and over a bundle of plumber's pipes. At that point, my way ahead was blocked by a solid stack of bricks, neatly packed, clean. To one side, tilted, lay a bathroom basin with bright and gleaming taps. Beyond the basin, its back to the bricks, sat a low round toilet bowl with a sun-bleached plastic lid. Unlike everything else, these things were not old, broken or used. They had all been abandoned brand new.

On days when Pa did not feel like working, he would say: Christmas comes but once a year, and, turning up the radio, he would lock the back door and go and fetch a bottle of brandy from the pantry. Happy happy! he'd sing, and take a heavy swig straight from the bottle. Then, holding the soft old bench cushion to him in a hug, he would begin dancing round the kitchen. Later, having fallen over once or twice, he would become quieter, almost sad, and, sitting on the bench by the stove, he would spend time cleaning his rifle. Taking it carefully to pieces, oiling it, and reassembling it, he would weigh the bullets one by one in his palm, before loading them into the clip again. Then, if he did not fall asleep, he would go and fetch the roll of plans from his bedroom.

Spreading the stiffly furled pages out across the kitchen table and using things like the sugar bowl, the radio, the brandy bottle and the box of bullets to pin down the four corners, he would say: Come, Rian, come. Climb up on the chair and take a look. You see? pointing to a tiny scratching of black ink at the foot of the first page. You know what this is? This is the town clerk's signature: H.H.P. du Toit. He's dead, now, too, old Mr du Toit. But this is my proof. Legal. These plans are legal. Home improvements. I had them passed just before you were born. I went to the town clerk's offices. I knocked on the door. An indoor bathroom with a toilet, I said. Tell me that's not an improvement, meneer.[4]

And he scratched his ear, old Hennie du Toit. He had cancer of the liver, but he worked on until only a few days before the end. He examined the plans, and looked up over the top of his glasses, and said: Well, Tok, your young lady is

4. *meneer,* mister, sir

going to love this, I'm sure. Tell her I say congratulations. With a man like you, she is bound to be happy.

Pa's voice went down to a whisper, and he coughed and poured a heavy dop[5] of brandy into a coffee mug. Lachaim, he said. It's what the Jews say, he told me, adding black coffee from the pot on the stove. To life.

Once, in ballpoint, he drew the door to the bathroom on the kitchen wall. Right here, he said, we will cut our way through. Tomorrow, he said. You'll see. We'll do it. All a man really needs is a hammer and a chisel. Give me the right tools, he said, and I can move a mountain. You know, he told me, these days you can get a power saw, the sort they use for cutting down trees. You kick-start it like a motorbike, and it screams like a mad animal, but you can slice through a brick wall with it like butter. It's never too late, never too late to try, said Pa. With great care, he drew the door with its handles and hinges on the wall, even adding heads to the screws. Then he returned to the plans.

Look, he said, and tapped at the heavy paper with his forefinger. Here, in the corner, you see, we'll get the hot-water geyser to stand. We can brace it up under the roof where it will be out of the way. We'll keep the gas bottle outside, okay? That will save space. We can knock two small holes through the wall, here, and lead in the pipes. Hot water on tap. And here we can place the bath with its smart new fittings in the modern style. I can't tell you how much your mother would have loved it. I can see her face now. Under the window, we can put the basin. We'll make the floor all smooth cement. I'll show you how. Not too smooth, you don't want to slip when it's wet. If it gets too cold in the winter, you can always put a towel on the floor. Or maybe I'll knock together with nails a frame out of wood, like the one I once saw at the public swimming pool, to prevent athlete's foot, and you can stand on it and drip dry. Why not, he said. I'll do it. I'll do it. It's never too late. I should have slapped it up quickly, before you were born. I've got the cement. I've got the bricks. I'm good with my hands. I could have done it. Why did I wait? Look. You see, Rian? You see? Again. Here is the geyser. Here is the basin. Here we can put the toilet, and drain it into the septic tank. I can dig a big tank. That is no problem. The problem is . . . forget it. There *is* no problem.

He took another swallow of brandy, and went over every detail again, point by point. The geyser. The toilet. The basin. The bath. After another few cups of coffee – brandy coffee – he began to run his fingers over the plans with his eyes shut, his lips forming words I could not hear or understand. Then he went and stood right in front of the door he had drawn on the wall, and stared at it. Jesus,

5. *dop*, shot, slug

I have sinned, he said, and he banged his head against the wall until his nose began to bleed, and he tried to wipe away the blood with one finger, but he looked
at the finger as if he could not really see the finger or the blood, and said, Annie.

Ahead of me now lay the bathtub, large and white and smooth, upside down.
I didn't look beneath it. (Snakes.) Here, too, lay the round white drum of the
geyser, just beginning to rust round the rim. The bathroom door, unpainted, its boards warping, stood leaning up against the bricks. If I had looked, I
would have found, too, plastic packets of hinges and screws and the like, still
unopened. And somewhere deeper in the dump, too, no doubt, the dominee's
milk-white mudguard. Instead, I found a piece of broken windscreen so shattered that it bent, heavy and smooth as water, as I lifted it. Green glints and
angles in the depths.

Stacked around the foot of the water tank lay the bottles – plenty of bottles.
Beer bottles, wine bottles, hard liquor bottles, pickle and jam jars, Coca-Cola,
tomato sauce and milk bottles. I found a square-faced gin bottle with a picture
on it that I liked: a boar's head like a firecracker exploding, all red and green
flames licking. The glass face was spattered with sand kicked up by the summer
rains, but I wiped the bottle clean on the leg of my pants.

'Look, Pa,' I called, holding up the gin bottle.

But Pa had climbed the iron ladder fixed to the side of the water tank and was
standing on the rim, his hands on his hips.

'Come on up, Rian! Quick.'

The rungs were so cold that I had to pull the sleeves of my jersey over my
palms as I climbed. Beside me, the windmill dropped its long steel-frame shadow over the parched ground. Morning glory, not all of it yet shriveled by frost,
had twined its way through the ladder and up the wall. In the round concrete
water tank, the water stood clear and still, in part a pane of ice.

'Never you mind a few goldfish,' said Pa. 'One of these days, I'll go and get
us a whole bakkie-load full of barbel, and dump them in here to breed. When
I was working on the Driehoek mines near Stilfontein – long ago, before I met
your mother – they put me in charge of the slimes dams. Once the ore has been
crushed, you see, and most of the gold has already been taken out, they must
pass the ore just one more time through the slimes dams. That is the final step
in the extraction process. They use cyanide to pick up the last of the gold that
didn't come out in the washing so far, you see?'

It seemed to me I could see. The slimes dams were deep and green with long
waving beards of weed, and at the bottom gleamed the gold, like a giant moon.

I nodded.

'Well, in some of the outer dams, barbel were breeding. You could hear them grunt when they hit the surface for air, or ate the waterflies. Barbel have got teeth as good as a watchdog's, you know. Still, you can't eat a slimes dam barbel. One day, one of the kaffirs from the compound caught one and tried, I don't know why. Tired of mieliepap, I suppose. Anyway, he nearly died. All the others thought it was witchcraft, and they began to kill one another – Zulus going for Shangaans, Shangaans for Pondos, Pondos for Xhosas, everybody killing everybody else – screaming and chopping with pangas[6] and kieries.[7] Blood and brains, arms and legs. But it wasn't witchcraft. It was barbel.'

Pa plucked a bloom of morning glory and sucked the tip.

'Like to try? It's what the bees eat.'

The tiny drop of nectar disappeared almost before it touched the tip of my tongue. Holding the flower between my lips like a little trumpet, I breathed the air.

Pa was quiet for a while. Then he said:

'Look, Rian. The hills.'

On the horizon, shadows of a blue barely deeper than that of the sky. In those hills, I knew, Pa used to go hunting leopard. But not today. A stray breath of wind across the veld set the windmill blades turning. The long shank of the piston came down with a grinding clank, and water spilled from the pipe into the reservoir. The windmill kept its face turned to the breeze.

'Come on. Bottles for Mr Abie,' said Pa.

We stood the bottles I had collected in a row on the plank.

'Like soldiers on parade, hey? One, two, three . . . how many have we got? Count, now, Rian.'

I touched each one with my finger to make sure, but before I had finished, Pa said: 'One too many? Is that a fact?' He pushed back his hat and rubbed his wrinkled forehead. 'Pass me the last one, there. That's right.' With a swing of his arm, he sent the bottle spinning high, and began to sing again, laughing, his voice cracking:

> *'And if one green bottle*
> *Should ac-cidentally fall. . . .'*

At the top of its arc, the bottle seemed to pause, to hang in the air. Before dropping to burst in the middle of the cemetery.

'Now,' said Pa. 'Let's go and get what we want.'

6   pangas – machetes
7   kieries – clubs

I STOOD WHERE I ALWAYS STOOD, on the seat beside Pa as he drove. The seat was a bucket seat lifted from an old MG sports car. The inside of the cab was painted red, pillar-box red, because Pa had once found a can of the paint in a broken down GPO van. Waste not, want not, he told me. But the paint had cracked and split across the MG's leather seats, and always felt sticky to the touch. You wait, Pa told me. I'm going to hot up this bakkie. I'm going to make it one of a kind. He loved to gun the engine until it shook, and then he'd throw back his head and shout above the roar: This bakkie is souped up. This bakkie is as good as a V-8.

Although it lacked a radio, the bakkie did have an aerial of its own. In honor of Oude Hoop, Pa had stuck a plastic orange on the tip. Ask Oupa Gert, he said. An orange on your aerial makes you come faster, go faster.

Today, before we left, he went and fetched his hunting rifle and stowed it in the sling behind the seats. Leaning out of the window as we swung through the gate, he banged at the door with the flat of his hand, and yelled:

'Wa-hoo! Crystal! Crystal le Roux!'

We turned on to the open highway, and then off again, and began tearing up the dust of a dirt road. In the back of the bakkie, my bucket rolled around. The bag of bottles jumped and rattled.

'Pa, let's go to Durban, Pa.'

'Right away, today?' He smiled at me. "Happy Days Are Here Again'?' he said. 'Why not?'

I put out my hand, the way I had seen him do.

'It's a deal, is it?' Grappling with the steering wheel, he leaned over and held me close for a second or two. 'Right you are then, Mr Man. After Oude Hoop, maybe. We'll see.'

The A.B. Abrahams Cash & Trading Store stood at a bend in the road beside a clump of mimosas. Beyond the waves of yellow blossom, you could see the green stems of the trees in the early morning light.

'Bloody weeds, those trees,' said Pa. 'They grow like wildfire. They'll shoot up through his floorboards one of these days, you'll see. Full of dust, too. If I was Mr Abie, I'd grub them up, root and garter.'

The shutters of the store were still up. We seemed to have arrived too early. Pa tapped at the front door.

'No luck,' he said, peering through the shutters. 'Let's try round the back.'

But at that moment, Mr Abie opened the door.

'I *thought* I heard. . . .'

'Good morning, Mr Abrahams!' said Pa, lifting his hat. 'If it's too early, just say the word.'

'No, no. Please. Come inside. What can I do for an early visitor? For two early visitors?'

Nodding to me, he smiled. I liked Mr Abie. He stood in the doorway, now, wiping his fingers on a big white handkerchief.

Pa held up the bag of bottles.

'I've brought you a little business.'

'So I see.'

'But if you haven't opened yet. . . .'

'No, no, not at all. Please. I've been up since four.'

'So early? Why?'

'It's the day the rabbi comes. Rabbi Podolski from Pietersburg. You know him, I suppose?'

'I can't say we've ever met.'

'Well, once or twice a month, the rabbi comes to bless the chickens. We like to get an early start. It's a long way back to Pietersburg, you know. He's doing me a favor.'

Raising his eyes to the horizon, Pa gave a low whistle.

'All that way just to bless your chickens?'

'Oh, yes. On a day like today, we try and do as many as we can. One dozen, two, maybe more. Pietersburg is a big town, you see. Bigger than this. Here, there is nothing, no market to speak of. But what can you expect?'

'Well, if ever you need,' said Pa, 'I can always spare you a couple of chickens.'

'Thank you. If ever I run out.'

Together, Pa and Mr Abie began to take down the shutters.

'Now, Rian,' said Pa. 'You don't want to get under our feet.'

Inside the shop, I could still smell the shadows of night. I could feel all the things pressing in around me – dead things, waiting. But shutter after shutter rattled and banged and was lifted away, and sunlight leapt across the floor. You could see the belly of a wheelbarrow with a solid rubber tire. You could see a sewing machine, SINGER printed in gold along its black wasp's waist. Bales of bloudraad stood towering over me. A gang of tin lanterns, bright and empty, their glass chimneys dusty, were strung from a loop of wire over my head. If one day the mimosas did come shooting up, I wondered, where would they stand? The floor underfoot was thick with trampled sawdust. Heavy bags of mealie meal lay packed in a slump around the wooden posts that held up the roof. From the roof itself hung a bundle of shiny new guitars, together with one large, stiff black bicycle, also new. You could smell the raw mealie meal and the sunlight and the paraffin that Mr Abie sold for five pennies a bottle – three, if you brought your own.

Sometimes Mr Abie used to let me siphon the paraffin from the drum in the back room. When the bottle was full, you had to add a screw of newspaper for the stopper. A bottle like that is as good as a bomb, said Pa. All you need is a match.

Now, at the door, I heard Pa say politely:

'After you.'

'No, no. Please,' replied Mr Abie. 'After you.'

'Dolly!' I called and went to look for Mr Abie's fat and lazy bull mastiff, who loved to spend all day sleeping in the sawdust behind the counter. But there was no sign of Dolly now.

Inside the glass counter stood a row of alarm clocks that looked as if they had all marched up there together and stopped. Each told a different time. Beside the clocks, and taking up most of the space, lay a wide white enamel bedpan, a chip the size of Pa's thumbnail missing from its rim. Secondhand, that bedpan, Pa had told me. Half of Mr Abie's shop, he told me, is secondhand. At the bottom of the bedpan lay a rubber bulb tangled in among a bunch of chalk-dusty rubber pipes. An enema! cried Pa. Shit a brick, he said, and laughed.

A brick? Was it possible? Huge. And hard. And dry.

My ears, my face, began to burn.

I pressed my face up flat against the glass.

Look, Pa. I'm a fish. I can swim through solid glass.

On the shelf below the clocks lay a tray full of little penknives with tartan handles. (I wanted one.)

'Fifteen bottles, fifteen pennies,' said Pa, swinging the bottles in the bag on to the counter.

Smiling gently, Mr Abie took his place behind the counter, and stood tapping the gold wedding ring he wore against the keys of the till.

'Cash?' he inquired.

'On the nail! Fifteen pretty pennies, please. You know what they mean when they say, 'A pretty penny'?'

'They mean,' replied Mr Abie, 'expensive.'

'You are only too right,' said Pa and smiled, crinkling the corners of his eyes and gazing, as it were, through the back wall. Then he leaned forward lazily across the counter on his elbows, and added: 'I don't mind telling you, Mr Abrahams. I don't mind telling you: I've had an idea.'

'Oh, yes? An idea.'

Mr Abie stepped back. His eyes, as he stood quietly looking at Pa, were large and dark and soft, but also drooping and sad. His face was very pale, and his chin all folds. On the back of his head, which was bald, he wore a skullcap with gold embroidery. (Why? I once asked Pa. Because of the Ten Commandments, he told me.) As you looked up, you wondered how he shaved each soft fold and wrinkle without cutting himself. But he was kind, too, Mr Abie. As soon as he saw me staring, he handed me a lollipop from the jar beside his till.

'A fine young man. How is he doing at school?'

'Only too well,' said Pa.

Mr Abie shook his head.

'Is it possible? Who can do too well at school?'

Me, evidently.

'No school today!' I said. Shouted.

'Really? In the middle of the week? Why, may I ask?'

'Because,' I said, 'we're going to Durban. But first, we're going to Oude Hoop.'

Mr Abie looked at Pa.

'Gert van Dyk?'

'Yes,' said Pa. He rubbed his chin and looked around. It seemed that he needed to talk.

'Pennies won't get you to Durban,' said Mr Abie.

'You're right,' agreed Pa, beginning to unpack the bottles from the bag. 'You are only too right. But what makes you think I care?'

'What *is* this?' said Mr Abie.

'Bottles.'

'I know. But why are you doing this?'

'I've got an idea.'

'So you say.'

They both stopped and looked at me.

Sticking the lollipop into my cheek, I asked:

'Where's Dolly?'

Mr Abie said nothing.

'Rian,' said Pa. 'Why don't you go and play outside?'

'Pa?'

'You heard me.'

I didn't want to. I wanted to stay and see the little flag that flipped up and said SALE! when Mr Abie opened the till. But I went out on to the stoep and hung as far as I could over the railing. I let my head hang down, and watched the spit slip from my mouth to the ground in a long slow drop, like blood.

Then I swung head over heels.

'Dolly!'

I didn't know why she didn't come when I called.

From the railing of the stoep, if you looked, you could see all the way down the dry winter's road. There was no one in sight. Not even a black man on a bicycle. Every time we drove by such a man, Pa would raise one finger and say: Mr Abie's customer! And if we drove by a black man with a guitar – going nowhere, it seemed, but walking along, playing the same few notes over and over – Pa would again raise his finger. You see? Mr Abie's customer!

As if Mr Abie ever had only one customer.

'Dolly!' I yelled at the top of my voice. 'Dolly!'

Then I jumped all the way down the steps and stood for awhile beside the bakkie, listening to the odd ticking sounds the bodywork made as it cooled and contracted.

After a while, I picked up a stick and wrote in the dust:

HAPPY HAPPY

To underline the words, I drew an arrow. And after that, another. Then I walked a little way down the road, trailing the stick in the dust. There was nothing else to do.

Sometimes, though, you saw a ship.

On Durban beach, if you looked out to sea, said Pa, you saw a ship. The funny thing was, the ship never moved. You could watch for as long as you liked, he said, but it just hung there, high on the horizon. If you looked away, if only for one moment, though, the ship was gone.

On the beach the sand was soft and white. Like mine dump sand, said Pa, only better, because sea sand is full of salt, not cyanide. There is no end to the beach, he said, and you can walk forever, if you like. Only, all along the edge, where the waves wash up, it's full of trash. Bottles and shells and plastic bags, and dead jellyfish here and there like big stones of glass. And oranges, Pa? Ja, ja, and oranges, too. Oupa Gert's burst oranges. We'll find them, if we look, you'll see.

But the first thing we'll do, he said, is hire ourselves a beach umbrella, a big one with stripes, and go in among the crowd (there is always a crowd) and find ourselves a place, and park. Whenever we want, we can go for a dip in the sea. Then we can come back to our towels, and lie around in the sun, and drip dry, and listen to all the stations on the transistor radio. One day, too, on our way to the beach, we'll stop off at Harry's Holiday Snapshots. What you do at Harry's is put your head through a board, and smile, and out you come – the Astronaut, or maybe the Abominable Snowman, or Old King Cole. You keep the picture, of course. Take it home with you. And then you can always see it, and laugh, and remember, and say, Those were the days. Outside Harry's, on the beach, is where they make the candy floss. You'll see. This blonde lady in a bikini comes and pours sugar into a big white washing machine, and it spins, and the candy floss sticks to its sides like lamb's wool. Then she wraps the candy floss round on itself like a big pink cloud, and you take a bite, and. . . . Mmm. Ja, said Pa, you wait. I'll buy you a blow-up surfboard, too, and you can go out on the waves, and hang on, and when the big breakers break, you can ride all the way to the beach, for free.

When, Pa?

One day. One day is one day.

So, why not today?

In my belly I felt a kick of excitement. You never knew with Pa. Or so you could pretend. Anyway, no school today, for sure.

I threw away the stick, and went all the way round to the back yard.

But Dolly was not there, either. Instead, on the ground in the sun sat three black women with dead fowls in their laps. The women were talking and laughing, and pinching up tufts of feathers. You could hear the rip and thump. You could see the way the skin stretched up before the feathers tore away.

As I watched, one of the women got to her feet, put her hand to her head and walked in a way that made me think of Mr Abie. They all laughed.

'Have you seen Dolly?' I asked.

The woman standing wiped her face.

'What you say?'

'Dolly. Dolly the dog.'

Hiking up her sleeve, the woman pointed. Behind us stood Mr Abie's storage shed.

'In there?' I said.

'Eh-weh.' Yes.

But my eyes were still too full of the sun, and at first I couldn't see anything inside the shed. I put my hands over my eyes, the way Pa had taught me, and thought of the inside of a dark box. All around me, I could hear the chickens. I could feel their warmth. Then, suddenly, right beside me, a chicken screeched and started to cluck. I dropped my hands. In front of me stood a tall black man I did not know, holding a chicken upside down by the legs. When the chicken tried to flap, he trapped its wings.

'Outa,' I said.

The black man said nothing. He looked down at me. He did not smile.

Beside him stood another man, a big, soft-looking man with a pale face and a beard. On the back of his head he wore a skullcap like Mr Abie's, except that this man's was plain black. His face was broad and quiet, thoughtful. Cupped in his hand lay an open straight-razor. A single tiny feather was sticking to his beard.

I wanted to say good morning to him, too – Good morning, rabbi – but he stood quietly looking over my head.

Then, talking to himself, the rabbi lifted the razor, and reached out with it and touched the chicken's throat. The chicken did not – could not – move, but its blood shot up in two thin lines like a fork.

Turning on his heel, the black man swung the chicken upside down over a long tin sluice that led out the back of the shed. The rabbi's lips were still moving, I saw, but I could not hear what he was saying. He was praying, I knew. I wanted to pray, too. In tongues. I am the Lord, thy God, thou shalt have no other God before me. What did it mean? And how many tongues could you have?

It was silent in the shed.

The black man shifted his grip. The fowl gave an abrupt, shaky flap of its wings. Its feet clawed and clenched. You could hear the trickling, the tapping of the blood.

The black man stood weighing the body in both hands. Then, as if satisfied, he slung it around to get rid of the remaining drops, and tossed the body on to the workbench, where a heap of others lay already. Reaching into a coop at his feet, he pulled out another screeching, struggling chicken.

This time I did not stay to watch. I went and stood outside the shed in the sun. After a while, I wandered round to the place at the back of the shed where the sluice stuck out. Here, the blood was trickling into a bucket, I saw. And here, too, stood Dolly, her big black wrinkled face looking profound as she lapped.

'Dolly!' I cried. 'No!'

But she would not listen. When I put my arms around her neck and tried to pull her away, all she did was give my neck and face a warm wet sloppy lick, before turning her attention to the bucket again.

I ran back round the shed.

Pa and Mr Abie were crossing the yard. Pa had his hands in his pockets. His face was shining and he was smiling. An idea. Mr Abie had his hands in his pockets, too, but he was not smiling. He was staring at the ground.

'Where have you been, Rian?' called Pa. 'Come and see the rabbi. Come. He's making the chickens holy.'

He reached out a hand but I pulled away.

'Rian. . . .' he said. A warning.

'Let him be, let him be, if he doesn't want to,' said Mr Abie. 'Tell me, Rian. Did you find Dolly?'

I shook my head. But Mr Abie seemed to know.

'Excuse me, Rian. Just a minute. You seem to have. . . .' Taking the handkerchief out of his pocket, he wiped the side of my face where Dolly had licked it. Then, turning to Pa again, he said, 'Money makes money, you know.'

'Telling me,' said Pa, grinning and jingling the coins in his pocket.

'It's the way of the world,' continued Mr Abie. 'Money makes money. But,' he shrugged and stretched out his hands, 'what do you expect?'

Turning his face up to the sky, Pa grimaced, winked, as if at an accomplice.

'By the way,' remarked Mr Abie, stopping at the door of the shed, 'you don't happen to know, do you, a good way of making sausages out of blood?'

'Me? You must be joking.'

Mr Abie smiled.

'It's only an idea,' he said, and raised his hand at Pa's back. 'After you.'

'No, no. Please. After you.'

I went back to the women.

They seemed very busy now. Their heads were down, and they did not look up or talk. Their hands moved quickly, stripping the fowls. A few feathers floated. Laid out at their feet in neat rows on newspaper were the bodies that had already been plucked. All still had claws, I saw, but the heads had been twisted off and dropped into the big pile of feathers. Skinny little things, the necks – limp, white-pink, and far too short. I tried, but could not see where the rabbi's razor had made the cut.

I said: 'Dolly is drinking the blood.'

'Dolly,' said the woman I knew.

Rapidly, she said something to the others again, and they all laughed. Hearing a word I understood, I repeated it.

'Inja,' I said. Dog.

The woman I knew smiled at me.

But suddenly, Pa was coming out of the shed again. He took me by the arm and began walking very quickly. I had to run. We went up the back stairs and through the store. It felt wrong, as if we were going backwards. We went in at the back door and round the counter and through the store, and down to the bakkie.

Pa took hold of the steering wheel in both hands.

'Time to get going,' he said.

But he did not move. He sat. My feet sank into the bucket seat. The paint felt sticky, cracked. All the windows were shut.

Pa smacked his head with his open hand, and hissed, and whined, clenching his teeth: 'Chickens! They're just chickens! Use your head.'

He began to knock at his head with his fist. Then he swung the door open and jumped out. Rolling his eyes, he tried to speak, to smile at me, but then he bent over abruptly and vomited.

'It's all right!' he called out at once, his voice hoarse. 'It's all right, Rian!'

But the stink of the vomit came up in waves, acid, hot. Would I have to vomit, too?

Pa spat and wiped his mouth on the back of his wrist. He pointed at the ground.

'You know what that is? It's just . . . I'm unfit, that's all. Unfit. You see, Rian? All I've got in my stomach is coffee. Filthy bloody black coffee.'

Again, he spat. Climbing back into the cab, he rolled the window down and started the engine. But at that moment, Mr Abie appeared on the stoep.

'Your bag,' he called, holding it up.

'Keep it,' said Pa.

'No, no,' said Mr Abie, coming down the stairs. 'I don't need it. But you, you are not well?'

'Me? Never felt better in my life. My apologies to the rabbi.'

'Rabbi Podolski?'

'That's right. My apologies to Rabbi Podolski. Please tell him I'm sorry, but. . . . Feathers. Oh, Jesus. I'm not going to hurl cats again, am I?'

Pa called vomiting hurling cats.

'A teaspoon of bicarb in water, perhaps?' suggested Mr Abie. 'It's the best thing, you know. Helps me, whenever I have a bilious attack.'

'One for the road?' said Pa. 'No. No, thanks.'

Mr Abie came closer. Leaning in at the window, he spoke very quietly to Pa.

'You know, I do not think it is wise.'

Pa looked up at him with wet, red eyes, and smiled.

'Mr Abrahams,' he replied, 'fuck off. I like you. I respect you. Don't get me wrong. But in this case, I know what I am doing.' He gunned the engine again, and said with a loose grin. 'This bakkie is as good as a rocket.'

'So I have heard.' Mr Abie was holding on to the door. 'What about the boy?'

'He's coming with me.'

'Is that a good thing?'

'Can you tell me what might be better?'

Mr Abie raised his brows. The skullcap shifted on top of his head. But he said nothing.

'Thanks for the pennies,' said Pa.

He let slip the handbrake, and tore up dust in a wheel spin, pulling away with a jerk.

When I looked back, I saw that Mr Abie was still standing where we had left him. He did not wave. He was staring at the ground, while all around him the dust was beginning to settle. The bag hung over his arm, and his face looked very white.

3

BLINKING IN THE SUN, more than half asleep, Oupa Gert van Dyk of Oude Hoop sat in his chair on the stoep. He looked as if he had been waiting for us all morning. His hands, folded together over the handle of his thick bamboo cane, were like fat bald puppies. His braces, dangling unhitched – maroon braces with black rosettes, I remember – were shriveled like fried bacon, while his paunch hung down in a bulge so huge that he had no choice, it seemed, but to sit with his knees wide apart. On one knee lay his hat, neatly brushed (no spots). On the other, his false teeth, wet and shiny, newly plucked from his mouth, and still trailing saliva. Here we are, the teeth seemed to say. And who are you?

Licking his lips, Oupa Gert leaned forward, his eye on Pa.

'Ja, neef,' he lisped. Nephew. A boer might pretend that you were part of the family, even if, like Pa, you were not.

Pa took off his hat.

'Oupa is well?'

The old man shifted his stumpy stick.

'Ag, ja, you know how it is. . . . Old age. Hot in the sun. Cold in the shade.'

Pa's reply seemed to stick in his throat.

'Hot!' he cried, or choked. 'Cold!'

He tried to strangle the laughter that started to trickle, to spurt out of his nose. (Was he going to vomit again?) But all he could do was stagger round weakly, whacking at his knees with his hat.

Oupa Gert sat back. Turning his eyes to the winter garden, he seemed to grow very remote. Whatever Pa was doing was of little or no interest to him, it seemed. But suddenly, even he, Oupa Gert, couldn't help being tickled. His mouth dropped open in a wide-split grin.

'Hee hee!' he said, clapping his hands.

I thought of a frog.

Pa was still staggering, crying out:

'Hot! Cold!'

I put down my bucket.

At the end of the driveway, I knew, stood the white cement lady. From the lip of the vase on her shoulder spilled a trickle of water, catching the light. Even now, in winter, the water lilies in the pond were in bloom, their spiky white crowns floating, delicate. How could my goldfish breathe, I wondered, hanging around in the dark among all those slimy, furred stalks, waiting?

'Pa.'

But Pa, who was still dancing, made a hard slicing motion at me with one hand. I knew what it meant. Shut up.

The first to stop laughing was Oupa Gert. Leaning forward again, his mouth set in a thin hard line, he pressed down heavily on his cane.

'To what,' he said deliberately. 'To what do we owe the honor of this visit?'

'Owe?' said Pa, abandoning the shuffle. 'Owe, Oupa? No! God knows, Oupa Gert van Dyk of Oude Hoop owes no man. No, not a penny.'

Oupa Gert shifted his stick again, and began drawing something (a circle?) on the red cement stoep.

'Ja, Oupa.' Pa stood very upright, holding his hat to his bosom as in token of respect. 'If you ask me, Oupa, I will tell you straight: 'It is not Oupa who owes us, but we who owe Oupa.' The first, the worst culprit is me, I know. But then there is the next man and the next, and so on and on, until all of us in the world around here could stand in one long line and cry: 'We are all, all up to the ears in debt to Gert van Dyk.' Ja, Oupa,' said Pa, as if Oupa Gert had agreed, though the old man glared and said nothing. 'I am the first and the worst, I know. But tell me, Oupa, what would Oupa say if I said to him now, and to his face: 'A man, to be a man, must take no shit'?'

'What,' said Oupa Gert, measuring his words slowly. 'What is this you are saying, neef?'

'No, nothing, Oupa. Only what Oupa has heard.'

There was a long silence.

'You know,' said Oupa Gert at last, and his eyes on Pa were a very fierce blue. 'You know, neef, I know you. I have known you now for many years. I knew your wife, the late Annie. I know your child, this little boy. We have ridden together in my motor car, you and I and this child, now and then. Still, you know, sometimes, when I look at you as I do now, it seems to me that I don't know you. Ja-nee, Tok Erasmus, after all these years, I don't know you. And then, you know, I begin to wonder.'

'Ag, ja, Oupa. As the Bible says, it is given to man to wonder. But in this case, there is no great need. After all, all I am saying is this: It is up to a man to pay his debts. A man must pay his respects to God and his neighbor. Fear God. Love thy neighbor. And so on. But in the end, a man must also look out for himself. Is that not so, Oupa? In the end, he must take care not to sink too deep in the shit, or else the worms, the fat white ones with the pointy noses – you know them,

Oupa? – will find him out. And then, as the Bible says, 'It is finished.' Ja, Oupa. That's the story. Today, I am here to pay you,' said Pa, putting his hand into his pocket, 'a pretty penny.' (You could hear the clink.) 'It is true, Oupa.'

Oupa Gert sat back as if to think. With one hand, he groped around until he found his false teeth. Fumbling, he slotted them into his mouth, though his jaws kept working even after his gums got a grip. Then he picked up his hat and put it on. Stretching his braces, he fixed the clips to his trousers. Then, hanging on to his cane with both hands, he came toiling to his feet.

'Oupa's back. . . ?' said Pa.

'My back,' replied Oupa Gert grimly. 'My back, neef, does not bear speaking about. Crystal!' he called, opening the door. 'Crystal, where are you?'

Just inside the front door at Oude Hoop stood an elephant's foot. Wrinkled like a tree trunk, hollow as a pot, it held a bunch of bamboo canes – Oupa Gert's spares – all leaning to one side, and ganging up, as it were, on a single, tightly furled, English umbrella. Somewhere deeper in the house, I knew, hung the head of a buffalo. Massive, bulky, black and hairy, its blunt muzzle raised, its heavy horns swept back, the buffalo's head seemed to listen, stock-still forever.

Who had shot it, I wondered. Oupa Gert?

I put my bucket down again.

At that moment the pebbled glass sliding doors beside us creaked and rolled back, clashing, flashing light – and Crystal le Roux stepped into the hallway. I remember her wide dark eyes, almost too wide, pained, her rich red lipstick, and her way of looking surprised.

'Hai, Tok, man! What cloud did you drop from? How come we never see you any more here at Oude Hoop?'

'Crystal,' said Pa, and didn't know in which hand to hold his hat.

Oupa Gert showed a row of regular, perfect teeth in a little grin.

'Coffee, Crystal. The man tells me he has got money in his pocket.'

'In fact,' said Pa, putting his hand into his pocket again, 'I am here to make a proposal.'

'Right away, Oupa,' said Crystal. 'Coffee. But ooh! I don't believe it! Who, tell me, Tok, who is this young man? Can it be you, Adrian Erasmus? Ag, my little boyfriend! How you have grown! Come, quick, and give your tannie Crystal a kiss.'

She stooped. Her lips were cool and soft, her eyes large and dark and shining. Close up, she smelled like my mother's face powder in the cut-glass bowl on the dressing table at home. I thought, too, of the bright water trickling from the cement lady's vase, and of the water lilies in the pond.

With a laugh, Crystal picked me up, swung me round and settled me on her hip. I could feel how slender she was, and how strong.

'Come with me to the kitchen, young man. You are my young man, aren't you, Rian? We've got lots to talk about, don't you think?'

'My bucket!'

'Oh, your bucket we won't leave behind!'

And she stooped gracefully to pick it up.

Unlike our kitchen at Magnet Heights, Crystal le Roux's at Oude Hoop was open and clean and full of light. (Ja, said Pa. Like a shop window. And Crystal, he said, is like the dressed-up dummy in the window.) An American kitchen, Crystal called it. A home improvement. Oupa Gert, she said, had hired Bult Kloppers, the building contractor from Pietersburg, to do the job. First, Bult and his boys had pulled off all that rotten old thatch with its dirt and spider webs and birds' nests, and put in its place a smart new set of tiles. Waterproof. Imported. Then they had remodeled the kitchen from scratch. Now, see, said Crystal, I've got a proper oven, and I can even bake a cake if I like. Also, we don't have to be afraid any more of every flash of lightning, or that the house will catch fire in our sleep. (Ja-nee, said Pa. Lightning. Isn't it a wonder what a fear of lightning will do for a fat old boer with too much money, once his wife is safely in her grave and his pretty young niece – his wife's brother's daughter – has come to keep house?) As for me, I liked the kitchen. You could run from one end of it to the other. Crystal said you could.

Today, though, I didn't run. I sat at the table and had my biscuits and milk. Beside me stood Crystal, grinding coffee in a little wooden contraption.

'What is that thing, tannie?'

'Hai, Rian! Don't tell me you've never seen . . . ? It's a coffee machine.'

The air was full of the rich bitter flavor of ground coffee.

A young black woman in a white uniform worked in the kitchen, too. She worked very quietly, laying out the cups, arranging the tray, while Crystal paid attention to me.

'Now, tell me, Rian. Why are you here, you and your Pa?'

'To visit, tannie Crystal. Today is the day, says Pa.'

'Oh, yes?' She concentrated a little, grinding the coffee. 'Why? What is so special about today?'

I dipped a biscuit and took a mouthful.

'Today we are going to Durban.'

'Durban? Why Durban?'

'To see the disappearing ships.'

'The what?' Crystal wrinkled up her nose when she laughed.

'The ships. You look up and they're there, says Pa. You look up again, and they're gone.'

'Oh, really? Where do they go?'

'I don't know.'

'What does your Pa say?'

'He says he'll lend me the binoculars, and I can look.'

'You'll look? Is that all you will do in Durban, then, you and your Pa? Just look?'

'No, tannie! In Durban, Pa says, you can have the time of your life. We'll swim in the sea, and lie on the beach, and listen to all the stations on the transistor radio. We'll have our own umbrella, too. With stripes.'

'Oh, yes, the stripes are important.'

'And one day, too, maybe, we'll get our picture taken.'

'Really? Will you send me one?'

'If tannie wants. What you do when you go to Harry's Holiday Snapshots, says Pa, is put your head through a board, and smile, and – snap! Out you come. Different things.'

'Like what?'

'Old King Cole. The Astronaut. The Bubble of a Snowman.'

'Hmm, yes, I can just see your Pa. I won't say as what.'

'Yes, tannie. And on the beach this lady in a bikini comes and makes candy floss in a washing machine.'

'In a what?' Crystal wrinkled her nose.

'A washing machine. The candy floss is pink like clouds, says Pa. You taste it, he says, and it's gone.'

'Pa says, Pa says,' she teased. 'What else does Pa say?'

'He's going to buy me a blow-up surfboard.'

'Lucky you! Do you know how to ride it?'

'Not yet. But it's easy. The waves do all the work.'

'Oh, yes? Is that also what Pa says?' Crystal tipped the ground coffee into a tall silver percolator, and shut the glass lid. 'And what else does Pa say?'

'Well, we are going to go and find Oupa Gert's burst oranges.'

'Oupa Gert's what?' Crystal cried, and laughed so hard that tears sprang into her eyes. 'Where will you look?'

'All over. On Durban beach you can walk forever.'

Crystal picked me up out of the chair and made me stand on the table.

'Tell me more,' she said.

'There isn't any more.'

'Oh, yes, there is!'

Drawing me close, she wrapped me in her arms, and pressed her lips to my ear.

'Mmm,' she said, and her lips parted (I felt them) and she slipped her tongue, warm and wet, into my ear.

I pushed away, rubbing my ear against my shoulder.

'Ag, no, tannie! It tickles!'

Crystal was laughing. You could see the laughter rippling, throbbing in her throat.

'My little man,' she murmured.

I looked into her eyes. I couldn't help it.

'I know,' she said softly. 'I know. Now, tell me, little Adrian. Two goldfish, is it? Or three?'

Too excited to speak, I nodded.

'Okay – three!' agreed Crystal, nodding, too, and smiling. To the black woman she said: 'Go and call Stompie.'[1]

Drying her hands on a towel, the woman went to the back door.

'Stompie!' she cried. 'Stompie, wena!' You, Stompie.

'Now, little Adrian,' whispered Crystal. 'Quick! Jump. Go and get your bucket.'

---

1. *Stompie*, cigarette butt

THE WHITE CEMENT LADY HAD NO FEET. Where her feet should have been, there was only a cement block. In a tangle around the block lay piled the water lilies that Stompie had dragged there with a garden rake. He had scooped up pond water in my bucket, too, and placed it beside the block.

Stompie was a very short black man with a face at once so heavy and so lined that you couldn't tell whether he was smiling or scowling. He stood, now, holding up the net – a long pole with chicken wire sagging between V-shaped prongs at the top – and looked down into the pond, which rocked and glinted in the sun.

If you looked down deep, you could see the goldfish.

'That one! There! Catch that one, Stompie!'

I pointed.

A red goldfish, not a bronze. Cutting away from the rest, it crossed the pond to hang poised as if questioning – gills going open and shut, fins gently waving – so close that you could almost have reached down and caught it in your hands.

'Him, Stompie, him!'

Stompie swung the long pole. Dipped it. But it was too long: he had to change his grip.

With a flick my goldfish was gone.

'Now, what?' I cried.

Stompie only frowned, or smiled, harder, and swept the net round slowly under-water. But all the many goldfish seemed only too easily able to lift, drift out of the way. Stompie stopped and stood still. Clearing his throat, he spat. The white clot of phlegm went dancing on the waters. As we watched, a fish or two came up to nibble at it, but not my red goldfish.

At the back door, Crystal had said:

'You hear what I am saying, hey, Stompie?'

'Miesies.'

'Three little fishes, okay? First, you put so much water in the bucket.' Using her hands, she showed him how much. 'Then, you put the fishes. Now,' she said. 'Tell me. What do you have to do?'

Stompie's face bunched up in a scowl (or a grin) and he replied, making the gesture of adding a fish to the bucket each time:

'One fish. One fish. One fish.'

'Good,' said Crystal. 'The bucket belongs to this small baas, baas Rian. You look after the bucket. You look after the small baas. Okay, Stompie?'

'Miesies.'

He had carried my bucket, which clanked because he limped – one leg was shorter than the other – all the way to the pond. At the rainwater tank round the back of the house we'd picked up the net. It was not meant for fishing, I saw, only for skimming fallen leaves from the water in the tank. Then he had led me through the garage where Oupa Gert's Mercedes, the sleeping tiger, gleamed in the half dark, and took up most of the space, and gave off a scent of expensive car polish.

Stompie was concentrating hard, now. His face was like iron, and furrowed. To me he did not say a word. Again, he swept the net round slowly underwater. The goldfish were skittish, and fled, but he tried to strike, anyway – leaning down on the pole at the same time, somehow, as heaving it up – and the net sprang from the waters dripping, empty.

In the meantime, my red goldfish had reappeared.

I pointed.

'Him, Stompie! Can't you catch him?'

Stompie ignored me. Swinging the net round, he dropped it back into the pond, aiming for a handful of goldfish which scattered at the splash. Next, he simply let the net rest on its prongs at the bottom of the pond, while he himself stood sullenly, or perhaps patiently, waiting.

You could hear the water trickling from the lip of the cement lady's vase. The sun cast a net of its own into the waters, wavering light through which, here and there, the odd goldfish passed with a glint. At the far end of the pond, most of the goldfish gathered together and lay low, as if slowly lapsing into a dream.

Only when all was at peace did Stompie again begin to move. Step by step, leaning first on this prong, then on that, he stalked the goldfish. They did not appear to notice, even when he edged, eased the net right under them.

As for me, I couldn't take my eyes off my red goldfish. A little apart from the others, it too stayed where it was. Suddenly, one or two fish shot away. The red goldfish hesitated for a beat of its fins. Beside me, Stompie braced himself.

'Him, him,' I murmured, prayed. Held my breath.

With a thrashing sound, the net came tearing from the waters – but this time, a single goldfish was flipping, twisting on the chicken wire.

'Yes!' I yelled. 'Yes, Stompie!'

I ran to look in the bucket – though I knew already, for I had seen when he turned on his heel to deliver the fish. A bronze goldfish was going round and round in a wild dash. As I watched, it slowed down and began to tread water, though not for a moment did it cease prodding at the bucket's sides. I thought of the sugar spoon at Magnet Heights. Once silver, the spoon had been licked so often that the underlying metal shone through, a sharp bronze. Teaspoon, I thought. Could a goldfish be called Teaspoon?

'Pasop!' grunted Stompie. His first word to me. Watch out.

The net swung up right at my face – I had not heard him strike – rusty chicken wire, the v-shaped iron prongs, and no fewer than two fish spun, flopped, dropped with a splash down into the bucket.

I couldn't believe my eyes.

'You got him! You got the red one, Stompie!'

Stompie was grinning, now, and no mistake. He held up three fingers. So did I.

'Yes!' I cried, elated. 'Yes, Stompie!'

My own now, the goldfish in the bucket went racing round, striving to get over and under one another, churning up the water. To me, they were a wonder, perfect, a miracle – bright bronze upon bronze, and red gold.

'Thank you, Stompie! Thank you, thank you!'

Still smiling, he half-raised a hand. Then he turned back to work. Slowly, he gathered up the water lily pads, and began to float them one by one upon the water, while I took the bucket by the handle and set out, staggering under the weight.

The water tipped and slopped.

The most difficult part was the stairs up to the stoep where Oupa Gert had sat. But I managed not to spill a drop when at last I placed my bucket beside the elephant's foot on the polished parquet floor.

'Pa!' I called.

There was no reply. The pebbled glass sliding doors stood wide, and I ventured further.

Somewhere, I could hear a murmur of voices.

'Pa?'

They were sitting together – Pa, Crystal and Oupa Gert – under the gaze of the buffalo's head. Noticing me in the doorway, Crystal put a finger to her lips, and rolled her eyes in a glance that I was meant to follow.

To one side, in an armchair, sat Oupa Gert. He had on a pair of big tortoise shell glasses, and was sorting through a tin box full of papers. (I had not seen it before, the box, but I knew it at once. Pa called it the Strongbox. Half of the Ysterberg, said Pa, was locked up in that box. A man might kill, he said, for what was kept locked up in that box.) Oupa Gert sat looking at me over his glasses, but his mind was still on his papers, you could see. His lips were moving, busy doing sums.

Opposite him, also in an armchair, sat Pa. He sat leaning back, his arms and legs spread wide, his hat completely covering his face. He did not move at all.

Crystal beckoned me to her.

'Come, little Adrian, come. Stand next to me.'

I went, looking back at Pa.

'What's wrong, tannie Crystal?'

'Wrong?' she asked as if highly entertained. 'No, nothing is wrong. Children should be seen and not heard, that's all.' Smoothing back my hair, she gave me a little kiss on the forehead, adding, under her breath: 'Did you get your goldfish?'

'Oh, yes!' I said. Loudly. I wanted Pa to hear. 'Three goldfish, tannie, just like tannie said. I've got them in my bucket at the front door. Does tannie not want to come and see?'

She touched a finger to my lips to seal them.

'Not now.'

Oupa Gert was looking at me sharply over his glasses.

'What is this?'

'No, nothing, Oupa,' replied Crystal. 'Oupa must do what Oupa is doing, not worry his head over the child. Let me look after him. He is excited, that's all. He has just come back from a visit to the fishpond, and he wants to tell us all about it. But he can't. Not now. Okay, Rian? Quietly, quietly. Can't you see Oupa Gert is busy?'

I could. I stood a little closer to Crystal.

Ice in winter, Pa had said.

Oupa Gert gathered another few papers from the Strongbox, and began to examine them. He took a pencil from behind his ear, and made a note.

'Thirteen thousand,' he remarked, 'and still counting. As you can see, neef, we are not yet quite at the bottom of things. One or two bills might still be waiting down there, you never know.'

Pa did not move.

Oupa Gert continued to spread and read the remaining papers, one by one.

From under his hat Pa remarked:

'Durban beach.'

'Oh, yes?' said Crystal, raising a dainty coffee cup to her lips. 'I hear from Rian, Tok, that you are leaving today for Durban.'

Pa stretched out his limbs even wider, and let them flop.

'This is it. Durban beach.'

Crystal wrinkled her nose in a little laugh.

'Ag, Tok! You and your jokes.'

And she sipped at her coffee.

Oupa Gert picked up a piece of paper and waved it.

'You see? What did I tell you?'

'What?' asked Pa from under his hat.

'Five hundred Rand, cash advance, January the seventh, last year – that's what.'

Pa said nothing. He did not move.

'I knew there was still something,' Oupa Gert went on smugly. 'It's a good thing I got you to sign that day, isn't it? Otherwise, where would we be, now? Sign on the dotted line, I said. Ja, you can't catch the old crocodile sleeping on his own lump of mud. Now,' he remarked, turning back to toting up the figures: 'How much does it all come to, plus interest?'

Pa let the hat slip down from his face. His eyes, I saw, were wide and staring, as if they had been open all the time under the hat. Without a word, he turned his eyes upon Crystal. He seemed somehow to be begging, pleading. I had not seen him look like that before.

Crystal, however, seemed simply not to notice.

'More coffee, Tok?' she said, and when he did not reply: 'Is that yes or no?'

Pulling himself together so quickly that his hat rolled off his chest and dropped to the floor, Pa said:

'It's yes! Yes, please, Crystal.'

And he held out the tiny coffee cup.

Let's go, Pa, I wanted to say. Let's get my bucket and go. If this is Durban beach, I don't want to stay. I want to go back to the paradise for snakes, the cemetery for cars. I want to climb the ladder under the windmill, and pour my goldfish into the water tank. Now, Pa. Come. Let's go.

After calmly refilling his cup, Crystal set the percolator back on the coffee table.

Pa shut his eyes as he drank.

'So good,' he said, and smacked his lips.

Above us hung the buffalo's head, grim, silent, filling the room with its present absence, its death. I did not have the words for it then that I have now, but to me it was sublime, that head – forbidding, dark like thunder, with wide unblinking eyes. And yet it was only dust. Dust, skull bones, horns, tanned hide, glass eyes, bits of wire. Just as words are only words. Sounds in the air. Marks on paper.

Oupa Gert spanked the tin box shut.

'Grand total, including interest owed,' he announced: 'Fourteen thousand, six hundred and fifty-two Rand and twenty-three cents.'

'Is that all?' said Pa.

'All?' The old man stared. 'Is it not enough?'

Pa smiled a fixed smile.

'No, Oupa.'

The old man cupped a hand behind his ear.

'What's this?'

'Ja,' replied Pa, 'Oupa heard right. I said it is not enough.'

Oupa Gert looked from Crystal to me, as for help. Then he looked back at Pa.

'In all my years of helping my neighbor,' he said slowly, emphatically. 'In all my years of lending a Rand or two here and there, and helping where I could, I have never, neef – never – heard a man complain before that his debt with me was not enough!'

'Ja, Oupa. In fact, from what I hear, our debt with you is always too much.'

'Too much? What is this you are saying, now? Here.' Oupa Gert thrust a few pages at him. 'Take your time. Check for yourself.'

'Ag, no, Oupa. I do not dispute Oupa's arithmetic.'

'What, then?'

Pa sat studying the tattoo on his forearm, smiling.

'You know, Oupa, it's a funny thing. Chop off a chicken's head, and at first it cannot believe it is dead. We have all seen it happen. Here, at your feet, lies the head with its comb, beak open in the dirt. And there, without a head, the chicken goes jerking, jumping, flopping around, holding up its wings, and trying to run – as if it would still get away from you if it could. While the blood squirts.'

'Of course, ja. Well?'

'Well, as Oupa knows – as I was explaining just a few minutes ago – on my way here today I stopped off to see Mr Abie Abrahams.'

'The Jew?'

'Correct. And as I was saying, today is the day the rabbi comes to cut the throats of the chickens.'

'I see. Get to the point, neef.'

'It is a curious custom, Oupa. Oupa should go one day and see for himself. He is dressed all in black, the rabbi, with his little flat hat, the size of your palm, on top of his head. All around him, the chickens go hysterical, and the feathers fly. 'Adonai! Adonai!' he says (the name of God). He blesses them, the rabbi, one by one. Then he cuts their throats. He uses a strop razor, not an axe. Ja, Oupa. I saw him today – Rabbi Podolski from Pietersburg. Just as I see you.'

'You and I, neef,' observed Oupa Gert after a silence. 'You and I, we are not Jews.'

'Still, Oupa. You know – if I look at you now, I see Rabbi Podolski.'

With a shrug Oupa Gert held out both hands.

'How so?'

Pa braced himself.

'I mean,' he said, and shook his head. 'I mean. . . .'

Slowly, he began to arch, to lift over backwards in his chair. He tried squeezing, pinching at his eyes – but no matter how hard he tried, he could not stop the laughter from leaking, as it were, between his fingers.

'I can't,' he protested. 'Look, Oupa. Look!'

Slipping out of the chair, he squatted on his heels. He put his hands on his hips, arms akimbo, and began to wag his elbows back and forth.

'Puk, puk, pu-uk!'

Then he went hopping round the coffee table, clucking all the way.

Crystal couldn't help it – she put her hands over her nose, and swayed back and forth, gurgling, shrieking almost, with laughter.

Pa hopped right up to her and cocked his head.

'Puk, puk!' he said. 'Chop?'

'No,' said Crystal, her eyes gleaming, welling with tears. 'Enough, now, Tok.'

'Puk-puk! Puk, pu-uk!'

Pa wagged his elbows. Hopped.

'Didn't you hear my niece say no?' demanded Oupa Gert. 'Enough!'

'Please, Tok,' urged Crystal softly.

But Pa only stuck out his chest, and flapped his wings even faster, and went hopping round the table again, back to his chair. Once there, he picked up his hat, and stood straight.

'Puk, pu-uk!' he said. 'My head.'

And put on the hat.

'Ag, Tok!' sighed Crystal, while the giggles still caught in her throat.

'Sit down, neef,' said Oupa Gert sternly, pointing. 'Sit down at once and behave again like a respectable human being.'

'Of course,' said Pa. 'Enough is enough. Not so, Oupa?'

'Or too much,' retorted the old man.

Far from sitting down, however, Pa stood rocking back and forth on his heels. He put both hands in his pockets and leaned back, and looked down at Oupa Gert.

'Ja, Oupa. Don't forget I've still got a proposal to make. But first things first, I agree. After all, there remains between us at this moment still the small matter of the money.'

'My money, yes. Well? I am waiting.'

'If Oupa lends a penny,' said Pa, digging into a pocket, 'then it stands to reason, does it not, that a man must return a penny?'

Out of his pocket he drew the pennies. He counted out three equal little piles, and placed the pennies neatly upon the coffee table beside the silver percolator.

Oupa Gert stared.

'What is this?' he asked, breathing heavily, his cheeks quivering. 'Another joke?'

'It is what they call a token payment, Oupa. Oupa says I owe – what is it, again – fourteen, fourteen and a half thousand Rand? I say no. It is not enough. Let me pay you fifteen, Oupa. Fifteen pennies.'

'A 'token payment'?' the old man repeated, mystified.

'Ja, Oupa.'

Oupa Gert continued to breathe heavily, and to stare.

'Tell me,' he said at last. 'Tell me, neef. What makes you think I will accept?'

'Well, as I was saying, Oupa ... Mr Abie says no, it is a bad idea, but I think not. You see, Oupa, I am full of hope. I woke up this morning, and I thought, 'Why not?' I got up and said, 'Today is the day.' I woke Rian, and I said, 'Come, child. Today is the day.' And I brought with me my token, my pennies. Which Oupa will accept, I think, as soon as I am properly part of the family.'

'Say again, neef?'

'Ja, Oupa. I hope soon to be Oupa's neef, his nephew, for real. Or, more precisely, his nephew-in-law.'

Crystal stiffened in fear.

'No, Tok!' she whispered.

'Go on,' prompted Oupa Gert.

'Ja, Oupa. Well, as Oupa can see, I am here to ask for the hand of Oupa's niece, Crystal le Roux, in marriage.'

Oupa Gert first opened his mouth, then shut it tight. You could hear his false teeth click. Then he tried to get up out of his armchair, but could not (perhaps his back prevented him). In the end, clutching his cane, he took a swing at the pennies, smashing into them, but also knocking over the tall silver percolator, which flung hot coffee around as it toppled.

'Over my dead body,' he swore, half-choking. 'Over my dead and stinking corpse.'

'That,' said Pa, stepping forward, 'may not be too difficult to arrange.'

Leaning down, he laid hold of the table by its short, squat legs, and, in a single movement, raised it high above his head.

'Don't!' screamed Crystal.

You could see the underside of the table – the bare, unvarnished wood. You could see the shadow flung upwards on the ceiling, like the shadow in the kitchen that morning. Or, it seemed to me now, like an axe.

'Crystal!' cried Pa. His eyes were very wide and dark.

'No, Tok,' replied Crystal. 'I'd never marry you. Never. Not if you were the last man on earth. Where did you get the idea?'

'That's my girl!' cried Oupa Gert, thumping his cane up and down on the carpet. 'That's my girl! My Crystal!'

'Your' girl?' said Pa, shifting his muscles in order to raise the table a fraction higher.

'Of course,' replied Oupa Gert. 'What did you think?'

Pa did not reply.

But the old man, looking up at him, seemed for the first time really to see.

With an exclamation, he began kicking, struggling, in an attempt to get the armchair to roll backwards. Upended as his knees convulsed, the Strongbox pitched to the floor with a crash.

I put my fingers into my mouth, but the sounds in my throat would not stop.

'Oupa! Tok!' cried Crystal. 'Stop it! Stop it at once! Can't you see you are frightening the child?' She tried to pull me on to her lap, but my legs were too long, somehow. And I wouldn't be pulled. 'Shh,' she said. 'It's all right, little Adrian.'

'Shut up, Rian,' said Pa.

Crystal placed her arms round my shoulders to protect me, or restrain me.

'Quietly, quietly, little big boy,' she whispered. To Pa she said: 'And you, Tok? What do you think you are? The furniture removals man? Put down the table.'

'Crystal – please! Listen.'

'No, not another word. First, the table, Tok.'

For a moment longer, Pa stood towering. Then he let go, dropping the table, but catching it again before it struck the floor. With a show of great skill he placed it on its feet exactly where it had stood before.

'Good,' said Crystal. 'What took you so long?'

'Crystal!' begged Pa, more desperately yet, it seemed. 'Marry me.'

For a little longer she sat looking at him. Then she lowered her eyes.

'You heard what Oupa Gert said. It is true.'

'Do you mean I have no hope?'

'Ag, hope!' said Crystal, and twisted her mouth in an ugly way.

There was a silence.

Nobody moved except Oupa Gert. Reaching out with his cane upside down, he hooked the Strongbox by the handle and hoisted it into the air, letting it dangle, if a little shakily, before dropping it flat on to the coffee table. Then he sat back again, folded his hands over the top of his cane, and pursed his lips.

You could hear the ticking of the clock on the mantelpiece.

I had not yet taken my fingers out of my mouth. In my throat there was a stiffness, a tightness, as of screaming, though the sounds had long since disappeared.

Oupa Gert sighed, and sat staring. He stuck a thumb up against the roof of his mouth, and began to push and twist at his false teeth – which popped out all at once, and lay, wet and glistening, in his palm.

'S'much better,' he mumbled, and leaned forward, placing the teeth on the lid of the Strongbox.

Where they squatted, rigid, facing him.

'Oupa's watchdog?' said Pa.

Smiling fatly, all gums and spittle, Oupa Gert simply repeated down to the last cent the sum Pa owed.

'Is that a lot?' he lisped, licking his lips. 'Or a little?'

'A lot,' Pa admitted.

'Good. We agree, then. You may expect to hear from my lawyer shortly.'

As if deaf to him, Pa put out a hand to me.

'Rian, come. Time to go.'

'Oh, no,' interjected Crystal. 'You are not going anywhere, Tok. Not until you do some explaining. But, Oupa – Oupa is all right?'

For the old man had at last succeeded, it seemed, in struggling to his feet. With the embrace of the armchair behind him, he stood stooped, bent over. Clinging to his cane with one hand, he waved the other.

'Get out.'

'Did Oupa not hear?' said Pa. 'Crystal told me to wait.'

The old man took a step round the table towards him.

'Get out.'

Raising his cane, he tried to prod Pa in the chest, but Pa knocked the cane aside, and when the old man tried again, twisted it out of his grip. For a moment,

Oupa Gert stood staring down at his empty hands as if he could not believe. Then he turned and headed for the door, moving in a slow and painful shuffle, wheezing and muttering.

'I will be back,' he warned us all, rolling his eyes.

Crystal waited until Oupa Gert had left the room, and then she said:

'What in the world is going on with you, Tok?'

'With me? No, nothing. Why, what should be going on?'

'I mean it, Tok. Tell me. I want to know.'

'No, Crystal, if you still don't know, go and look in the mirror.'

'You never said a word – not a word – to me before.'

'Did I have a chance? You know how it is, don't you? If I look into your eyes, I am gone.'

'Gone?'

'Drowned, ja. Finished and klaar. I feel light in my head, and I go round and round singing songs like you hear on the radio.'

'Ag, Tok.'

'Then, when I'm back at Magnet Heights, I knock my head with my fist, and say: 'You're better off without her. Can't you see? Forget her, man. Forget her.' But it's no good. The nights are cold, the days are long.'

'Why didn't you speak? It's not so impossible, you know.'

'How? Just tell me.'

'Well, first you could talk about this and that. Your broken cars' business, for instance. I would listen. 'Really?' I would say, and: 'Is that so?' Then, once you saw you weren't 'gone', you could go on. You could talk, say, about the drought. The dust. Holes in the roof. How the hens are not laying. And so on.'

'You're right, those hens – good only for the pot! And as for the cock.' Pa put his hands on his hips, arms akimbo. 'Puk, puk!'

'Oh, no! Not again. Don't start. But you did make me laugh.'

And she laughed again – a little nervously, but a rippling laugh.

'Leave him,' begged Pa. 'Leave the fat old ballie. Today, now, at once. Walk out. You can do it. Why wait? Come with me now, home to Magnet Heights.'

'Now?' she said, sitting back and folding her arms. 'Right now?' She smiled, and rocked, tapping one foot. 'Tell me, Tok. Did you come here today to pick a fight?'

'Go and ask your old Oupa that question, not me. After all, who started it? Him or me?'

'He didn't come here today, Tok. You did.'

'And what did I do? You saw. Here I stood, my hat in my hand, my child by my side. 'Oupa,' I said, 'forgive me my debts, Oupa, as you one day too may be forgiven Finished and klaar – finished and done with yours.' And what did he do? He opened up the Strongbox. No, Crystal. The man is a stone. He feels nothing for his own people. Look at him. Look how he walks – one foot in the grave – but will he stop? No, not until he has got the whole of the Ysterberg in his pocket. Why? Because he wants to pull us all down with him when he goes. I ask you: Is it right? Is it right that a man like him should be sitting on me, on my head? That is why, as soon as he started his nonsense today, I said: 'You see, Oupa? This is what happens when a stone meets an iron fist.'

'I see,' said Crystal briefly. 'You did not come for me. You came for yourself.'

'No, no – for you, I came for you. You know what I hoped.'

'Yes, yes, I know. Be quiet, now, Tok.' As if distracted, she sat staring at the carpet. 'Just look at this mess. Coffee, beskuit, all over the place.'

'Don't worry, if he does his share, I will do mine. As soon as he comes back, we'll clean it up.'

'Oh, no, you won't. What do you think there are servants for?'

'Well – do you want Rian to run and call someone from the kitchen?'

'No, thank you. I know when to do what in this house. Stay where you are, little Rian. Don't move. Now, tell me, Tok. Do you love me?'

'Do you still ask?'

'I do, I do. I want a straight answer, too.'

'My heart is in your hands, Crystal. Look.'

'Is that a straight answer?'

'What do you think?'

Crystal smiled. Tilted her head.

'I think you are a schemer, Tok. I think you are in love with nothing so much as your own lies.'

Shaken, Pa stepped back and wiped his face with his forearm.

'How can I prove to you you are wrong?'

'You can't. Don't even try. If you do, I won't listen. Oupa Gert said he would be back, remember? And he will.'

'So what? What can he do?'

'You never know,' observed Crystal quietly. 'What if he has gone for his gun?'

'Rian,' said Pa, and caught me by the wrist.

And for the second time that day we were going back very quickly the way we had come.

Crystal kept close behind us.

But Oupa Gert, it seemed, had not gone for his gun.

He was standing just inside the front door, beside the elephant's foot. He had taken out two of the canes – one for his left hand, one for his right – and now stood leaning on both, fascinated, it seemed, by what he could see in the bucket. At our approach he looked up.

'You!' he said, his cheeks shaking, and lifted a cane to point at Pa. 'You! Behind my back!'

'Oupa, no!' cried Crystal, stepping in between. 'It wasn't him. See? It was me.'

'You? This whole bucket full of fish?'

'Me, yes, Oupa. As you can see.'

Oupa Gert shut his mouth grimly. Then, lowering the cane, he dipped it into the bucket, and – holding her gaze with his own, his eyes cold and curious – deliberately overturned the bucket. The water hit the tiles with a broad splash.

My goldfish went flipping and twisting at his feet.

'Oh, no, no! Does Oupa not see?' cried Crystal, distraught. 'I did it for the child. For this child, who has no mother. 'After all,' I said to myself, 'Oupa has so many goldfish – and in his heart he is so good, so kind – he will surely not miss one or two.' And now, look. Look at what Oupa has done.'

'Let's look,' he said, and poked at the fish with the tip of his cane. 'Let's look at what Oupa has done. Let's count. Tell me, little boy. How many fish do you see? One? Two? No, come let's look again. One. Two. Three. Am I right?'

'Half right,' Pa put in. 'Three little fishes, ja. Not a whole bucket full.'

Awkwardly, flat on their sides, my goldfish lay quivering, flipping.

I stood looking at Pa and Oupa Gert. For fear of the sounds' returning, I put the fingers of both hands into my mouth, and held the back of my tongue down hard.

'Tell your Pa, little boy. Tell him it is going to cost him. After all, are these just any old goldfish? Any old goldfish you can go and pull from the bottom of a pond in a bucket? Oh, no, they are not. Not at all. Tell him. Go on. Say: 'What you see here are prize goldfish. From the Rand Show. And they don't come cheap. Not these days. Not at Oude Hoop.' Now, little boy. Watch. Did you ever see a goldfish pop?'

With a fixed little smile he placed the rubber-capped tip of his cane on the belly of one of the fish (my red goldfish – its flat bright eye, its gulping mouth), and pressed down hard. The fish's guts burst out.

'If that is what you do to a prize goldfish,' observed Pa, 'if that is what you do, Oupa, then the question is: What will you do to the real prize?'

'Oh, yes? And what is that, may I ask?'

'No, don't tell me Oupa doesn't know, Oupa. It's Crystal.'

'Crystal? To Crystal,' Oupa Gert smiled again, all gums and spittle. 'To Crystal I do what I like. And,' he added, still smiling, 'I like what I do. It's true. Ask her. Ask, if you don't believe me.'

'I will, Oupa. But wait. Tell me, Oupa – would Oupa himself not like to go pop, perhaps?'

'Tok! Thank you,' said Crystal sharply. 'You've had your say. Go home. Go home at once.'

'You heard the lady,' gloated Oupa Gert, his smile broader, more gleeful than ever. 'The lady you asked to marry. You heard what she said. Go on. Go. Get out.'

We went out the front door and down the steps. Pa walked rapidly up the gravel path, pulling me along.

'A boer makes a plan,' he told me. 'A boer always knows what to do.'

The bakkie was parked not far from the white cement lady. Throwing open the door, Pa reached inside and lifted out the hunting rifle.

'Beautiful thing,' he murmured, running his fingers over the stock. He worked the bolt once, rapidly, to check that the rifle was loaded, and yelled: 'Come out, Gert van Dyk! Bring your gun. I am ready.'

The house remained silent. Nothing moved.

Pa was restless. Leaning back on one heel, he pointed the rifle at the roof of the house and fired, though to no obvious effect.

'Plug it full of holes,' he said and laughed, and swung round, his aim going all over the place.

His next shot broke the vase on the white cement lady's shoulder. The vase exploded, leaving only a few clots of cement sticking to a brass pipe from which the water still trickled. Then he sheared off half of her head with a single bullet, and with the following shot smashed one breast, and knocked away most of that shoulder.

Lowering the rifle, he shouted again for Oupa Gert.

The house remained as silent as before.

'All right, Oupa. You'll see. A man can wait.'

He walked up and down, waiting. Twice more, he put a bullet through the roof. A spurt of red dust flew up each time.

'Bloody wig,' said Pa.

Otherwise, nothing happened.

Still staring at the house, Pa said quietly:

'How about a little joy ride, Rian? Target practice can wait.'

I tried to hang back, but he took me by the hand. All the way to the garage, I walked beside him in terror. What if we bumped into Stompie? What if he was hiding in a corner, or lying curled up under the Mercedes-Benz?

In the end, though, Stompie was nowhere to be seen. Only the great car stood gleaming in the half-dark.

'There's the luck! Keys waiting. Hop in,' said Pa.

The leather of the Mercedes' seats was slippery, cold. I stood breathing through my mouth. For a moment, I seemed again to see my red goldfish – its bright round eye, its gulping mouth. I saw, too, the way its fins had stirred as the broad rubber stopper on the cane burst open its belly. (But I did not cry – neither then nor later.)

'Cream of the cream,' said Pa, backing the Mercedes into the driveway. 'This is class. This is the power, hey, my lightie. Who can beat it? Hundreds of horses under the hood.'

White horses, crowded together, I could almost see. How did they all fit in?

Pa stepped on the accelerator, and the Mercedes picked up speed. We hurtled round the front of the house, and he was still accelerating. Then he braked, skidding so hard that the car dragged into a broadside. Rubber stank, hot and black. You could hear the gravel getting ripped up, but even before we stopped, he had shifted the stick into reverse. Looking over his shoulder, he drove backwards, while the gears moaned in high agony.

'Here we go, now. Hold tight.'

More slowly, and far more carefully, we went rocking backwards across the softness of flowerbeds. Suddenly, the rear wheels dropped away, and the whole front of the car tipped up. The chassis grated on concrete.

'Out! Get out.'

We left the Mercedes just as it was, its rear end half-sunken among the lilies of the fishpond. The white cement lady, newly battered and broken, bullet-pocked, stood as she had before. Water still spouted from the bared brass pipe on her shoulder.

Pa cupped his hands around his mouth.

'Oupa Gert, come out! Come out and look! See your Mercedes swim!'

We waited again, but only to make the point, it seemed, since he never did appear. Pa sat down on the bumper of the bakkie, and began to rub his face with his hands. He looked very tired. He kept the rifle upright, gripped between his knees.

'And you, little Rian?' he said. 'How are you?'

'No, fine, Pa. It's just my throat.'

'Thirsty? Me, too. Tell you what.' He stopped rubbing his face, looked at me through his fingers, and grinned. 'How about we go grab a few of those export oranges? The sweetest, the juiciest you'll ever get, believe me. Better in our bellies, don't you think, than at the bottom of the sea?'

5

It was as though I had been awake for years as I stood next to Pa on the front seat of the bakkie. (In a way, I think, I am standing there still.) We took the back route, the shortcut, across the Oude Hoop lands. I stood with my neck bent, looking out through the dust-streaked windshield. Tree after tree went rocking by. If I looked, I could see, too, in the gaps, how the trees went on and on across the plain in rows, as if forever.

Pa, it seemed, was only too happy. He drummed at the steering wheel with open palms, or gripped it so hard that the bones of his knuckles showed white. He also kept singing out:

'Happy, happy!'

And he kept looking back as if expecting, or daring, someone to come after us. But no one did. The lands were deserted. Even Oupa Gert's orange pickers, who should have been all over the place, were nowhere to be seen. Perhaps (like Stompie?) they had disappeared in reaction to the gunshots.

What we did see, here and there, was a tall bright water sprinkler. Trying to catch sight of the little rainbows at play above the briskly efficient, glittering jets, I looked up each time. But no little rainbows appeared. It seemed that the day was barren, although we were driving hard.

With a grin, Pa reached over and ruffled my hair.

'Looks like I'm going to have to put a brick on your head, Rian. If I don't, you're going to grow right up through the roof. And then where will you be?'

'Me, Pa?'

'You, ja! Of course, you!' Pa laughed aloud. As if in a conspiracy with me, he leaned over and murmured: 'Don't forget the barbel. A whole bakkie-load of barbel, like I promised. Okay? We'll go and dump them in the water tank to breed.'

Blunt barbel mouths breaking the surface to grunt. In the depths of the tank, sinuous black shapes, teeming.

In my belly, the sounds I had swallowed lay like ice.

'Va-room!' yelled Pa, choking on his own laughter.

And veered too close to a tree.

Branches loaded with oranges thrashed, bumped, and went scratching, dragging across the windshield. Still laughing, he tore free of the leaves again, and swung us back on to the bumpy track.

Don't worry, he told me. If anyone was a liar, it was Oupa Gert. Just look at him, the fat old ballie. What could he do all day but sit in the sun and scratch? At his age, and with all his aches and pains, he couldn't get it up, for sure. Not even with a hot cookie like Crystal. His only hope, it seemed, was to use his stick as a stand-in. (For what, Pa? No, little Rian, forget it. One day, maybe, I'll tell you. One day, when your head has gone through the roof.) As for the Rand Show, what did the old ballie think? If he, Pa, had been to the Show once, he had been twenty times – maybe more. At Easter time, he said. It was easy. You paid for your ticket and you walked through the gate. And what did you see? The latest and best in the whole of South Africa, that's what. Imported goods, too, mind you, not only homegrown not-so-goods. Of course, Pa added, no one could claim to have seen every last item, but he for one had seen plenty. Plenty. Prizes? Ag, prizes galore. But never, he said – not once ever – a prize goldfish.

Ja-nee, he sighed. There was no show like the Rand Show. It was high time, he added, for him to go and visit it again. After all, he hadn't been for years. You couldn't help knowing when the Show was on. You could be driving far away, say, at night. And suddenly you would see it . . . the whole sky, full of search-lights. And you knew, without a doubt, that the Show had begun. Once, he told me, he had tracked one of those lights down, and examined it up close, parked where it was on a corner. It was like a big round drum, half as big as a motor car, with little white fires burning inside it, behind plates of glass. Soldiers stood working the searchlight, swinging it round, looking up at the stars.

Ja, said Pa. No doubt about it, the Rand Show was a big thing.

Once, for instance, he had seen this big black bull called Sonop.[1] Smooth-skinned, as black as night, and so huge, so heavy, that his heels cracked the pavement when they led him to drink. It took not one but two big strong kaffirs to lead him, said Pa. Big strong kaffir bastards, the kind who could snap your neck between finger and thumb, but on either side of that bull they walked on tiptoe, each one holding a pole fixed to a ring through his nose. They knew, if all he did was shake a fly from his ear, their poles would go flying, they wouldn't have a chance, and all hell would break loose. He must have weighed well over a ton – Sonop, black Sonop. His eyes were like pools, except for the rims, which were pink like raw meat. From one of his horns hung the ribbon for first prize. When at last he got to the trough, he snorted and groaned and made a sound like a bugle blowing, and then he lowered his head, pulling those two big kaf-firs almost off their feet. Then, once he had drunk all he wanted, he stood for a long while without moving, his mouth still dripping, his nostrils opening and

---

1. *Sonop*, Sunrise

closing. Only when he was ready would he turn and go back to the stall. In the meantime, said Pa, he stood like a mountain.

Your time will come, too, little Rian, don't worry. I'll take you to visit the Show one day soon, you'll see. When, Pa? Ag, no, little boy, man! Don't always ask, When? Mark my words, on the day that we go, we'll visit the pavilion of the Chamber of Mines, where the gold gets poured. What happens is this. First, they take a pot and put a bar of gold in it. Then they let the pot sit inside a furnace for a minute or two, until the gold is like water. Then they pour it into a mould. In the meantime, the Master of Ceremonies talks. He holds a microphone, and talks into it, and shows you slides. This is a reef, he says, and this is gold-bearing ore. This is a stick of dynamite, and this is the fuse. Here is how we do deep-level mining. This is a gang drilling at the rock face. And so on. Until at last, Now, ladies and gentlemen, he says, we are ready. One moment, please. Watch. He gives the mould a knock, first this side and then that, and turns it over, and, clunk! Out falls a clean bar of gold. Better than pennies, hey, Rian? If you can pick it up with one hand, you can keep it, they say. And you, Pa? Did you pick it up? Ag, no, it's only a joke. Nobody can keep it, even if they do. Do you think I'd go and ask old Gert van Dyk to forget what I owe, and give me his Crystal for a bride, and everything, if I had walked out of the Show with a bar of gold in my pocket?

You'd think, Pa went on after a pause – because the Show is so big – if you step inside, you might never come out again. After all, you can walk around for days and days and still not see it all. But you can't get lost, don't worry. Wherever you go, you will see the Tower of Light. It is made of concrete, the Tower of Light, and whitewashed. It stands halfway up the hill, with loudspeakers hanging in a string around the top. What the loudspeakers do is call you back. Look, he said, let me show you how. With a smile he spoke into the hollow of his hands, making a mock-up of the echo: Rian Erasmus! Calling Rian Erasmus! Come at once and meet your father at the Tower of Light.

I laughed. It was almost as though I could see myself climbing the hill to meet him.

'I will, Pa.'

'You will, will you? When?'

I thought about it.

'One day.'

'One day? One day is one day.' Pa threw back his head, and his face went all wrinkled as he laughed, or winced. 'Ja, we know all about that, don't we? And now,' he added, 'it's time for an orange, don't you think?'

We parked just beyond a set of sprinklers. I watched him go stepping quickly from tree to tree, plucking the oranges, which he dropped down into the front of his shirt, giving himself a lumpy belly. Back in the bakkie again, he undid his buttons, and the oranges rolled out.

'Whoa! Too many!' he said.

He did the peeling for us both.

'Valencias, that's their name. Thin skins, you see? But full of juice. Here, try this one.'

Cold, bright, rich with juice. I ate four more oranges. Pa himself, I don't know how many. He threw the peels out of the window. Behind us, we could hear the sprinklers turning with rapid little jerks, as though repeating, 'In a jiffy, in a jiffy...'

'Sticky?' said Pa, examining my fingers. 'Here, look. Do this.'

He held up his hand and licked at his fingers, and I did the same.

'Still not quite right? Never mind. Just wait.'

Far out of our way, at the other end of the plain, lay the Oude Hoop irrigation dam, a long stretch of muddy water held back by a low concrete wall. We drove there now, rattling along, flat out. Dust boiled up in a pillar behind the bakkie and stood like a sign for all to see.

On a slope above the dam we stopped.

Pa rested his head for a few moments against the steering wheel.

'What's right is right,' he observed slowly, his eyes shut. 'Don't you agree?'

'Ja, Pa.'

He opened his eyes again.

'Come. Let's get out.'

He took my hand and led the way along the top of the dam wall, counting his paces aloud. Every twelve paces, a sluice gate – an iron panel the color of mud – stood slotted into the concrete. After two or three such gates, he squatted down on his heels and rinsed his hands in the water.

I did the same.

'You know,' he remarked in a voice so low that at first I thought he was talking to himself, 'I regret only one thing. When I walked out of that room, after Crystal said Oupa Gert had gone for his gun... Did you see? The Strongbox was lying by itself on the table. I could have stopped and turned round and picked it up. And why not? Oupa Gert can't keep straight in his head himself any more all that he keeps in that box. I could have brought it here, and packed it full of stones, and thrown it into the dam. Let it take all our troubles down with it. And not only our own, either. The troubles, too, of every poor, hard-working boer from here to the other side of the Ysterberg. Let them all sink forever. Just think. If old Gert van Dyk can go and dump shiploads of oranges out at sea, and only grow richer, then why can't I come and chuck away one bloody black box full of bad debts?'

Shutting his eyes tight, he knocked at his forehead with his fist. Then he ducked down, scooped up water, and rubbed it around his face and neck.

'Ja,' he said, and sat dripping, his eyes wide open again. 'I ask you. Why not?'

On the way back to the bakkie, he stopped and kicked at the iron pegs that held one of the sluice gates in place.

'Look,' he said, pointing with his toe. 'Here, right here, is an idea. You see? If all these oranges are going to drown, anyway, then why shouldn't we pull up these plates, you and I, and let the waters roll? Why wait for Oupa Gert to do the job? Flood the fruit at the root! That is what I say.'

Squatting down on his heels again, he used both hands. He pulled and jerked, but the pegs were jammed too tight.

'Bring me a stone,' he urged.

But even when I did, and he hammered it at the pegs, they would not budge. In the end, he tossed the stone over his shoulder into the dam, and laughed, and shouted in a voice so high that it cracked:

'Happy, happy!'

He was happy all the way home, too, I remember. At first, he beat out the time on the steering wheel, and sang songs he had heard on the radio. He also sang a song or two that no one had ever heard on the radio, like:

> *There's a rooster*
> *In your bloomers,*
> *Tant Meraai.*

Then he fell silent for a long time, and stared straight ahead from under his hat. Taking the most direct route, he drove all the way back to Magnet Heights without stopping.

Seraphima was at work in the kitchen, drying dishes, when we burst in through the back door.

'Yoh, yoh!' she cried out in alarm.

'Halleluia! Hamba wena,' said Pa. Go, you. Leave.

He flung the rifle down on the bench, and took off his hat.

'Baas?'

Pa snapped the sweat from his forehead with one finger.

'Christmas comes but once a year,' he stated with a crooked grin. 'You heard what I said. Go on. Go. Get out.'

She did, too, in a hurry, frightened, taking with her a twist of sugar in brown paper and a few thick slices of white bread. Pa watched her go. As soon as the screen door slapped shut, he went and fetched the bottle of brandy from the pantry.

'Lachaim!' he said, and held the bottle high, and took a first long straight pull.

Forced to catch his breath, he shuddered, gasped and stood pounding at the wall with the flat of his hand.

'Do as I say,' he urged hoarsely, rolling his eyes (a joke). 'Not as I do.'

He swallowed another shot of brandy, and shuddered, and drank a shot or two more, and spat.

His eyes were watering. With a grin he wiped the tears on his forearm. Then he sat down on the bench, and leaned back, and laid the rifle across his knees, and stroked the solid wood of its stock.

For a while, he stared at the wall where the door to the bathroom stood outlined in ballpoint.

His lips kept moving, but he made no sound.

Then, abruptly, he got to his feet, and went staggering down the passageway to his bedroom. When he reappeared, he had the roll of plans under one arm, and the urn with my mother's ashes in his hands.

'What are we waiting for? Let's do it, Rian. Haven't we got everything we need, already? Bricks, cement, hand basin, bath, the lot. Okay, then. Let's make a start. We'll give these plans one last quick once-over, just to make sure. Okay? No more delays! Now, let's see.'

With odds and ends – the sugar bowl, the brandy bottle, the urn, the palm of his hand – he pinned down the plans at the corners. A fly alighted on the paper. He fumbled to grab it in his fist, muttering: 'Die, fly.'

And stood staring at the spot where it had been.

Already, I felt trapped in the immobility of the long afternoon ahead. Reaching up, I unlatched the screen door.

'Ag, no, little Rian!' Pa objected. 'Where do you think you are going, now? No, man, you can't go outside. Can't you see? First things first. We've got work to do. Listen. What I want you to know is this. It's never too late. Never. Today, you watch, I'll do it – I'll not only try, I'll do it. I'll knock a hole through that brick wall with a cold chisel, so wide that the sunshine will jump in. By this time next week, we'll be able to open that door, you and I, and walk right through. You with your towel, me with mine. Durban? Ag, Durban can wait. Durban will always be there. Durban won't run away. Ja-nee, take my word for it, my lightie. Home is where the action is. Just look at what we'll get. A long bath to lie in, hot and cold running water, a proper flush toilet, everything. Ja, believe me, everything. Just like your mother always wanted.'

He took another swig of brandy, and wiped his mouth on the back of his hand. I looked at the floor.

It seemed that I could see all that would happen laid out before me in the re-peat- pattern of the linoleum. As always, Pa would first spell over the plans again in laborious detail. He would drink, too, without stopping, and talk. The sky's the limit. There is nothing a man can't do, if he sets his mind to it. When a job is your own, do it alone, and do it now. Give me the tools, and I will move the world. We fix it or we fucks it. Etc.

At some point, too, in order to show me how completely a man could (and should) throw himself into Christmas, he would scoop up the plump dusty cushion from the bench, and hug it close, and begin to waltz. Listen, my light-ie. Listen. Your mother's favorite. 'The Blue Danube'. La *la* la la la, la-la, la-la.

Later, too drunk to dance if not, perhaps, to talk, he would lurch across to the bench again, and sit down, and pick up the rifle. With great but unsteady care and concentration, he would take the rifle apart, oil it and clean it. Then, un-erringly, he would put it all back together again, and check its moving parts. He would toy with the bullets for a while, weighing them in his palm, and rolling them around, before reloading the clip, and setting the rifle to stand on its butt in a corner.

Then he would either sink into a slump and pass out, or go and fetch from the top of the cupboard the pictures of the lady in the ostrich feathers. Back at the table, he would thumb through the pictures, and snap them together, and fondle them. (Hey, lovely thing!). In the end, he would leave the pictures lying scattered and forgotten, and pick up the funerary urn, and cradle it in his arms, and stare at the floor, and rock back and forth, and press his lips to the cold por-celain, and murmur to it. Suddenly, groaning and crying out, he would get to his feet and go stumbling across the room, and start banging his head against the wall. His nose would bleed. Wiping it with one finger, he would stare at the blood, but not see it. Annie, he would cry, the tears trickling down to collect round his chin, and his lips twisting back. Annie.

At present, though, all he did was stand and take further little nips at the bottle. You could almost hear him thinking.

'All right,' he agreed at last, eyeing me sidelong, and waving the bottle. 'Go, then. Go outside and play. But don't go far. And come when I call you, okay?'

He swigged again, his eyes shut.

I went outside and stood in the hanging tire. Leaning back steeply, I forced the swing to move. In the stillness of the dry winter afternoon, the pepper tree leaves whispered and shook. The branch above me rocked. Ou Willem the baboon hopped up on to the roof of his kennel to watch.

I was swinging high when I heard the screen door flap.

I looked back over my shoulder. Pa, I saw, was standing on the steps, and holding out to me the little transistor radio.

'Come, little Rian. Take it. You can listen to any station you like. Okay? Like Durban beach.'

But it seemed that my swing was going too high to stop, and in the end he had no choice but to come all the way down the steps to the yard, and sling the radio in a fork of the tree, himself.

I waited only until I heard the screen door flap again. Then, hugging the tire between my knees, I let myself hang. Overhead, the rope creaked and rubbed. Sleepy-sweet music came oozing from the little radio. Almost at once, though, just as I knew it would, the swing lost height, and began slowing down. As soon as I could, I dropped out.

I didn't care if Pa saw. (In a way, I know, I wanted him to). Without looking back, I headed straight across the veld to the one place forbidden me, the paradise for snakes.

My aim at first was to find more bottles. There were plenty left lying around the water tank. Penny a bottle. This time, I made no effort to count, just stood the bottles in a row on a plank. Then I cast around for stones, which I packed together in a pile.

Bottle number one burst like a bomb—a bright, hollow, splashing sound. Bottle number two stood tall, unscathed, for a moment. My stone had swung wide of the mark (perhaps I was trying too hard?). But the next hit the bottle square in the face. Deliberately, I went on to smash every bottle in the row, however many of them. (Look, Pa!) Soon, nothing was left but broken glass, thick and glittering. I tried balancing on a bottle butt, and walked around on the litter of broken glass, just to see what it felt like. Then I turned my attention to the ladder at the side of the tank.

The rusted rungs were warmer now. With wide-open faces the morning glory watched me as I climbed. Above me stood the windmill, gaunt and motionless. There was no wind.

I stood where we had stood that morning, Pa and I, on the round white concrete rim of the tank. All around lay the winter veld, sun-bleached and dry, while in the distance rose the hills, so blue as to be almost one with the sky. Between my lips I held a flower which I kept tilting up and down, breathing through the tip. Where in those hills, I wondered, was the leopard? And the lightning bones of the witch?

I leaned forward and dropped, or spat, the flower from my mouth. Ragged, slightly torn, outspread, the morning glory floated. My goldfish (long fins waving, round mouths opening and shutting, O) would have come swimming up now, I knew. Leaning over, I tried to look down deeper yet, but all I could see was the shadow of my own head, spokes of the sun around it.

I put my finger into the water. It was very cold and still.

There was nothing left to do but to climb down again.

I took the long way round to the corner where the abandoned building materials were stacked. I stepped up on to the barrel-back of the gas geyser, and jumped down on the other side. Using a plank as a lever, I managed to turn the bathtub right side up. (Dank, the earth, but still no snakes.) A crust of sand clung all round the rim, while the inside shone smooth and white. I climbed into the tub, and sat cross-legged on the floor, and waited.

I do not know how long I waited (it seemed to me a long time), but Pa never did come to find me.

It was full broad afternoon when I made my way back to the pepper tree. The radio hung in a fork as before, talking to itself. The baboon lay on his side in the sun, not really asleep, for his paws twitched now and then.

I flopped on my belly in the swing.

Welcome, said the radio. Whoever you are, wherever you may be, stay tuned. We have a pile of platters, oldies and goldies, just for you. I rocked round slowly, letting my shoes drag in the dust. This is your favorite station, Springbok Radio. It's three o' clock on the dot. With you in the studio today and every day, ready and waiting to take your calls, is your host, yours truly, Johnnie Walker. A deep voice, his, rich, warm, and smug. (A bedroom baritone, Pa used to say.) I swung round, rocked, hung down. Let the blood drain into my head.

A jazz jingle, the theme tune, rose up and under, female voices capering, as it were, through the words: 'Mr Walk-er wants to–play'.

Johnnie Walker was the name of a whisky, too, I knew. On the label a cheery man in old-fashioned clothing stretched his legs in a long stride. Whose customer he? Not Mr Abie's, for sure. And I am who? I swung round, rocked. Weight of the stone in my hand. Bright flash of the glass as it shattered, a fountain. From the brass pipe in the broken vase water still trickled. Only half a face she had, the white cement lady who kept an eye on me. Where, she asked, where now is Stompie? Each time the rifle cracked, red dust sprang up from the roof. Tannie Crystal's nose wrinkled up when she laughed. Hai, Rian, don't tell me you've never seen...? The coffee at Oude Hoop, freshly ground, smells rich and dark. My little man, she whispered, and held me close. Her breasts were soft and rounded. Her throat throbbed when she laughed. Into my ear her warm wet tongue went teasing, probing.

Was that not Pa, now, calling?

I jumped out of the swing and stepped back, straining to hear.

'Pa?'

The air was very still.

In the dust outside his kennel the baboon lay stretched out flat on his side, his paws twitching against the flies.

'Pa?' I cried, and listened.

No reply.

I ran up the stairs and into the kitchen. The screen door clapped shut behind me. I tried to see, but my eyes were still too full of the sun.

'Pa?' I said. 'Pa called?'

The Place of the Skull

I

After Pa shot himself, I ran down the back steps into the yard. The baboon stood up at the end of his chain and shrieked, barked. Where are the witch's stones?

I can't stop running–not now. I thrash my way through waist-deep veld grass, the breath tight in my throat. Small seeds of grass are sticking to my face. The sun is in my eyes. If I could, I would speak in tongues. Adonai, Adonai. My legs are brutally heavy, unwieldy–I stumble and plunge and almost pitch headlong. The grass wraps itself like snares around my feet, and I have to kick, twist, wrench myself free. At the same time, I keep throwing myself from side to side in an effort to dodge, to zigzag. In the small of my spine there is this freezing feeling. I expect at any moment to be shot.

If I were to stop now and listen, I'd hear the growing gush and roar of the bush fire. The kombi will have made of every dry grey tree surrounding it a blazing torch. The balloon has gone up, all right. Sky-high. Somewhere soon must be the path. First I will cross the dried-up little spruit, then I will climb to the top of the madala's ridge. (And then what? Look down? The Great Rift Valley, they say, is visible from the moon.) If I were to stop now, I'd hear the branches crack. The heat must be tremendous.

When Pa shot himself, he was flung bolt upright. Bits of bone and other stuff got spattered across the back wall. The rifle kicked out of his hands and came clattering towards me across the floor. I stood where I was, just inside the screen door. I could see the twin halves of his brain, laced all over with blood, where the bullet had taken off the top of his skull. (Gleaming, the brain, and wrinkled like your palms when you have lain too long in the bath.) I could see, too, the pale band round his forehead where his hat had kept off the sun. Then he collapsed, sprawling flat on his back across the stove. You could hear his blood hiss. You could smell the burning flesh and hair.

Jesus could never have walked here. His feet were too soft. And white. As for me, my feet are black beneath the skin and hard, hard as horn. Tant Koba told me so. When she lifted me out of the tub and wrapped me in the folds of a clean soft mealie meal sack, and stood me before her on the bench. Come, my little kaffir, she said (kaffir, a term of endearment). Come, let me dry you. Give me your foot. Hard, she said, rubbing it in the cloth between her hands. Hard as horn. Little Rian must know, little Rian has got real little kaffir feet.

Where the path is I don't know, but the bank of the little spruit is suddenly underfoot. I can't stop–not now. I step over the edge and go skidding, sliding, very nearly sprawling my way down the side. Red dust and small stones come showering down after me. I half-expect Bamford, stumping along with his shotgun for a crutch, to loom over me against the skyline. Looking back, all I see is this thick and growing column of oil-rich black smoke. Did I do that?

Adonai.

The sand of the riverbed is harsh and white, like salt. The pockmarks of goats' hoofs are everywhere, as well as the odd spurt or scattering of pellets. Bone-dry, stocked with boulders, the watercourse lies outstretched before me. Place of the skull. Noon. My tackies scuff the crust of the sand, breaking it. No doubt, if you were to kneel down here and dig–scoop with both hands–water would eventually seep in. Is this it, then, Pa? Durban beach.

Just the spot to pitch a jolly holiday umbrella. With stripes.

What would Pa do on the beach all day if he did not sit on his towel and look out over the rolling waves, and sing along with the transistor radio:

I want you, you, you,
No one else will do, do, do. . . .

Not too long after the funeral Crystal le Roux came to visit. She and Tant Koba sat together in the front room and drank tea. Oupa Gert had passed away, too, said Crystal. Is that so? said Tant Koba politely, though her glance was sharp. Of what did he die? He fell, replied Crystal. He was going down the passageway to the stoep, when his stick slipped and he fell. He broke his hip in two places, here and here. She showed where. Ag, ja, sighed Tant Koba. So it goes with the old folk. One day the earth calls them and they fall. Yes, said Crystal. Of course, she added, I telephoned the doctor at once. That nice new young doctor from Pietersburg, Dr Bothma. Him with the moustache and the little round glasses. Does tannie not know him, perhaps? Me? said Tant Koba. I take no interest in nice new young doctors. Not at my age.

Yes, well, said Crystal. Oupa's nose was bleeding, so I ran and got ice from the fridge. Ice can help, Tant Koba agreed. It did, said Crystal. At least, it stopped the blood. Then I rolled him on to a bed sheet, and called the meid[1] from the kitchen, and together we pushed and pulled him all the way to the front room. It was a struggle, but in the end we got him to lay down and wait on the sofa like a decent human being. Dr Bothma, when he came, took one look at the hip

1. *meid*, maid

and told him he had no choice, he had to go to hospital at once. Hospital? said
Oupa Gert. What for? Stubborn! Ag, tannie, stubborn is not the word. Men,
remarked Tant Koba grimly. I know, said Crystal. Oh?

How do you know? asked Tant Koba. The same way as tante, said Crystal.
Go on, said Tant Koba after a pause. You were saying, about Oupa Gert.

Yes, said Crystal. The doctor explained it all so nicely. Listen, Oupa, he said,
we are going to have to break Oupa's hip again, and put it back together with
pins. I've heard of that, put in Tant Koba. Stainless steel pins. Like knives and
forks. Yes, said Crystal. It's the latest thing. Pins give the bones a chance to knit
properly. It would have worked, too, in this case – Dr Bothma said it would – but
does tannie think Oupa Gert would budge? He just lay there, blowing spit bubbles through his gums, and rolling his eyes up at the ceiling. Is that all you
doctors can do? he wanted to know. Break what is already broken? If Oupa is serious about wanting to walk again, Dr Bothma said, then Oupa had better make
up his mind to come with me to hospital right away. Over my dead body, said
Oupa Gert. Let's hope it won't come to that, said the doctor. And he got up, and
stood smiling a little under his moustache, and clipped his black bag shut.

It took Oupa Gert four days to die. I sat beside him, and wiped his face with
a washrag and cleaned him like a baby. But the hip – ai, tannie, the hip! You
should have seen it. All black and blue and swollen. He died in terrible pain.
Towards the end, he couldn't pass water. I brought him the bucket, Tok's bucket that he left behind on the day of the goldfish (Oupa Gert liked to make water
in it), and he tried, but nothing came. I thought it was gangrene, but the doctor
says no. He says that Oupa Gert's prostate gland had blown up as big as a football, and it shut off the bladder, which burst. An old man's problem, Tant Koba
remarked. Ja, said Crystal with a sigh. What the Lord giveth, observed Tant
Koba. I know, said Crystal, and took a sip of tea. She was wearing a hat with
a little black veil, and she had to lift her veil, while her nose looked white and
pointed, as she put her lips to the cup.

After another sip, she added: You can keep this place, you know, tannie. Tok's
place. I don't want it. In fact, I have already phoned my lawyer and told him to
drop the case against you. After all, I am a wealthy woman now. Oupa Gert left
everything he owned to me. I don't need your money. Money? said Tant Koba,
carefully wiping the bottom of her cup on the rim of the saucer. What money?

This sand is a slog. Slow. I am sweating. On Durban beach you can walk
forever. Because the sea is salt, not cyanide. I will walk on into the sparkling
light. Fallen fruit will turn to salt, tons of it, salt to sand. As soon as I get to the

madala's kraal, I will tell him: Time stands still here, madala. In this heat nothing can move. Believe me. Throw away your watch. It's no good. Junk for jewels.

If I had binoculars, I could stop and rake the horizon.

I do not see the disappearing ships.

At first, after the sun in the yard, the kitchen was dark. Pa? I said. Pa called? I stood still. I put my hands over my eyes, as I had been taught, and thought of the inside of a black box. I thought, too, of the Strongbox sinking through the standing waters of the dam to settle in the mud at the bottom. If only Pa had taken it from the table at Oude Hoop, he and I could have packed it full of stones, and shut the lid and sealed it tight. He could have climbed up and stood on the dam wall and shouted, 'Wahoo!' and swung the tin box round his head and chucked it out into the middle of the dam and let it sink.

But Pa never did.

When I lifted my hands and looked up again, I saw him. He was not singing or dancing any longer. He was standing before the coal stove at the far end of the kitchen. He had raised the rifle to his shoulder and was aiming it at me point blank.

I did not move. I could not.

You wanted to kill me, too, Pa.

I never told anyone.

I throw myself down flat behind a boulder and lie still. Wait. In the flash floods of summer this boulder must cleave the churning, foaming waters. Red with the rich topsoil, the floodwaters go rocking, swirling by, choked with floating debris of all kinds – broken branches, plastic bags, tussocks of grass, the odd drowned dog. (Me?) In the strip of shadow cast by the boulder I sit up. I pull off my tackies, strip off my socks. I stuff the socks into the throats of the tackies, knot the laces together and hang the tackies round my neck.

I am ready at last for the trail.

I stand up, look back.

No sign yet of Bamford. Why not? To one side of the towering black column a low bank of thick white smoke has begun to build up. The bush, too, is burning, then. Long folds of white smoke come flowing down into the gully, where they hang around like ghosts. Okay. So, what did he do? Give up the chase from the start? Why should he, when in a hop or two after his first, failed shot, he could have reached the camp table, grabbed up the shotgun shells, stuffed a couple into the chambers, swung round and had me in his sights again before I had cleared twenty meters? Unless of course he decided to go tottering round to the deck-chair in order to collapse into it, to nurse his big toe, swig down another neat whisky and watch the fireworks.

And Vicky? Why did I hear no outcry, nothing, from her? When the kombi exploded, what did she do? Catch up her shirt and hold it to her? Run? If so, where to? Straight into the bush, like Bucs? Who has by now himself walked how far, the warrior?

I will have to go back to the camp, sooner or later, I see. But not now.

Now, I break away from the boulder and sprint, my toes spurning the hot sand. I exult in my newfound strength and pour all my energy into veering from side to side again, a moving target. I cross a long slope of bare rock, take a bend in the channel and go crashing through a brake of tattered reeds. I half-expect the tarentaal[2] to start up with a racket again – safe, this time, from me, though they, too, will soon have to flee the fire. I am its herald. My every touch could as well be a crackling flame. Then, through a last rickety screen of reeds, I catch sight of a place I seem to recognize. Wasn't it here that Bamford and I first saw the goats?

I rush out into the open with a yell. Only, a stitch in my side keeps coming and going. I am thirsty, and the tackies round my neck knock into one another and smell of sweaty rubber. I push on, running hard, regardless, determined to gain my second wind.

On the far side of the riverbed lies the path, I remember. I take it. I am the kudu. I bound from stone to stone, mounting ever higher. My blue body races, light as a shadow. Soon I will stand at the top of the ridge and look out over the plain. My gaze will rest on the horizon. I will stand like a statue, the fires far below no more than a flicker in my eyes.

It was Seraphima who found me. I was hiding under the tractor, Pa's iron cow. I sat up against one of the giant rear wheels, making myself as small as I could and watching a slow drip of oil stain a patch of grass. It grew late and the shadows began to lengthen, but I did not move. I watched a tiny ladybug, her shell bright red with black dots, go creeping up a grass stem until she teetered on the very tip, and whirred away in flight. I listened, too, but all was still. The air was sheer, like a wall. At times I dared not breathe.

Then suddenly Seraphima's bare feet were beside the tractor, and her face. She called out my name, and grabbed me. I tried to cling on to the wheel, but she was too strong. She stood up and held me to her bosom and ran. I felt very high up. I felt I might fall.

2. *tarentaal*, guinea fowl

Steep, this slope. The path loops back on itself, twists round a massive boulder. Just ahead, flowering aloes lift blossoms as pale in the sun as red hot iron. Winded, I stop for a moment. I step off the path and lean against the boulder. My breath feels broken, burning in my chest. My T-shirt is wet and sticks to me.

A hippo's head, boiled in a washtub, looks huge, bloated. Her ears are little folded pouches, one cocked stiffly, the other crumpled flat. Her eyes, swollen lumps, dull as lard. Sweat, or condensed steam, stands out all over her head. Broad and bulging, her lips seem to be smiling, parted slightly. If you look, you catch a glimpse of tooth bone in the gap. All you can do now is wait, until the idea fixed in her head is ready to trickle like a drop of sweat. What is it? I whisper. What is it, Madam Hippo? Beaded with fat and frothing, the water bubbles up around her lips. She has no voice, I know, so I lend her my own. Better, she says (or bubbles), better not to have been born at all.

I spit – with some difficulty, my mouth is so dry – turn away from the boulder and look out over the plain.

The bush fire, advancing at what seems like a leisurely crawl, has burnt in a wide ragged crescent away from the wild fig, which stands untouched, as green as ever. The kombi is nothing but a knot at the foot of its column of black smoke. I see no human figures.

Bamford could not have gone far, for sure. Not with that foot. I can take it easy from now on, then. Walk. Already I am more than halfway to the top.

Seraphima carried me, clutched to her breast, all the way back to the house. The kitchen was full of people, some sitting, others walking up and down. The lamp had been lit although it was not yet sunset, and the doors and windows stood wide, perhaps because of the smell. Here he is! they cried when Seraphima and I appeared. Poor child! and, Thank the Lord! But as soon as she put me down, they told her to leave. Go, they said. Go. You have done a good thing, my girl. Now you may leave. (And when she did, a man muttered: Swart gat. Black arsehole.)

I was surrounded by legs. A very big man stooped down and put his hands on his knees and stared at me, face to face. His face was round and red, his moustache ginger and turned up at the corners. I know you, he said earnestly, but you don't know me. I am Detective Sergeant Kloppers of the police force. How do you do, Rian? You can call me Oom Sakkie. He held out a hand. I did not move. I said, Where is Pa?

Oh, the lamb! shrilled a woman sitting at the table. The innocent! The poor little lamb! It was the dominee's wife, Tant Hattie. She was sitting beside the dominee, Roelofse, he of the devil's tongue. The dominee was not looking at me but down at his own straight fingers. Both he and Tant Hattie were drinking coffee from the white cups with the blue flowers, my mother's favorites, which Pa never used. On the other side of the table stood our neighbour, Kot Kotze.

It was Kot who had found Pa, in fact. His bakkie had developed engine trouble, it seems, and he had dropped by in the hope that Pa could take a look at it. Hullo, how are you? he had called and stepped in through the back door.

The rest of the people in the house were police.

Kot stood staring at me helplessly. He must have been crying not long before. His cheeks still bore the grubby marks of tears.

Pa's body had been rolled up in a couple of blankets – one for the head – and left on the floor of his bedroom. They never showed me, but I knew it was there.

With a troubled frown Detective Sergeant Kloppers spoke: I am very sorry to say, Rian. . . . He is dead. Your Pa is dead.

I know, I said.

You do? That is interesting. Very interesting. Tell me, little boy, he added. What else do you know?

His eyes were small and round and bright. He waited.

At the top of the ridge, I abandon the path and strike out as far as I can along the stony spine. Small scraggy bushes grow here, and sparse grass. If you look up at the sky, you see nothing, not even a bird. A thin wind blows. I walk among rocks that aeons of wind and rain have hollowed and carved into fantastically distorted shapes. Before me stands a giant decapitated soldier in armour, sunk to his waist in the ground, his torso all twisted against the violence of the blow. Beyond him again a tall but deserted throne rears its rigid back. I almost expect to find weapons – discarded maces, battle-axes, shields and swords. Instead, what I come across is a perfectly flat expanse of rock, circular in shape. I pace the diameter. Fifty meters exactly. Fool. How could your stunt with the kombi have helped Vicky?

I seek out an overhang, a smooth slab of stone leaning up against the sky. At end of day you could take shelter in a place like this, put together your own small fire of sticks and grass, and roast such small creatures as you might have trapped – lizards, birds, bush rats. No doubt, you would sometimes go hungry, but you could also live very wholly, very simply. Stooping, I explore to the end of the overhang where I discover a curious deep hollow, large enough to hold me, in the rock. On impulse I climb into it. The walls are smooth and cool, dry and rounded, like eggshell. I lie back, shut my eyes.

And again I am an old, old man, older than any other on earth–withered, gaunt, white-haired. My face and fists are like rock, my staff shod with iron. I lie, not breathing, suspended in space and time. I know that the day will come when I will enter this iron world again, strike iron on iron. My eyes are black pits. My lips move wordlessly. It is my fate to reveal in a flash of lightning the darkness all around.

I allow myself to drift on currents of sleep that seem to lead irresistibly ever deeper into solid rock. At the same time I become aware of a slight weight, warm and soft, that I appear to be holding close to my chest. At first I think I must have picked up again the dove that I shot. I expect to find its feathers sticking to my bloodied fingers when I look down. What I see, cupped in my hands, is no dead bird, however, but a hot, wet, slippery, still palpitating–almost, indeed, convulsing–torn-out heart. (My own or another's? I cannot tell.) I hold the heart tight for fear it might hop out of my grip like a frog. The muscles collapse. I do not let go, but squeeze it to a pulp. Blood drips and trickles between my fingers and down my forearms. The smell is raw and very close. In the meantime the flesh of my hands seems to have turned translucent, like glass: I can see all the bones and veins. What now? Will I have to swallow this crushed and sticky heart? I cannot move, for the rock is also, I discover now, the black iron stove in the kitchen at Magnet Heights. Pa, I say, Pa. Can't you see I am burning?

I am awake again–if indeed I have slept–awake and cramped and cold in the hollow of the rock.

Oh, Jesus, Jesus, I mutter and beat the back of my head on the rock.

I want to go to the madala.

I ease my way out of the hollow. My right arm is numb from being pinned under me, and I have to work the stiff fingers to get back the blood. Sitting in the thick dust of the floor of the overhang, I undo the knot in the laces of my tackies and put the tackies back on.

It seems to me the time is right to try and argue my case. Look, madala, I will say. Today is the day of the big fire. You see how the smoke stands? It is a very big fire, yes. But fire sweeps clean. That is its beauty. Come the rains, and all will be green again, madala, fresh and young.

The first thing Tant Koba did was to wash the blankets in which Pa's body had been wrapped. There is nothing, she stated with some severity, nothing in the world that a little soap and water won't fix. Accordingly, she soaked the two blankets in the washtub, and rubbed at them with a stick of blue soap, and trod on them, barefooted. You see? she said with a laugh. This is how they press wine in the Cape – tramp and tramp to make the juices run. She rinsed the blankets thoroughly and hung them up on the sagging fence of the fowl hok to dry. A person can't allow two such good blankets to go to waste, she remarked. Ja-nee, she added, and now that it seems as if winter doesn't want to come to an end, and also because this old house is like an icebox, especially at night, it seems to me a couple of extra blankets can only come in handy. She ironed the blankets, folded them and pressed them to her face. Clean as clean can be, she said. Sun and air, that's all. There you are, smell for yourself. To me, though, it seemed as though a stale aroma of blue soap still clung, a rank and fatty smell that stuck in my throat.

She spread one blanket across Oom Frikkie's bed, the other across mine. And that night I dreamt of an awkward trampling of feet in the passageway, and of something heavy being dragged, that bumped, while a wine bottle dropped (I heard the glass shatter), and I awoke with a cry to find Tant Koba standing at the foot of my bed. Do not be afraid of the dead, child, she said. She was holding up a lighted lamp. Her face was daubed with cold cream, her hair crowded with paper curlers. The dead cannot harm you. The living, yes. Fear the living. But not the dead.

I find the path again with ease and make a rapid descent, but only when I reach the bend where I paid for my skinning knife with less than a handful of cash do I gain a clear view of the madala's kraal. What I see stops me in my tracks.

Three hulking trucks – Army trucks, not GG – are parked up against the low mud wall. Knots of young white soldiers with guns at the ready have sprung from the trucks and fanned out all over the courtyard. As I watch, two of the soldiers kick down the door of the closest hut and disappear inside.

I step behind a thorn tree. With great care I scan the whole area.

What is this? A forced removal?

The madala himself, still dressed in his greatcoat, is sitting flat on the ground in the space between huts. I do not see his kierie. Perhaps it has been taken away? A small group of soldiers is standing guard over him. They look almost casual, toying with their rifles and chatting. On the ground beside the madala kneels the young woman who served us tea, and beside her again is another woman I have not seen before. Both the women are shrinking or leaning towards the madala, while as many as four small children are clinging to the woman I do not know, and screaming and crying. Where was she earlier, then?

Away from the kraal, maybe. Anyway, by the look of things she is the mother. Meanwhile, the young woman I know is holding one arm raised as if to protect her head. I wonder if the soldiers have hit her.

Now, shouts erupt above the crying and screaming of the children, and the two soldiers emerge from the hut, driving before them the young man in the vest, my messenger. They club him with the butts of their rifles and kick him. He falls to the ground where they continue to club and kick him.

My heart contracts with pity and rage. I have no idea what to do. Go down there and try and remonstrate? Oh, yes? And say what? Excuse me, kind sirs, but what you are doing is wrong?

Here, nothing short of a machine gun could stammer out all that needs to be said.

One of the trucks backs up, turns and reverses into the baked mud wall of the kraal, which bursts and collapses. A number of soldiers clamber up on the canopy of the truck and sling a chain over the thatched roof of the hut. At another shout the truck goes lumbering forward again. The thatch is torn off and dragged to the ground. Then, while the chain is being thrown round the walls of the hut and secured, the soldiers who have been beating the young man drag him to his feet. They prod him with rifle barrels and force him to climb into the back of another truck.

The first truck, the one with the chain, rolls forward and the hut, torn from its moorings, collapses. There is a great deal of dust. Through it all I see the madala getting cuffed and shoved into the back of the truck that already contains the young man. Behind the madala follow the two women and the children, still clinging and crying.

Another hut collapses. I stay where I am and watch as the soldiers methodically demolish the entire kraal. Only when the trucks have driven away, bumping and swaying across the veld, do I descend and go to the kraal myself. The dust cloud has not quite settled. I walk across the rubble. There is nothing to be seen but a single stray fowl, unexpectedly bold, venturing out to peck at the dirt. I pitch a chip of dried mud at it, and it scoots with a squawk and a cluck. I climb to the top of the highest mound. Am I the King of the Castle? I look around me, and then I stumble down again and fall to my knees on another heap of sticks and thatch and broken baked mud, and whisper, Christ!

I do not know what to do.

2

I HAVE TO TREAD CAREFULLY. The ground is still hot and smoking in places and if I set a foot wrong could easily burn through my tackies. All around me
the blackened landscape stretches away, flat and bare. On the horizon smoke
is still rising. I feel as if I have never been here before. I feel as if I am the sole
upright thing in the middle of a vast circle of fire. To right and left of me the
charred and smoking remnant of trees stick up, while the entire plain is dotted
with stones, not to mention the odd, bared ant heap.

The kombi, when I get to it, is just as I thought it would be – a burnt-out
wreck, blasted, gutted. It stands tilted to one side, its barrel body scorched
and blackened, the letters, ACE-TV, still faintly visible on its sides. The windscreen, which must have shattered if not melted in the heat, has left a cavernous
hole from which a strand of smoke still comes twisting up. The tires have not
stopped smoldering, and the stench of burning rubber is so thick it makes me
want to gag.

I stand staring. What is left of the tires look like strips of charred flesh sticking to the wheel rims.

Coughing, retching, I turn away.

A gleam on the ground catches my eye. It is my goat knife, dropped, I guess,
when I went to light the fuse. I pick it up, wipe the blade on the leg of my jeans,
and stow the knife back in my belt.

Little as there is of it, the rest of the camp – the collapsible table, the deck-
chairs – has escaped the flames. Here, where the wild fig spreads its branches,
the eye of the storm would seem to have held its own – if a fire storm has an eye.
I cross to my camera, which stands as I left it, locked off on its tripod, the lens
uncapped.

I check, but all seems in perfect order. No ghostly images have been brand-
ed into the video tubes, and the batteries register close to a full charge: the DC
power must have shut down automatically. In a minute I am panning over the
camp, widening my focus to take in the razed landscape. Where exactly Vicky
and Bamford happen to have disappeared to, I do not know. Nor do I care. I am
simply glad of the space they have left me, glad to be able to move about freely
at last. When I try and trigger a recording, a signal tells me that the tape is full.
I set it to rewind.

What I've got to get hold of at once is water. Under the table stands the fifty-litre canister, its level low. I take it out, lift it up and shake it. Less than a litre left. I turn the tap and allow the trickle to go straight to the back of my throat so that I can swallow without shutting my mouth. I drink as much as I can, then splash a bit of the remaining water over my face.

Only now do I realize how hungry I am. I take handfuls of the birthday cake and cram my mouth full. I eat potato crisps and peanuts, too. Wrapped in its blood-browned newspaper, the goat's meat lies where I dropped it, attracting flies, while the Wonderboy skull squats on the lid of its black velvet box, the guest of honour: How many millions of years old?

I drink more water. The canister holds very little, I see. A cup or two.

I am busy pushing more of the moist rich birthday cake into my mouth when I hear, clear and weak, almost a croak, Bamford's voice, saying:

'What took you so long?'

I swing round.

But for the roots of the wild fig, some nearly knee-high, I would no doubt have caught sight of him before. He is lying back between them as in a bath tub, still quite naked, halfway round the other side of the tree.

I approach very carefully. Where is the shotgun?

'Digby?'

He does not reply. His head sticks up and his eyes shine, gazing at me. I am so close that I can hear his labored breathing. And only now do I see the blood. All down his left side and into his crotch as well as over his legs, it has blackened or dried into a crust. Across his belly it seems to have been more thinly smeared, as by his own hands, while in a fist-sized hole just under his ribs, where it is ringed by a black fur of flies, the blood still glistens, wet.

I give a low whistle.

'Bamford, you dumb fuck. What have you done to yourself this time?'

His breathing is harsh, and he stares at me with resentment.

'Do you think,' he says, 'you could give me a drink of water?'

'What happened?'

'Nothing. An accident. The shotgun.'

'What did you do? Trip over your own feet?'

'What did *you* do? Behind my back! One big bloody bang, and the next thing I know, fire, fire everywhere.'

'Where is Vicky?'

'Sweet Jesus. Here I lie, just as you see me, and all you can do is ask about Vicky?'

'She is not hurt, too, is she?'

'Oh, fuck her. Fuck Vicky. She's gone, man. Cleared out. Left me. Long ago. And you? Where the hell did you go?'

'Me? Nowhere. Over the ridge and back again.'

'What for?'

'I thought you saw. I ran.'

'Oh, lucky man! You ran. While I crawled to the trunk of this tree, and lay here, bleeding like a pig – you ran.'

'What did you want me to do? Take your picture?'

'I've been gut shot. Understand? Gut shot.'

'I didn't pull the trigger, Digby. You did.'

'Don't tell me you watched, because you didn't. I know you. What you are is a bloody arsonist, man. Because of you, this place got toasted. Take a look around, for fuck's sake. Why did you do it? Tell me. Why?'

'Because of you.'

'Oh, no. Now we are getting nowhere, going round in a circle. Here I lie, flat on my back, the shit shot out of me, and I look up at the top of this tree and realize I don't understand a thing. Not a thing. Tell me again. Why did you run?'

'I didn't want to get shot.'

He gives a gurgle of laughter, which makes his chest quake, but also wrenches his guts with ferocious pain.

'You? You didn't want. . .?! Christ,' he groans, panting and trembling, 'you little shit. Who would want to shoot you?'

'You.'

'Me?'

For a long moment he stares at me, his eyes bright with malice, as if he would speak. Then he shuts his eyes, and his head goes rolling round on his shoulders, showing his sweaty white throat. He slumps back as if boneless, to be propped up by the great tree roots. What little life he has left is draining out of him, it seems, and all this talk has not helped.

'Wait,' I say under my breath.

Here and there, not far from one of the deck-chairs, lie the clothes he tossed off at the party. I pick up his T-shirt and try to tear it into strips, but the cotton proves too tough until I use the goat knife.

I crouch down beside him again, wrapping the cloth in loose loops round my hand.

'Water,' he begs hoarsely.

'First let's put a bit of pressure on that wound, okay?'

'No. Not now. It's hard . . . hard enough to breathe as it is.'

'We have to avoid further bleeding.'

'We'? Who, may I ask, in this case, are 'we'?'

'You know what I mean.'

'Don't patronize me. You have no right.'

'I'm only trying to help.'

'Oh, go piss in the ocean.'

'Tell you what. Let me bind up that wound, and I'll fetch you some water.'

He stares at me fixedly.

'Do you know what you are doing?'

'Sure. I'm trying to stick a piece of your own T-shirt round your belly like a band-aid. All I want to do is to keep out the dust and dirt and flies and crap. Won't you let me give it a try?'

He holds his breath and then quite suddenly relents:

'Oh, all right. Go ahead, man. Do your worst.'

He has bled very heavily. There are pools of blood among the roots. I wad up a portion of the cloth and press it to the hole in his side. Flies buzz around my hand, sticking to the blood. I try to wave them away.

'Christ!' he whispers, and his mouth gapes wide in a show of agony.

'Turn over,' I tell him. 'Good side down.'

'Oh, yes? And which would that be?'

'The one opposite to your wound.'

'What's so good about it?'

'It doesn't leak.'

He does not stir a finger to help, but lies watching me as I struggle to wind the strip of torn T-shirt around and under him. Whether his inability to move is due to the fact that death has already begun to bear its full weight down upon him, or to no more than a decision on his part to passively resist, I cannot tell. Anyway, done at last, I get to my feet and stand beside him.

My hands are covered in blood. I wipe them on the back of my jeans.

'Listen, Digby. I've had an idea. I'm going to go back to the road. All you have to do is hang on, okay? I'll be as quick as I can.'

'All the way back to the road . . . on foot? Why?'

'There is no other way.'

'The question is: Why go at all?'

'To try and get hold of a doctor, an ambulance, maybe.'

'Forget it, my friend.'

'Why should I?'

'To begin with, it will take forever.'

'I know. But it's your only chance.'

He tries to smile. His lips are putty-colored.

'Fat,' he replies. 'Fat chance.'

I take his pulse, which is feeble and very fast. He watches my face closely.

'I am dying,' he says.

'Oh, no, you're not. You'd be no problem if you were. The trouble is you're as strong as an ox, man. You could lie around like this for days. Me, if I had a hole that size in my belly, I'd be upstairs by now, playing a harp.'

He says nothing for a long while, staring at a root.

Then he says:

'Kill me.'

I look down at him. Fold my arms. Smile.

'Good idea. I'll cut your throat, shall I? Then I'll chop off your head, and stick it on a stick. I'll hold it up high, your head, and wave it this way and that when I carry it back to the road. Flag down a passing car.'

'Don't mock me, man. I'm gut shot.'

'And I am trying to help, remember? Look, I'm sorry, but the bad news is, you're going to live. All you have to do is hang on, okay? I'll be back before dark. Or just after, maybe.'

'So that's the plan. Running away again, I see.'

'Sure. All the way back to where we came from, if I have to. Why, what else would you like me to do? Sit down beside you and hold your hand?'

'You know very well what I want you to do. You know why, too. It's not the death, it's the dying. To be dead is nothing. I'm not afraid of my own corpse. What I can't do is just lie here, hour after hour, and take it, the pain.'

'I'm not going to kill you, Digby. Forget it.'

'In Christ's name, man! You could always say I asked for it.'

'You asked for it, all right.'

'Do it, then! Do it, and be quick. That's all I ask.'

'Too late – I can't. Not now.'

'Ha! Is that your final word? I don't believe it. You, the big bold bloody arsonist who only this morning would have given his left ball to settle old scores with me. For a chance, mind you – let alone an invitation!'

'True. But that was a long time ago, now. Before the fire. And besides, at the party I didn't need an invitation.'

'Afraid now, are you?'

'Me? No, I'm not afraid, Digby. You are.'

'My God. If that's what you think, give me the knife – I'll do it myself.'

'No.'

'Look. Don't make me beg.'

'Oh, come on, Digby. You're not going to die and you know it.'

'You're lying. You're a coward, and you're lying. I am dying, and we both know it.'

'Anything you say, professor.'

'Oh, no. Nothing. Nothing that I say . . .'

He shuts his eyes and I listen to the rasp and rattle of his breathing. Then, just as I turn away, his eyes open a crack.

'Water.'

I go at once and fill a paper cup.

Returning, I put a hand beneath his head, and raise it slightly so that he won't choke. His hair is thick and sweaty.

I lean forward and touch my forehead to his.

'I want you to know,' I say, 'I hit the kombi, yes, but I had no idea that you'd get shot instead of me.'

All he can think of now, it seems, is the water, which spills down his chin as he swallows.

'More.'

I bring him another cup, and he finishes that in a few shaky gulps, too. Then he lies staring. His eyes are very wide, dark and deep.

'. . . 'll do the trick,' he mutters.

I say nothing.

What I am trying to do is to weigh up my chances. From here to the high-way is no easy walk, I know. At least four, maybe five hours, straight. I'll have to cross the path of the bushfire, too. Then, as soon as I can, I'll need to stop a car, hitch a lift back to the town, and seek out a doctor. (I check my watch. It's ten minutes past one.) After which, I'll still have to find my way back here again in the dark. Midnight. It will be midnight, maybe later, by the time we get back.

'Cold,' Bamford moans, and I hear his teeth chattering. 'It's cold under this tree.'

'It's your own fault if you're freezing,' I scold cheerfully, on principle (sympathy can undermine). 'You want to hang around without pants on, don't you?'

'No, no . . . body temperature sinks in response to severe . . . severe blood loss.'

'Oh, yes? That's no excuse.'

I go and collect his jeans and underpants. The jeans I try and pull on to his legs, only to find that the slightest movement – let alone the bending of his knees, which I do not attempt – sends a jolt of pain to wrack him. I stop, therefore, and simply drape the jeans across his upper thighs. The underpants I crumple up and tuck as a pad beneath his head. I take off my T-shirt, too, and spread it over his chest.

'Now you look like a clothes horse.'

He is breathing through clenched teeth. He seems not to hear, but raises his head a little again and glances around wildly.

'What time,' he says, panting. 'What time is the shoot?'

'The shoot? We won't miss it, don't worry.' I squat on my heels beside him and place my hand on his. 'You hang on, okay? You're doing fine. The shoot can wait.'

He shuts his eyes and lies still for a moment. Then his eyes snap wide open again, and he seems almost frantic.

'Did you see it?'

'See what?'

'There, on the table. There! Exhibit A.'

'The skull? Why, what's wrong with it?'

'Is it safe?'

'Oh, yes. Safe and sound, lording it over all the party goodies. Do you want me to bring it to you?'

'No, no, can't you see? I should never have risked it. Not the real thing. And to think, all the time I had a replica – perfect, a plaster cast – locked up in my office, in a glass cabinet.'

'Plaster, white plaster? A fake?'

'No, listen, it's not what you think. It's perfect, the spitting image, even to the weight and feel of petrified bone. A sculptor made it, moulded it.'

'Sounds good. Maybe we'll use it next time.'

'Yes, yes. Next time . . . !'

Loosely at first, but then harder and harder, he begins rolling his head from side to side.

'Take it easy,' I say, slipping my hands between his temples and the buttress-like walls of the roots. 'Easy. You don't want to damage the tree!'

'Listen,' he hisses through clenched teeth. 'Did I say it right? You heard me. You watched. Christ almighty, almighty Christ! Did I do it, say it right? Did I? I tried, tried, tried. Did my best. Over and over. All I wanted to do was to polish

. . . polish my performance. You saw me. I saw you see me. Was I good? Tell me: Did I do it right? 'It's real,' I said. 'Wonderboy is real. Here we have it – the fact, the hard and staring fact. This is no stunted, brutish, ape-like thing, but man, man as we know him: tall, upright and conscious. Man, in whose brain the cosmos is born to self-awareness. Against this skull there can be no arguing. We came first, you and I. Out of the blue! Let us not be afraid, therefore, to look into the mirror and declare: I am the crown of existence, the living upshot of chance and time, of a moment of mystery that will never return. Aeons before the knuckle-dragging root-crunchers went shuffling and grunting their way up an evolutionary cul-de-sac, man, the star of the show, sprang into being here, right here in South Africa.'

For once, there is no faulting his command of the script.

'You've said it all, all right. Loud and clear.'

He stares at me wordlessly for a moment.

'What have you done?'

'Me? What do you mean?'

'Where have you put it – the skull?'

'It's right there on the table, as I told you. Look, let me bring it to you.'

'No, listen. What you must do now, at once, is take it and store it in my bank vault. Let me give you the number: eight, three, five, oh. . . .'

'I don't need the number, Digby.'

'You will, you will. After the funeral. . . .'

'Hey. You're not going to die, remember?'

He stares at me. His lips move. Still shaking with cold, he manages to roll on to his back and gasps, snores. I rearrange the clothing on his body, and sit still for a while. Suddenly he raises his head again and stares around vacantly.

'What happened to the ambulance?'

'It's on its way. It won't be long, don't worry.'

He shuts his eyes and breathes through his mouth, his lips twisted back.

'My guts,' he whispers. 'Oh, Jesus, no! I'm not – not going to. . .'

A slow paroxysm seems to grip his body, and he groans, screams. But I hear other sounds, too – a distinct squirtling or puttering – while a thick stench arises. I lean away, try not to breathe.

He opens his eyes and begins to plead: 'Believe me, never before in my life has anything like this ever . . . ever happened to me. . . .'

Ashamed – of him? of myself? – I sit upright again. Breathe normally.

'It doesn't matter. Let it happen. I'll clean up afterwards.'

'You must understand, I didn't mean to . . . you know . . . believe me. . . .'

'You're wounded, man. It's not your fault.'

Again the paroxysm grips him, and he groans. Thick and rotten, the smell hangs round me, settling, it seems, to the roots of my hair. I bend my head and wait, willing to submit, openly and with all patience, to the squalor of our common humanity.

'It's okay,' I say to comfort him. 'You hear? It's okay, don't worry.'

He flinches as I pat his shoulder – flinches, shudders and rolls his head.

'Eight, three, five, oh, oh, eight, six . . .'

I watch the blood that has long come seeping through the makeshift bandage. Now and then I strike out vainly at the flies. I remember, too, the goat – the blood-drenched curly white hair of his neck, the fixed golden stare of his eyes.

'You're going to be okay,' I repeat. 'Just hang on.'

I wait until the movement of his bowels has come slowly, sluggishly to a halt, then go and fetch a packet of serviettes from the party table. I stop for a moment and split the cellophane seal with my teeth, only too pleased to have laid hold of so ample a stack of fresh, clean, tissue-like paper.

'Here. Let's try and make you a bit more comfortable.'

I ease him up and over on to his good side. Heavy and helpless, he goes sagging, half sprawling. His buttocks, small and moon-white, are all smeared and spattered. Worse yet, the bulk of the load has squeezed its way up between his thighs, I see, where it clings. I hesitate. Under the full onslaught of the stench, I cannot but object aloud:

'Do I have to do this?' But I brace myself. 'Here we go!'

Using large bunches of serviettes, I begin to wipe. Rapidly, I drop one pinched-up bunch after another.

'Shit-logged,' I remark in an effort at good cheer.

Shaking his heavy head, Bamford moans:

'No-o-o . . . !'

'This won't take long. I promise.'

But the job proves stickier than I anticipated. No matter how hard I rub, vile stains remain like old yellow bruises. I fetch a bottle of whisky from the table, soak a handful of the serviettes, and rub again – and at the very first swabbing his skin comes clean.

'There you are now. It's all over.'

Taking him by the shoulders, I let him roll slowly over again. He drags for breath, groans. Livid, sweaty, he lies staring at me without really seeing. I call his name but he does not respond. Alarmed, I slap at his cheeks. He rolls his head and mutters something I can't catch.

'Say again?'

He does not stir, but his lips twist away from his teeth:

'Too... too tight, this bandage. Please... could you...?'

The bandage, such as it is, is in fact quite slack. Still, I undo the knot slightly.

'Better?'

'Thank you, yes.... Much... much better.'

He shuts his eyes and lies without moving, his mouth half open. As I stand beside him, listening to the hitch and struggle of his breathing, it occurs to me that he may be sinking into a coma. If so, my presence can make precious little difference now (if it ever did). I stoop, gather together the bunched-up, used serviettes. Balancing the bundle lightly, I walk far out into the burnt stretches of the veld.

With a whoop I throw the lot high for the winds to take and scatter. Then I kneel and scour my hands with sand and soot. Having not yet let go of the bottle, I am able to rinse quickly, too.

'Here's luck!'

I take a mouthful of the whisky, which bursts, hot and fierce, down my throat. I cough, rock back on my heels, blink away the tears.

Before me lies the blackened plain. Tall columns of smoke hang in the distance, silent. I look up into the sky. Birds up there the size of pinheads, wheeling in a long slow tireless wheel. If they are what I think they are. After all, what is this fire-ravaged stretch of veld now but a vast *table d'hôte*, as it were, of tasty treats for scavengers? As they hang up there, what do they see, I wonder, the vultures? Do they fix their telescopic focus on the world below only to discover, say, a porcupine, still crawling, though scorched of its spines? Do they know at a glance the difference between a rounded rock and a tortoise baked in its shell? What else can they possibly see? A hare, maybe, doubled up and seared to the bone? Here and there a twisted snake? A whole warthog or two, horribly burnt? A greater kudu, fallen to the flames, its charred bulk a feast for a week for the entire flock? And what if they have already sighted that once-famous expert on *homo erectus*, or *sapiens*, is it, Digby Bamford, lying here under the wild fig, dying?

African magi, *sangomas*, teach, I am told, that in its death throes the spirit, animal or human, is cast out into the sky in a widening spiral. Drawn into this spiral, vultures descend as they do, slow wings outstretched.

I check my watch again. Twenty to two. Many hours yet to midnight. What will the full moon look upon, I wonder, when at last she comes rolling over the horizon? What but this desolate plain, black as a shadow, where nothing moves save a hulking hyena, limping along, chuckling and screaming as though trying in vain to hug to its ribs some insane secret, while jackals drift round at its heels or drop back into the night, their cries like splinters of ice. And you are about to commit Digby Bamford to the tender mercy of such creatures as these, are you?

I return to the camp.

I walk slowly, tapping the bottle against my leg. Now and then I stop and take another swig, thinking. My head is ringing. I am beginning to feel solidly drunk. In a tribute to pure reason I lift the bottle high, squint at the sun, and recall step by step the classic syllogism: All men are mortal. Socrates is a man. Hence, Bamford, too, is mortal. In fact, at this moment Bamford is busy checking in his mortal chips. If you stand where you are and strain your ears slightly, you will hear the slow, strangled rattle and slur of his breathing. From the corner of your eye, if you look, you will catch sight of his corpse – or what is about to be his corpse – beached high and dry among the wild fig's roots. Aye, very like a whale.

I do not go back to his side. Not immediately, anyway.

What would be the point?

Instead, taking my time, I return to the camera. Idly, I set my eye to the viewfinder and trigger the playback. (The tape has long since rewound.) For a minute or so a set of bars in monochrome holds steady, then comes a plunge into blackness and white lightning, and up flicks Vicky's image – clear-cut, perfect, like a diamond.

'A relic!' I assert and take another swig. 'From before the flood.'

I wipe my mouth on the back of my hand.

Too bad I have seen it all before. Too bad I don't care. (But watch it again I will. I will watch every move, every gesture.) What if by chance you have at heart a secret yen to help humankind? What would you do, if only you could? Treat time like a videotape, spin it back on itself, erase what you don't like, take multiple retakes, stop only when 'what I did' becomes identical with 'what I wish I'd done'? Oh, yes. You *wish*. Too bad you know already exactly what will happen. Too bad you know, too, that nothing you know can stop it from happening all over again. And the upshot is? What God Himself knows. Omniscience is far from omnipotence. Knowledge is *not* power.

I take another swig.

'Well,' I conclude, 'I'm not God. All men are fucked.'

Vicky smiles, looking straight into camera. Only a little too slack, her breasts rise and fall quickly with her breathing. Pale penny nipples. Her face stays tensed up against the sun, which makes her look quite shy and ordinary, like the girl next door; or rather, a not-so-young, naughty housewife playing at backyard porn. She grimaces now, or giggles. (In the absence of sound it is impossible to tell which.) She shrinks to the left, and I look closer. She is not quite out of the frame: a smooth pan, almost unnoticeable, reclaims her. But now Bamford's body jumps across the screen – broad and white, his back. He clasps her to him and strikes up a waltzing stance. His mouth moves. I know what he is saying: Ta da!

I lift my head, step back, look around. I need to breathe, to catch my breath. The old ache, the old pain, has me by the throat. But this time there is no small bird tapping out its rich, sweet cry of blood. There is only the burnt-out kombi, its insides still smouldering, and beyond, in a huge emptiness, the fire-ruined plain.

When finally I put my eye to the viewfinder again, I see that he has placed the shotgun like a horizontal bar under her chin. He is whispering in her ear, too, while forcing her to face the camera. This I have not seen before: I must already have left for the kombi. The seconds tick by. They both stand smiling fixed holiday-snapshot smiles. Watch the birdie! Aren't we cute? A blissful pair. But now something happens. That it happens off-camera makes no difference. (The camera itself, I am pleased to see, withstands the shockwave from the exploding kombi, and does not rock or sway, not for a moment.) Bamford is thrown off balance. He tries to steady himself, but his foot fails him. For a moment it looks as if he is going to keel over. But all he does is lose his grip on the shotgun, which goes sliding, tumbling down from Vicky's chin to her collarbone, against which it bumps, while his arms flail the air. Very deftly, neatly, almost as though she has practiced the move, she reaches up and catches hold, and in a single swift movement turns, just as he regains his balance. Her back is to camera. The shotgun is slung lower now, at hip level. She stands still. There is no sound, but from slight movements of her shoulders I can tell she is speaking. All Bamford can do, it seems, is shake his head and raise his hands as if to say: Hey, wait! Me, I'm just a helpless, harmless old fat fellow, see? Now, he is speaking, but only a lip-reader would be able to make out what he is saying. Vicky keeps the shotgun pressed to her hip in a snug, tight fit. But suddenly she is shaken by the recoil – and Bamford falls bang out of sight, knocked clean off his feet by the force of the blast.

'No!' I yell out loud.

It can't happen like that. I won't let it. Too stunned to move, I murmur (from force of habit, perhaps): 'Okay. Let's try it again, that take. One more time.'

In fact, if this were a real movie, the whole scene would have to be reshot – at least, until we got the dramatics right.

WANTED: ACTION (HARDCORE)

Listen, Digby, don't just fall over flat. Screech a bit, first. Stagger. Lurch from side to side. Hold your guts. Squeal. Show us your teeth. Hiss like a kettle. Look down in disbelief and try to stuff the blood back in again with your fingers. We've got to see how slippery it is, see? We've got to see the look in your eyes. We've got to see how your knees buckle, how your face goes all doughy and dumb with dismay. We've got to watch as you slowly topple over. Good, that's better. Now, say something. Anything. Say: Please! Or: Help! Or: For God's sake! Or choke, as the blood comes trickling from the corner of your mouth: Why me, my love?

In reality, Vicky is left standing with the shotgun. She gives a single quick glance over her shoulder, into camera. Then she, too, steps out of the frame. The camera continues to record, but only to show the bush beyond – not even the fire, or not as yet – while I say under my breath: 'My God.'

I can't believe what I have seen. I spin the tape back, review it in detail, but I have made no mistake. I slow the tape down, let it drag by, frame after frame. I switch to the portable monitor, and the action leaps out at me, a tangle of limbs. The colour values, too, are all awry. Naked skin blooms a rich pink, teeth show an edge, ice blue. Still, there can be no doubt.

She shot him. Deliberately.

He knew it, all right, but didn't tell me. Why not?

'Bamford!' I yell.

I run back to the tree. He is lying as I left him, dragging and gasping for breath.

I grab hold of his shoulder. Shake him.

'Why didn't you say? Why didn't you tell me? She shot you! Vicky shot you!'

He snores and screams, groans, and drags for breath. I sit down next to him. I push and shove him until he rolls slowly over on to his good side again. In that position, he may speak, perhaps. He did so before. But all he does now is snore, puff out his lips and groan. I wish to speak to him myself. I say in his ear:

'I know! I saw!'

He is deaf to my words.

It takes him about an hour longer to die. There is nothing I can do but sit beside him in the shade of the wild fig and wait. Occasionally, I push him around again or shout in his ear.

Later, I watch the vultures come dropping, one by one, from the sky. At first all you see are their shadows skimming the earth, then the ungainly-looking birds themselves come sailing down to land on their heels and go skipping, running for a short distance. They stop and bob their bald heads and peer up and around. A thin whitish fur seems to cling to their necks. They shuffle their wings and sit hunched.

'Why don't you fuck off, you dirty bastards? Go on. Fuck off. Fly!'

Once or twice, I try and chase them, and they sail away on outstretched wings, but never far. In the end, I give up. I tell myself to ignore them, to pretend they don't exist, grotesques, freaks of nature that they are. At one point, however, moved almost to pity by the sight of their shriveled, skinny crops (or simply out of curiosity, perhaps), I get up and pitch into their midst the rank chunk of goat's meat: a consolation prize.

I watch as they squabble briefly over it. They buffet each other with their wings, rap and hammer down with horny beaks, and rip and gouge. As soon as one bird dares to hook or snatch the chunk from another, the others pounce and wrest it away. All hobble and dance over the battered piece of meat, which grows ever smaller and more ragged. Dust gets kicked up. Soon, the last scrap is gone. Then, with no sound but a soft rattling of feathers and the odd click of a beak, the vultures settle down again – a dozen or more of them in a wide, ragged half-circle.

As for me, I put my hand on Bamford's body. It is cold to the touch, chill.

'Dead,' I say aloud, feeling the weight of the word at my fingertips.

I sit looking down at his face. Were it not for the cluster of flies, the whites of his eyes would show. Flies trickle around his open mouth, too, or stay fastened to the corners. I try to wave them away but they stick. In the end, since there are simply too many, I no longer try to ward them off. Instead, I turn my attention again to my T-shirt, which is still wrapped around his chest. I tug it away from him, put it back on. After all, I tell myself, he won't be needing it any more. Then I sit down close beside him.

'You fool,' I whisper in his hairy ear. Yell: 'You fat fucking fool!'

In my fury, I fall upon him, beat him with my fists. I slam at his ribs, hoping to crack them, make them cave. (They don't.) Finally I fall back again, breathless, wretched, shaky. I cover my face with my hands and, I don't know why, begin to cry. For my own father I did not cry, not once. But now, for this buffoon, this dead fat fraud of a professor, Digby Bamford, I cry. Hard, wrenching sobs that tear at my throat, and turn at length into a string of hiccoughs, then into nothing but a hollow pain behind my breastbone.

For a while, I sit staring. I feel very distant, very empty.

All right, then, I tell myself. That's that. Up you get. On your feet. The least you can do now is to scratch out a grave for him.

I try. But the ground turns out to be too hard and stony, the knife too light. In the end I am left with the huge weight of the corpse bearing down beside me. I fold the heavy hands across the chest, set the ankles together, and make an attempt to shift the body as a whole. Almost immediately, I have to admit that I don't have a hope in hell of dragging or rolling it into a hole, even if I could dig one. The next best thing, then, I decide, is to pack stones over it and hide it from sight. No pyramid of Egypt, this. A crude cairn, at best. But as long as it proves obstacle enough to thwart the assaults about to be launched by bird and beast, then, crude as it may be, it will do – at least, until such time as the undertaker's shiny black limousine comes rocking and swaying across the veld in order to claim his swollen – and by then no doubt stinking – corpse for a belated bourgeois burial.

There are plenty of stones around, of course, bared by the fire. One by one I carry them back to the tree – scorched, cracked and blackened stones. I pack them in as solid a pile as I can. It takes a long time. For fear of what the vultures might do if I turn my back, I don't range too far. I would hate to find the whole flock of these greedy creatures surrounding his carcass on my return. I can just see them craning their necks, burrowing into his entrails, gorging on the fat, blood and other slippery stuff, smearing their feathers, gloating, croaking, all but crowing over him.

I toil on through the early afternoon, fetching and carrying stones.

Each time I pause, I tell myself:

There you are, then. You've found them at last. The witch's stones.

Broad, sharp-edged, unwieldy, the stones wear away at my skin, causing my fingertips to bleed. In order to continue, I wrap my hands in the torn remnants of Bamford's T-shirt. Gradually, the mound grows, a sprawling heap, a five-pointed star. To my mind, it is more than a halfway house for a corpse. It is a monument to a failed idea. On top, its staring sentinel and crowning point, I set the Wonderboy skull.

Tired, but thankful to be done, I sit down to wait and catch my breath.

Far out towards the horizon, a single pillar of smoke leans toward the sky, while the land around is flat and blackened and bare. All I can smell is the bitterness of the charred wastes before me, the emptiness borne on the wind.

Behold thy kingdom. All yours, it lies around you, as far as the eye can see. And who lit the match?

A wisp of smoke still goes twisting up from the hulk of the kombi.

I take a mouthful of whisky, and allow it to leak, little by little, down my throat. Check the bottle. A good round tumbler or two to go yet, I'd say.

Without really wanting to, I find myself staring at the vultures again.

'Why don't you leave, little birdies? Fly, fly, fly. Go on. Go. You've lost your dinner, can't you see?'

Shuffling, bunched together, they sit, evil geniuses of the feast. They crane their necks, doting, their hard eyes bright and glittering. Or tilt their heads, critical, I fear, of my every word.

3

BLUE. A very particular and wondrous blue – hummingbird blue, I'd say, or possibly cobalt – her shirt catches my eye. She is far away yet, I see, just this side of the dried-up little spruit. Ahead of her, bared to the sun now like the stones and the ant heaps all around in the burnt-out veld, the path goes winding away, quick as a snake.

I get to my feet. Lean back against the tree trunk.

If I weren't so drunk, I'd leap up, spin round, and sing out. I'd yell: Happy, happ-ee-ee! I have enough good sense not even to try, though. My legs would only stumble, get tangled up, and topple me.

I raise both hands above my head. Wave.

'Here!' I cry. 'Over here, Vicky!'

She pays me no attention at all. She does not even look up. No matter. I slide down to a sitting position.

What I could (and should) do, I know, is make a more concentrated effort yet to drive off the vultures. I could, for instance, pelt them with stones. Or try. Plenty of smaller stones, half the size of my fist, are lying around here. If I could hit just one of the birds on the breastbone, say, or lower down, between the legs, I'd shock the whole lot of them, send them all packing. By what right are they hanging around, anyway?

Admittedly, the main problem is me. I am in no fit state to move. My limbs are inert, like logs at the bottom of a swamp. My mind, however, has stayed keen and clear – like ice, I'd say, except that it seems to me more like flame, an invisible flame, lit by the whisky. I feel I could talk on demand, volubly, intelligently, for hours. In fact, demand or no, I feel I would *like* to talk volubly, intelligently, for hours.

For want of better company, I decide to embrace, so to speak, the crowd around me again.

'Well, my friends? What do you think? Look. She is back. Vicky. Alive. Unhurt. Listen, I know how hard it is for you to think of anything but the next bite to eat, but why not try, just this once? Forget this fresh carcass of your fantasies. Swivel your heads round that a-way, that a-way. See? No, you're not looking. You are too narrow-minded, too stubborn. What names shall I call you? Psychopomps, ushers to the underworld? Black shrubs sprouted from hell? Two-legged urns for the dead? Or just good old garbage guts? Me, I could snap your picture, or pour out words like coins in a new-minted shower. I'm a poet. Or used to be, once upon a time. You don't believe me? Ask Vicky. She will tell you, for sure.'

At the sound of my voice, one or two of the vultures shift uneasily, but the rest sit tight. I lift the bottle. Shall I pitch it at them?

Not before it is empty.

I take a swig, a whole mouthful, and swallow.

What will she think of me, then, when at last she arrives? Here I sit, my hands still wrapped in scraps of Bamford's T-shirt–soot-soiled, slightly bloodied, white rags. Which will seem to her a sign of what, I wonder? Wounded innocence? Purity of heart? Surrender?

Wishful thinking. (I am very drunk.)

Oh, I admire her, all right. I admire her very much. Now more than ever, perhaps. Looking out across the stretch of burnt veld, I see the sunlight on her hair, the patch of blue that is her shirt. Even at this distance, I am conscious of the way she moves. It is as though each muscle and bone of hers is mine, or mine hers. I am able to scan the path up ahead through her eyes, to select each step in terms of her neat logic. It is as my own, too, that I feel her balance and poise, her cool, bold and newfound self-confidence.

I have seen your photograph.

It seems I may be moved to sing, cracked voice and all:

I want you, you, you,
No one else will do, do, do. . . .

I may also begin to weep big tears. Or fall asleep again without knowing it. Only, don't, I caution myself, don't vomit. Or, if you do, make a good job of it. Lay it all out before her in a gush. (This is me, see? This vile, acid, festering mess.)

Ants are trickling all over the pile of stones in search of a shortcut to the deconstruction site. If they have their way, in a year or two, Bamford will disappear underground, all but his bones.

Lachaim.

I sprinkle out the last of the whisky, a gift to the chthonic gods. The bottle I should pitch at the vultures, let it go smash. But I can't, it's too good: Johnnie Walker, Black Label. Expensive tastes you once had, professor. And now you are dead. I stow the bottle in a crotch of the roots, and slide a little further down the bole of the wild fig.

The toes of my tackies stick up. The longer I stare, the more unintelligible they seem – chalk-white, bulbous, looming like space junk – objects of dread I'd like to refute. Or hide.

When I look up again, she is a lot closer. I feel suddenly wary if not fearful. What shall I say to her? Hello, there, remember me? I'm the guy who lit the fuse, yes. I'm the guy who tore the clothes, who sprang the catch, who

   tripped the trap,

     burned the bush,

      blew the lid,

       flipped the bus,

        snapped the pics,

         slipped up again

and left you. Oh, yes. That's me, all right. Quite the guy. Do you know, I was well on my way already, headed for the hills, while you were still busy pumping birdshot point blank into Bamford? Ran right to the top of the ridge, yes. Bumped into the hippo's head at a bend in the path. You won't believe how much she has grown. Big as a boulder. Big as a house. Anyway, she sends her regards, hopes you are well. As for me, I'm glad to see you. Sit down, why don't you? Mind the heap of stones. A pity the whisky's finished, it looks like you could do with a drop. You're right, I am full of questions. Did you catch much of an all-over tan? Are you *yourself* at last? How does it feel, your trigger finger? Satisfied, or does it still itch?

I wait until she is not thirty meters away, rounding the kombi, before I call out:

'Vicky! Are you all right?'

More restrained than I, she does not reply. Avoiding the charred tussocks, choosing gaps of open ground, she continues to walk with grace and quiet dignity. All trace of coltishness is gone. Her eyes are lowered, her face smooth and still, expressionless, or – stubborn, is it? In the crook of her arm, she cradles the shotgun.

'Too late,' I remark, not slurring at all – which pleases me no end. Maybe I'm not so drunk, after all? 'He's dead and buried. See?' I hold up my rag-encased hands. 'I buried him myself. Didn't dig a hole, I'm afraid. Couldn't. In the end, all I did was stick these stones on top of him, like candles on a cake.'

Close enough to step on my toes, she stops and stands looking down at me. When finally she speaks, her voice is low and tight, cutting: 'What do you think you are up to, Rian?'

'Sorry, I guess that was a cheap shot, about the candles and the cake. I should no doubt have used a cliché. At least, it ruffles no feathers, a cliché. It may even help to smooth things over, who knows? In the world of the cliché, nonentity rules. Surprise is out of the question. Of course, if I were to adopt it, embrace it as a preferred part of speech, I might even learn a thing or two. Like the banality of being good. Or, how to be vacuous, mild and kind. Okay, then. I rolled these stones down on top of him like an avalanche. I dropped them on him like a ton of bricks.'

She puts her head back and studies me with narrowed eyes.

'Are you drunk?'

'Me? No, drunk is not the word. I'm happy. Hap-py, yes! Thankful! Here you are, safe and sound. I was beginning to think I might never see you again. I mean I fucked up, didn't I? Big time. Could have killed us all. Talk about out of the frying pan, into the fire! Well, it happened. And it was bad – I don't dispute the fact. All the same, here I am, back again. Relatively unscathed, as they say. And so are you. Maybe we should throw a party? Sorry, that was a cheap shot, too. The truth is, certain things simply can't be smoothed over. Take Digby's grave, there at your feet. It's a rude, crude thing, I know. Undug. Unholy. Unfit to house him or anyone for long. But it will have to do. For the meantime, I mean. To keep his fans from picking his bones.'

'Oh,' she cries, 'those horrid birds!'

For a full minute she says nothing. Her face is taut, a mask. Then at last, very quietly, she lets drop a biting question: 'What kind of man are you?'

I try to sit up, but can't. Instead, I smile. High above me, the leaves of the tree, caught in a breeze, stir, scattering sunlight like coins, new-minted coins, all over us.

'Funny, you know, but every now and then I ask myself the same thing. When I'm shaving, for instance, and I look in the mirror. You, I say. You with the face. Tell me. What is your excuse?'

'Go on. It had better be good.'

'Oh, but it is, it is! You, I say. You with the big brown eyes. Haven't you heard? Today is the day. Of Judgment, that is. Christ and trumpets. Flaming clouds. Blood and tears. No place to hide your skinny shanks. Any moment now, the dead are going to rise up, and point their fingers, and say: You! We died because of you.'

'I don't think so. The dead have more important things to do.'

'Like what?'

'Like staying dead. Look, Rian, if all you are going to do is make up a lot of morbid nonsense, forget it. Don't waste my time.'

'You too have more important things to do?'

'I do.' She shifts the shotgun on her hip. 'I want to get moving, get out of here. This is a terrible place.'

'It is. I agree. Burnt veld, corpse and vultures. At your feet, this hopeless drunk. Happy, he says. Happy, happiee-eee! Jesus wept. Bitter tears. And then they nailed him. Looks like I set the whole world on fire, doesn't it? And now comes the aftermath, the interminable aftermath. Well, we don't have much choice, do we? We have to carry on. It's twenty k's from here to the road. No way that we can make it before dark. Then, once we get there, we'll have to wait, God knows how long. Hitch a ride back to town. Contact the cops. Come back here with a mortuary wagon. Load up. Carry on.'

'Is that your excuse?'

'Is what my excuse?'

'Fate. You talk as if there's no choice, it's all fate, and we can't do a thing about it. Well, then, who is responsible? My God, Rian, look around you. Look. What kind of man could do a thing like this?'

I look, all right, but I'm also growing more used to the sight. Burnt veld is burnt veld, after all. Not uncommon in winter. Moreover, by bracing myself on the wild fig's roots, I manage at last – despite the tilt, as it were, of the turning earth – to sit up.

'A fool kind of man, maybe?' I say with a laugh.

'You're not at all sorry for what you've done, are you? Look at you, sitting there in a heap, grinning from ear to ear, only too pleased with yourself. Pleased, yes, and proud. But let me let you in on a little secret, Rian. You could blow up fifty kombis, you could set fire to the bush from here to Mozambique, and you'd still leave me cold.'

'I would, would I? Okay. So much for me. Talking of cold, what about Digby? Poor old Digby. Poor old blubber boy, poor old bragger. Who knows, maybe he was a great man? In which case, I guess it may even do him good to be dead. Don't the great tend to grow in stature once they are dead?'

'Stop trying to change the subject.'

I shrug. 'Okay. It's me you're after, I know, not Digby. But Christ, Vicky, he died hard! You should have heard him screaming.'

She gives the stones a fleeting glance.

'Should I? I don't see why.'

'Why not? I sat beside him, held his hand. He was terribly strong, you know. He hung on. It took him hours and hours to die. He had crawled here to the tree, was lying among the roots when I found him. Gut shot. He wanted me to kill him. Begged me to, in fact.'

'And did you?'

'No, Vicky. You did.'

She fixes me with a hard, sharp gaze. Her eyes are a rich, deep blue. (Look into them at your peril. You could disappear in those depths, drown.)

I scarcely notice the breasts beneath her shirt, itself a vivid blue, and buttoned to the throat. But I do see how difficult she is finding it to breathe. As if by reflex, her grip on the shotgun tightens, and I can sense how the barrels, which have been pointing down all along, begin slowly to tilt up.

She does not speak.

I watch her face.

At the same time, I cannot but be aware of the shotgun's focus passing over my groin, my belly, the center of my chest, to my chin and finally my forehead. If I were to lean forward, I could take the imprint on my skin. Perfect. Cold metal. A double zero. Here it is, then, the kiss of death. You have lived through this moment time after time. What now? What if, as Bamford preached and Madam Hippo agreed, the dark to come and the dark from which we all already have come, are identical?

I am sweating. A slow, cold sweat. At the same time, I seem to feel the alcohol steadily dwindling, withdrawing from my veins. I'll be sober again before I know it. Already my mouth is dry, my head beginning to ache.

I force myself to look up.

Conscious of nothing but her own accusing gaze, she stands holding the shotgun to my head.

'First,' I go on doggedly. 'First, you said something to him. I saw. Then you shot him.'

'You saw, did you? What did you see? I saw you ducking, running away.'

'Later, when I came down from the ridge again, I saw it all, from beginning to end. The whole show. If you like I'll let you see it, too.'

She glances over her shoulder at the camera, while the shotgun swings round and dips down to point at the ground again.

'You videotaped it?'

'Automatically. The camera was on at the time. It didn't matter that I wasn't there.'

'A camera can lie.'

'Oh? How so?'

'You could do things to it.'

'I could, maybe, but I didn't. Listen, Vicky, I don't blame you. Believe me, if I'd had the balls, I would have shot him myself. Or cut his throat. I had the opportunity, didn't I? More than once. And if I'd done it, I'd have said the same thing: 'Not me, sir, I didn't do it. Uh-uh, you've got the wrong guy. Sorry.' I'd go even further, and spout a boatload of sentimental bullshit about how undervalued he was, how huge a loss we have suffered as a nation, now that he is gone, and so on. And in a way I'd mean it, too. Not because I happened to like the lazy arrogant old bastard, but because, as he lay here bleeding, dying, all I could feel was this terrible pity. Aren't we all, all, ultimately, utterly innocent in the end? Do you know what I mean?'

'No, I don't. Not at all.'

'I mean, no matter who we are, no matter what we have done, we all just die. We are born, and we die. Okay, that's a platitude. Forget it. I'm probably asking the impossible, trying to say things that can't be said. Or that I don't know how to say. Too dumb, maybe. Tongue-tied. Listen, I may as well tell you, the trouble is, it doesn't look like an accident – not for a moment.'

'Why? What does it look like?'

'What do you think? You had the shotgun. He didn't. He was no longer a threat to you, but you shot him, anyway.'

'Then it wasn't what it looks like. I know exactly what happened, and it wasn't murder.'

'Oh? What was it then? Suicide by girlfriend? Digby using you to shoot himself?'

'Oh, for God's sake! Let me be and let me think.'

She shuts her eyes, shakes her head. With her free hand she begins to toss back her hair, which, I see now, is straggly, dusty. She has taken the strain, for sure. Her face is colorless to the lips.

If I could, I would hold her close. It's all right, I'd say. It's all right, my love. If you want, I'll get rid of the evidence. I'll chop up the tape, bury the pieces.

Leaning back and away from me, she puts a foot on one of the big stones and tips it, rocks it slightly.

'He is here? Digby is under here?'

The question is childish, painful. I suspect I was not even supposed to hear it. I pretend to be deaf or distracted, absorbed in a scrutiny of my fingertips, which turn out to be skinned, scalped – quite a sight. While a slow ball of anger rises and settles in my throat.

Too bad, I tell myself. The joke, whatever it is, is on you.

I look up at her again.

'For sure. One big tub of white flab. If you don't believe me, I'll unpack a few stones, and you can see for yourself.' I hold out both hands as though I am lifting, weighing, if not juggling a stone.

'No, don't! I don't want to see.'

'I won't strip him naked, never fear. You don't have to see things like his fat little dick, squashed flat as a frog on the tarmac. Or worse, the size of the hole you blew in his side. I'll only unload a few of the stones on his face. Just enough to prove to you it's him, all right. Him. Digby Bamford. Dead.'

The thing is, I'd topple over if I tried to get to my feet, let alone tried to pick up a stone. I'm all talk and no action, and she knows it.

'I told you I don't want to see.'

'You're not like me, then. I always want to see.'

'You're only too right, I'm not like you!'

As if simply indifferent, but in fact quite cold and hostile, she turns to leave, hitching the shotgun higher on her hip. In an attempt to detain her, I add a casual comment: 'He told me what a good shot you were, you know. Better than he was himself, he said. If you ask me, he was very proud of you.'

'Oh, I was proud of him, too! Just think. A man like him in this place, at this time. He had his faults and foibles, plenty of them, I don't deny it. But he did what no one else in this bloody fascist country could do. He made the whole world sit up and take notice of us, beyond politics – though they shut him up in that tight little box soon enough. And, yes, I did find him personally attractive. He was so big and bold and brave, so witty and intelligent. He seemed to relish just being alive. And he always made me laugh. Besides, as I told you before, he was always very good to me, very sweet and kind. Except when you were around. You brought out the worst in him, the very worst, each and every time.'

'As he did in me, for that matter.'

'But why? Why did the two of you hate each other so?'

I look at her. Just look.

'No!' she retorts rapidly, almost under her breath. 'No, forget it! I can't and won't be held responsible for your behavior.'

'Oh, come on. Why take it personally?'

'Why not? Don't tell me you don't mean it personally.'

'Who cares? As I see it, even dead, Digby wins.'

She lifts her chin. Considers my words carefully.

'Not always. Not with me, at any rate.'

I laugh. I can't help it. 'If he had, he wouldn't be lying here now, huh?'

'No,' she replies, more distraught than I expected, 'that's not what I mean. That's not what I mean at all. I'm sorry, but I don't want to go into it right now. I can't. What good would it do? It was an accident, a tragedy. I couldn't help it, don't you see?'

'No, well, I don't. What would you say happened, exactly? He was mauling you, and...?'

'I don't remember. He said something, and I said something back, and then.. . The gun went off. He screamed.' She looks away, unable, it seems, to meet my eyes. At the same time, she begins to finger, pick at the silver filigree work in the shotgun's stock. 'That's all.'

'Is it?'

'Yes, it is. I'm sorry. I'm so, so, so sorry, I feel sick.' She pushes a stray wisp of hair away from her mouth. 'Listen, I don't want to talk about it, think about it now. Okay?'

'All right, my love, all right. I won't push it.'

'Good. I have other things on my mind. More important things, if you want to know. Whatever you do, don't try and force me.'

'I won't. What would you like to talk about instead?'

She pauses, and – for the first time, it seems – her eyes are drawn to my mittens. She stares, fascinated.

'What happened to you? Did you burn yourself?'

'Not me, no. I'm not so incompetent, I hope. Which is not to say that it couldn't happen, of course. Chance is the dance, as they say. One life, one chance. Well, I took my chance, all right. The kombi rocked. You saw.'

'Any fool could drop a match.'

'Sure. Strike, flick and that's that. It was only much later, when I was busy putting together the Great Pyramid here, that my hands got rubbed a bit red and raw, and I had to wrap them up. All that fetching and carrying was hard labor, believe me. Stone after stone after stone.'

For some reason, her attitude toward me seems almost to be softening, though. It is too much to hope for, I know, but if only she would recall how fond of me she once was – simply allow the thought to slip through her mind – a smile might even touch her lips.

Looking down, she puts a foot on one of the stones again.

'You packed,' she notes quietly. 'You packed all these stones on top of him. And you went on packing them, you didn't give up, even when your hands began to bleed?'

'Why, what else could I do? Let his flock of hungry house guests go hop on their host as the main course?'

She glances over her shoulder. The vultures have not moved.

'Oh, those horrid, horrid birds!'

For a moment longer she stands over the stones, thinking. Then, as if determined to put an end to an intolerable situation, she turns on her heel and goes to the table. Pauses. Draws from the canister a half-cup of water.

'Not much left,' she observes.

'No,' I say. 'There was little enough when I arrived.'

'When was that?'

I check my watch.

'Two, two and a half hours ago. It feels like forever, though.'

She nods. Sips at the water. I watch her throat move as she swallows. Though I'm still too drunk to get to my feet, I can't help feeling happy.

'Vicky.'

'What?'

'Nothing. Just Vicky. You're back. Where did you go, what did you do when you left the camp?'

She sips more water, and swallows. At the same time, she makes walking movements with two fingers in the air, adding:

'All the way round the ridge.'

'Oh, no, my love –'

But she slams down the cup.

'Oh, for pity's sake! Can't you stop pretending? I'm not your love. I never was. You don't love me, Rian. You never did. What am I to you? Oh, don't worry, it's not your fault. You never had a chance. Just think. What have you ever loved? A picture on a wall?'

'The question is not what, surely. It's who. Who have I ever loved?'

'All right, then. Who?'

'Only you.'

'Is that so? Look. Read my lips.' She leans forward at the waist, points a finger at her lips, and only too distinctly speaks the words: 'I'm – not – your – love. But wait, there's more. I – don't – love – you. I never did. Get it?'

'Most of it.' With an effort of will, I overcome my sprawl, sit up again. 'All but one word.'

'Love,' I suppose?'

'No, 'never'. You wanted us to get married, remember?'

'Oh, for God's sake! What's wrong with you? Are you caught in a loop, a time warp? Grow up, man! Get a life. Listen, it may be news to you, but all those years ago, when we went to Magnet Heights, I was head over heels in love, but not with you – with Russell. Russell MacKay. Rusty. Remember him?'

'The playboy? Of course I do.' I try to avoid the blow by blinking, but it's no good, I feel sick to stomach. In a flash, too, I seem to see again his sloppy attempt to kiss me on the nose. Quelling the urge to tell her about it, I lean forward, only to land up accusing her lamely, with a twisted grin: 'You called him a doggy old man. You said he made you sick.'

'I did, I know. The problem was, I was really wild about him, crazy. I would have done anything for him, anything. I was in love. As far as he was concerned, though, I was just a little girl. He had the money to make a stunning catch, like a Jackie Onassis. He took me because I was there for the taking, the cherry on top of this huge big deal he'd clinched with my father. Big for my father, that is to say, not him. A few hundred thousand. He soon got bored, of course. Dropped me. If it hadn't been for the fact that I was on the rebound from him, I would never have wanted you.'

With a jerk she breaks open the shotgun. Scrabbling together a handful of shotgun shells from the table, she fits a couple into the breach. I catch a glint of bright brass, and relief goes flowing down my spine to mingle with my present sense of uncertainty.

'You didn't tell me,' I say.

'What are you talking about?'

'The gun. You knew all along but you didn't say a word. After Bamford, you didn't reload.'

'No, of course not.'

She snaps the shotgun shut. Next, with what seems like a careless glance back over her shoulder, she begins to study the vultures.

'No!' I object, suddenly realizing. 'You can't shoot sitting ducks.'

'They're not ducks.'

'Vicky! Don't!' I plead, and come stumbling to my feet. Absurd as it is, I have nothing to dissuade her with but a little weak irony: 'Honestly, they're really quite nice when you get to know them.'

She pays me no attention at all. Pausing only to push a few extra cartridges into her jeans' pockets, she steps out of the shadow of the wild fig.

The afternoon is growing cold. A gust of wind sweeps across the empty veld, sending tiny bits of charred stuff flying into my eyes, making them water. On the horizon the pillar of smoke stands as motionless as before. I should not let her do it, I know. I should not hang back like this, holding on to the tree. What I should do instead is go staggering, stumbling out after her, crying: Vicky! No! Wait! (Who cares if I fall on my head?) Better yet, I should stride boldly ahead, cut her off, deprive the butcher of her prize. Here I am, see? Mark my defiance. Note the pallor of my bony brow, the doughty set of my jaw, the flicker, like lightning, of my bright and sunken eyes. Who am I, if not the dread guardian of this burnt-out circle of hell? Go ahead, then, I dare you. A left and a right – me and the birds. A massacre, a mess. It's what you really want, isn't it? Blood all over the place, lumps of flesh, feathers. Ready? Raise your gun. Go on. Blow us away. I am waiting.

It may be a bit too late for me to play the part of martyr or messiah, however. She has already crossed most of the open ground. Quite casually, as if out for nothing more than a Sunday afternoon stroll, she seems to be heading for the kombi, or rather, the path beyond. What she is really doing, of course, is circling round, closing in on the vultures.

Even now I could (and should) rush out into the open. I could and should stagger this way and that, milling my arms wildly, yelling: Hey, you! Birds! Scoot! No doubt, if I do, I'll go and fall slap on my drunken face. If so, however, I will refuse to stay put – dribbling, whining, and grinding my teeth, eyeball to eyeball with the ground. I will force myself up on to my hands and knees. I will forage around, grabbing up sand and twigs, not to mention the odd stone, to chuck at the huddled mob.

All right, then, why don't you? Why not let go, and stand up to her, just like that? I could, too, if I didn't sag back in a slump, and let my head go lolling, my eyes fixed in a trance. Am I trapped by this tree? What is wrong with me? Am I sick, lame, lazy to the bone? Or is it no malady of body or soul, but something else, something distinctly cerebral? What am I, a pale and preachy Prince Hamlet? If only I were much drunker than I am, I could collapse, roll over and pass out. Better to fall headlong down a black hole, and land up flat on my back, sprawling, snoring away the afternoon, than see myself for what I am – a puny thing, a weakling, a worm.

A fitful gust shakes the tree. Gaps in the foliage offer ragged glimpses of a sky so empty in its depths, so remote, it reveals to me nothing if not my own emptiness.

'Vicky!' I cry out, or try to – it seems I have no voice.

Vertigo (that is to say, my own drunken mind) compels me to look down again, to stake my claim to solid ground. A step or two away, shielded from sight by the stones, and probably beginning to bloat by now, lies Bamford's dead body. What else is there to see? Scorched earth, yes. Scorched earth forever. And to my left, stranded, tilted slightly to one side, the fire-blasted shell of the kombi.

At first the vultures stay clustered together. Edgy, distrustful, they keep a sharp eye on Vicky. For her part, the shotgun snug in the crook of her arm, she moves with such simple modesty, such self-effacing docility, you would think butter wouldn't melt in her mouth. And nothing happens. Except that one of the birds stretches out its skinny neck and starts to scratch under its chin, or no-chin, with a hooked claw, desisting only when thoroughly satisfied. Then, shuffling its feet and shuddering its feathers, it composes itself, and blinks. Vicky stops. Using her hip as a base, a fulcrum, she swings the shotgun round and up, and triggers both barrels. The hard double thud dents my eardrums, and goes rolling out across the veld.

'Wahoo!' I yell, overjoyed.

She has aimed deliberately high and wide. Not a single one of the great scrawny birds has been hit, but they break ranks in a panic, anyway. Scrambling to one side or the other, half-tumbling over backwards, recoiling at the same time as trying to flap, they begin to drag and rack themselves up into the air.

Somehow, I don't expect them to go too far.

Vicky is actually smiling, I see. A spot of red glows high on each cheek. She is breathing quickly, too. Swinging the shotgun along at her side, she comes sauntering back to the table.

'Jolly, jolly good show!' I call and clap my hands – one, two, three times – as I prop myself up shoulder-wise against the tree trunk. We are so close now that she could reach out and press the shotgun to my head if she liked.

She gives me a curt, cool glance.

'What are you trying to do? Sound like Digby?'

'Digby? Who was Digby? Me, look at me! Here I stand. On my own two feet. Sober as a judge. Wise as an elephant. Strong as an oak.'

'Oh,' she replies, mimicking me with three slow handclaps. 'Jolly, jolly good show!'

Round the far side of the table are the deck-chairs, just as we left them. She takes the first to hand – none other than the one we caught her sunning herself in this morning, an aeon ago, Bucs and I – and sits down again, while an image of her, naked, flashes through my brain like a razor.

'Christ!' I whisper.

Quick to notice, she watches me with narrowed eyes.

'What's wrong?'

'Nothing.'

'Are you sure?'

'Sure, I'm sure. I'm trying not to think, that's all.'

'For you that oughtn't to be too difficult!'

'It's not,' I reply. And it's true. As suddenly as it came, the image is gone. I shrug, smile, spread my arms wide.

What is more, no invisible bird is now crying, blood, blood, in the thorn trees. For there are no thorn trees – only, at odd intervals, a stump sticking up like a charred finger, smoke still trickling from its tip.

She tucks her legs up, crosses them like a yogi, and lays the shotgun straight across her thighs. 'Here,' she says, patting at the seat of the deck-chair opposite. 'Come and sit here. I have something to tell you. Something important.'

'Are you sure? It's a long trek back to the road, remember. Even if we leave right away, we're going to have to walk on into the night.'

'You're wrong. It won't be a trek. Of course, on our way here we had to take the long way round. But on foot we don't. In fact, if we cut straight across that way,' she says, and points, 'it won't take too long at all. It's only about five k from here to the highway. We'll easily make it before dark.'

I look the way she is pointing, but it's at a right angle to the sand road, and seems to make no sense. Suspicious, I ask: 'How do you know?'

'A little bird told me.'

'A little bird called Bucs?'

'You're obsessed, you know. You really are.'

'Oh, no, I'm not. I'm joking. Sorry. I didn't mean to upset you. In fact, if you really want to hear about it, I don't care a fuck.'

All I have is a dull headache, a dry mouth. (Nothing, it seems, can beat the threat of having your head blown off to wipe the last iota of alcohol out of your blood.) First, then, I lean away, let go of the tree trunk. Next, without swaying, let alone tripping, stumbling or landing on my head, I step over the bulwark of the roots. Upright, concentrating as from a telescopic height (my feet, it seems, are at the far end of a tunnel), I walk the line, the straight line to the table.

After my hollow in the ground, the deck-chair feels lightweight, only too taut and formal. I place my hands on my knees, lean forward.

'How kind of you, my lady, to invite me to tea.'

'On the contrary, good sir. How kind of you to grace us with your presence.'

'What is it you want to tell me?'

'In a moment. I have a question or two first.'

'So do I.'

'Tell me. What happened to Nando?'

'Nando Killing Boy? Now, there's a funny name, don't you think? Nando Pretty Boy. Nando the Hero. Nothing. He left. Why do you ask?'

'Did you bully him?'

'Not in the least. I didn't have to. He got cold feet all on his own. Told me he wasn't a mad dog, and pushed off.' I jab a thumb in the direction he went when he disappeared. 'Out of sight, out of mind. A hundred years ago – that is to say, this morning.'

'A mad dog?'

'A porn star. A stud. Evidently he didn't like the role.'

'Oh, good for him! You see, I was right. He *is* a decent human being.'

'Believe it or not, I agree. He's a prince, our Nando, a right royal prince! A diamond in the dung, so to speak. Who in the world can compare with him? No one in this camp, and that's a fact.'

'Is that supposed to be a deliberate insult?'

'No, not only you. We're all in the same boat, aren't we? You, me, and Digby. We are, in a word, the indecent.'

'Don't you dare refer to me like that!' she cries, her face aflame. 'Or to Digby. Speak for yourself, if you are going to speak at all.'

'Me? Sure. I'm a mad dog, all right. A mutt. Owoo! But Bucs, now, Bucs is a joy to behold. Let's say it at once: Bucs is beautiful. So quick, so supple, he takes your breath clean away, doesn't he? No doubt about it, he's priceless. But, better yet, guess what? Surprise, surprise! Our Bucs is a mensch. A decent human being. He has backbone, our Bucs – a bit rubbery, I guess, too supple-to-wobbly, too dodgy and flexible, but backbone it is.' I sway my arm this way and that, rotate my wrist, but hold up a clenched fist. 'When push comes to shove, he will not be seduced. Or forced. Or treated like a fool. Try, and he shies away.' I drop my arm again. 'A gentle, sweet guy, it seems, moral to a fault, a pure bloody saint. Scared shitless, too, if you ask me.' I twist my mouth in what I hope is self-reflexive ridicule. 'Which is why he ran away and hid.'

'Good God, do you blame him? Look what you wanted him to do.'

'What *I* wanted him to do?' I pause for a moment. Then, in a parody of a lumbering Afrikaans accent, I propose: 'Listen lady, I didn't do nothing. Me, I just work here.'

'Oh, no, you don't! You're his boss, Rian Erasmus. He'd do anything you asked.'

'*I* asked him to disappear, did I?'

'No, you didn't. All you did was ask him to do horrible things to me.'

'Listen, lady, don't get me wrong. I know what you are thinking. In a way, it all depended on me. I was the nerd with the knowhow. Who else around here could shoot a movie, any movie, let alone a little skin flick? Most of the time, though, I was just the skivvy, the go-between. It was my job to run up and down with messages. First from the makulu baas ¹ to the black boy, then from the black boy back to the makulu baas. Make no mistake, it was Digby who was the boss. It was his big idea, your fuck fest.'

'I don't care if it was. You chose to play along, didn't you?'

'At first, yes. Pretended to, anyway.'

'But why play along at all? Why even pretend? Give me one – just one – good reason.'

'I wanted to see.'

'Oh? What did you want to see?'

'What you would do, my love.'

She draws a sharp breath. About to speak, she checks herself. We are still sitting facing each other, as we have been all along. Now, using only one hand as if to prove the strength of her wrist, she lifts the shotgun, balances its butt on a strut of the deck chair, and lets it stand – a gesture of command. Next, in a tightly controlled voice, she makes distinct her stance: 'Listen to me. Listen carefully. I would never have done the things

Digby said. Never. I don't, I couldn't even *think* of things like that.'

'But you played along, too, didn't you?'

'All I did was take off my shirt.' In a single rapid movement, but careful to be exact, she lays the shotgun down again, flat across her thighs.

'Funny, you know,' I remark, staring up into the tree, 'but when Bucs and I came back from the ridge –'

---

1. *makulu baas*, great big boss

'Oh, that! That was different. I didn't expect you back so soon. In any case, what *I* did isn't so important. It's you, Rian, you. It's what you did. You said it yourself, didn't you? You were the nerd with the knowhow. Good God, what did you think you were doing? Did you *think* at all? What did you expect, you and Digby, telling Nando to have sex with me, a white woman, in front of camera? Against my will, too. They hang black men for that in this country, you know.'

'White men, too.'

'For rape? White men, sometimes. Black men, always.'

'Okay, I don't dispute it. I don't defend it, either. This is South Africa. I know what happens here. So do you. I could maybe tell you a thing or two. Just a few hours ago, for instance, I saw quite a sight. I'll tell you all about it, later, maybe. In the meantime, listen: Aren't you forgetting something? The Big Bang. Ka-blam! Up went the kombi, sky-high. So? No go for the sex show! And who did it? Who went and pricked Digby's bubble? Who? Before you turned round and popped his fat belly yourself, I mean.'

'What you did was awful. Nando was right to run. I'm glad he ran, or rather, walked, off into the bush. How could he know it wasn't a trap?'

'Look, Vicky, I'm sorry, okay? I'm sorry I scared Bucs into the bush. I'm sorry I blew the kombi to hell and gone. I'm sorry I set fire to the trees and the grass, sorry I scared you out of your wits, sorry above all that you went and tore Digby a new arsehole, which killed him. Okay?'

She sits up very straight in her chair. Even her fingers on the shotgun are stiff, straight, rigid, I see, as she responds with low fury: 'What a stupid, puerile, not to mention foul-mouthed, thing to say. I didn't do anything to Digby!'

'No, you didn't. You shot him, that's all. Here,' I gesture. 'Just under the ribs.'

'I did not. You know I did not. You know what happened. You saw.'

'Oh, yes, I saw, all right. Over and over again, I saw. I played that tape frame by frame, time and again, until I knew exactly what it was that I saw.'

'Ka-blam went the kombi, as you say. Bang went the gun. That's all. An accident, that's what you saw.'

'I'd still like to know what you said to him.'

'Nothing. I said nothing.'

'No, Vicky. I'm sorry, but—'

'Stop it!' She kicks at me, having freed one leg from her yoga pose, but the shotgun begins to slide. She has no choice but to grab hold of it, and, once it is properly secured, sit cross-legged again.

'Stop what?' I ask.

'Stop saying you're sorry.'

'All right, all right, I will.'

My mouth is dry, my headache worse. After a moment, I ask her to pass me the water. As she does so, she shakes the canister lightly.

'Why is there so little left?'

'There wasn't much left this morning. Also, when I got back to the camp, I thought I was alone, and I drank quite a bit. Mind you, when I found him, I gave him his fair share.'

She stares at me, incredulous.

'You gave him water?'

'I did, yes. Two cups full. He asked for it.'

'He had a severe abdominal wound, and you let him drink?'

'Sure. Why not?'

'Water would kill him, that's why not.'

'Says who?'

'Says the whole wide world, that's who. Oh, you fool! You absolutely total bloody fool! Don't you know you never give a man with a stomach wound anything to drink?'

I smack my forehead. 'Aha, I see! How dumb could I be? It's not the gaping hole in your belly that kills you. It's only water, a little sip of water.'

I take my own sip of water.

'Oh, yes,' she replies. For a moment she is silent. Then, with a wisp of a smile, she looks at me. 'I didn't kill him, Rian. You did.'

'Of course! Who else?'

'Oh, yes, it was you, all right. You. He was so strong. You told me yourself how strong he was. Just think. If he hadn't had all that water to drink, he might be alive right now.'

'Alive and kicking! On his back like a beetle. Good old Digby. A belly full of birdshot wasn't quite enough to bump him off, was it? Never mind. A drop of water did the trick.' I sit back. Rub my face. The cloth covering my hands is stiff, grimy. I'd like to peel it off. Instead, struck by an idea, I stop. 'That's what *he* said, you know. Just before he died, he said: 'It'll do the trick.''

'What trick?'

'The water trick. Oh, yes. Believe me, my love. When he drank from that cup, he knew what he was doing. He knew what he was doing, all right.' I look at her, give a crooked grin, and carry on in a singsong: 'I killed him, you killed him, he killed himself.'

'Very clever. Cute. You think you have it all off pat, don't you?'
We are both silent for a moment. Then I say:
'Vicky.'
'Yes.'
'Like it or not, you're going to have to view the tape.'
'I don't see why.'
'Nobody is going to believe you, that's why. Your best bet would be a plea of self-defense, manslaughter. But I wouldn't count on it, if I were you. In this country they hang white women, too, remember. Not often, maybe. But they do.'
'For a shooting accident? I doubt it.' She shrugs.
'So do I. No one, not even Bucs would hang for that. As I keep telling you, though, the last thing it looks like is an accident.'
'I don't care. I know what happened. So do you.'
'Vicky. Please. View the tape.'
'Stop pushing me. I told you, I don't want to see it.'
'Your story, you know, it's a bit like Digby's belly. It just doesn't hold water.'
'What a repulsive thing to say! You really do fancy your way with words, don't you, Rian? I have come to hate you. Do you know that?'
'I do, yes. I also know there is nothing much I can do about it. I still want you to view the tape.'
'No, *you* listen,' she says. She drops both hands on to the shotgun, grips it. Seems on the verge of snatching it up, wielding it somehow, but simply stays tense. 'I will never live through that scene again. Never. No matter what you say, no matter what you do. I won't. I can't. Get it?'
I lean back in my chair. Think. Finally I admit: 'Okay. I get it.'
'You do?'
'No doubt about it.' I get up from the chair. Yawn. Stretch.
'Where are you going?'
'Nowhere. I've got to take care of a thing or two, that's all. It's meltdown time.'
'Meltdown time?'
'Yup.'
The vultures, it seems, have disappeared, after all. I scan the sky, but there is nothing up there, no circling specks. If only I had turned my back on the camp earlier, walked out on it, and not looked back. Then I could long ago have disappeared into the wild blue yonder, like Bucs. Bucs and the birds. Where is he now, I wonder? High on the ridge, maybe, hiding behind a boulder, safe from us at last. Or better yet, well on his way home, stretched out in the back of a bakkie, or sitting up comfortably in a car. (If so, may he forget all about us at once,

and live happily ever after, amen!) From here to the highway is no great distance, it seems. Five k's or so, she said. An easy walk, and he knows the way.

But who of all the whites sailing by in their smooth and shiny cars, or for that matter in their beat-up old bakkies, would stop and offer a lift to a guy like Bucs, a lean young township black with a sullen mouth and mirror glasses? None this side of hell. Not one.

I pause, run my fingers over the camera, tap at the hard plastic and chrome. (Kiss it goodbye, I tell myself, and mentally I do.) Then I squat on my heels by the VCR and wait for the tape to be flipped out. In close-up the laces of my tackies appear oddly inexplicable, as things that are things always do. The same goes for the trampled and scuffed red sand. What I would most like to do now is to scoop up the equipment, carry it back to the party table, slam it down in front of her, and say: Here you are, my love. Watch.

With a clatter the VCR ejects the tape, and I pick it up. All the way to the kombi, I expect to hear the scorched metal creaking, contracting as it cools, but it does not even tick. The thread of smoke from the cab is still going straight up into the air. By now I ought to be used to the smell of burning rubber, but the closer I get, the more thickly it cloys, rough on my tongue, black at the back of my throat. Spittle wells up, thick and sticky. I swallow it, vow not to puke – hold myself rigid.

Not daring to touch any part of the blistered metal, or for that matter the rim of shattered glass where the windscreen once was, I look in. It is like looking into a cavern – dark, empty, bigger than I expected. Everything is twisted out of kilter, seared, charred, almost beyond recognition. Only the tight-wadded padding in the seats, or what is left of it, seems still to be smouldering. Below the steering wheel's stump, the coiled springs of the front seat glow thin, orange-red.

I toss the tape on to the closest coils.

'What are you doing?' cries Vicky.

I don't reply.

I spit in at the seat. The saliva sizzles, hops, is gone. The videocassette folds slowly, crumpling in on itself, and collapses into a cat's cradle. A blue flame comes rippling up. The black plastic begins to drip. Ultimately, when it cools, nothing will be left but a crust, a lava-like lump.

It is time for her story to come true, perhaps.

Aware how open, but also how empty, powerless, my hands are in their shells of cloth, I return to the party table. I take my seat again, tip back my chair for the sake of the sway, the easy, light and carefree feeling, and she says: 'You know what, Rian?'

'No, what?'

She smiles. 'All you know is how to destroy.'

I look at her, just look, for a long moment. Then I let my chair drop forward to peg its feet to the ground again.

I tuck my hands into my armpits, hug myself lightly.

'But you do believe me now, don't you?'

'Oh,' she says with an ironical little smile. 'You want the benefit of the doubt, do you?'

'I want every benefit I can get. Far more than that, though, I want you.'

'You're so transparent, Rian. Like glass. I can see right through you.'

I try to reflect her smile back at her, rock myself.

'Where did we go wrong, you and I? I'd like to know. I'd like to turn back the clock, to begin all over again. Because... You know what, Vicky?'

'No, what?'

'I love you.'

She considers me without a word. At length, very quietly, she lets drop a final comment: 'Then don't make me the excuse for the things that you do.'

I say nothing. I look up at the sky. I would like to touch it, just reach up and touch it, that blue. Let it decant its openness into me, flow in through my fingertips, and dissolve all thought, all feeling I own, I am. Mid-afternoon, winter. Only too open and empty, the sky, a pale or bloodless blue, fading to white at the horizon's rim. It makes me feel how distant I am from myself, how close to vanishing point.

Well, what now? What is it you see up there, now? Immeasurable height, or depth? (Am I falling?) My throat is aching, dry.

I lean across the table for the canister, turn it upside down, shake the last few drops into my mouth. Then I toss the big plastic bin away from me, at the pile of rocks, the cairn. Against which it bounces and rolls.

'That,' I remark, 'is that.' I place my hands on my knees again, lean forward. 'Now, if you don't mind, I'd like to ask you a couple of questions.'

She shuts her eyes, looks weary.

'What is it you want to know?'

'Why did you stay with him? Why did you agree to do anything he wanted? Why did you degrade yourself, submit to it all? Why did you act the cute little Lolita all the time?'

'Why not?'

'First tell me why.'

'I told you. He was always very sweet to me.'

'Oh, sure, he was, wasn't he? I'll never forget how sweet he was when he saw you were camera shy. How sweetly he used his superior weight against you. How sweetly he held the shotgun across your breasts, your throat, and got you to turn when you didn't want to, and face the camera. How sweet of him, too, to try and get you to say that you wanted the shotgun to be – what was it – 'reaming your cunt'?'

'He was drunk.'

'And you, Vicky? What about you?'

'I understood him.'

'Ah, yes. A complicated man, our Digby.'

'You're right. He was.' She looks away. Then – she can't help it – she looks down at the stones again, but as if really seeing them for the first time. 'You'll never understand, but he never did a thing to me. He never lifted a finger. Let alone,' she concludes wryly, 'anything else.'

'I don't get it.'

'Oh, yes, you do,' she insists, giving me a steely glance. 'This time you do. This time you get it, all right.'

'Jesus. You don't mean that he didn't, that he couldn't . . . ?'

'Don't pretend you didn't know.'

'I didn't. I really didn't.' I laugh. 'Well, well. Who would have thought? What a joke. It's pathetic, really. Ridiculous. So Digby's dangler only dangled. Talk of a little thing! I'm sorry. I don't know why I didn't know, but I didn't. It should have been obvious all along, I guess, but somehow I simply didn't know.'

'Well. Now you do.'

'Yes. Now I do. And when I think of it now, it makes complete sense. Poor old Digby. Poor old droopy. It's so pathetic, it's absurd. A hoot, as they say. A scream. Christ, how fucked up everything is.'

'Yes, isn't it?' She shakes back her hair, passes her fingers through it. Looks at me steadily, then adds: 'Now, do you mind if *I* ask *you* a question?'

'Give me a minute. I –'

I lean forward, press the heels of my palms into my eyes. Stay like that. My eyeballs ache. I see floating sparks, flashes of light. At the same time, for no reason I can fathom, I seem to see again my own saliva, bright as blood, slipping in a long slow drop from my lips, as I hung head downward from the stoep at Mr Abie's. I feel, too, the way the railing pressed in under my ribs, stopping my breath.

HAPPYHAPPY

Words I ought long ago to have slurred over with my foot, or trampled on, stamped out. It is better not to have been than to be, O my father. Here I hang, then, upside down, or so it seems, under this tree. One day I will write a book called *Zeno's Trap*. Or, maybe, *No Way Out*. One day I will walk with both eyes shut straight into the sun. In this world that has burned. Which I can still smell. Char dust, I call it. (What matter what I call it?)

If I had a stick now, I would write in the dust, in smaller letters, far smaller:

> *my defeat and my shame*
> *hot in my belly*
> *to me,*
> > *like a child*

But I have no stick.

Somewhat drunk in the head yet, I drop my hands, sit up.

'That's it,' I say. 'I'm through. No more questions.'

'Good,' she retorts. 'At last.' She tosses back her hair, smoothes it with her fingers, shuts her eyes for a moment, then opens them wide, as if to accuse me to my face: 'Did you see the terrorists?'

'The *what?*'

'The terrorists. White soldiers. SADF. They surrounded a kraal on the other side of the ridge, and pulled it down, flattened it. I saw them. Did you?'

'Oh, them! Yes, I saw them, all right. Couldn't help it. Had a grandstand view, high up on the ridge. I saw them hit the kraal, smash into it, pull it down with their trucks and chains. I told you I'd seen quite a sight, remember? Only, I didn't say what. Well, that was it. The attack on the kraal. But you, where were you? I didn't see you.'

'On the ridge, too, lower down. I didn't see you either, for that matter.'

'You didn't see me, I didn't see you. We both saw what happened, though. A forced removal. White soldiers with guns. Talk of a total onslaught!'

'That was no forced removal, Rian. It was something else. A forced removal is too routine for them to turn out the army.'

'Well, whatever it was, they went about it pretty thoroughly. Reduced the place to rubble. Carted the madala and his whole family away, too, God knows where.'

'The who and his family?'

'The madala, the old man. Name of Jonas. Very old man, ancient. I tried to pay him for his goat this morning, but he wouldn't accept my money.'

'What goat? What are you talking about?'

'It's a long story.'

'It would be: It's yours. Talk, then, but be quick. Look at the sun. I don't want to waste any more time.'

A white flame of ice, the sun. Or an ulcer, an open ulcer in the sky.

I give her a truncated version of events.

She listens attentively, her eyes narrowed, her face pale. She does not say a word. Even after I have finished, she remains silent.

'That's it,' I say. 'That's the whole of it. Unless you want the details.'

'No, thank you. Not now.' In a single movement, she uncrosses her legs, gets up from her chair, and stands, looking down at me. 'On your feet. Come.'

'Where to?'

'I have something to show you.'

'I see. And for this we have time, do we?'

'For this we do, yes. On your feet now. Come.'

Clumsy on my feet (still pretty drunk, as, to my chagrin, I realize I am), I follow her to the path again. If there were in this world a god benign enough toward stumbling drunks, I would ask him to grant me one wish, and one only: the ability to step clean out of my body. I'd do it at once, then, step out, stand aside, and watch the dumb, lumbering, brute of a thing go staggering on a pace or two, veering this way and that, its senses too blunt to register what has happened, its stupefied limbs giving way at last, so that it goes keeling over to collapse. Then I'd seize my chance. Laying hold of it by the heels, I'd swing my body up and round, and heave it, fling it as far as I could. Let it go sailing helplessly, both eyes wide and staring, in a short, steep flight across the veld. Let it land, and go tearing along flat on its face through the stubble. Let it grind to a halt, and lie there forever, outstretched, dishevelled, like a sack full of broken bottles. (I'd do it, too, if I could. Drunk as I am, I'd do it.)

4

It seems a very long way from the camp to the little spruit. In the end, though, we stop, and stand side by side on the bank, looking down. It is quite a drop to the dried-up watercourse below.

I'm out of breath, glad of the break. She is so close I can smell, almost taste, the tang of her sweat.

'What now?' I ask.

Too fascinated, to lift her gaze, she gives only a nod.

'We jump?' I say. 'From this height? Without a parachute? Wahoo!'

'Stop it, Rian.' She touches my arm, looks into my eyes. 'Would you still like to know what I said?'

'You mean, when you ... ?'

'Yes. When I shot him. Would you still like to know?'

For a moment I do not speak. I can feel my own heartbeat. What I would really like to do is to cup her face in my hands, and kiss her dry unpainted lips. I would like to hold her, crush her, and whisper in her hair, her ear: You see, my love? You see? We two are one. In spirit, I mean, the true identity. Let no one (not even you or I) attempt to set us asunder.

In the end, though, all I say is: 'Yes. Yes, I would like to know.'

Still smiling slightly, she hesitates. I can feel the warmth of her body.

'I said,' she continues in a voice so low it is only a breath – I have to lean over to hear it. 'I said: 'Happy birthday, you fat fuck!'

Before I can react, she takes a few steps to one side, then follows a twist in the path down the side of the bank. My head spinning, I take the same steps, half expecting to fall, though I don't. Poor old Digby. Poor fat fuck. What did you say back? Not that it matters. You're well out of it now, and no mistake. And me? Me, I'm in the thick of things.

At the bottom, the dank smell of clay closes over me, a smell of shadows.

'This way,' says Vicky.

We cross a sandbar in sunlight, and begin to push our way through the reeds.

From here, the overhanging bank does not look quite so high. Glancing back, I can't figure out why the flames did not take the leap, why they simply went playing along the verge until they died out. If a single tuft of burning grass had toppled down here, or if even a few scattered sparks had begun to drift, this place would at once have been set ablaze, these reeds ravaged, razed to the ground.

'It's all so dry around here,' I remark. 'It should have gone up like that!' I snap my fingers. 'I wonder why it didn't.'

'I really have no idea,' she replies.

Her mind is set on the struggle with the reeds. Mine, however, is still full of the fire. I can see how it would have gone racing through, eating up these stiff dry crackling reeds in a single voracious sweep. Nothing, I know, could have forestalled the spread of the fire, save the wind itself. But if the wind had swung round (as it did), turned on its heel, and blown again from the opposite quarter, it would have sent the fire whipping, tearing flowing back on itself. Or blown it clean out.

'There,' says Vicky, and points. 'Look.'

All I see is a long low boulder, polished by the vanished waters, half buried in among the reeds.

'Why, what's there?'

'You'll see. Go on. Go closer. See what you find.'

I begin to press my way through the reeds again, while she stays close behind, taking advantage of the passage I open up. Even in winter the sun has baked this place. The reeds rattle, clash, and make stiff screeching sounds as I push them over, trample them down. Finally, only a screen, thin as the fingers of a skeleton, stands between me and the boulder. Wary of the leaves, which, though shriveled, are sharp as razors, I part the dry stalks, and step through. The reeds clatter, click. Behind me, the leaves whisper as though scandalized. And there he is. Smaller than ever, it seems. Or maybe it is just that the bunny jacket looks larger. His eyes, fixed on me, are wide and shining. He doesn't move, or make a sound. A whitish scurf of dried snot is sticking to his upper lip.

'The mfaan!' I say, and add, in an effort at irony: 'Uh-oh. Here's trouble.'

'Do you know him?' asks Vicky.

'Not really, no. Bucs calls him the mfaan. He's the madala's grandson, or great-grandson, or even great-great. . . . I don't know his name, but he's the little goatherd who saw me shoot the goat. I guess you could say he knows me better than I know him. Where did you find him?'

'Round the back of the ridge. Rian, never mind about the goat, I think he saw the whole attack – everything – just as you and I did. When I found him, he was crying, trying to hide. I picked him up and brought him here.'

We stand, Vicky and I, looking at one another through the reeds, while at our feet, almost in a ball, the little mfaan stays curled as tight as he can, staring, too scared to move.

'You picked him up? You mean he trusted you?'

'I'm a woman, remember.'

'Yes, but you are white. And you had the shotgun. You still do, as a matter of fact.'

'I left it leaning against a tree. Besides, I spoke to him very quietly, gently, for a whole long while before I dared to approach.'

'Even though he understands no English?'

'It doesn't matter. Like any child, he understands kindness, concern, and goodwill when he hears it.'

'You brought him here, then, and left him? You never thought he might run away?'

'No. Why should he? Where would he go?'

'This is home ground for him, remember. He must know plenty of good places to hide. Come to think of it, though, I would like to know one thing. Why didn't you bring him back with you to the camp?'

She looks at me very gravely.

'Because of you.'

'Me?'

'Yes, you! Of course, you. I had to find out if you were still dangerous.'

'I see. Of course. And am I?'

'Do you think I would have brought you here if I thought you were?'

I look at the mfaan again. He stares back at me. I smile at him, but he edges a little way into the reeds, as though he would like to be smaller yet.

'What now?' I ask. 'What are you going to do with him?'

'Take him with us, of course.'

'Where to?'

'We'll see.'

'Oh, yes, won't that be fun? If I shut my eyes, I can see it already. Two whites, strolling down the state highway, hand in hand with a black child. Welcome to sunny South Africa! What do we tell the cops?'

'Why do we have to tell them anything?'

'We don't, I guess. But still, you know, we might, just to be polite. 'Look,' we could say, 'we have nothing to declare, except one fat old professorial corpse. You can dig him up at dawn tomorrow, if you like. That hole in his belly was an accident, okay? Not anyone's fault.' 'And this?' they will ask, because they are boere, thick in the head, and to them, the kid is more suspicious than the corpse. 'Oh, this,' we will say. 'This is our little black buddy. We call him the mfaan. Say hello to the nice white gentlemen, mfaan.'

For obvious reasons, I keep smiling, and hardly move, but talk in an undertone as I say all this.

'Oh, for God's sake!' Vicky retorts. 'I hate these morbid fantasies of yours. You know I do, and yet you always. . . . Look, do you want to help, or not? Because, if you don't –'

She swings the shotgun, points it in a dismissive gesture. I understand. If I don't, I can go away and die.

'No, believe me, I do want to help. I only wish I knew how. You see – just look at him – I'm pretty sure he hates me.'

'With good reason, don't you think?'

'Yet, you know, I'd never do him any harm.' I go down on one knee, open my arms. 'Hey, mfaan!' I call. 'Come to me, my lightie. Come.'

He gives a strangled little whimper, his eyes rolling, and tries to curl up completely in a ball.

'Don't frighten the child!' cries Vicky.

She steps forward herself. Treading lightly, carefully, she moves toward him, making soothing, cooing sounds as she goes. He allows her to pick him up, and she settles him on her hip, where he looks quite big. While she herself looks lopsided, overloaded.

'Pass me the gun,' I suggest. 'I'll carry it for you.'

'No, thank you. Never.' She hikes the mfaan a little higher, more comfortably, on her hip. 'Let's go.'

Halfway up the bank, she undergoes a change of mind, however, and turns to me. 'Take him from me now, will you?'

'Sure, if he'll let me. Here, put him on my shoulders.'

The little boy struggles, clings, as she tries to pass him to me. I reach up, get hold of him under the arms, and lift him.

'Hey, take it easy!' I say, as he kicks.

Only when Vicky pats his head, however, and talks to him again in baby-talk ('Soo-soo-soo-soo') does he begin to calm down and accept being placed on my neck. Even then, he stays crouched, hunched up, his whole body tensed against me.

I come slowly upright, clasping his small ankles to ensure that he won't fall. He hangs on to my hair, clutching at it, until I get him to clasp my forehead.

'It's okay,' I say. 'It's okay, mfaan.'

I take a single step higher.

'Hurry up,' calls Vicky, already at the top of the bank.

I don't want to. I move with care, step by step. I feel very tall, top-heavy, as I climb. The mfaan hangs on tightly. His small body stays tense, and he digs his heels into my chest, while I continue to steady him, my hands on his feet. His pants smell of pee, but at least they aren't damp. And the soles of his feet are hard, exactly as Tant Koba once said.

'Ja, tante,' I say aloud, smiling. 'Tante was right. Hard like horn, these little black feet. But, you know what, tante? This little boy (if only tante could see him), believe me, he is the real thing. More real than me, ja, tante. The mfaan we call him. Another charge of God.'

I feel less drunk, more happy. Grinning broadly, I crest the bank.

Vicky notices. Looks at me closely.

'What's wrong?'

'Nothing. Just thinking of my old aunt, tant Koba. You remember her, don't you?'

She shrugs.

'Not really.'

With that, she turns her back, and sets out along the path again.

It is mid-afternoon now, and cold. The sun seems both to have retreated to a great distance, and to be standing quite still. We do not speak again, but carry on in single file, Vicky some little distance ahead. The tree, I see, has begun to stretch its shadow across the plain, while the burnt-out wreck of the kombi stands stark, stranded. The thread of smoke that rose from the cab is no longer visible. The fire inside must be dead.

We do not go back to the camp itself. There would be no point. As we follow the path round the kombi, I catch sight of my camera, attentive on its tripod, waiting for me, but I don't give it a second glance. I overlook, too, the table with its load of party trash, and the vacant deck-chairs angled around it. Instead, I marvel again at the tree.

'Would you believe it!' I say at the top of my voice, slowing down, and staring into the rich green foliage. 'Not a single leaf got licked when the balloon went up.'

My impulse is to add that the rags tied in knots up there remind me of nothing so much as Tant Koba's curlers. But Vicky, I know, is not listening. I know, too, that I am not nearly as entranced as I am pretending to be.

What I am trying to do is avoid the stones, the whole crudely packed pile of them. In particular, I am trying not to think of the corpse in its cradle of roots – the gross white bulk of it, shrouded as it must be in shadow (except for scattered bright spots where daylight falls upon it through chinks). I seem to see, too, the wound in its side, wide open, crusted with blood, a glittering black. Where once there were flies, now there are ants. Palpably, too, in my own body, I can't help but feel how lumpy, dented, and, in places, how oddly flattened, the dead flesh has become beneath the static pounding of the stones.

Stones are stones, I tell myself. The sky is the sky. The dead are the dead. And that is that. But no neat little tautology packs the power to withstand, let alone exorcise, the images crowding my head. I stop where I am, then turn and stare hard at the stones.

'Hey, look!' I call. 'Look, Vicky! Over there! Right there! Do you see?'

She turns, glances round once or twice, then again at me.

'What is it?'

'The stones, the witch's stones. You see? I told you I would show them to you some day. And today is the day. There they are, see? All in a heap, just as I promised.'

'The what?'

'The witch's stones.'

She gazes at me unwaveringly for a long moment. Then, as though stiff with astonishment, she remarks: 'I don't know what you are talking about.'

I grin weakly, merrily.

'You don't get it?'

'No, I don't.'

I keep on grinning, as if it's only a joke, after all. Sweating though I am, I feel cold. The sky overhead is empty. No birds up there, nothing. I shiver.

Out of the blue, a cross-wind hits the camp. The tree gets side-swiped, buffeted, rocked. The leaves thrash and surge, but have nowhere to go. Stripped from among the foliage, little prayer cloths come whirling about us like so many torn and tattered white butterflies. A slight lull follows. We catch our breath. Then the next gust hits us head-on, and the mfaan huddles close. I turn my back, raise my hands in a vain attempt to shield him from the dust.

Just as suddenly as it arrived, however, the cross-wind is gone. All is still again, still and clear.

'It's okay, little big guy,' I say. 'Okay, okay.'

He hangs on tightly. A slight hitch in his breathing – a hiccough, brought on, I suspect, by his long fit of sobbing – keeps making his small body jerk.

'You sound like a bird,' I tell him, and pat his small feet. 'You chirp.' In what is becoming a refrain, I add: 'It's okay, little big guy. It's okay, okay.'

I try not to jolt him as I take long, somewhat stilted, strides in my haste to get back to the path. I'd even like to sing to him, but what could I sing?

I – a warrior?

I try again to spit, but my mouth is too dry. Soot and grit have settled between my teeth. When I swallow, all I get is the bitter aftertaste of the fire.

'Vicky,' I call. 'Hang on. Wait for us, will you?'

She pretends not to hear. Intent, it seems, on making up for lost time, she does not slacken her pace. I don't have a hope in hell of catching up, though I try my best.

'It's all right, mfaan. It's all right, little mister.'

On the horizon, under the weight of the wind, the pillar of smoke is leaning to one side – about to fall, in a silent, slow-tumbling avalanche. Otherwise, nothing moves. Not a bird. Not even a dust devil.

Late afternoon sunlight bathes the burnt-out plain in a golden stillness, like peace. We press on.

Me, half-drunk, with the little boy on my shoulders.

Vicky, slender, graceful, single-minded, the epitome of self-control. On her hip, dipping and tilting, riding high, the shotgun.

And all the while her shirt is blue. A very lovely blue. Bluer than ice, or sapphires. Hummingbird blue. Or possibly cobalt.

I shut my eyes. My throat aches. Not far to go now, I tell myself. Not too far to go to the road. (And then? Once we get there, what then?)

In the meantime, the mfaan has begun to trust me, it seems. Enough, anyway, to slump, go to sleep on my shoulders. I shift my muscles slightly to keep him secure. Glance up at the sun.

Don't think. Walk on.

AN ARMY TRUCK. The road is deserted, but for an army truck.

Far away as I am yet, I get the sense that it has been dumped, drawn up under a flat-topped thorn tree and dumped, left standing at so steep a tilt that it seems about to keel over. I study it.

No soldiers around, either. I keep scanning the bush to left and right, half expecting a bunch of them to come bursting out at me, yelling: 'Halt!'

Fear, I tell myself, and question whether I need it.

No doubt, if I were Bucs, I would get off the road at once. I'd duck, dodge, crouch down behind a tuft of grass and hide – do what it takes to save my own precious butt. But I am not Bucs. I will not run and hide. To the contrary, I will continue to walk down the very middle of the road, an open target.

Ever since I left Vicky and the child (or rather, since they left me), I have had this need to keep moving. Where to, I don't know. My only fidelity now is to the road, or rather its backbone, the broken white line. All the same, I cannot help feeling that I have somehow stepped over an edge – perhaps *the* edge – and that I am now in free fall, headed straight for the truck.

The sun is not yet down, but the moon has appeared, very high in the sky, and so pale it seems almost translucent. I look around. Long shadows slash at the earth, and the first chill of evening has begun to sink its grip to the roots of the bush. Ahead of me, glints as of metal appear on the tarmac.

An army truck.

Fall and fall as I may, in the end I walk right up to the truck without incident. I step onto the bumper, and look in through the semi-circles the wipers have cut in the windshield's dust. The cab is empty.

I press my palms to the hood in an attempt to judge how much heat has ebbed from the engine. Little is left, and the air is thick with the smell of oil.

I lean back, cup my hands round my mouth.

'Hullo, hullo! Anybody home?'

No reply.

Next, as if upon a childish impulse, I rock back and forth, but the stiff springs do not give, the truck does not topple. I would need the strength, or perhaps the weight, of ten men, to roll this dumb monstrosity over. And why not? After all, it could well be one of the gang of three that tore down the madala's kraal.

I drop to the ground again. Rap my knuckles on the mudguard. Thick iron. Dull sounding.

'Come on!' I sing out. 'Come on, open up! Show your face.'

Except for the shrilling of cicadas, however, all is silent. I turn, look back the way I have come, lean up against the truck. Think.

It did not take us as long as we had expected to reach the road. For a while we followed the path, our shadows stretching out behind us. Then, when the wild fig had at last disappeared from sight, and nothing remained all around us but the bare emptiness of the plain, we stumbled upon a donga which, like the little spruit earlier, had acted to stop the flames in their tracks. And Vicky paused – long enough for me to catch up, anyway.

'Kind of you to wait,' I remarked.

'Shall we cross?' she inquired.

'Shall we stay?' I retorted (quite wittily, I thought).

We walked a short distance along the bottom of the donga – dry as a bone, the winding rut of it, and no more than thigh-deep. Within a few steps of the other side, we came across another path which took us to a patch of dense scrub, all stunted grey bush bristling with long white thorns. More slowly, carefully, we pressed on. Not half a kilometer into the scrub, however, we caught in the distance the long tearing sound that a car makes at speed on a highway.

'There's the luck!' I announced. 'Five k's? It wasn't even two.'

I smiled but she did not respond. Her face was taut, pale. She gestured with the shotgun.

'Put him down.'

'He's sleeping.'

'I don't care. Put him down.'

I slid the little boy from my shoulders. Slack, sleep-heavy though he was, he went tottering over to her at once. She squeezed him to her side, murmured a little baby-talk.

'What now?' I asked.

'Now, *we* go that way.' She gestured to the north. 'And *you* go that way.' South.

'I don't get it.'

'It's very simple. You go one way, we go the other.'

'But why?'

'I don't want you with us, that's why.'

'Why not?'

'Because I don't.'

'Wait a minute, Vicky. You're not aiming to cross the border, are you?'

'Maybe I am. What's it to you?'

'Well, to begin with, it's a long way from here. A very long way.'

'We'll survive. And there will be plenty to eat and drink, once we get to the other side.'

'How will you do it? You don't have a passport, papers. You are not going to try and cross the river, are you?'

'Well, I'm not going to walk up to the first border guard and say: "I'm sorry, sir, I know it's illegal, but won't you let us through?"'

'Then you are going to try the river! That's insane. It's not only too wide, it's packed with crocodiles. Now you see them, now you don't. But they see you, all right. They see you, and grin to themselves with all their teeth.'

'Give up, Rian. You're wasting your breath. You're not going to talk me out of it. We'll go, the child and I. We'll cross the river, and we'll be safe.'

'All right, my love, all right.' In an effort to reach out to her, I took a step forward, but she stepped back, slipping the safety catch. 'What's this?' I said with a laugh, raising my hands in the air. 'A hold up? All right, if your heart is set on it, go. But let me come with you.'

She smiled a crisp little smile, and slowly shook her head.

'You never really get it, do you? All right. Let me explain in words of one syllable.' She gestured with the shotgun, first at my chest, then at the road. 'That way. There. *You. Go.*'

'Wait a minute. Think. What will you do when he wants his mother, Vicky? Not you, his real mother. He still has one, remember. Okay, so the army's got her, got the whole family, now. But they won't kill them. Why should they? They'll just go and dump them in the veld, somewhere. Some-godforsaken-where, I grant you. Still, it wouldn't be impossible for us, you and me, to find them. And once we did, we could give the mfaan back to his mother, reunite the family. Don't you think that that would be a good thing to do? The only good thing to do?'

'No, I do not. You know as well as I do, small children die when they dump them out there like that.'

'Very small children, babies, die, yes. And very old men and women. It's the madala who will die out there, not our mfaan.'

'"Our" mfaan? Forget it. He's not yours.'

'He's not yours, either.'

'I told you, forget it. I will *not* take him back. I will never, never take this child back to a place where men like you are only too eager to crush him, kill him, dump him in the middle of the veld to starve.'

'Men like me? You are very sure of yourself, aren't you? Open your eyes, Vicky. Open them wide. Look at what you are doing. You are kidnapping that child, not saving him.'

'Listen. I am going to count three. And if you're not gone, by then... One.'

'What about my question, the one I asked you way back among the reeds, where we first discovered little Moses?'

'His name is not Moses. Two.'

'Let me ask you again, then: What do I tell the cops?'

'Anything you like. Tell them I'm dead. Tell them I've gone to the moon. Tell them I'm in black, black Africa, now, and they might as well give up trying to find me. Racists don't have an easy time of it there. Tell them that. Tell yourself that. And don't you try and follow me, either. If you do, believe me, I won't hesitate: I'll kneecap you. You think I won't? Just try me. Three.'

Once she had spoken, there was silence. I stood listening for another car on the road, but there was none. I did not move. She pointed the shotgun at the middle of my chest.

'Go!'

I said nothing. I put my hands in my back pockets, looked around. The leaves of the tree beside me were a pale silver, very narrow, and delicately pointed. Ants were busy trickling up and down its bark.

Then I looked straight into her eyes.

After another long, tense moment, she lowered the gun.

'Suit yourself,' she remarked. 'Stay where you are. But we are leaving, the child and I. And if you follow us, I swear....'

'Don't worry, I won't. I've got a bright little idea of my own now. I'd like to see if it works.'

'A bright idea? You?'

'Oh, yes. It's bright like a diamond, my idea. It glitters. You want to know how I found it? A little bird told me in my ear.'

'Oh, really? What did it say?'

'I don't see why I should tell you.'

'Why not?'

Our role reversal made me smile.

For a short while longer she stood, eyeing me speculatively, tempted, it seemed, to raise the gun again. Then, with a shrug, she took the little boy by the hand, and set off down the path.

I watched until her blue shirt was out of sight. Then I began to make my way stiffly off the path and through the last stretch of thorn scrub to the road. I was very thirsty. My mouth was very dry. My hands in their wrapping of rags felt hot and swollen. As for my bright idea, it did not exist, let alone glitter like a diamond. What is more, no little bird had spoken to me, not even to tell me my name. At best, I was cold stone sober. At worst, an automaton, plodding onward, putting one foot mechanically in front of the other, while thorns hooked and jabbed, and once a branch struck me across the face.

A final obstacle, a barbed wire fence sprang up just short of the road, but sagged, caved in, as I trod on the lowest strand. I set out along the verge, but when loose gravel made me slip, decided to take to the middle instead. Fixing my gaze upon my feet, I kept count of strip after strip of the measured white line in the hope that I might ultimately be hypnotized. Also that I might thus hoodwink myself into believing that I was in fact getting somewhere, so that (in fantasy, at least) I would be able to walk all the way round the bulge of the world, and at last get back to where I had started. In the meantime, if a car came along, I couldn't miss it, and it couldn't miss me. We might even collide.

Standing now, however, in the shadow cast by the army truck – aware how massive, overbearing, gaunt, and empty a thing it is, how blunt an instrument of power – I can't shake the impulse to attack it, wreck it, somehow . . . but how? I put my hand to my belt, a helpless gesture. The knife is gone, I know. I must have lost it way back. Not that it would have been of much use, except to dig some scratch-marks into the paintwork – though its blade might just have been sharp enough to slash the tires.

I step back into the road. Move on, I tell myself. Walk. What point is there in hanging around? Abandon this place. Let go, accept the *status quo*, leave.

Except that Vicky was right, wasn't she? Kids in the townships don't give up quite so easily. They have nothing, no weapons to speak of, but no fear, either. In their running street battle with armed killer cops, they grab up any old junk they can find – sticks and stones, broken bottles, half-bricks – and hurl these at the enemy's head. The cops, who obviously 'feel nothing' about gunning them down, like later to crack jokes about their tired trigger fingers. But the kids keep coming. Not with a drunken and staggering yell, like your, 'Happy, happie-eee!' but a rallying cry so direct, wrathful and demanding it shakes the entire land, magnetizing the oppressed, inspiring them to cohere, to solidify into the masses who will one day roll forward to overwhelm and destroy this present order. Power! is the cry. Power to the people!

AMANDLA!
AMANDLA NGAWETHU!

You know, too, don't you—I tell if not taunt myself—you know, don't you, where such determination on the part of the very young (some not even ten years old) comes from? An unshakable belief in the slogan of the party underground, the graffiti which at every turn proclaims the fact that

VICTORY IS CERTAIN

Nothing, not even death, can stop those kids. Comrades, they call themselves. Fighters. The shock wave of the future. Hear us, they chant. They dance the toyi-toyi, kicking up dust, and surge forward, singing, clapping in unison. Daubed on the flaps of cardboard they hold up high is their vow of collective self-sacrifice:

OUR BLOOD WILL WATER
THE TREE OF LIBERATION

(And it will, it will. Wait. You will see. It is only a matter of time.)

Go on, then, I urge myself. Go on, why don't you? Grab up a handful of stones, say, and smash in the eyes of this bloody Goliath. Hit its headlights, tail lights, the lot—above all, that staring front windscreen. Who cares if the damage you do is less than a pinprick, ludicrous or worse in this uneven struggle? You might at least make your protest heard. Or rather, seen. Go on, I tell myself. Declare, if only symbolically, how much you, too, object to White Might.

Ah, how feeble, a voice in me says. Forget it. Nothing in this country is as lame as white-on-white protest. The truth is, bra', if you want to make a real impact, you're going to have to use your head.

Very well, then, I will.

Taking my time, I circle the truck once, twice. Stop. Check the petrol cap. In a single twist, it lies cupped in my palm. And all at once my heart is in my throat.

If I were to strip the rags from my hands, and knot them together, I'd have a short fuse, ready to blow. One spark, and this truck, too, would erupt, self-destruct, and be done with. All I need is a match.

I bend down, breathe in the fumes.

'This is it,' I tell myself, and take another deep breath.

My head begins to swim.

Then, at my feet, I catch sight of a few scattered orange peels, fresh ones. I rub my eyes, stare. A funny feeling down my spine tells me I am being watched.

Slowly I straighten up, look round.

And there he stands, a very big man, the soldier, not five paces from me, leaning up against the tree. His arms are folded, his beret flattened and pushed far back, as if he recently needed to scratch, and – to hell with it – let his curly black hair spring out over his forehead. How long he has been there, I don't know, but he may well have witnessed my every antic. What seems to me most striking, however, is not his face – inflamed as it is, burnt by the sun, and pitted, too, with acne scars – but the fact that he is wearing a pair of those mirror sunglasses, exactly like Bucs's.

I give him a nod.

'Middag,' I say. Good afternoon.

He raises his chin slightly, but does not say a word.

'I didn't see you,' I explain. With a glance at his sleeve, I add: 'I didn't see you, sergeant.'

Just then, the petrol cap slips from my hand, and goes hopping, rolling around at my feet. I have to stoop to retrieve it.

He waits, watches, as I grope along the side of the truck in order to twist the cap back on. Fixed in the mirror lenses, I am nothing if not agitated, a contorted midget.

Only when the petrol cap is in place once again, and tightly secured, does he speak.

'Ja,' he says, his lips stiff, almost motionless. 'Ja, and you? Who are you?'

I tell him my name, and he repeats it.

'Erasmus, ja. Adrian Erasmus. You make a lot of noise – do you know that, Adrian Erasmus?'

'Yes, I know, sergeant. But I didn't mean to disturb the sergeant. You see, when no one replied, I thought –'

'You thought? I know what you thought. You thought you could help yourself to a bit of free petrol, that's what you thought!'

'No, I didn't, I–'

He raises his head as if to examine my every word.

'Ja?'

'I was checking, that's all. As the sergeant can see for himself, I don't have a container, a can or anything, to carry petrol in.'

'Checking, you say? What were you checking?'

'Well, you see, sergeant, I was walking down the road when I saw the truck. I couldn't understand why it was leaning like this, all to one side, like it wanted to fall over. I thought to myself, 'What can be wrong?' Then, when I got here, I made a noise (as you call it), to see if anyone was around. But it didn't seem that there was. It occurred to me then that the truck might be empty, dry. So I looked, sergeant.'

'You looked, ja. I saw. You took off the petrol cap, and you looked. And what did you see?'

'Not much,' I admit with a grin. (The midget reflected back to me in the mirror lenses is an idiot, I see.) 'You can't really tell too much like that.'

He gives me a little lip-curling grin in return.

'You're right. You're right, my friend. You can't. Like that you can't. So why try?'

'Well,' I press on quite recklessly, 'to look is not the only way, of course. Sometimes, if you bang at the petrol tank, you can hear.'

'Hear what?'

'You don't know? Wait.' I thump at the side of the truck with the heel of my palm, bend my head as if I'm listening. My hands are sweating. The tips of my fingers are burning, stinging. 'There. Do you hear?'

'What am I supposed to hear?'

'That.' I thump again, once, twice. 'See? But you don't have to worry, sergeant. Everything is okay. You haven't got a belly full of petrol, maybe, but you haven't pissed it all out yet, either.'

'Oh, yes? What is this you are trying to tell me? That I can't read a petrol gauge? That I must go and bang on this truck with my fist to see what is in the tank?'

'No, I was just–'

'No, my friend. I've got eyes in my head. I can see for myself. And I see you now. Now, right in front of me, I see you, ja. I see who you are, meneer die meneer.' Mister the mister, that is to say, mister the pompous gentleman. 'When I looked, I saw you coming. At first you were far away in the distance, so far, and so small, you looked like a fly. But a fly is no worry. After all, a man can always wave a fly away from in front of his face, or catch it in a clap of his hands. But the closer you came, the bigger you got, and the bigger you got, the more you made me think. 'And now?' I said to myself. 'What now? Why is that man walking down the middle of the road? Does he not know where he is?'

'There weren't any cars, sergeant,' I respond. Too glibly, perhaps, since he pauses for a beat, a warning to me not to chip in.

'I know. But there could have been. In any case, my friend, it is not just cars that are the problem. It is always possible to see a car, or hear it, and jump out of the way. There are other things, too, besides cars, to watch out for. Ja, Adrian Erasmus. You were taking your life in your hands when you came down the road like that. No white man does such a thing, not in this part of the world. Not if he knows what is good for him.'

'Why not? What is wrong in this part of the world?'

'Terros.'

'Terrorists? Here?' I make a show of looking up and down the deserted road.

'Here, ja. Right here.'

'Says who?'

'Says me, my friend. I know, because I catch them. I wait, I watch, and I catch them. At night, they slip across the river in twos and threes, or they come on their own, alone, like you, now. They think I can't see them, but I can–I'm not blind. They bring their guns, they bring explosives. By day they hide in the kraals around here, by night they move on, looking for people to kill. People like you and me, my friend. Innocent people. Or better still, people like your wife, your children. Mine, too, if they get the chance.'

I smile at him cheerfully.

'Lucky for me I've got no wife or children, then, I guess. But is that why you are here now–to catch terrorists, sergeant?'

'Not only now, no. Day in, day out. I am never *not* here.' He shakes his head. 'Ja, my friend, if it wasn't for me, and people like me, then people like you wouldn't sleep easy in your beds. South Africa would be like the rest of Africa, full of blood and shit, rape and murder. There would be nothing but mad kaffirs all over the place, running around, waving sticks and stones, guns and knives, killing and chopping and stealing. *You* wouldn't be safe, I wouldn't be safe. Nothing and nobody would be safe.'

'And it's the army's job to keep an eye on things, you say, sergeant?'

'More than an eye, my friend. More than an eye. We keep the peace, me and my troopies. We look out. We look around. We do the job for you. We clean out every terro nest we can find.'

'You must be very busy.'

'We are, ja. Already this morning we cleaned out one kaffir kraal. There, up that way.' He points.

'Catch any terrorists?'

'Today? No, not one. Why, I don't know, but today, not one. Sometimes, you know, it happens like that. You look and you look, but you don't always find what you want.'

'I see. Got away from you, did they?'

'The answer is no, my friend. No, they did not. Terros don't get away – not from me, they don't. When I catch them, they die. *They* know it, and I know it. If I see them, it's overs kedovers,[1] finished and klaar.[2] No two ways about it, the terro who meets me is as good as dead. To his face I call him a dead man walking.

'This morning we looked high and low, me and my troops. We went through all the huts, one by one. We shook out dirty kaffir blankets, we kicked over ugly kaffir pots, we even looked down inside those stinking holes they dig for latrines. Nothing. No terros. Not a single one. In the end, then, what could we do? We picked up the kaffirs from that kraal, and stuck them in the back of a truck. Then we took our tow chains, and pulled down the walls of the kraal. You should have seen it, my friend. In five minutes we knocked that whole place flat. Sticks and straw, dust and dried cow shit, all gone flying. They won't come back again, those kaffirs, not in a hurry, they won't. There is nothing to come back to. Just broken pots and bits of rubbish that will all go under the grass again as soon as it rains. Ja, no doubt about it, in the end we set a good example, me and my troops.'

'And who do you think you will impress with your 'good example', sergeant?'

'Who do *I* . . . ?' Checked by the question, he pauses, stares. Then, very softly, as if he cannot believe my audacity, but may be prepared to pretend that only some sort of ignorant sentimentality stands in the way of my understanding, he continues, barely moving his lips: 'Listen to me, meneer. Listen carefully. Don't tell me you feel sorry for a kaffir. If you do, then you are making a big mistake. A kaffir is a kaffir. He is not like you and me. You can take a kaffir out of the bush, but you can't take the bush out of a kaffir. It's no good to try and say to him, 'Please,' and, 'Thank you.' No, what you've got to do is bliksem him,[3] – hit him like lightning – 'bliksem him so hard that he knows who you are. Then maybe you've got a chance. Then, if you say to him, 'Jump!' he will jump. Ja, I'm

---

1. *overs kedovers*, final (meaningless rhyme)

2. *klaar*, Afrikaans, finished; meaning: final, the end

3. *bliksem him*, hit him like lightning

telling you: In this case, I don't just 'think', I know. Slip up once, just once, and treat a kaffir like what he is not – a decent person, a Christian soul – and you will see what will happen.'

'Why, sergeant? What will happen?'

'You still don't know? Let me tell you again, then. Listen. A kaffir is a terrible thing. He is a thing without a brain. Chop off his head, cut it open, and what will you find? Nothing. A handful of worms, maybe. Snot and bone, and one big empty hole. I ask you: What can a man do with a thing without a brain? Ja, *you* know and *I* know. Nothing! A man can do nothing. Except, as I say: Bliksem him, bliksem him so hard that he won't forget. And then, if he still forgets (because he will), bliksem him again. And again. And then, if he shows you he still doesn't know who you are, kill him, break his neck, throw him down the pit of his own latrine, and let him rot. Ja-nee, my friend. White man on top, kaffir on the bottom. That is the way it is in this world, and that is the way it ought to be. It is also the way that it must stay. We can't afford to take chances. Not now, we can't. This is the land of our fathers, and of our fathers' fathers, and of their fathers again, who fought for it. If we don't want to lose what we've got, the ground under our feet, we've got to set an example that sticks.'

'Sounds like a tough job, sergeant.'

'You're right, ja. It is a tough job. But what can a man do? If the terro doesn't sleep, then how can we? If we shut our eyes once, just once, we will die. He will kill us all. We can't walk around with our head in the clouds, like you did when you came down the road. No, what we must do is make a plan. It's not so difficult, if you think of it. We wait for the terro, it doesn't matter how long. We wait for him, catch him, and rub his face in the shit.'

'We', sergeant? You keep saying, 'we', but when I look around, I see only you.'

'We', ja! Me and the others.'

'Where are they now, the others?'

'Out and about. In the veld. On patrol.'

'On foot?'

'No, in the other two trucks. There are two other trucks, twenty-five troopies in all.'

'That's a lot of troops and trucks, all right. Still, there is one thing I don't quite see. Why did they decide to leave you behind here, alone? You and your truck, sergeant?'

'No, never mind me, my friend. Never mind my truck, either. It is you who have got some explaining to do. Where do you come from? Where are you going? What were you trying to do, jumping up and down on the bumper of my truck, and shouting like you were mad in the head?'

I laugh a little, shake my head.

'At last!' I remark. 'I'm glad you finally asked. In a way I've been trying to tell you all along. You see, something has happened. Something bad, sergeant.'

'Oh, yes?'

'Yes. There has been an accident.'

'An accident? A motor car accident?'

'Not a car, no, a kombi.'

'A kombi, a car – what is the difference? But is that why you are walking? Because of the accident?'

'It is, yes. Because I had to.'

'Why didn't you tell me before?'

'I did. At least, I tried. Over and over again I tried. But, with all due respect, sergeant, I couldn't get a word in edgewise.'

'Well, then, now is your chance. Talk, my friend. Go on. Talk.'

'I will,' I say, and stop. My throat tightens, and I suddenly wish I were at vanishing point, so far down the road that it would seem totally empty. 'Look,' I say, 'I *want* to tell you what happened. You can see I do, can't you, sergeant? The thing is, there is a lot to tell, and I've been walking a long time. Listen, do you mind – could I have a drink of water?'

'Water?' He rubs his chin, while the glasses, ill-fitting, tilt slightly on his nose. 'No, now that is a problem. Water I haven't got. We finished all the water this morning. It is thirsty work, believe me, scraping a kraal down flat. Everyone drank. Look what I have got, though. Oranges! A whole bag of oranges.'

Not nearly a whole bag, I see, as he swings it up – a loose string bag of oranges with half a dozen or so crowded into the bottom. To judge by the peels scattered around his boots, he has eaten all the rest. Pleased with himself, he hoists the bag up triumphantly, and crosses to the truck.

'Strydom,' he says, putting out a hand. 'Georg Strydom. From Zeerust. You know, Erasmus, you don't have to call me 'sergeant'. After all, you are not a troop. Call me Org.'

'Org. Pleased to meet you, but –'

I open my hands, display my rags.

'And now?' he demands. 'What now? What is this that you did to yourself?'

I am the midget in the mirror again, I see, and as such, suspect.

'No, nothing, sergeant. Org, I mean. It was the accident that did it, not me. Honestly, Org, don't worry.'

'Me? Worry?' Curling his upper lip, he smiles slightly. 'If that is what you think, my friend, then you don't know Org Strydom.' Shoving a hand into the bag as into a sleeve, he rummages around. 'Here.'

I take the orange, thank him.

'I'm not going to eat it, okay? Just pulp it for the juice.'

'Do what you like, my friend. It's a free country. There is plenty more where that came from.'

Cool to my palms, like a blessing, the orange comes wrapped in the aura of its own keen scent. Oude Hoop. The flat muddy waters of the dam, dead still under the sun. Cracked concrete of the wall. Pa's forearm, where the lines of the tattoo kept shifting, spreading. A dagger. A hood. Down the tunnel of trees, flashes of dark and light, and the bakkie barreling along–leaves, leaves, thick with dust, splattering, shattering against the glass. Again and again, unable to arrest or deflect the bamboo cane descending, I see the blunt rubber cap on the tip pressing down, grinding, and the goldfish's guts bursting out. Cahoots. We are all in cahoots. Oupa Gert on the stoep, his mouth wide open in glee–his toothless gums, his stringy spit. In both plump fists the wire-bristled brushes he wields in buffing, scuffing at the suede of the panama hat. For the ladies. We do it for the ladies. You see, neef?

I set the orange down under my heel, and begin to roll it back and forth, while Org shakes another orange out of the bag. Ripping off a flap of peel with his teeth, he lets it drop with a vigorous flip of his lips. Digging his thumbs in, he tears away all further peel. Juice leaks, trickles, as the orange splits open. He picks out three or four segments, and pops them into his mouth. Chews. Swallows. Gazes raptly up the road before he speaks:

'There, up that way. Did you see? Never in my life, no, not in all my born days, have I ever seen a fire so high. When it stood up over the trees, it was like the Red Sea in the Bible. Only, in the Bible, they had more of a chance. A man can swim in water, but not in fire. When it was gone, it left nothing standing–not a tree, not a bush, not a blade of grass. In the end, everything, everywhere, as far as the eye could see, was like one huge black hole. If you look now, you can still see some of the smoke, lying flat on top of the trees over there.'

And you can, I see. A wreath of smoke, ghostly, has spread out across the tops of the trees.

'Yes, I did. I saw it, all right. Only, it didn't look quite so big to me.'

'You? Where were you?'

'Pretty close, at one point.'

'Us, too! Or no, not just close – we were caught in the middle. On our way back, the wind blew round, and it started coming at us through the trees, like it was stalking us, the fire, and about to jump. You should have seen then what it was like. This side, that side, every side, higher than the truck, higher than the trees.'

'Yet here you are, safe and sound, sergeant. How did you manage to escape?'

'No, I don't know. My eyes were stinging, and the smoke was thick, like wool. It caught in my chest, I couldn't breathe. But I just pushed the pedal flat, and drove blind like that, until we got away.'

'On your way back, you say? From where?'

'I already told you where. The kaffir kraal, the terro nest.'

'Oh, yes, of course! How could I forget? The terro nest without a terro in it. Which reminds me, you know. What did you do with the people?'

'The people? You mean the kaffirs.'

'Yes, all right, the kaffirs. What did you do with them?'

'You know, you ask a lot of questions, my friend. I thought you were too thirsty to talk.'

'I am.'

I lean down, pick up my orange, toss it from hand to hand, squeeze it, hold it at eye-level – all in an attempt to make it, not me, the object of attention. Shapeless, slack, and bulging, it yields easily to piercing by my thumb. I put my head back, and let the juice spurt into my mouth. A sunburst, sweet. I continue to squeeze, allowing my mouth to fill again, slowly, brightly, with the juice.

Org, beside me and brooding, begins to instruct me further in his ideas of realpolitik.

'Ja-nee,' he argues, 'a man must do what he must do. A kraal kaffir is no real problem. Put him in his place, and he will stay there. Bliksem him, and he will jump. But with a terro it is different. Him I have to kill. When I catch him, I take him on a little walk into the bush. Not far. Just a little way. He walks in front, and I walk behind. Then, when we have gone far enough, I put my gun up against the back of his head, just where it joins the neck, and, ka-pok! One time. End of story. Still, you know, a man must be fair. I always give him a chance. In fact, I give him two chances. Either he can talk, or he can not talk. If he talks, I kill him. If he doesn't talk . . . Ja, well, I kill him, too. A terro is a terro. He can't complain. He knows the rules. With a kraal kaffir, on the other hand, it's not the same. Him I put in the back of the truck, then I ride away, and chuck him out in the middle of the bush, where he belongs. There he can sit, and scratch in the dirt for another mud hut, if he likes. As a rule, I don't kill him. He is not a terro. Ja-nee, I know him, and he's not. But today, let me tell you, there is one kraal kaffir who, if I catch him, I will kill. Ja, Adrian Erasmus, as true as I am standing here, if I catch the kaffir who started that fire, I will shoot him dead. No question about it. Not a word, either. Not a chance, nothing. Just one bullet. Here.' He slaps the back of his head. 'Ka-pok! And why? Because the fire he started nearly killed us all, that's why.'

I delay dragging at the juice. Swallow. Listen to him with great care.

'Don't try and tell me,' Org continues. 'Don't even think you can tell me he didn't know what he was doing. He knew. He knew from the start. It was just too much trouble for him to clear a piece of ground, make a hole with his finger, and plant a mealie pip. No, for him the only answer was to chop and burn, burn and chop, until there was nothing left, only red sand, and everything else, black like his own black skin. I know him, that kaffir, I know him only too well. I know just what he did. This morning he got up, and took a stick from the fire where his mealie pap sits and cooks, and went and dropped the stick in the grass. And, *goosh!* Up shoots the fire, sky-high. Next thing, the wind gets hold of it, and it starts jumping around like a mad dog, biting at everything that stands in its way. And the kaffir? What about him? Does he say to himself: 'Look at what I have done. I'm a no-good black bastard, I should go creep into a hole, and curl up, and die'? No, how could he? He's got no brain, like I said. All he wants to do now is to go home, and sit in the sun, and eat his mealie pap, and drink his potbelly full of kaffir beer. And tonight, as soon as he is finished sticking his long black pole into his fat black wives, he will roll over, and snore in the dirt. The fleas and the lice don't worry him. Nothing worries him. What does he care, the black piece of shit, if the whole world burns?'

Georg Strydom, sergeant first-class in the South African Defense Force, leans back against the truck, and folds his arms.

'Org,' I object, squeezing the last drops of juice from the flattened orange into my wide-open mouth. 'Who knows how the fire started? It could have been anything. The sun through a piece of broken glass. Lightning hitting a tree.'

'Lightning hitting – ? My friend, it hasn't rained in these parts for the last four years. Where is your lightning going to come from?'

'Out of the blue! Just like that!' I laugh, snap my fingers. 'It happens.'

He smiles stiffly, gazing over my head.

'I'd like to see it.'

'I have,' I say. 'I've seen it.'

'You have?' He shows his teeth again in a little grin. 'All right. Call me, next time you do. I'd like to see it, too.'

'For sure. You wait. Lightning will strike, you'll see. In the meantime, do you mind if I have another orange?'

'Help yourself.'

'Patience,' I tell him, as I collect the orange, drop it, and begin rolling it back and forth under my heel again. 'If you're like me, you soon learn that if there is one thing in this world that you've got to have, it is patience.'

'If I'm like you? Why? I'm not like you, my friend.'

'I said if, Org. *If.*'

'I heard you, ja. So? Who and what are you?'

'I'm a photographer. Wildlife. I'm here because of the animals.'

He takes my word for it, nods his approval.

'Then for you this must be the Promised Land,' he says, serious, impressed. 'Everything a man could ever want to catch on a camera is running around here in the bush – rooibok, blesbok, warthog, zebra. Even, now and then, a giraffe. Me and my troops, we see plenty of them every day. Sometimes, we shoot them, too.'

'Ka-pok?'

'Ka-pok, ja.'

'Well, Org, I may use only a camera, but in the last few days, I've shot... Let's see. ' I count on my fingers. 'A leopard. A lizard. A kudu bull. The kudu, only this morning. You should have seen him, though. Horns – magnificent.'

'Ja-nee, but for me,' he replies, 'for me, a kudu is not just a pretty picture. He is a bakkie load of buck meat. If I see him, I go for my gun. 'One kudu, one bullet,' is what I say. I drop him in the dust, skin him, and take what I want. His horns I sell. His meat I eat. Or make biltong. The parts of him I don't want, the offal, I throw into the bush for the jackals to cry over.'

'Right, but for me again he was perfect – the perfect pic. You should have seen how he stood. Head up, eyes wide and dark, silent. And those horns, going up and up in a spiral against the sky. He was male, Org, male all the way to the bone – the blood, the muscle, and the bone. Male, too, as male should be, if you ask me. Gentle, and noble, full of deep wisdom, and quiet. If only I've got all that into my picture, believe me, I'm a happy man.'

Org yawns, and presses his fingers up under his glasses to rub at his eyes.

'Ja,' he agrees carelessly. 'I hear you, Mr Photographer. But listen. What about your camera?'

'What about it?'

'Where is it now?'

'Where I left it, back at the scene of the accident.'

'The accident! Now you are talking. I want to hear all about it, all about the accident.'

'Now?'

'Now, ja. Right now.'

'Org... Honestly, I'd like to, but –'

'No, my friend. No buts. Your throat is no longer so dry, is it?'

'No, it's not.'

'Well, then. Talk. It will be better for you if you do.'

The moon is higher yet, I see, and smaller. Clean and gleaming like polished bone, the cap of a cranium, say, it hangs in a sky that has changed, too, gained in depth, become bluer yet, like gentian. Night is coming on. Who or what am I in that infinite expanse, I wonder. I feel so distant from all things, not only the moon, that I might as well be suspended in space at this point, no more than a split hair, invisible, spun from glass.

'I can't,' I reply at last. 'I'm sorry, Org, but I can't. Not now. Not yet. I can see it all clearly, just as it happened, but I can't talk about it yet. Which doesn't mean that I won't ever be able to, of course. I will talk – I'm sure I will. Just let me get to it in my own way, at my own pace. Don't try and hurry me, okay? Things happened that I don't find so easy to talk about.'

'What things?'

'You'll see, I promise.'

'Oh? When?'

'I don't know. Just give me a chance.'

Org shrugs, and wiggles his little finger irritably in his ear. For the meantime, he lets me be. We stay as we are, then, side by side, neither of us moving or speaking. Gradually we sink into a more profound silence, spellbound, it would seem, by the shrilling of the cicadas. Then, as though I have simply allowed my mind to wander in pursuit of quite other things, I ask:

'Ever read a book called *The Soul of the White Ant?*'

'The what?'

'*The Soul of the Ant*, the *White Ant*. Ever read it?'

'No, not me. I'm not a big reader of books.'

'You're not, I'm sure, but this one you'd like. It's by the poet, Eugene Marais. Remember him? He wrote bitter little lyrics like: 'O koud is die windjie en skraal.'[4] Boer War poetry. We had to learn it off by heart at school, all of us kids, remember?'

'No, I don't. Him I don't remember.'

'Let me tell you, then. After the war over the gold, Marais went and lived on his own in the veld. Spent hours, days, years, studying ants, white ants.'

'What for?'

'Who knows? Distraction, maybe. His wife had died, and the war left him sick and tired of human beings, so it took his mind off things, maybe. Also, he had been dosed with what doctors in those days thought was the miracle drug, morphine, and he'd landed up an addict. Finally, he killed himself. Said he needed to shoot a snake, borrowed a shotgun, went out into the veld, and blew his head off.'

'Is that so?'

'It is, yes. But by then he had written *The Soul of the White Ant*, so in a way it was okay. It's brilliant – his best book by far. Poetic metaphysics in the guise of pure scientific observation.'

'Meta-.... *What* is this? What are you saying?'

'Me, I'm not saying anything. It's Marais, Org, all and always Marais. Look, he says. Go on, take a close look at an ant heap. It's not just a big lump of dried mud with all these tiny little creatures running in and out like clockwork. Go on. Look closer. Stick around, be patient. Analyze the way it is structured, and you will see: It's like a living organism, a body. And like a body, it needs a mind, a soul, to keep it organized. The worker ants are like the blood, the red and white corpuscles of the blood. The queen is like the brain. And when the ants get wings, as they do sometimes after a thunderstorm, and start swarming through the air, then they are just like the spermatozoa in sex.'

'No, now why bring sex into it?'

'I didn't. Nor did Marais. As always, it was there all along. But you're right. Sex is not so important. The real point is this: It's about us, Org. *The Soul of the White Ant.* It's about us, you and me – not to mention your troops, your wife, your children. You do see, don't you? Take the poetry, twist it a bit, stretch it, and – ka-pok! It's politics. The body is the body politic. The soul at stake is the soul, if that is the word, of the white South African.'

'Ag, no, man. Don't talk shit.'

4. *'O koud is die windjie, en skraal.'* 'O cold is the wind, and thin.'

'You don't like the idea?'

'No, I don't. In the first place, an ant is just an ant. It's got no soul. In the second place, an ant hill is just an ant hill. It's what you keep trying to say it is not–mud, a big lump of dried mud. Break off a piece, and you will see. It's hard and dry like beskuit, the mud, and full of little holes like a man could make with a drill, except that there are too many of them, you'd never do it. No, Adrian Erasmus. If you ask me, this Marais of yours got it all wrong, sitting alone in the middle of the veld and watching those ants run round his feet. It seems to me he had sex on the brain. Like you do, too, maybe. Sex and politics.'

'Maybe!' I laugh. 'Okay,' I concede. I have to be careful. I have been talking too much. 'Okay, I won't argue with you, Org.'

'No,' he insists. 'No, you won't. Because I am right.'

He helps himself to another orange, splits it open, bites it, sucks at it, slurps up the juice and the flesh. Once he has finished, he gives another wide yawn, and stretches to his full height, before settling slowly back on his heels.

'When I was a lightie,' he recalls, having pondered awhile, 'some days, after school, I used to go into the veld with a spade, or just an iron fence post, and look for an old ant heap, and stay there all afternoon. If the ants move out, a snake moves in. The ant heap is hard, like cement. You hit it on top with the fence post, or the sharp side of the spade, and it starts to break, to crumble in pieces. It's also got roots. If you use the spade, or the fence post, and get it in just right, you can turn the whole thing over. And then you will see the roots, because ants build down under the ground much more than they build up on top. Sometimes, there is also a hollow under the ant heap. Maybe an aardvark digs it. Or a ratel.[5] And that is where the snake, if there is a snake, likes to hide.

'Where I lived as a lightie, it's most of the time a rinkhals, the black snake who likes to stand up on his tail, and spit. He spreads his hood wide, as wide as your hand, and spits in your eyes. You've got to be careful. The clever thing to do is to wear goggles, like in a swimming bath. Then, when you are digging, you sweat, and the sweat gets in your eyes, but you don't take the goggles off. You turn the ant heap over with your spade, and all of a sudden, there he is, the snake. If he is angry, he will spit. But if all he wants to do is get away from you as quick as he can, he will jump out. Snakes can jump, ja–far. He will jump right over your feet, and then you will have to run fast if you want to catch him. But if he gets too much of a fright, he will play dead, the rinkhals. He will lie flat on his back, and stick his jaw out to one side. Then you can pick him up, stick him in a bag, take him to the snake park, and sell him. There they will keep him, and

5. *ratel*, badger

milk him for his poison, to make serum. Of course, you don't *have* to run and catch him. You can just kill him, if you like. Chop him to pieces with the spade, or smash him up with the fence post.

'Ja, when I was a lightie, I used to break open ant heaps and catch the snakes curled up inside. These days I break down kaffir huts to catch terros. If you think about it, though, it comes to the same thing.'

I have sucked my second orange dry. I tear it open, pick at the pulp.

'Org,' I say in the last light of the sun. 'I know who started the fire.'

He pauses.

'What is this?' he says softly, his lips barely moving, reflections rippling, spilling in the mirror orbs. 'What is this you are telling me?'

'I know what happened. It wasn't an accident.'

'How so?' he breathes.

'I haven't been able to tell you,' I say, 'because of your sunglasses.'

He stiffens, touches the rim of the sunglasses with his fingertips. I wait for him to say something, but he does not. It is as though he is dumbfounded.

'Those sunglasses,' I say. 'The terro wore them. Or a pair just like them.'

'The terro?'

'A swanky township lightie. He shot up our camp.'

Org releases pent-up breath in a rush, almost a whistle.

'Tell me,' he whispers. 'Tell me now. The whole story.'

'I will,' I say.

And I do.

I spin it out of the air. Some of it is true, some not. I tell him what he wants to believe, and what he will believe. I tell him what *I* want him to believe, too. And he will believe me, I know, because I know his world. No blame for him – he is a blind force acting on blind belief – but for me? For me there is no going back. Not now that my bright idea has finally occurred to me, and my words arise effortlessly, in a shining stream.

There were four of us on this trip, I tell him. Two camera crew, one talking head, and one girlfriend. We drove up here in a kombi piled high with equipment, our plan being to shoot some on-site footage for a lecture series on evolution, called *The Rise of Man*. No big deal, really. Canned instruction for undergraduates.

Org nods.

As you know, I say, my first love is wildlife. But, of course, for my bread and butter, I have a day job. You could call me a jack of all trades. I'm a cameraman, scriptwriter, producer, everything, even a gofer, for the university's video outfit, ACE-TV. I seem to spend my life patching together tape after tape for classroom purposes, like this one. Not that I am complaining, I tell him. On this particular occasion, for instance, I found myself working side by side with the distinguished professor, Digby Bamford.

'Ever heard of him?' I want to know.

'No,' replies Org, his face stiff, motionless. He is listening with total attention to my every word.

'A pity,' I say. 'Not that you should have, but. . . .'

Once upon a time, I say, the whole world knew Digby's name. Way back in the early sixties, he dug up a prehistoric skull that caused quite a stir in scientific circles. I will spare you the details, I say, but on the strength of that skull, he put forward a bold argument. Man came first, he said. We, or creatures in our spitting image, happen to have been roaming the veld around here a million years or so before things like the shambling ape-men of Olduvai Gorge reared their ugly heads.

'The *what* sort of things?' demands Org.

I spend a few minutes trying to explain, but he shakes his head.

'Ag, no, man. Enough. Just tell me about the accident.'

'Okay,' I say.

So, then, the professor came up here with his skull to shoot a video. It was real, too, the skull. I saw it, held it, I say. He needed it, he said, as back up. Proof, solid proof. Well, I add, that skull is out there now. Stuck on top of the pile of rocks I built over his corpse.

'He's dead?' says Org.

'Oh, yes,' I say. 'The terro. . . .'

'Ja? Talk quickly now, my friend, if you know what is good for you.'

'Trust me, Org. I will. Honestly. But first, let me tell you a bit more about the girl. The professor brought with him for company a girl. Vicky. Vicky Daintree. Young, very pretty. More than just company, if you know what I mean.'

He nods. He knows.

Listen, I continue, don't get me wrong. You would have liked Professor Bamford. Everybody did. Okay, so he had his faults. He was a bit of a boozer, a womanizer, too. Know him for a day or two, though, and you couldn't help appreciating how big-hearted, generous, and full of ideas he was – exactly the kind of guy you'd like to have around, not only on a video shoot, but anywhere, any time. He made jokes that kept us all in stitches. Better yet, he wasn't stuck up like most big shot intellectuals. No fat ego at stake. He was the star of the show, all right, and he knew it. But he was also modest to a fault. For instance, I say, he used to get all tongue-tied and embarrassed when the camera was on him. He'd sit there like a lump, pink-faced, choking on his own words. I had my work cut out for me, just trying to get him to relax and look natural.

There is a brief silence as Org takes all this in.

'How did he die?'

'I'm getting to that. But before I do, I'd like to tell you one more thing.'

Avoiding technical jargon, I go on to explain that there is more to shooting an instructional video than simply getting the pictures straight. For sure, I point out, you can't do without a neat set of visuals. After all, you have to be able to staple together a logical narrative, shot by shot. In addition to high quality pics, though, what you need is high quality sound. On this shoot, it was my ACE-TV crew mate, Bucs, who got to monitor sound. He turned out to be pretty good at it, too. Headphones, eyes on the dial, he could pick up every word, clear as a bell. His real name, I add, was Nando Killing Boy Ndhlovu, though he liked to call himself Bucs.

'The terro,' says Org.

'Yes,' I admit, 'but we didn't know it at the time. It wasn't all that obvious. He didn't come paddling across the Limpopo with an AK-47 in one hand, and a limpet mine in the other. In fact, he was so quiet and peaceful, you hardly noticed him. When he wasn't at work, watching over sound levels, he liked to hang around, listening to Reggae on a little tin pot tape recorder. He never once missed his cue. If the professor had anything to say, I could rely on Bucs to be ready to point the mike.'

'You let a kaffir do that? How come?'

'It's the university's big idea, not mine. Preparing for the coming change.'

'Ja, well, forget the university. It's full of kak. No change is going to happen. Talk. Tell me how the terro got the professor.'

It happened during a break in the filming, I say. Late this morning. Vicky and the professor climbed into the back of the kombi, and shut the door. At first, they were very quiet in there. Then we began to hear certain sounds, little cries and whimpers, moans, even a scream or two. Me, I say, I got up and walked to the far end of the camp. As for Bucs, he didn't move. He switched off his Reggae tape, sat back, and tilted his head. Of course, I should have told him not to, I say. I should have told him to leave them alone, respect their privacy. No decent person eavesdrops on others making love. I was still trying to get as far away from the kombi as I could, I say, when Bucs jumped up, grabbed the shotgun (it belonged to the professor, but like a fool, he had left it lying around the night before), Bucs grabbed the shotgun, threw open the kombi's sliding door, and shoved the gun up against the old man's head. Listen to me, Professor Digby, he said. Listen. If you don't want to die, then you'd better pull out now, and let me fuck the white chick. Those were his exact words, I say. Pull out now, and let me, Bucs, fuck the white chick.

'And did he?' asks Org. His voice is hoarse.

'Bucs? Not then, no,' I reply. 'Maybe later. I don't know.'

'Go on.' Org's lips barely move.

I had never before heard Bucs speak so many words at once, I say. For an instant, or maybe less, the professor and Vicky stayed just as he'd caught them, locked in a tangle on the kombi's back seat. Then, stark naked as he was, I say, the professor bounced up. In a huge rage, reckless, he threw himself at Bucs, who shot him in the stomach.

'Kafir-r-r-r!' cries Org, trilling the r in his fury. 'And you?' He points a finger squarely at me. 'What did you do, Erasmus?'

I pause, realize I am shaking. Running, I tell Org. I was running. Yes, I ran back at full tilt, faster than I had ever run in my life before, but still I arrived too late. The gun went off just as I got to the kombi. I grappled with Bucs, wrenched the shotgun out of his hands. He ducked, doubled up and ran away into the bush, dodging from side to side. I aimed, I say. I pulled the trigger, but there was only a click. The shotgun was empty.

'And then?'

And then, I say, I did the wrong thing. I should have reloaded, I know – reloaded, gone after him, and shot him down. Instead, I tried to help the professor. Wounded, bleeding heavily, he had staggered away, collapsed under a tree. What we should have done, Vicky and I, was bundle him into the kombi at once, and set off to find a hospital, a doctor. Instead, we knelt beside him, and did what we could to stop the blood. We ripped up a T-shirt, pressed it to the hole, and tried to bandage his belly. Not for a moment did we think that the terro would dare to set foot in the camp again, but that, of course, is exactly what he did. He must have doubled back, I say, and hidden behind a tree, or an anthill, maybe, to watch us. Then, I say, as soon as he saw how intent we were, how completely distracted, he took his chance. The next thing we knew, the kombi exploded. Somehow – with a bunch of burning rags, I guess – the terro had ignited the petrol tank. Flames went rolling across the ground, and up into the thorn trees, and the fire began to spread.

'Just like you said,' I tell Org. 'Like a mad dog, snapping and biting at everything that stood in its way.'

'No, never mind what I said. What happened to what's her name, the girl?'

'Vicky?' I say. 'Nothing. Or nothing, at that moment.'

She stayed, I claim, right beside the professor. She did not budge until he died. She held his hand, she wiped the sweat from his brow, she dipped a cloth in water and wiped his lips when he cried out with thirst. She really loved him, you could see. He loved her, too, no doubt. Not that it helped. With a load of birdshot in his guts, the old man lay twisting around in agony. He tried not to scream, but in the end he couldn't help it. He bit his lips, he arched his back, tried to stay rigid, but couldn't. And then as he twisted from side to side he began to scream like a maniac, at the same pitch, over and over again, while the blood gurgled and sucked in his wound. Finally he just lay there, I say, wheezing and staring, but only because he had no voice left. Meanwhile, the wind drove the fire away from us. I watched it. I stayed beneath the sheltering tree, and watched. I wish I could have gone to fetch help, but how could I? It would have meant leaving Vicky alone. We waited a long time. Not only was the professor incredibly stubborn, he was also incredibly strong. It took him hours to die.

'Ja, so he's dead. But the girl, tell me about the girl. Where is she now?'

'Gone,' I say. 'I don't know where.'

'You don't? Now tell me. How did that happen?'

Vultures, I say. I looked up, and vultures were circling. The sight made me so uneasy, I went out in search of stones to pack over the body. Then, while I was away on one of my forays, Vicky took the shotgun, pocketed a handful of shells, and set off on her own into the burnt-out veld. Grief, I suppose. Half-insane rage. She aimed to track Bucs down, I think, and kill him, I say.

'Who could blame her?' mutters Org. 'Not me.'

Even though I was anxious to follow at once, I continue, I still had to pack the last of the stones. In my hurry, I managed to chafe and tear the skin from my fingertips. But at last I did go after her. It wasn't easy. I had to cast around for her tracks. Most of the time, I could only guess which way she had gone. I walked and walked across nothing but burnt grass, scorched earth. Finally, however, I pushed my way through a patch of dense, unburnt bush, and found the road. I carried on walking, and then I saw the truck.

'Ja,' says Org, 'and I saw you.'

'But I never found Vicky. She is out there somewhere, now. And so is the terrorist. Who knows what has happened? And here I stand,' I conclude, 'unable to do a thing about it.'

'Maybe. Maybe not,' replies Org. 'You never know.' Casually (it is, after all, too dark for them to be of any use), he removes the mirror glasses, and drops them into the pocket of his shirt. 'Come. I've got something to show you.'

He leads the way round the back of the truck. Telling me to wait, he climbs up over the tailgate, stoops in under the canopy, and moves off into heavy shadow. I hear his boots go clanging on the iron floor.

As for me, I stand looking up the road. There is nothing to do now but think. I seem to know (in a way, I seem to have known all along) what I am about to see. My heart is beating with slow, heavy strokes. Not a single car has passed in all this time, I reflect. The tarmac glistens, exuding a little warmth. Otherwise, the cold is sharp, biting. I shiver.

O my bright idea.

I stand where I am, waiting.

My mouth is dry again, my throat tight, constricted.

From the back of the truck, I hear a series of rapid thumps and thuds, as of kicking. This is followed by a brief silence, then a shuffling, dragging sound.

I want to call out: 'It's okay. Leave him.'

But I don't.

In a moment Org stands towering above me at the tailgate again. He does not speak, but stoops down, stays almost hunched. Seems to be engaged in a struggle with something at his feet. Until with a grunt, a jerk, he heaves up.

And something comes tearing through the air, rushing by me in a sudden flailing. To slam down hard, flat on the ground.

For a moment I can't move. Then I squat down beside it. It is lying face down. No, *he*. He is lying face down.

'Bucs,' I whisper. 'Bra' Bucs.'

I am afraid to reach out, to touch him. He is breathing, I see, but shallowly, with difficulty. He must be in great pain. Is this what you want? I ask myself. This beaten, broken man? For shame.

Tentatively, I put a hand on his shoulder, which is wet and sticky with blood. Then, just as Bucs raises his voice, Org leans over the tailgate with a clank that knocks out all other sounds.

'Special delivery! One township terro. Happy now, my friend? We caught this one on the road not far from here. You should have seen him – fancy as you please, walking along like he was out to smell the flowers. Like he was as good as anybody, you or me included. I took one look, and thought: 'That is no kraal kaffir, that.' We pulled over. We wanted to ask a question or two, but he didn't cooperate. Gave my troops lip.'

'And?'

'What do you think? My troopies wanted to finish him off, then and there, but I said no. 'Let me take him back to the camp,' I said. 'Give the professionals a go. You watch. He'll talk.'

'What if he gets away? Or if someone saves him?'

'Him? This one? Over my dead body.'

Org seems to be grinning. The dark bulk of his torso blots out part of the night sky, but I can see his teeth. The moon appears to be growing from the back of his head.

'Go on. Turn him over,' he urges. 'Check. Did we catch the right one?'

I brace myself, hesitate.

With an effort, I lean forward, turn him on his back.

His face is suddenly very close to mine. The mouth is open, swollen, smashed. Blood glitters. Every tooth may well be broken. He smells, too, of raw urine. His pants must be soaked.

'Bucs. Bucs, bra'. It's Rian. Can you hear me?'

He makes a creaking noise in his throat. His lips puff out, tremble, begin to stretch into what looks like a smile, but actually must mean terrible effort. One eye is open and staring (though not seeing), while the other, crusted with blood, remains swollen shut.

'Ri,' he cries in a cracked, reed-thin voice. 'Bra' Ri.'

'It's okay, bra',' I say softly. 'Okay, okay.'

I pat his shoulder, get to my feet. Wipe my hands on the back of my jeans. Go on, I tell myself. It's what you wanted, isn't it? Look. Look closely. Can you stand the sight of what you have done?

For shame.

'And now?' says Org. 'What do you say, my friend?'

I give a nod.

'It's him,' I say. 'It's him, all right. You got him. You got the bloody terrorist.'

6

I T   I S   S O   L O N G   A G O   N O W that our speed steadied out that we seem almost stationary on this flat and unchanging road, en route to the military camp. When we will get there, I do not know. Nor do I ask. The headlights of the truck, two balls of glass I should have smashed, but didn't, cast a sharp glare on the tarmac, while the solid white line down the middle unwinds endlessly into the night.

Org, beside me and driving, is morose, silent. I can smell his sweat. It must have been more difficult than he expected. When he returned from the bush, he walked wearily, pausing often. He carried his rifle like a yoke upon his shoulders, and patches of sweat, dark in the moonlight, had spread out from his armpits.

Opening the cab door, he climbed up into the driver's seat.

'Org,' I said in dry acknowledgment and greeting.

In the pallor of the light from the overhead lamp, his raw slab of a face looked livid. Giving no sign that he had heard me, he reached out and slammed the door. Then, seated as he was, he bent slowly forward until his forehead came to rest on the rim of the steering wheel.

'What's up?' I asked.

For a moment he did not move. Then, rolling his head to one side, he stared at me. His small eyes seemed restless, dull and furious, but he did not speak.

'A hard day's work?' I gibed, but again he did not seem to hear.

Earlier, he had come clambering down over the tailgate to land right beside Bucs in the dark.

'I knew it!' he exulted. 'I knew it was him, all along!'

Then, with a sudden high shriek of: 'Kaffir!' he began hopping up and down, trampling upon Bucs.

I feared he might die on the spot, but Org, it seemed, had no intention of killing him right away. Restraining himself with some difficulty – clenching and unclenching his fists – he stood over Bucs, who lay huddled, groaning and retching.

'Stay like that, kaffir,' he said. And to me: 'Watch him. I'm just going to go and fetch what we need.'

For some reason, the cicadas had fallen silent. I stepped back from the truck, and looked up. The first stars glittered faintly. Between and beyond lay nothing but darkness, a depth without end into which I longed to fall, and go on falling. I could not see Bucs where he lay in the solid block of shadow cast by the truck, but I could still hear him. He kept moaning, crying out weakly:

'Ai, my baas! Asseblief, my baas!' Please, I beg you, my baas.

Under my breath I told him to shut up. I felt paralyzed, stifled, unable to do a thing. What now? There was no way out. I was going to live; Bucs was not. This bright, moody and ambitious young man whom I had called bra', brother – this township kid – was about to die by my word, if not my hand. For what? I asked myself. One last gesture toward Vicky, so that no suspicion might fall on her, ever? Ah, what would she say if she knew? I know, don't tell me. She would look me in the eye, and say: You are a coward, Rian Erasmus. A coward, a liar and a cheat. In a word, a traitor.

Before long, Org returned. Brushing by me, he stood over Bucs again, coolly loading and cocking his rifle.

'Kom, kaffir.' he said. Come. 'Time to go bye-bye. Up. Get up on your feet.'

'Wait,' I interjected. 'I don't think he can move.'

'Him? He can move, all right. He can move if he wants to. What he would most like to do is play dead, like a rinkhals.'

'No, I mean it, Org. Listen. He's been too badly beaten –'

'Kak, man.' Crap. 'Who is in charge here, Erasmus? You or me?'

'You are, but –'

'But? But what?'

'I told you. He's too badly hurt. He can't walk. For all we know, he may have broken bones.'

'My friend, listen. If one day I want your opinion, I'll ask for it. Right now, I don't need it. In fact, I don't even want you around. I don't need you watching me. I know what I am doing. Understand? It won't take too long. Go and get into the truck, and wait.'

Finally, obedient not to Org but the iron logic of the end I was pursuing, I did as he said. What dictated was need, necessity. This was not spineless submission, or culpable complicity. No. At stake was survival, over and beyond the question of right and wrong. Survival, my credo. Or, as Vicky would say, my excuse.

It was cold, and I sat with my hands pressed between my knees, resisting the steep slant of the seat. Beside me, tangled in the bag that I'd picked up on my way, lay the last couple of oranges. Across my knees, a constant reminder of its owner, rested the little tape player, which I had found on the floor when I climbed in. Poor loot, I'd felt, for Sergeant Georg Strydom of the SADF. What did he want with Bucs's shiny toys – his mirror sunglasses, his cheap portable tape recorder – anyway? And how could he, good racist that he was, not feel contaminated by the touch, the feel, of a black man's private property?

Despite his assurances to the contrary, it took Org a long time. As he sat in the truck now, his forehead leaning on the steering wheel, he seemed exhausted, dispirited. He shifted around, first opened his mouth, then shut it again.

'Yes?' I prompted.

For a moment he said nothing, though he still stared at me with malevolence. Then, slowly and distinctly, he said: 'You. You, Erasmus.'

'What about me?'

'You know what you did, and so do I.'

'What do you mean?'

'Your terro friend talked.'

I paused just long enough to give weight to my reply.

'My – terro – friend?'

'Him, ja. Nando Killing Boy.'

'Nando, huh? Well, well. What did he say?'

'Plenty.'

Org twisted the key in the ignition. After a short tremor, the engine caught, turned over, and began to labor. With a rapid spin of the steering wheel, he got the truck to right itself, to come down hard and square on all fours, so to speak, and then go trundling round in a wide U-turn, and mount the highway again. The headlights flicked on, the canvas canopy flapped and cracked, and we picked up speed.

'Bucs talked, you say?'

'That's right, Erasmus. He talked.'

'Funny, you know, but he didn't look in the best of shape, the last I saw of him. How come he suddenly started to talk?'

Org bit at his thumb nail, reflecting.

'It's me,' he concluded, spitting out a fragment of nail. 'My terros talk to me. 'Talk,' I tell them. 'Talk, and I will let you go.' Only the real hard cases don't. The cheeky ones try not to, but they don't get it right. I don't take kak from a terro, and they know it. All I want is information. So, if I know that they know, and they still try to give me cheek, I cut off their fingers, one by one, starting with the pinkie. Usually, before I get to the thumb, they see the light. Mind you, tonight your terro was easy. He gave me no lip. When he saw he was going to die, he cried big tears. He said you were his friend. He wanted to talk to you, he said. I said no, that was impossible.'

'I see. What else did he say?'

Org looked at me askance. Again, he opened and shut his mouth. Then, as if to put some actual distance between himself and the question, he drove on for quite a while without a word. Finally, he leaned back, and in a low flat voice, rigidly suppressing his rage, let leak the facts from the corner of his mouth: 'He said it was you, not him, Erasmus. You who started the fire. He said that you and the other one, the big baas, wanted him to do ugly things to the white madam, but he wouldn't. He ran, he said, but not far. He stopped under a tree and watched, he said. He saw you tear up some clothes and make a rope, and dip it into the kombi's petrol tank, and set it on fire.'

'And you believed him?'

Realizing at once that he had blundered, Org had no choice but to backpedal.

'No, my friend. *You* know, and *I* know, a man can never believe a kaffir. His head is too full of shit. A kaffir can tell me what really happened, he can swear with his hand on the Bible, and I still will not believe him. A kaffir is a kaffir, and a kaffir always lies.'

Only too delighted to press my advantage, I challenged the obvious contradiction.

'Oh, yes? Even when you cut off his fingers?'

'Ag, no, man! That's different. Don't get me wrong. Listen, let me put it this way. If a white man says to me that such and such a thing happened like this, and a kaffir says no, it didn't, it happened like that – then, I ask you, who do I believe?'

'Who?'

'You, of course. Not the kaffir. Never him, no. Here,' said Org, fumbling in his pocket, and handing me a small plastic-clad book. 'I brought you this to show you. A memento. Just so you know.'

I recognized it: Bucs's pass book – his *dompas*, as he would have called it – the labor document that all black people must carry at all times on pain of arrest. I took it from Org, and tried to flip it open, but the pages were stuck together, tacky with blood.

'What do you want me to do with this?'

'Keep it. Burn it. Swallow it. Do what you like with it, my friend. It's yours now.'

I managed to shove, twist the little book into the back pocket of my jeans. Later. I would think about it later.

'Ka-pok,' I said softly.

'Ka-pok, ja!' agreed Org. 'One terro, one bullet. That's what I always say.' In lieu of stretching, he tried to ease his muscles by shifting his shoulders. Then he calmly checked both the rear view mirror and the road ahead. 'With this particular kaffir,' he added, 'believe it or not, it nearly took me two bullets, one after the other. Ka-pok-pok! Why, I don't know, but he died hard. No terro I have known has ever taken so long. Ten minutes, by my watch. I put the bullet in the right spot. Just here.' He tapped at the back of his head. 'But he kicked and rolled, rolled and kicked, so long that I thought he was going to jump up and run round in a circle. What I did wrong, I don't know. Hit a nerve, maybe. Or a whole bundle of nerves. It just goes to show you, though, a kaffir's got no brain. Otherwise, it would have been finished and klaar, overs kedovers, the moment I pulled the trigger. But don't you worry, Erasmus. He's dead, your friend. Kaput.'

'What?' I said. 'Me, worry?'

Ignoring, or perhaps simply failing to notice my mockery, Org sat thinking to himself, pondering.

'I didn't piss on him,' he recalled with regret. 'Sometimes we do that, you know. Piss on a dead terro, in the face. Or shit on him. Sometimes, my troopies will cut open the stomach, or cut out the heart, and shit down in the hole. Or, if we know the terro's comrades are in the vicinity, we hide a hand grenade under the body. Then, when they try and pick him up, bang! A big surprise.'

Again Org shifted his shoulders to combat cramped and aching muscles. Patting at the steering wheel in an attempt to drum up energy, he yawned widely, loudly.

'You know what, my friend?' he said, musing. 'It looks like it's my turn now. I'm getting thirsty!' He opened and shut his mouth, making sticky, smacking sounds. 'Do me a favor. Peel me an orange. To sit around like this and do nothing is putting me to sleep.'

For some reason, I concentrated on peeling the orange in a single, continuous spiral. Juice got onto my fingers. Acidic, it stung.

Org fastened on the orange as soon as I offered it. Juice dripped. With his mouth full, he thanked me.

In pursuit of a little relief, I pressed my fingertips to the legs of my jeans. It seemed as though every thread in the fabric stood out, abrasive, electric, competing for attention with the slim pressure of the pass book in my back pocket. I made a pact with myself to keep the *dompas* on me always. Penance for this night.

The rifle shot, when finally it came, I remembered, was hard and flat, concussive. It jolted me upright, where I sat waiting in the cab. My mind went blank in sheer terror. What had I done? I tried to pray, but the words would not come. Even after the sound of the shot had vanished, I sat straining to hear more.

'Good,' sighed Org, busy wiping his fingers on his pants. The orange I had given him was gone. 'How many left?'

'Just one. It's yours, if you like.'

'I do like. The same again, my friend. Peel it, okay?'

Carefully, meticulously, I peeled the last orange. In the end only a couple of lengthy, twisted peels lay curling beside me.

Org ate thirstily, tearing the orange to pieces, and then lapsed into silence.

It is so long ago now that our speed steadied out that we seem almost stationary in the dark. I try staring at the tarmac. My hope is that the rushing blur beneath the headlights will scour my brain, and leave me fresh again, wide open to everything, keen and clear of sight.

At the same time it seems that a terrible loneliness has descended upon the starlit veld.

> *O koud is die windjie*
> *en skraal. . . .*

Where, I wonder, in all that darkness, are Vicky and the mfaan? What chance, if any, do they have of crossing from this land to the next, faced with armed border guards at either end of the bridge, and the ancient peril of crocodiles in the river below? And what has happened to the madala? Where is he now? And what of the young man with the looped and ragged vest, and the woman with the lovely mouth? In what desolate corner will they end up? I know I will never know, and it is futile to wonder, for nothing I can do will bring them, or anyone, back again.

As for Bamford, out there under the wild fig tree, I can only too easily picture him, belly up, the mound of his naked white corpse holding up (upholding?) the mound of stones, topped by the fossilized skull. And then there is Bucs. But of him I cannot think. Not even as I know him to be, in the dark, not too far from here. Not now, anyway. I find it impossible to imagine that he is dead.

Org rubs his eyes with his fist. Yawns.

'Ag, ja,' he declares, a propos of nothing. 'Never mind. That's how it goes in this old life. What more can a man do?'

A night wind has sprung up, and the lumbering truck takes the strain, head-on. Most of the time, it feels four-square, solid, a fortress on wheels, the truck. Now and then, however, buffeted by a gust, it feels as though it is sailing along on tiptoe, about to be lifted, blown away into the night – while the canvas canopy rattles and shudders over the shadows in the back, and I try not to think.

With nothing else to do, I pick up the little tape player, press it to my ear. Turning the volume so low that only I will be able to hear, I switch it on. Strident, tinny music. And then, only too predictably, the catchy, corny, repetitive refrain:

> *I – a warrior*
> *You – a warrior*
> *We – a warrior*

I listen attentively, turn it up slightly. I lean my head back, shut my eyes. My head is throbbing with the beat. My lips form the words, but I make no sound.

I know that I may never speak.

PETER ANDERSON hails from South Africa, but currently resides in North Texas where he is an associate professor of English at Austin College. The author of a previous collection of poems, *Vanishing Ground*, his poems have appeared in numerous literary magazines and have been anthologized in both America and South Africa, including recently in places such as *I Go to the Ruined Place: Contemporary Poems in Defense of Global Human Rights* and *Against Agamemnon: War Poems*. His stories and creative nonfiction have also been published and anthologized in both countries. *The Unspeakable* is his first novel.